MERCEDES LACKEY

CLOSER TO THE CHEST

THE HERALD SPY BOOK III

TITAN BOOKS

The Herald Spy Book III: Closer to the Chest
Print edition ISBN: 9781783293766
E-book edition ISBN: 9781783293773

Published by Titan Books
A division of Titan Publishing Group Ltd
144 Southwark Street, London SE1 0UP

First edition: October 2016
1 3 5 7 9 10 8 6 4 2

A CIP catalogue record for this title is available from the British Library.

Printed and bound in Great Britain by CPI Group Ltd.

Did you enjoy this book? We love to hear from our readers.
Please email us at readerfeedback@titanemail.com or write to us at
Reader Feedback at the above address.

To receive advance information, news, competitions, and exclusive offers online,
please sign up for the Titan newsletter on our website: www.titanbooks.com

CLOSER TO THE CHEST

THE HERALD SPY BOOK III

Also by Mercedes Lackey and available from Titan Books

THE HERALD SPY
Closer to Home
Closer to the Heart

THE COLLEGIUM CHRONICLES
Foundation
Intrigues
Changes
Redoubt
Bastion

VALDEMAR OMNIBUSES
The Heralds of Valdemar
The Mage Winds
The Mage Storms
The Mage Wars
The Last Herald Mage (March 2017)
Vows & Honor (September 2017)
Exiles of Valdemar (March 2018)

THE ELEMENTAL MASTERS
The Serpent's Shadow
The Gates of Sleep
Phoenix and Ashes
The Wizard of London
Reserved for the Cat
Unnatural Issue
Home from the Sea
Steadfast
Blood Red
From a High Tower
A Study in Sable

To Betsy Wollheim and 30 years with DAW.
Here's to 30 more!

1

Mags slumped over the table, his posture calculated to reflect indifference rather than defeat or weariness. This was not the sort of place in which to display any indication of weakness. This might not be the worst tavern in Haven, but it was certainly in the bottom third. The room was barely big enough to hold six tables; Mags was sitting in the corner at the rearmost one, with his back to the wall. The chimney smoked, leaving the already-dark room further obscured by haze from about chest-high up to the black rafters. The rushes on the floor hadn't been changed in years, and probably housed entire self-supporting populations of mice and bugs. And there was a thin film of grease on everything. The beverage selection was limited to stale beer and sour wine, and the food selection—well, Mags wasn't putting *that* to the test. The best he could have hoped for was that the pocket-pie he'd ordered, and was slowly crumbling to bits, was mostly crust with a smear of gravy inside. The worst, well . . . the probability that the meat inside was dog, cat, or rat, was very high. The choice of food here was bread and a substance alleged to be cheese, pocket pie, boiled eggs of uncertain age, or bread alone.

Fortunately he wasn't hungry or thirsty, having fortified himself for his little fishing expedition before he arrived.

So both the pie and the beer were going, by sleight of hand, into the rushes at his feet. No one would ever notice. Except perhaps the indigenous wildlife, which would come harvest his sacrificial offerings and hopefully not crawl up his legs.

"Harkon!" The greeting included a hearty slap on his back, which he'd braced himself for the moment he heard his assumed name called. The speaker slung his leg over the bench and joined Mags. "What're you doin' in this scummy part'o town?"

"Bizness fer the Weasel," Mags replied, clanking wooden mugs with the newcomer. "You?"

The newcomer snorted. "Debt collection." Merely from the way the fellow intoned those words, Mags knew the errand had ended in failure.

"Done a scarper, did 'e, Teo?" Mags said with sympathy. "Bad luck fer ye. 'Ere." He tipped his mostly full wooden tankard into Teo's mostly empty one. "Least I kin do." Teo wasn't bad, as the hired thugs around here went, and neither was his boss, who had, more than once, extended a little more time to debtors who needed it, and whose interest rates were more than reasonable even by the standards of Willy the Weasel's pawn shop. Teo had also proven to be a good source of information more than once, and Mags liked to keep him "sweet."

8

"Ye ain't all bad, Harkon," Teo said gratefully, and looked meaningfully at the pie lying on the slap of wood that passed as a plate. "Ye gonna et—"

"Here, I got about all I kin stomach," Mags replied, shoving the greasy slab of wood that held about three fourths of the "pie" at Teo, who grinned and took it. "So aside fr'm yer coney doin' a scarper . . . ?"

Teo ate, and talked, and Mags got a refill for both of them—and again, tipped most of his into Teo's mug—and listened.

Teo loved to talk—and he knew Harkon could be trusted to keep his mouth shut. They were off in their own little corner of this dank hole, with everyone else avoiding the area around two known toughs, so Teo could gossip like a laundrywoman and no one would care or pay any attention. Since Mags rarely got over to Teo's part of town—the slums around the Tanner's Quarter—every bit of information was potentially useful.

When Teo finally ran down, Mags got refills for them both again, and a second pie for Teo, who seemed to have a stomach made of boiled leather. No fear Teo was going to get drunk, not on *this* slop. "Yer a generous fren' Harkon," Teo said with gratitude.

Mags shrugged. "Nuncle's payin'. I kin afford t'be generous."

Teo laughed.

Since this was *precisely* the reason Mags was here—to collect street-gossip—he wasn't any too eager to chase Teo away. The man was good company, even if he did look like a battle-scarred alley cat, and at least, unlike a lot of the denizens of this place, he was clean. In fact, he was fastidious. That had been one of the things that had drawn Mags to him in the first place. Mostly, he played bodyguard for his employer, especially when the man took money to the goldsmith for safekeeping. A goldsmith could always afford more protection for his place than a small-time moneylender ever could.

Teo actually performed as much of a service as a bodyguard merely by standing there and looking intimidating as he did by using his fists or other weapons. Tall, strongly muscled, visible scars on face and arms, a jaw like granite and a skull to match, thick brows, and black hair cut shorn-sheep close to his scalp, he did not look like someone one of Mika Tarneff's customers would want to cross—and those intimidating looks scared off most would-be robbers as well.

Teo's gossip today was useful, even if there was nothing urgent in it. In fact, it was useful precisely *because* there was nothing urgent in it. Most especially, there were no "Nah, ye ken, I heerd a strange t'ing t'other day . . ." which was generally a sign that there was something amiss, or about to go amiss. Things were exactly as they should be for summer. Stinking, of course; the Tanner's Quarter was at the downwind side of Haven, always stank, and it was twice as bad in the heat of summer as it was in winter. No one lived there that could possibly afford to live elsewhere. It wasn't filthy; in fact, there were weekly inspections to make sure the entire Quarter was as clean and vermin-free as possible, because if disease started there, it would spread like wildfire. But the process of tanning itself was noxious, and after the hides were cleaned of decaying flesh and fat, the first step required the use of urine, which was collected all over the city every morning for that purpose. The stink of urine was everywhere, even on the coldest day. Frankly, Mags could not imagine living somewhere that stank of piss night and day, but Teo swore you got used to it.

It was just one more of the things that reminded him on an hourly basis of his incredible good luck; it might not have seemed that way when he was a little mine-slave, but every day since he'd been carried off by Dallen and Jakyr had been a day when he'd enjoyed a ridiculously good life. Well, apart from people trying to kill him. But the mine had been full of perils, and if anything, the attrition-rate among the mine-slaves was twice that among the Heralds.

"Ye look about as fur away as th' Pel'girs," Teo observed, breaking into his thoughts. "I arst ye twice if'n ye're aight."

Mags shook his head. "Long night," he observed. "Will took't inventory. 'Ad a notion there was stuff missin'."

"And?" Teo prompted.

Mags laughed. "Turned out, we 'ad more damn stuff'n 'e 'ad in 'is books. 'E's 'appy, fer sure. 'Tis like some'un give it to 'im free."

"If Willy ain't 'appy—"

"Ain't nobody 'appy," Mags finished for him. There was a clutch of young layabouts at the table nearest the door, grousing and carrying on. He jerked his head at them. "Like thet lot. Yammer, yammer, yammer th' whole time I bin here, 'bout they's sad, sorry lot."

Teo snorted. "Whingin' like a lotta liddle girls, 'cause they cain't get none. *I* ain't got no prollem gettin' wimmin, an' I look like a beat mule. Mebbe iffin they treated wimmin proper, gels 'ud gi' 'em the time'a day."

"Is *thet* wut they're on about?" Mags asked, curious now. He listened. And sure enough, Teo was right. They were complaining bitterly about how women treated them. Which is to say, women treated them like the ne'er-do-wells and lazy louts that they were, and not as the all-conquering kings-of-the-world they *thought* they were.

This group of about six young ruffians evidently considered it their natural born right to be feted like gifts from the gods and were complaining mightily because that wasn't happening.

At the moment, the subject being harped on was that, somehow, women in general, and a couple of girls by name, "owed" them sexual favors by the mere fact that they were men, and that was the only purpose women had.

Mags listened with growing disgust and astonishment as they waxed as eloquent as a lot of louts with pus between their ears instead of brains could. This, it seemed, was not mere hubris, it was theology. This lot had either invented a system of belief wholesale, or had found someone who would preach one to them that they embraced fervently. At first, Mags was of the opinion that they'd made it up all on their own but the longer he listened, the less sure of that he became. Their cant was repugnant, but too internally consistent for a lot of rattle-brains like them to have concocted in what passed for their imaginations.

So who's telling them what they want to hear and calling it Holy Writ? That was a good question.

Women, it seemed, should "know their place," and that place was to be told what to do by men. Evidently, some god had created men in his image, and women were an afterthought, created to serve men. Women should be pretty, serve, and provide sex, and not be heard, or think for themselves. A woman's duty was to make sure she was always attractive and pliant, and do everything a man told her. She certainly wasn't to "take a man's job," or compete with a man in any way. In fact, she wasn't to work outside the home at all, unless it was to the advantage of her man, and as ordered by her man. She must get a man as soon as she was able—"the younger, the better," growled one.

"Aye, get 'em little and get 'em trained up right," spat another. "I got no use for anythin' above thirteen."

"Them Holderkin down south's got it right," agreed a third. "A man kin hev as many as 'e wants, an' thirteen, no later, is when they go to the men."

Well, the others wanted to hear all about that, and the fellow was happy to oblige. Mags felt anger and disbelief in equal measures rising in him, until he was suddenly aware that Teo was making a very strange noise.

He glanced over at his friend. The bodyguard had his fist jammed up against his mouth, and was making a strangled sound as his face turned red. Now a little concerned, because Teo had never shown signs of being prone to fits, Mags poked him with an elbow. "You aight?"

Teo looked up, trying to keep his face from being seen by the gang of layabouts. "Holy balls," he choked. "I ain't niver seen so much stupid i' one concentrated place i' me life!"

"Aye, bu—" Mags said doubtfully.

"Lissen t'em! They ain't one uv 'em got a pot t'piss in, an *they* thin' iffen they was down i' Holderkin territory, they'd be wallerin' in wenches!" Teo's face got redder as a chortle broke through. "What they'd *be*, is like th' mangy mongrels sniffin' at th' fence whilst th' prize hound gets put t' the bitches. I seen the Holderkin wi' their passel'a Underwives, an' they all be *old*, wi' *money*, an' wi' tight bizness connections and plenny uv' favors from given large t'their priests. Rat's asses like them? Farm drudge *if* they was lucky, an' not put t' turnin' th' water-wheel or suchlike. An' closest they'd get t'wimmin is a straw-dolly, iffin they could get the straw."

All the time Teo was talking, he was having more and more trouble controlling himself, and when he got to the word "straw," he couldn't manage it anymore. He broke out into a guffaw, and Mags couldn't help it, because though he might have been uneducated, Teo had a certain way with words, and Mags could just *see* those layabouts, sniffing sadly after a gaggle of girls supervised by their lord and master, and *he* broke out into laughter.

Now the entire group turned to stare at them. That only made the two of them laugh harder.

The leader, who, on a good day, with a rock in each hand, *might* have weighed as much as Teo's thigh, stood up and glared at them belligerently, hand on the thin strip of pot-metal he called a "sword." "Somethin' funny?" he growled.

"Oh, aye," Teo howled. *"High*-larious."

Now all of them stood up, and put hands on their weapons. Mind, those weapons mostly consisted of clubs, with a couple of knives. Teo wiped his eyes, and Mags managed to get himself under control, and both of *them* stood up.

Now, Mags had been a small boy, and he was still not a tall man. But as he stood up, all *his* weapons became visible as he cocked his elbows back and tucked his thumbs into his belt, pulling back his long vest a trifle. Short sword, long-sword, and across his chest an entire bandolier of knives. All of them in old, worn sheathes and possessed of hilts with plenty of wear on them.

As for Teo . . . he topped the tallest of the others by a head and a half, his shoulders were broad, his chest matched his shoulders, and he had *two* bandoliers of knives, an ax, a sword, and a club twice the size of the ones the layabouts were sporting. And of course, there were the scars. Not just on his face, but, since his chosen attire in this warm summer weather was a sleeveless moleskin jerkin, there were plenty of scars lacing across the highly defined muscles of his arms.

Teo reached up and gave a final chuckle as he wiped away a last tear. "Oh, aye. Funniest t'ings I heerd in ages. Be ye a comic show? On account'a I'd pay t'hear all that palaver agin."

The would-be toughs had shrunk back once Mags and Teo had revealed their true natures, and now the ones at the rear were stealthily making their way toward the door, leaving their erstwhile leader and two of his friends standing there uncertainly. The leader tried to bluff anyway, unaware he was being rapidly deserted. "Th' hell ye say! I say—"

Now he looked around. And the speed at which his bravado ran out of him made Teo laugh all over again, reaching out to support himself on Mags' shoulder.

"I . . . ah . . . say . . . oh . . .no . . . we was jest . . ." He began backing up, as his two final friends made their escape. ". . . jest . . . talk—" And here he fell over a bucket and tumbled into the noisome rushes.

Teo lost it. He doubled up and howled with laughter again, as the poor fool scrabbled backward, away from the giant madman, managed to get to his feet, and tore out of there, running as fast as his legs would carry him.

Teo collapsed, choking with laughter, back down to the bench. And that was when Mags made up his mind that it was time to put Teo to the test. He'd known Teo for the better part of a year now. He knew Teo was kind to children, animals, and generally all weak things. He knew Teo was as generous as a man of slim means can be—if he'd been in the same position just now as Teo, it would have been *Teo* tipping beer into *his* mug, and passing over the uneaten pocket pie. He'd entrusted Teo with several small secrets, and Teo had not betrayed them.

:I agree,: said Dallen in his mind. *:He's proven that he is trustworthy, he's good at your back, and he deserves something more in his life. Besides, I like how he thinks.:*

Well, that settled the matter.

"Teo, ye got some time?" Mags asked.

"Aye. Boss ain't 'spectin' me back any time soon, an' I don' reckon on gettin' a happy welcome when I tell 'im 'is coney done a scarper."

"Good," Mags said. "Nuncle ain't at th' shop right now, an' I got better beer by a sight than they got 'ere. Not ter mention, I gotta nice quarter-wheel uv cheese, some nonions, some reddishes, bread from this mornin', an' some pears what ain't too bruised."

Teo perked right up at the mention of the beer, and it was clear that by the time Mags got to the pears, his mouth was watering. By Mags' reckoning, a man as big as Teo was probably often hungry. "Reckon thet sounds real good," Teo said, tentatively, proving that Mags was right. "Wut's th' ketch?"

"The ketch," Mags said, slapping him on the back (and not moving him an inch), "Is thet I got a bizness proposition fer ye, an' I want ye feelin' good when I make it."

"Then I'm yer man," Teo declared. Mags chuckled, and led the way back to "his" part of town.

* * *

:This might be the only time in the history of Valdemar that there has been two King's Owns,: Amily thought, from her place behind the Prince on the dais.

:That's not . . . entirely . . . true,: Rolan objected mildly. *:You are the King's Own. Your father is merely providing guidance to you, and advice and friendship to Kyril. You are still the King's Own. The only King's Own.:*

:It's true enough, so far as everyone else is concerned,: she replied, glancing over to where her father, Herald Nikolas, stood where she should have been, behind the King. *:Just look at that. And look at* them.: She let her gaze drift across the room, apparently idly, actually noting the place and expressions of each and every person in the Court, from the courtiers ranged on either side of the aisle to the people waiting at the end of it for their turn to be presented, to the Guards standing at stoic attention at their appointed places. *:If you said "King's Own" to any of them, they'd respond with "Herald Nikolas." And you know that I'm right about that.:*

Silence for a moment on her Companion's end, while she automatically checked the newcomers nervously approaching the Throne. Were they *too* nervous? Were there slight bulges in their clothing where a weapon might be? She wished for the thousandth time that her Mindspeaking ability extended to reading *people's* minds as well as animals.

Like Father. . . .

:Do you resent this?: Rolan asked.

No bulges, and their nerves were all because it was clear that the clothing was new, stiff and uncomfortable, and Lord Meriman, his wife, and twin daughters had never in their lives been to Court before and now, at the last minute, they were all overcome with the conviction that they hadn't practiced their Court bows *nearly* enough and they were going to look like fools—

Amily moved just enough to catch the eyes of both Lord Meriman and Lady Felicity, and she smiled, warmly, reassuringly. Their eyes widened with surprise, then a little flush appeared on their cheeks, they smiled tentatively back and they relaxed, just a little, with the feeling that they had a friend on the dais. Prince Sedric, who had taken this all in, smiled warmly as well, further relaxing them. Then it was their turn, and they pulled off their Court bows flawlessly, the girls with the artless grace of the young, the Lord and Lady with confidence. Nikolas murmured something to the King, and the King congratulated the couple on their recent anniversary.

Then they moved off, flushing with pleasure and the success of their presentation, and it was on to the next, a stodgy old self-confident Guildmaster who clearly felt he was the equal to or the superior of anyone here. No weapons, but an outfit that was only a hairs-breadth from being so ostentatious as to be in appallingly bad taste. The corner of her father's mouth quirked just a little.

:*No,*: she decided. :*Not really. I'd have been so far out of my depth if I was in his place right now that I'd have been half in a panic and I would never remember all the things I'd been supposed to memorize about these people.*:

But . . . yes, she did resent it a little. Because, once again, she was *Nikolas's daughter* first, and not only was she not generally thought of as the "King's Own," if she wasn't wearing Whites people would forget she was *Herald* Amily.

On the other hand . . . the alternative to this situation would be that her father would be dead, and she'd be struggling—and probably failing—to take his place.

And the most important part of that equation was, *her father would be dead.* Even if she had resented this situation a hundred times more than she actually did, she would *never* want that. Even now, when she remembered how near a thing it had been, her throat closed up, she went cold all over with the echo of that dread, and she started to shake.

He's very much not dead, she reminded herself, and shook it off. She cast her eyes over the crowd again, and wondered if anyone out there suspected her mixed feelings. Or if there were those who thought that she *should* be champing at the bit with resentment.

:Of course there are. People do like their gossip,: Rolan said tolerantly. *:And you know if there is nothing to gossip about, they'll make something up.:* She managed to not roll her eyes, but she heartily agreed with Rolan's statement. That was perhaps the one constant here at Court.

Court was being held today in the Greater Throne Room, which tended to get used unofficially for any time large numbers of the courtiers wanted to mingle together and weather or season rendered the gardens less than ideal. Officially, it was used to greet important visitors to the Kingdom, like Ambassadors or even the occasional—never in Amily's lifetime—Visiting Royals. Since the royalty of other lands never visited Valdemar unless there was a possible war or marriage-alliance on the horizon, she was just as glad such a situation had never occurred in her memory. It was also used for these twice-monthly formal Receptions, those occasions at which people were formally Received by the King. This could be when they had been elevated in status, or had a new family member to present. It could also be when they had never officially presented themselves to the King; there were plenty of highborn who lived so far from Haven that the journey to Court and back was a once-in-a-lifetime occurrence. When merchants and craftsmen rose to the level of Guildmaster, they came to be presented, at least the ones in and around Haven did. And there was an odd subset of people who had risen to great fame in one way or another—poets or other writers, for instance, famed artists, famed inventors, people who had done something extraordinary, or heroic—who could ask to be presented as well.

Strangely enough, no one in any of the three Collegia ever seemed to see the need for presentation. Perhaps that was because they had been up here on the Hill for the better part of their lives, mingled with the Court a bit (sometimes a great deal more than just "a bit") and saw the Royal Family at its most casual. Once you have seen the King ducking his head in the watering trough outside Companions' Stable after a hard workout, or had trounced the Prince yourself in a bout under the eye of the Weaponsmaster— well, you didn't lose *respect* for them, and they didn't lose one particle of the honor to which they were due, but you didn't have that peculiar sort of awe that made the regard of a crowned head a rare and special thing.

The last of the highborn who would spend the warmer months here at Court were just now trickling in for the summer season; like the time around Midwinter, this was an opportunity for arranging marriages. For some, who wanted to keep a sharp eye on their estates, Spring meant planting and birthing, Summer brought haying and harvests, and the noble who felt anxious for his land did not want to leave it at such a crucial time. For others, Spring meant melting snow and rains and bad roads, and they didn't care to leave until traveling was less arduous.

And here came Duke Henley, who was in the latter group. He didn't need to be presented, since he was very well known to the King, but he never lost the opportunity for a formal exchange of greetings. "He thinks it's his right," Nikolas had explained to her this morning. "As if the King has a certain number of allotted fractions of candlemarks to acknowledge the importance of certain highborn, and he is bound and determined to get his share."

As she had expected, he bowed to the Prince, ignored her, greeted the King effusively, and Nikolas in passing. *Then again, for most of his life, Father was King's Own, and that's what he's used to.* She tried to remember anything about him other than what her father had told her, and failed. *I wish, back when I was tucked up in a window seat at the back of the Court and hardly anyone but my friends even acknowledged my existence, I had spent more time paying attention to what was going on at the front of the room. It would have been the perfect time to learn about* everything *and* everyone.

But then, who would ever have thought the little scholarly cripple would be a Herald, much less the King's Own? Certainly not her.

Duke Henley was certainly taking every single one of his self-allotted fractions of a candlemark. The King seemed more amused than anything else, and no one was showing any impatience. She relaxed a little, and once again wished she could Mindspeak with others. The Prince and her father, at least. And behind Duke Henley she could see the unmistakable figure of old Lord Anslott, who did not approve of mere females doing *anything* other than being

"Proper Wives and Mothers of the Race." At least Duke Henley would only ignore her. Anslott would snub her if he thought he could get away with it. Lord Jorthun had observed once that "If Anslott ever had a single original thought in his head, the poor thing had probably died of loneliness before he ever got a chance to articulate it." Everything Lord Anslott did, said, or thought was dictated by umpteen generations of Anslotts before him.

:And isn't that the saddest way to live?: Rolan asked. *:You should really feel sorry for him. Every time he sees a new thing, he shies like a nervous colt, then takes the bit between his teeth and bolts for the safety of the barn. His whole life has been lived in a state of fear, because even* his *world changes, fight it tooth and nail though he may, and there is nothing he can do to stop the change.:*

She chewed that over in her mind a while. None of that had ever occurred to her. She still didn't *like* Anslott, but . . . given the circumstances, she could feel sorry for him.

A bit.

And the Duke was bowing himself down the aisle, and here came Anslott, his face fixed in his perpetual scowl, doing his best to look right past her.

:All right. I feel sorry for him. But not too much. If he's going to live in terror, he brings it all on himself, after all.:

"So gen'rally, all I needs t'do is keep m'ears open an' pop by the shop oncet or twicet a week, an' tell ye whut I heerd?" Teo said, as he cleaned his fingers of sticky pear juice by the simple expedient of licking them clean.

"Tha's all. Tell any on us here, it'll git back t'me an' Willy 'ventually," Mags replied. "Iffen ye come acrost anythin' particular juicy, git here soon's ye kin. There'll be extree fer that. Otherwise, it's a reg'lar siller a week, an' more iffen it turns out t'be a lead Willy kin sell." This would be Teo's last "trial," before Mags revealed his identity and recruited him into his network of informants and helpers. If Teo brought leads that Willy the Weasel could sell to thieves—well, Mags would keep him on as a source, but never let him into the network. But if Teo did the opposite—brought warnings Willy could take to the Watch and Guard, well, that would be the last sign he could be trusted with Mags' true identity.

As for leads on things that had nothing whatsoever to do with criminal activity, well, those could be sold, and the Weasel's pawn shop did a brisk business in them. Who was likely to hire, for instance. Who'd just been sacked, and for what reason. A load of shoddy goods to beware of. Adulterated goods of any kind. Someone cheating and selling short. And . . . though this was unlikely to come within Teo's purview, who might be having an affair with whom, and whether or not it was an open secret. There were a great many pieces of information that were worth *something* to *someone*, and over the years, the pawn shop, which had started out merely as a front for Nikolas's information ring in the city, was now not only self-supporting, but making a profit.

"I'm yer man," Teo proclaimed, offering his hand to shake on the bargain. Mags took it and shook it without hesitation. What was a little clean spit between friends, after all?

"Oh," Mags added. "Meal's part'a th' deal. Thet way, iffen ye takes yer meal-break t'come report, ye ain't gonna go short."

Teo's eyes lit up at that, and Mags hid a smile. Not a smile of satisfaction, exactly; although it did make him very satisfied to be able to improve Teo's life. More like a smile of mingled satisfaction and commiseration. When he was down here, wearing Harkon's face and character, he *lived* as the real Harkon would. He understood scrounging for pennybits and even pins, and saving to buy old clothing that was not *too* worn or in need of patching to wear, or could be mended. He knew all about having to choose between a beer in winter and an extra bit of wood or coal for the fire to cook a bit of a hot meal or drink or both *and* huddle over to keep warm enough that getting to sleep would not be a shivering ordeal. He'd just made Teo's life that much better, with a good free meal he didn't have to pay for once or twice a week, and an extra silver piece at week's end. Teo would be much better rewarded if he joined Mags' circle of helpers and informants, of course, but even this small addition to Teo's income meant some better clothing, better food, more fuel in the winter, perhaps even a new cloak or blanket for his bed.

Teo cheerfully took his leave, and Mags checked with the two burly former actors who were currently manning the shop—these fellows were part of *Nikolas's* network, and he had first recruited them back when he was Mags' age, and they were still playing minor parts. They had nothing for him to investigate, and aside from that loose talk in the tavern, he had nothing to report.

A quiet time in Haven then. It wouldn't last, of course, but he'd enjoy it while it did.

He made his way to the stable where Dallen waited; walking openly for several blocks, then, once he was in a position where he could vanish off the street without attracting attention, he did so, and made the rest of the journey covertly, by way of back alleys. Once at the extremely busy inn where he kept his disguises and Dallen could idle his time away in one of the loose boxes reserved for Companions until Mags returned, he vanished into a hidden doorway and a secret room only he, Nikolas, and the innkeeper were aware existed.

Once "Harkon" was disposed of and put away in the proper chest, Mags emerged as his proper self and trotted round to Dallen.

:So, not very exciting, but at least you've made a bit of progress with Teo,: Dallen observed, as Mags saddled and tacked up his Companion. *:I can't say I'm displeased with "not exciting.":*

"I was thinking the same thing," Mags replied, hiking himself up into the saddle. "I might actually get to spend some good, relaxin' time with Amily tonight, especially since she's not going to be eatin' with the Court."

If the *King* had been eating with the Court, it went without saying that so would Amily. But that was only two or three times in the week at most; this was one of the nights when the King and his entire family dined alone, leaving the rest of the Court free to do as they pleased.

Heralds were a relatively common sight in Haven; he did his best never to go back up to the Hill on the same route twice, just to make sure that he "blended in," so to speak, with all the others whose duty took them down into the town every day. But there were still a few people on every route who knew him by name. A pocket-pie vendor whose wares Dallen particularly favored was on one of them; a flower-seller he liked to patronize on another. It couldn't be helped; much as he would have preferred to be able to go to and from his life as Harkon completely invisibly, it couldn't be done.

Tonight's route, however, was the busiest at this time of the evening, and everyone on it was far too engrossed in his or her own affairs to pay *him* any attention. So he escaped notice, and once he got up among the mansions and town-homes of the highborn, there was no one about other than servants, for whom Heralds were no novelty, and whose duties precluded gawking even if he'd been riding an Ice-drake instead of a Companion.

The Court was finally over. The King shooed her off, retiring to the privacy of his own quarters with an expression of relief. The courtiers dispersed; some few going to their rooms and suites in the Palace, most returning to their sumptuous homes up here on the Hill. In the absence of any formal entertainment scheduled for tonight, some would return to mingle in the Greater Throne Room or the Great Hall or the gardens. Others would have entertainment planned at their own homes. And Amily would have a rare evening off.

She cut through the gardens to get to the quarters she shared with Mags—quarters not in Heralds' Wing, in the suite of rooms formerly reserved for the King's Own, but a nice, cozy sitting room and bedroom attached to Healer's Collegium. The gardens were empty, or nearly, at this hour, and Amily took her time meandering down the path that would end at the greenhouse-end of Healer's Collegium. *:It seems like the only time I ever get to see the gardens is when I'm eavesdropping or following someone. I would never have guessed there are actually flowers here!:*

:Your sarcasm is wasted without a proper audience, Chosen,: Rolan replied with amusement.

She chuckled. *:You'll do,:* she replied. *:You appreciate it.:*

She left the ornamental Palace gardens for the more practical gardens and lawns around the Collegia. The "new" arrangement still had the odd feeling of unfamiliarity. Until just before Mags had arrived here, there had only been two Collegium buildings, not three. The Herald's Collegium, still looking a little raw and new, at least to her eyes, was where an ornamental fishpond had once been, an oblong water feature that had been one of those things that seemed desirable in theory and on paper, but in practice had proved to be something else altogether. It was, sadly, deep enough to swim in—chest deep on a tall man to be precise—which made it a hazard to small children who didn't know how to swim and could not touch the bottom. It had been stocked with colored carp, but the Trainees *would* persist in trying to fish for them, or tickle them, neither of which pursuits made it the picturesque, placid bit of tamed nature it was supposed to be. Or worse, Trainees and courtier's offspring alike *would* throw things into the pond that were not good for the fish, or overfeed the fish, both of which pursuits ended up with pathetic little discolored corpses floating in the water or discarded on the stone curb surrounding it. Then the gardeners would have to pull all the dead fish out, making sure none were left lurking on the bottom to surprise someone with a terrible stink when they finally rose. And the gardeners would silently curse the miscreants, and curse the job, and go to complain to the Seneschal that they were *gardeners,* dammit, not zookeepers or fish-keepers and this was *not* properly part of their duties. Then the

Seneschal would agree, and promise to stock the pond only with pretty waterlilies, until the next courtier decided the pond looked too quiet without some fish, would present his offering to the King with a proud smile, and it would all begin again. The whole farce seemed to be on about a three year cycle.

So when it was decided to replace the old Heraldic Trainee system of Senior-Herald-and-"apprentices" with the same Trainee-Collegium system that the Bards and Healers used, the fishpond was sacrificed without a backward glance.

No one missed it, though now and again it still seemed strange to see a three-story-tall building rising there. Four, if you counted the kitchens and storage rooms in the half-basement.

She would have known she was out of even the informal gardens and into the practical ones belonging to Healer's Collegium even if she'd been blind. The scent of flowers gave way to the sharper and more complex scents of herbs, and "home" was in sight, the greenhouse attached to the rear of Healer's Collegium. Just past the actual greenhouse itself were two sets of rooms; drying and stillrooms for the preserving of herbs and the making of medicines, and the suite of bedroom and sitting room given to whoever volunteered to keep an eye on the greenhouse and let the actual gardeners know if anything was amiss. Up until recently that person had been a Healer, or at least a Trainee—generally someone who was primarily an herb-Healer. But Amily had been loath to dispossess her father of the rooms he'd had as King's Own for as long as she had been alive, and none of the herb-Healers at the Collegium had wanted to take over Bear's old rooms, and she had gotten them when Bear had essentially "gifted" them to her.

Then, of course, once she and Mags had gotten married, there was no need to move out; *his* old quarters in Companions' Stable, were obviously not suited to a couple who were both full Heralds, much less the King's Own.

She went in through the greenhouse entrance with a sigh of relief that no one had come running up to her with some purported emergency, or to complain about something—no one to her recollection had ever come running to her father with petty complaints, but people certainly seemed to take it as read that they could do so to her.

The greenhouse had all its windows propped open, with a nice, gentle breeze coming through. She took an appreciative breath of the damp, green smell and went on in.

"Just in time!" said Mags, from where he was sprawled on a padded bench. "I'm starving."

2

The dining hall was full; full enough that there was a steady babble of conversation echoing off the ceiling, and Mags had to look hard to spot some room for himself and Amily at one of the long tables. Spring and summer tended to bring more Trainees to all three Collegia. For the Bards and Healers, the reason was obvious; it was easier to travel then, and Spring in particular made people inclined to make new beginnings. Why there should be more *Herald* Trainees in Spring and Summer, however, Mags could not think—

:Simple, if it's not a screaming emergency to fetch our Chosen, we'd rather wait until good weather,: Dallen said, as he and Amily took their places at a table that had just been cleared. Mags chuckled; Amily gave him a knowing look. They had scarcely sat down when a server bustled up with mugs and a pitcher of cold, clean water and another of herb tea, followed by a second server with wooden platters, bowls,

and so forth, and a third with food. As usual, the aromas were enough to make anyone's mouth water. The Collegia never stinted on food and always made sure they had excellent cooks. The meals might not be the fancy stuff served at the Palace, but they were always perfectly made and tasty.

As they served themselves from common platters and bowls, Mags caught a few words of conversation behind them that sounded *very* familiar; in fact, it could have been a repetition of the sort of animated conversation he and his mates had had a scant three years ago. The subject was Kirball, of course. As he concentrated a little to make out what they were saying through the babble of dozens of voices all speaking at once, he figured out that the Trainees behind him were discussing the best sort of strategy to use against a team that had someone with the Fetching Gift when they themselves didn't have anyone of the sort. Oh, it was tempting to lean over and give them a bit of advice, but Amily caught his eye and shook her head. "Let them work it out for themselves," she mouthed. He sighed a little, but nodded. And she was right; the only way for them to learn to work together was to actually *do* it . . . even if it was a bit disconcerting that they didn't recognize that (former) Trainee Mags, the first ever star of one of the very first four Kirball teams, was sitting right behind them.

But before he could feel too much of the sting of not being recognized, he felt a slap on the back as someone slid in next to him, on the side not occupied by Amily. "You'd best have saved some of those dumplings for me, old horse," said Pip as he made a grab for the bowl full of dumplings, chicken, and gravy. "I shall be aggrieved otherwise."

"Well, if I'd known you was back, I'd've et it all," Mags teased, handing him the basket of bread, and snagging a roll for himself. "When did you sneak in?" When Pip had taken the bread and set it aside, Mags handed him the new peas.

"I was right behind you on the road up the Hill, if you'd'a looked," Pip replied, filling his plate with dumplings and chicken, then reaching for the peas. "I said to myself, 'that ass looks familiar,' and my Companion says, 'it should be, you were behind it on the Kirball field often enough,' and that's how I knew it was you." He paused long enough to shove a huge spoonful of dumplings into his mouth and let out a sigh of happiness. When he'd chewed and swallowed, he sighed again. "I've been South. Sheep country. Mutton, lamb, mutton, everlasting mutton. They've got chickens, but they don't trot 'em out even for Heralds. It's mutton pie, stewed mutton, hashed mutton, mutton chops, mutton roast, and for a little variety—mutton ground up and stuffed into pocket pies! Sheep's-milk cheese. Mutton-fat instead of butter. Oh, and barley-bread, and barley-porridge, and never a sign of wheat. They do have every kind of root you can imagine, and plenty you can't, and peas and lentils and beans, but their idea of how to flavor 'em is . . . mutton fat. Almost no herbs that aren't for medicine. Not a sign of a fish. Not a glimpse of a goose or a duck. Now and again, they let loose of one of their precious eggs, and they *stare* at you while you eat it, to make sure you appreciate their sacrifice, I guess." He shook his head woefully.

"It could have been worse," Amily pointed out. "It could have been goat."

Pip shuddered. "It *was* goat in some places. At least where it was goat, the cheese was good. I am *so* glad to be back. Still. The weather wasn't awful, and the good thing about sheep-country is every bed I had was a nice fat wool mattress. Yes," he said, at Mags' look of astonishment. "In the Way-stations. Nice, tufted, wool mattresses, *and* wool blankets if you please, all put up with some sort of herb to keep the moths away. So if the food was enough to make you weep with boredom, I slept good."

"Sounds to me like you made out all right," Mags observed, as Dean Caelen took a seat opposite them and silently began helping himself. "No disasters?"

"Nothing worth talking about," Pip replied. "Just the usual lot of foolishness you get all the time out on circuit. Quarrels to break up before they become feuds. Boundary disputes, sheep claimed by three different people. Gossipy old hags and interfering old men trying to run everybody else's life for 'em. Runaway younglings, abandoned girls halfway to birthing, lost littles, claims of curses. People not liking the new laws, people wanting old laws changed right that moment, people wanting this, that, or the other, and me having to put their best case for them." He waved his hand vaguely in the air. "The usual. Which is to say, I am very damn glad I don't get the kind of excitement that *you've* gotten."

Pip had been a tall, lanky, brown boy, and he had become a tall, lanky, brown man, and he looked very handsome in his Herald Whites. He'd always been one for spending as much time out of doors as possible; being a Field Herald clearly suited him.

There were more than one or two of the older female Trainees watching him out of the corners of their eyes, and several of the younger ones who were looking at him as if they were star-struck; Mags smiled to himself, though he felt a little sorry for them, for they had no hope at all. No full Herald would ever dally with a Trainee; it was considered very bad form. Pip would pretend not to understand any outright advances, although he'd be quite polite and not at all condescending about it.

Dean Caelen, the head of Herald's Collegium, smiled a little as Pip stopped talking so he could concentrate on eating. "Perhaps East on your next circuit?" he suggested, buttering a slice of bread. "We'll try and keep you out of sheep country, but from the sound of it, you do a good job with country-folk."

"Nobody complained, at any rate," Pip offered. "We might be highborn, but we're country highborn; more squire than Duke, if you take my meaning. My Ma is sort-of the peacemaker back home for everyone all around. Less than a judge, not a Herald, but more than just the manor lady. People were in and out of the manor, all day, every day, taking their troubles in with them, and mostly leaving those troubles behind them. Maybe some of it rubbed off."

Dean Caelen nodded. Like Pip, he was brown of hair and eye, but unlike Pip, he did not give the impression that he was a coiled spring, ready to bounce off at the first hint of something to release all his pent-up energy. Instead, he had an air of quiet, unruffled confidence that was very soothing to harried or troubled young Trainees.

"We'll talk that over later, when we've had a chance to review all your reports," the Dean told him. "Meanwhile, enjoy your leisure. If we get someone injured out in the Field that needs replacing, your holiday may not last long."

"So how is the latest crop?" Pip asked, raising his eyes from his food long enough to cast a skeptical eye across the dining hall. "They look a bit grubby."

As those discouraging words met the ears of the nearest young ladies, they looked flustered and crestfallen, and quickly turned their attention to their food.

"I expect we looked a bit grubby at that age," Amily pointed out, and chuckled. "I wager every new crop of Trainees looks grubby and unfinished to the ones that were here before them."

"That's because they *are* unfinished," the Dean observed with a smile. "It would be rather astonishing if they were not. We wouldn't need the Collegia, and we wouldn't be calling them Trainees now, would we, if they came to us ready to be put into Whites and on to the job?"

"You have a point," Pip chuckled. "Although, I have been lending half an ear to the grubby lot behind us, and take it from me, they have a *lot* to learn about Kirball. I hope they are farther along in their Trainee studies than they are in game strategy. Unless their opponents are just as bad, they're going to fall flat on their noses."

But Mags had heard something more than faulty Kirball strategy as he had been listening to those young (*so* young!) Trainees. He'd heard a kind of careless freedom, freedom that gave them the ability to see a game as the most important thing in their lives at that moment. "Innocence" probably wasn't the right term for it . . . but he couldn't think of a good word. Not "ignorance," either, unless you subscribed to the notion that "ignorance is bliss," which he did not. Ignorance was dangerous. This . . . was more like the carefree certainty that right now, they would be so safe in the hands of their elders that they could concentrate on what they pleased.

"Didja ever wish you could go back?" he asked, wistfully.

Pip gave him an odd look, as if he had said something

incomprehensible. "Go back? To what?"

"Bein' a Trainee again," Mags elaborated. "When things was simpler. When the worst thing that happened was failin' a test, or losin' a game."

The Dean chuckled. "Only if I could do so from the perspective of my older self, so I could *enjoy* the contrast," he replied. "Because, remember, when you say 'the worst thing that happened' it literally *is* the worst thing that can happen to these younglings, and it can seem devastating. They haven't had experience of anything worse, a lot of them. And, trust me, that makes them feel just as miserable as if what had just befallen them was an adult-sized disaster."

"An' hell, Mags, maybe that's how it'd be for me, but *you* had some pretty adult-sized disasters when you were a Trainee," Pip observed, as Amily nodded and passed him the bowl of chicken and dumplings again. "And what you came from? Three-quarters starved, near beaten to death, and a slave in the mines? You sure you'd want to go through all that again?"

"You got a point. I wouldn't," Mags admitted. "Still, I'd kinda like to know what it was like t'have been a normal Trainee, though. Like you, say, or Gennie."

"Define *normal*," the Dean replied dryly. "From my point of view, the entire Collegium is composed of people with issues, anxieties, and quirks. Some of our Trainees might come from homes of wealth and status, but that doesn't mean they've had an easy time of it. And as for those that have, well, suddenly finding themselves without personal servants and all the good things that come with rank is quite a shock to their systems!"

They all chuckled at that, and with that as the opener to a new conversation, Amily encouraged the Dean to talk about some of the more amusing "quirks."

Mags quietly ate, and considered all that, and with a burst of nostalgia decided, on the whole, he *would* like to come back here all over again as a Trainee. Provided, of course, that as the Dean said, he still had his adult perspective, and had *not* had the parentage he'd had. The idea of spending four or five years with nothing more life-challenging than classes and games . . . sounded rather heavenly.

Nothing more engrossing than classes, nothing more desperate than exams, and nothing more exciting than Kirball . . .

Then again . . . not bloody likely. Even if he could have somehow sloughed off his own past, if some magic had given him a regular family, the Dean was right, and who was to say whether or not some *other* drama would have cropped up?

And even if he'd had a normal family, there would still have been Lena's wretched father, the unfortunate Bard Marchand, who had single-handedly made a wretched mess of her life and had betrayed the King with his carelessness and pride. And there would have been Bear's horrible family, and all the messes and misery they had caused. The Karsites would still have been sending their spies and agents here. And who knows? There still might have been a missing Sleepgiver "Prince," and the Sleepgivers *still* could have turned up, taking jobs for the Karsites with an eye to getting paid while looking for their missing heir.

There was no telling how that might have ended, if he had not, after all, been the "missing Prince." The only change likely would have been considerably less grief for him, since he wouldn't have been a foreigner, and there wouldn't have been any ambiguous visions from the Foreseers involving *him*. Or, rather, there would have still been ambiguous visions from the Foreseers, but it wasn't likely that anyone would have interpreted them as involving him . . .

:This would be entertaining speculation for a writer imagining alternate versions of history,: Dallen reminded him dryly. *:But it didn't happen that way, and we are here, and your life is scarcely wretched now, is it?:*

The others were still being entertained by the Dean, and he smothered a smile. *:True, horse,:* he replied. Look how things had turned out, after all! He was *married*, for heaven's sake, to the loveliest and most patient and dearest girl he had ever known. A girl he could count on in any situation, and who would always be honest with him. Someone who would not pout and feel offended when the job took his attention and time from her. And rather than being faced with the perils of Field duty, he and Amily had positions here, in Haven. True, you could not call what they did *safe*, since nothing a Herald did was *safe*, but they were in the safest possible place to be a Herald. And they weren't moving all the time, the way Heralds on Circuit were. They had a real home, together with all of the creature comforts that meant. Any possible separations would be temporary at worst. There were scarcely any Heralds in the entire Heraldic Circle who could say that.

Life, in short, was rather good.

:Yes it is. It will be even better if you bring me a pocket pie,: Dallen prompted.

:Sorry, not on the menu tonight,: Mags replied. *:You'll have to make do with pears.:*

There was a long pause from Dallen. *:I take it back about life being good.:*

* * *

Mags and Nikolas had turned over the day-to-day running of the pawn shop to their hand-picked half-dozen ex-actors and retired Guards. They still went down to it several times a week, but generally only to check in on things, and seldom stayed to work the counter. This wasn't one of the nights when Mags had planned to do that, and since the King was having one of *his* nights with his family, there was nothing formal for Amily to attend. As a consequence, he was about to suggest a stroll down by the river, when Dean Caelen stopped them as they were all picking up their plates to take them to the serving hatch for cleaning.

"Some of the Bardic Trainees put together an informal concert for tonight," he said. "They're having it at the Yew Garden." The Yew Garden was one of several gardens inside the Palace walls; this one was particularly suited to informal concerts, being far enough from the Palace itself that those who were more interested in gossip than listening to music would probably not make the effort to attend, and would instead stroll the Rose Garden or one of the other flower gardens, chattering away about—whatever it was courtiers found to gossip about. *Each other, mostly. . . .*

"I think we should all go!" Pip said, happily. "Just what I need for the end of my first day back here!"

Mags and Amily exchanged a quick look, but it was clear to each of them in that glance that they both wanted to go. Pip was right. No matter what kind of day *anyone* had had, short of one filled with tragedy, there could be no better ending to it than a night of music. If nothing else, being friends with Lena had taught them that.

However, the wearing of white uniforms did come with a certain hazard—and by common consent, they all went back to their quarters to get something to sit on before re-gathering on the terrace to go down to the Yew Garden.

Of the many benefits of actually *living* here, one was that Mags and Amily had plenty of storage, and could keep things around that had only one purpose—like an old rag rug good only for picnicking and similar pursuits, and a couple of cushions covered in a patchwork of leather from worn-out tunics that would hold up under any amount of outdoor abuse. When they met up with the rest, it was clear that Pip had just grabbed his sleeping roll, something he might later regret when the time came to spread out his blankets on whatever bed he'd been given. Sharing his bed with ants, for instance, was probably not high on his list of "ways to get a good night's sleep."

The Yew Garden was just that; a garden full of yew trees that were kept clipped into pleasing shapes. Some people went so far as to have their yews clipped into the shapes of animals; tradition held here, however, that the trees should merely be abstract and ornamental. At one end of the garden a curve of hedge as tall as a house gently framed a half-circle of paving. Tonight this paving held lanterns and lamps a-plenty, and six Bardic Trainees—and far more instruments than Mags cared to count. In order to be admitted into Bardic Collegium, would-be Trainees had to demonstrate two out of three things for qualification: Bardic Gift, compositional ability, and exceptional ability on at least one instrument, the voice counting as an instrument. It was Mags' impression that most Trainees had all three; in order to become a full Bard, after all, they had to create and perform a musical work of sufficient quality to be deemed a "master" piece, so even those with the Gift had to learn what they lacked.

Given the number of different instruments waiting to be played, it was pretty obvious that this set of six was a proficient bunch.

White shapes began to ghost into the Yew Garden; the fence around Companion's Field was never meant to keep the Companions *in*, it was more to keep other things *out*. Plenty of Companions enjoyed music, and it seemed they had gotten word of this little concert, too. Two of them ambled over to the spot where Amily and Mags had spread their rug and placed their cushions. Rolan simply folded up his legs and laid himself down on Amily's side of the rug, but Dallen blew into Mags' hair, meditatively.

"Hey!" Mags objected.

:There were no pocket pies,: Dallen said mournfully. *:Life is not worth living. I shall eat yew.:*

"Go right ahead," Mags said without pity. "An' I'll tell the Healers y'ate yew, an' they'll come and force a purge down yer throat, an' ye'll get t'spend all night with a bellyache."

Rolan snorted, and Amily giggled.

:Heartless,: Dallen sighed.

"Y'might have a bellyache anyway," Mags continued. "Since you et not less'n a half dozen pears. Might've been more."

:I never!: Dallen exclaimed, indignantly.

:I counted,: Rolan interjected. *:He's right.:*

Dallen's head came up and he stared at Rolan with indignation. *:You traitor!:* he gasped.

:You didn't share,: Rolan pointed out.

"Hush, both of you," Amily put in. "They're about to start."

And so they were. Dallen grumbled a little, folded his legs under him, and elected to make a backrest for Mags and Amily. Mags put his arm around Amily; she smiled and snuggled as near as was physically possible.

The six Bardic Trainees in their rust-colored uniforms were a mixed lot. There was a very tall young man, who surely would be going for his Scarlets soon, and a serious-faced, long-haired girl in the skirted version of the uniform who looked to be about the same age, and four younger ones who were more or less androgynous, and at the moment, distinguished only by the differences in their coloring. Mags had assumed the oldest boy would be the leader, but rather to his surprise, it was one of the younger four who they all looked to for direction when they finally settled with their instruments.

Well, they're not Lena, he thought to himself, after two short numbers. *But they're pretty good.*

:Lena is a Master's Master,: Dallen pointed out. *:And once she got over her shyness, she proved just that.:*

Mags couldn't help but smile at that. It was the first time Dallen had ever said anything like that about Lena, and to hear a *Companion* say that Lena was just that good . . . well it made him feel warm all over. *I'll remember to write her and tell her.*

Then he just relaxed with his arm around Amily and enjoyed the music. Despite their fierce concentration, it seemed to him that the musicians were enjoying themselves, too. He could tell that Amily was having a wonderful time—and he could tell which people here—at least of those he could see—were really music lovers, and which wished to be *thought of* as music lovers. The little thing in full

Healer's robes sitting all alone, for instance, who bobbed her whole body a little in time to the fast pieces as if she was dancing, and swayed slightly to the slow ones—she was enjoying every note. But the fellow with the fixed, stern expression, who visibly winced at what he supposed were mistakes—you couldn't call such a person a music lover. Mags would bet he'd probably spend a considerable piece of time tomorrow, buttonholing someone to describe in detail everything that these youngsters had done "wrong."

:Actually, he'll just have to seethe about it until the next time, I'll bet,: Dallen replied with amusement. *:By this time everyone he knows is well aware of what he's like. They'll either avoid him, cut him off, or ignore him while nodding vaguely until they can escape.:*

Mags nearly choked on a laugh. Amily looked curiously at him, then smiled. Rolan must have told her what Dallen had said. As if to confirm that, she reached back and gave Dallen an approving pat.

The entire group of Trainees didn't play the entire time; they took it in turns to solo, duet, or trio, as well as performing as six. And it wasn't all instrumental music; they sang as well. They all had good, strong voices, though none of them was the sort to take your breath away, and if any of them had the Bardic Gift, they didn't demonstrate it. Frankly, Mags didn't particularly miss that; people actually *using* the Bardic Gift could get you so wrapped up in the performance you wouldn't notice if it was mediocre—a fact that was probably lost on Milord Critic sitting on the bench beside the pyramidal yew.

As a finale, they played a very complicated original piece for gittern, harp, viol, lute, flute, and hautboy. Although they didn't announce it as such, Mags figured it must be an original. If so, whoever had composed it was clearly talented.

At the end, they got up and bowed, and the tall young man cleared his throat when the applause finished. "That's the end of what we had planned, but we're just going to hang about and play around for a while longer. If anyone wants to join us, you're welcome, and if anyone just wants to stay and chat, we won't be offended."

That last brought an appreciative chuckle from several of the listeners, Mags and Amily especially, since they had, more than once, been the recipients of one of Lena's irritated plaints about people who considered the musicians at court events a sort of musical background that could be talked over. And what Master Bard Lita, the Dean of Bardic Collegium had to say on the same subject was . . . vivid.

The Dean, who had been sitting as near to the musicians as he could get, and Pip, who had placed himself where he could stretch out on his bedroll, both picked up their things and moved to join Amily and Mags. A few moments later, as if drawn by some unheard signal, they were joined by Herald Jakyr, Amily's father Nikolas, and Lita herself.

"Well, what do you think of them?" Lita asked, as Jakyr spread out a rug nearly as battered as the one Mags and Amily were sharing, and she dropped some flat cushions on it for them both to sit on.

"They're good," Mags said. "Have they been playin' together long?"

"One week," Lita replied, satisfaction coloring her voice as they all exclaimed in surprise. "And the three youngest haven't been here for more than six months. That last piece was composed by the oldest lad. Trainee Dani's his name, and we expect great things of him."

Mags chuckled. Lita gave him an odd look. "What's so funny, my lad?" she asked. Ever since they had all traveled together, with Bear and Lena, combining an attempt to hide Mags from the Sleepgiver assassins trying to find and kidnap him with Mags' Field Year, the Master Bard, though technically far senior to anyone except Amily, tended to treat them all rather like family.

"Oh, Amily and Pip an' me were sayin' at dinner as how the current lot of Herald Trainees looked a bit . . . grubby," Mags replied.

Jakyr laughed, and Lita waved her hand in the air. "Of course they look grubby," she agreed. "My six over there got polished within an inch of their lives before we let them come out here for their concert; give them another couple of candlemarks and at least the three youngest will look like they've been rolling in the grass. The First Years all live in the moment, or at least, the ones that come to us as younglings do. Even *you* lived in the moment to a certain extent, Mags."

"Huh," he said, thinking about it. "Reckon I did. Mostly, it was enjoyin' the food, and havin' a real bed, an' good clothes. Now that I think about it, I kinda lived in the moment a lot."

"Especially at mealtimes," Jakyr chuckled.

"Living in the moment is all well and good when you're merely reveling in taking a second helping of apple pocket pies," Lita sighed. "The problem comes when you are living in the moment and doing mischief. *My* lot don't have Companions in the back of their minds giving them the scolding of a lifetime if high spirits turn into something potentially harmful."

Mags raised an eyebrow at her. "Is this gener'lly a problem with your Trainees?"

Lita made a sour face. "Marchand isn't the only Bard or Bardic Trainee with a monumental ego and monumental self-centeredness to match monumental talent. We haven't got one like that *yet* this year, but we're only halfway through the year. The last one . . ." She paused. "Let's just say the amount of drama he caused made it very clear that no amount of talent *or* Bardic Gift was going to make up for his first six months alone. We turned him out to fend for himself and find what teachers he could. And before we did that, we got the Healers to shut his Gift down."

Mags blinked. "Ye can *do* that?" he asked, both fascinated and revolted.

"It takes a Mindhealer, and you have to convince every senior Healer at the Collegium, but yes," Jakyr told him, a little grimly. "Perhaps you aren't aware of a rather mordant saying among the Healers? *Those who know how you are put together can easily take you apart.* It's not done often and it's *never* done lightly, but it is possible to shut down nearly every Mindgift there is. The closer those Gifts are to Empathy—and the Bardic Gift is very close indeed—the easier it is for the Healers to close it down."

"Huh." Mags considered that. "Reckon it's a good thing we got Companions, then."

"And it's a good thing anyone with Bardic Gift is generally identified quickly and sent here," Lita replied. "Though I do wish there was a Bardic form of the nagging conscience that is a Companion."

"But that doesn't always work either," Amily pointed out. "Look what happened to Tylendel!"

Before Mags could think of anything to say, Dallen put in his word. *:That will never happen again,:* he said, and the tone of his

Mindvoice was such that Mags would never have dared to argue with him. And from the looks on the faces of Amily, her father, Jakyr, and the Dean, their Companions had said much the same and with the same emphasis to them.

Which led to a moment of extremely awkward silence, as Lita looked around at their frozen faces. "Well," she said, finally, breaking that silence. "I do believe the Companions have had the last word."

"They generally do," Nikolas replied, dryly.

"But that just underscores what I've been saying, and emphasizes something else that occurred to me that I dearly wish the Bardic Trainees had," Lita continued. "Certainty. That's something that Heraldic Trainees and Heralds *always* have. They *know* what they are doing—the job, that is—is the right thing to do. If I had a copper for every candlemark I've spent reassuring anguished Bardic Trainees—yes, and Bards too!—who are caught in the stranglehold of a crisis of conscience, I would be the wealthiest woman in the Kingdom. Do you realize how rare that sort of certainty is in life?"

Mags snorted. "Oh, sure, we know we're doin' the right *job*. But that don't help with other things. 'Specially not personal stuff. We muddle through that all on our lonesome, an' let me tell you, when you're used to bein' told what's what, an' all of a sudden the critter you're relyin' on for advice clamps his horse-teeth down an' won't say a word, it's downright aggravatin'."

:Shall I call those Trainees over to play sad songs now?: Dallen said, mockingly. *:Would you like a handkerchief to sniffle into?:*

:Quiet, horse.:

"Ye-es," Jakyr replied, ruefully. "As I know all too personally. You can feel the weight of disapproval, but of *what*? They won't say. And you don't find out until *after* you've made a hash of your personal life."

"As I was told rather sternly when I was a Trainee, it is not the Companion's place to interfere in our personal lives so long as we are not affecting anyone but ourselves," Nikolas said, with a long look at Rolan, who only snorted. "Though it seems to me that they are very *flexible* in that interpretation."

:We're right here, you know. Rolan and I can very well get up and leave you without backrests.:

"And then we'd just be talking behind your backs," said Mags, Nikolas, and Amily, all at the same time, while Caelen nearly choked on a laugh.

"It's all right for you," Jakyr added, looking remorsefully at Caelen. *"You* have never put a foot wrong in your life."

"But for a Herald I have led an extraordinarily dull life," the Dean replied serenely. "The most adventure I ever had when out on circuit was fleeing from a troupe of bandits."

"No ill-conceived romances? No misplaced trust? No hijinks or shenanigans?" Jakyr inquired, looking incredulous. "Dear gods, Dean, you are a dull fellow."

The Dean bowed his head slightly, acknowledging the fact. "But then, what I was actually doing out in the field was very time consuming. I didn't even have time for a life, much less getting myself into trouble. The circuit I had required an unbelievable amount of personal managing. It was all little villages, with no central authorities at all, so *I* was what passed for a central authority. The Border had just been expanded—at their request—to include them, and they were incredibly anxious that they not do anything wrong and somehow cause us to withdraw our protection again." He spread his hands wide. "Ten years of that made it clear to Herald Parthen that I was capable of handling his position, so he put in my name as the sole candidate and when he died, I suddenly found myself managing the Heraldic Trainees, and I managed us right into the new building and the methodical training system."

Huh. So it was Caelen behind changin' from the old way t'the new Collegium way. That was something Mags had not known.

"So you gave up havin' a life t' do the job," Mags said aloud. "But if we ain't got a life, how are we s'pposed to understand regular folks that *do* got a life?"

"Ah—now there's the question, isn't it?" the Dean countered.

"Perhaps we shouldn't expect to have a life," Jakyr sighed. "But you're right, if we don't have *something* apart from being a Herald, how can we expect to treat people with—" He waved a hand vaguely.

"Compassion for their foibles and follies and mistakes?" Amily offered.

"Something like that. We can't exactly go around being little plaster gods, after all," the Dean agreed. "Which is probably *why* the Companions don't interfere in our personal lives. You can't have sympathy for someone else's mistakes if you've never made any yourself."

"I thought you just said that you had no life while out on circuit," Jakyr retorted.

"Ah!" Dean Caelen held up a finger. "But I didn't say a word about my Trainee days, now, did I?"

* * *

The conversation drifted on to Trainee pranks; Mags and Amily had nothing to contribute, really, but the Dean, of all people, turned out to have been a notable jokester. Finally someone noticed that the musicians had packed up and gone, and so had almost everyone else, and the group broke up. The Companions ambled back over to their stables, being perfectly capable of opening the stable door and tucking themselves up in the stalls, and Mags and Amily shook out their rug, beat the ants out of their cushions, and headed back to their rooms.

"That was fun," Amily said, in tones of immense content. "I wish we could have evenings like that more often."

"Ah, but didn' Caelen say Heralds don't get a life?" Mags retorted with a chuckle. "Though I reckon we have more of a chance at it than most."

"Well . . . yes and no," Amily replied thoughtfully. "When you think about it, most people spend almost every waking moment working, just to keep a roof over their heads and food on the table. The mere idea of being able to have a whole evening to listen to music and talk with friends would be as fantastic as flying to the moon to them."

Mags already had his arm around her shoulders and he gave her a squeeze. He didn't have to think about it too hard; he knew, from his forays down in the poorer parts of Haven, and from his own past, that she was absolutely right. "Reckon we ain't so bad off, then," he replied as they got to the greenhouse door. "Reckon it's 'cause Caelen an' Jakyr an' even your Pa had it good as kids?"

"Very likely," she replied, as they tossed their burdens into the box by the door where they were usually kept. "Going down into Haven to help Bear opened my eyes to quite a lot. Sometimes it opened my eyes to things I would rather not have been aware of—but then, Rolan Chose me, and now I know it's a good thing that I found out about abuse and hardship that made me angry and unhappy."

He smiled in the darkness of the sitting room, and was about to say something, when she put her finger against his lips. "And right now, since we have the option, I would rather not talk about anything unpleasant. We're actually in our rooms together at the same time, there's nothing wrong, and the night isn't that far gone and *nothing* had better interrupt what I have in mind!"

And since she made it quite clear what she had in mind . . . he was not about to make any objections.

3

Once a seven-day, if his little collection of urchins had nothing urgent to report, Mags collected them all together and took notes on whatever they had gathered since the last time they'd reported to him. Today was that day, and he turned up in the morning, before breakfast. Before the runners went out, he came to Minda's place to collect his information. He sat on a stool in the middle of the former shop next door to the Weasel's pawn shop and gravely took down notes as each child faithfully recited the "doin's" to him. Most of what they told him was redundant, most of it was information he already had from other sources, but this was all training for *them*, and he took down every word, and at times stopped to question them more closely about details. He always took the reports of the "senior" children first, the ones who had been in his service longest, so the newest could learn by listening. There was a lot for them to learn, and not just what it was that Harkon wanted them to watch for. They learned how best to give a report, and what details Harkon would want. As the others listened, they also learned how to make reports that were concise and clean. They learned from his responses what he considered valuable information—including what things he felt were worth paying a little bit more for.

He had a new group this time, another lot of seven bedraggled urchins he'd taken wholesale from yet another idiot who thought he could get away with running a gang of mistreated child-thieves. This lot hadn't been allowed to do anything yet other than eat, rest, and accustom themselves to the idea that with Aunty Minda and Harkon, they'd never be beaten (unless they had transgressed one of Minda's few rules), never be clothed in rags, never sleep cold and rough, and never go hungry again. Gradually Mags would integrate them into his runner network, unless they proved to be uncommonly bright. In *that* case, he'd assign them to schooling exclusively, for a literate youngster could get any number of superior jobs, and a literate informant in a runner's job was priceless. Already he had half a dozen youngsters in apprentice positions around the city, another half dozen had places as servants among the highborn, and he looked forward to the day when he'd have as many informants as Nikolas did. One of his prize pupils was Coot, from the first gang he'd liberated. Coot was the lad in charge of the day-to-day operation of the runner-service now, with all the runners reporting to him at his very own office in what had once been a hot-sausage-stall squeezed in between two prosperous inns. As a sausage stall it had not been able to compete once one of the two innkeepers had taken a notion to open up a window on the street selling leftover meat on loaf-ends, and jugs of beer—bring your own jug. As the counter of a messenger-dispatching service it did a brisk business.

The runner-service was turning a profit, too, now, and Mags was very proud of how Coot was handling it.

So now, this new lot of skinny, bruised, ill-treated littles was getting to see "how things was done fer th' Cap'n"—the "Cap'n" being what the very first group had decided to dub him, probably because the ultimate authority they had known (and feared) on the street was the local Captain of the Watch.

They never called him by his real name, and never referred to him as a Herald. Most of them had never seen a Herald except at a distance before Mags had revealed himself to them, and *all* of them knew that the fact that "Harkon" was also a Herald was a secret none of them was to divulge.

Not that anyone would likely have believed it if they had. Harkon had too definite a reputation down in this part of Haven for anyone to do more than guffaw at such a ridiculous notion, and probably send the child off with a box to his ear for being an outrageous liar.

One by one, the rest came up to him, made their reports while he took notes, and collected their pay. The newcomers watched the others interact with him wearing varied expressions ranging from skepticism to awe—the awe when extra copper bits and even a small silver piece got-doled out. Finally the last of them had made his report, and the lot swarmed Aunty Minda, who decreed that "Ye kin et, now," and began ladling out porridge and cutting thick slices of bread and giving them a smear of butter and jam. The new littles had been here long enough to know that the food wasn't going to vanish, no one was going to take their shares away from them, and there would be plenty to go around, so while there was the expected jostling that would go on in any group of children, be they low or highborn, there was no frantic scrambling to get a share of the food. In fact, some of the new ones had begun to make friends among the established group. Both groups mingled together to eat; it was easy enough to spot the new ones by how thin they were, and how their "new" clothing was much too big for them.

He liked to stay—pretending he was going over his notes—to watch them eat. Of all the things he had done, rescuing these children from near-slavery and terrible hardship made him the happiest. He couldn't claim to have been personally responsible for rescuing his fellow mine-slaves—that had been due to Jakyr and the other Heralds—so he did his best to rescue and support as many other wretched little mites as he could.

The last of them were just mopping up the last bits of porridge with their last bites of bread when one of the seasoned runners came bursting in, frantically looking around, his face suffused with mingled alarm and relief to see that Mags was still there. "Harkon!" he exclaimed, "Hatchet, Dog-Billy, an' Rufus is on th' way here, wi' some paid bully boys, an' they reckon t'—"

Mags held up a hand, to quiet the boy and hush the rest of the children, who reacted with terror to the names of their former captors. "It don' matter none what they *reckon* t'do, because they ain't gonna do it, an' they're gonna be sorry they tried. Pagen, git th' Watch. Minda, git the littles below. Trey, git up i'rafters; I wants a witness." As Minda pulled up a hatch in the center of the floor and herded the children down into it, the runner obeyed Mags' orders to him, and scrambled up into the exposed rafters where he could observe, safely out of reach, and escape through the door in the roof at need. While they all did as they had been told, Mags sauntered over to the fireplace and removed a small lead ball from a cracked bowl of more of the same. These balls were small enough to conceal in his hand, but larger than the round clay balls the children played rainy-day games with. Definitely too large to be swallowed, and just about the right size to use as shot in a sling for a strong child, which was what a very select few of the children were allowed to do.

While he was there, he also took up a staff that had been leaning against the mantelpiece. Of course, he *could* use the weapons he had on his person, but he didn't actually want to kill these men.

:I've sent a Herald to alert the Watch,: Dallen told him.

:Good, I sent Pagen off after them, and Minda will send someone, too, so this will give us a head start.:

The cellar was not a potential trap; a properly made tunnel ran between it and the cellar under the pawn shop. Minda would send the most responsible of the children up into the shop to first alert whoever was working there, then run off over the rooftops to find the Watch just in case Pagen couldn't locate them quickly. When Mags was through with the three instigators, the Watch would have a nice little package to take off to gaol.

He was absently regretting now that he'd gotten a little bit lazy with these three; in all his other forays into thieves' dens to free their child-gangs, he'd taken care to beat the thief-masters to a bloody pulp before announcing to the lads that *he* was taking over the gang.

That had been more than enough to prevent any retribution. But his reputation had begun to precede him, and with this lot, he'd decided to wait until the thief-masters had gone before he broke into the filthy, drafty hovels they were keeping their gangs of boys in. Once there, all he'd done was to make sure none of them were actually chained up and announce he was there to recruit them, figuring the children would follow him without needing to be terrified into doing so. It had worked all three times; the decent prospects for redemption had all been more than willing to go with him, while those with stickier fingers had scarpered off. *Not* turning their erstwhile master into a quivering heap on the floor set a good example, he'd told himself, and he had been sure that Harkon's reputation would make those "masters" think twice before having a go at him.

Evidently not.

It was quite out of character for them to turn up in broad daylight, but then, he reckoned they intended to make a "statement" about Harkon's fearsome qualities or lack thereof, and how *they* did not intend to let him take what was "theirs" and flip a finger at them.

So it appeared he'd have to beat them to a bloody pulp after all.

:My, aren't we self-confident.: He ignored Dallen's sally for a moment, as he planned out his moves. The three bosses would be leading their hirelings. They wouldn't be able to go through the door three abreast, so they'd have to let one lead, then the other two would have to squeeze in behind the first. They'd never been here, so they would take a few moments to get oriented and focused on him. Those few moments should be all the time he'd need.

:The only question I got is whether or not their hired thugs are gonna pile

on me after I get the three bastards down,: Mags replied. *:I'm figurin' they won't. I'm figurin' they got paid enough t'make a show, but not enough t'risk gettin' hurt.:*

:And if you're wrong?: Dallen asked. *:Purely an academic question, of course . . . :*

Well, he'd tie up the door taking out the leaders, and that would buy him a bit more time if the mercs got enthusiastic. Time was all he needed. The Watch was already on the way.

:By then, I reckon the Watch'll be here, so likely at the worst I'll get off with some bruises.: He might have added more, but just at that moment the door crashed open, and there they were, Hatchet, the grizzled, greasy-haired brute, coming first through the door and ending up in the middle, Dog-Billy, the filthy, ugly one squeezing in on the right, and Rufus, the bald, scarred fool on the left.

Of the three of them, Dog-Billy was the most dangerous, because he was no little crazy, and utterly unpredictable. Besides that, there was not a single soul in all of Haven who would mourn if he died, and he was so foul Mags really didn't want to touch him, even with a six-foot pole. So it was Dog-Billy who got the lead ball pitched into his throat before Hatchet could open his mouth to say anything.

Dog-Billy went down choking, clutching at his crushed larynx, as the hired thug that had been crowding in behind him stared in dumbfounded disbelief. Hatchet and Rufus were staring, too, but not for long. Mags took two long strides toward them and drove the end of his staff up between Hatchet's legs before the bully-boy had any idea what he was doing. As Hatchet doubled over, clutching at his abused privates, Mags reversed the staff and brought it down on the back of his head, felling him. And before Rufus had time to react,

Mags cracked him alongside his head, dropping *him* to the ground.

There were six hired thugs standing there just outside the door now, staring at him in shock. He grounded the staff, and looked them up and down.

"So, what'd these idjits give ye?" he asked calmly. " 'Cause I kin do better."

They exchanged a look, equal parts shock and calculation. Finally the rightmost one answered. "Five copper each in 'and. Five more when—" He shrugged, saying without words, *well,* that *isn't going to happen.*

Mags dug into his belt-pouch and came up with six of the smallest silver pieces, each one of which represented twice what they had each been paid already. He tossed the coins at them; they snatched the money out of the air. "Get out," he suggested. " 'Less any on ye either wanta *meet* th' Watch or *bring* the Watch."

It appeared that none of them were interested in either prospect; the doorway shortly held nothing but air.

With Hatchet and Rufus unconscious, Mags examined Dog-Billy without touching him. It appeared that he had figured out how to breathe again, so maybe Mags hadn't actually done him permanent damage, but he was still choking and gasping, his hands still clutched his throat and tears of purest pain were cutting furrows through the grease and dirt on his face. "Guess, ye'll live," he said with regret, picking the lead ball up from where it was rolling around a little on the floor, just as the Watch arrived.

Now the Watch of this district knew him; knew him not only as Harkon, but as Mags, so they didn't argue when he loudly proclaimed that the three men on the floor had come there to "interfere with m'bizness," and had tried to attack him. Mind, that actually was telling the strict truth—they had, and they had. In Mags' mind, it was always better to tell the truth than make something up you'd have to remember later.

It did help, of course, that Trey was in the rafters, loudly seconding everything Mags said. Not that they would doubt the word of a Herald, but Mags wasn't being Mags at the moment, so a witness would come in handy if one of the three raised objections in front of a judge.

Therefore the Watch had no reason to make any sort of objection to anything Mags asked, and what he asked was that the three bullies be taken off and locked up, and let the law handle them. They just trussed the three thugs up and carted them off. When the whole group was gone, Mags pounded his staff on the hatch, signaling to Aunty Minda it was safe to come up again.

But before anyone but Minda could emerge from their hiding place, he tossed the staff and the lead ball to Trey, who had scrambled down out of the rafters, and left, smiling a little, but only to himself. Standing there to be congratulated and fawned over by a pack of littles was not in Harkon's nature, and it would reinforce that, and enhance his reputation, if he stalked off as if felling the three thugs by himself was inconsequential. There had been no witnesses but Trey to the fight, but the arrival and departure of the Watch would surely bring the curious flocking to find out what had happened.

The result was that he was well out of the way by the time a crowd started to gather around the door, and out of sight by the time Trey began his story, which would likely be much embellished. Although the fight hadn't made much noise, the arrival of six stout fellows of the Watch was not something that would pass unnoticed in this part of town. The departure of the Watch with three notorious gang-masters trussed up and in considerable pain would bring just about everyone out to see what was going on. Mags wasn't particularly concerned about repercussions; the three thugs didn't have any friends in this neighborhood. In fact, since the general opinion hereabouts regarding Rufus, Dog-Billy, and Hatchet was "good riddance to bad rubbish," the only reaction to seeing the trio hauled off would be "who did 'em and how did it happen?"

:Well, this isn't going to do Harkon's reputation any harm,: Dallen observed. *:Well done, by the way. How did you know you'd take them by surprise?:*

:All three of 'em like to speechify before they beat a feller up,: Mags replied. *:They'd 'specially want to speechify in front of the young'uns. It'd make it easier t'herd 'em all up and drive 'em back t'whatever bolt-hole they're using now.:*

He was pretty sure what had been their plan after that; divide the littles up according to their own pecking order. The next order of business would have been to start beating the younglings, then put them back to work as thieves again once they were suitably cowed and broken.

Which just showed how short-sighted and stupid they were, first, that they would assume that beatings would keep youngsters who'd seen a better life in line, and second, that they'd go right back to the risky business of running a ring of thieves and pickpockets. Moronic, really, when they could just as easily have taken over Harkon's messenger-service to a safer, if smaller, profit. But he reckoned that simply wouldn't occur to them.

:Honestly I'm pretty pleased it was those three. I've been expectin' some

blow-back for a couple of moons now.: He took to the back alleys; too risky to go running over rooftops in broad daylight if you weren't a youngster.

:You have *been breaking up gangs that rely on children and then stealing the children, so to speak,:* Dallen agreed. *:But why are you pleased it was these three?:*

:They ain't as sneaky as some of the others. They came at me, 'stead of ambushing me. They got no friends in my part of town, and I didn't have to get . : . radical.: Nobody had died. Not that he'd have mourned Dog-Billy, not that *anyone* would have mourned the loss of Dog-Billy, but on the whole . . . Heralds weren't supposed to kill people like low-life criminal scum. Bandits in a battle, certainly. The enemy in wartime, absolutely. Those assassins that the Sleepgivers had sent after him, no question. But not petty thieves. And there were some gang bosses he'd "robbed" he *would* have to kill if it came to a fight.

This time, he hadn't needed to do that.

As for the next time? He'd worry about that when it came to it.

One problem at a time, that was his motto. Too bad he never got to live up to it.

A few times a moon, the King held private audiences in the morning. These were reserved for people who didn't need the official, royal presentation in front of the entire Court, nor did they have anything they were asking for or needed attended to. But at the same time, the people who requested this sort of presentation were much more important than the ones that had the official presentations before the Court. These were occasions for those people to introduce themselves to the King without being under the eyes of anyone else; for both parties to size one another up, and for more to be exchanged than a few simple words of welcome. Ambassadors, for instance, when they first came to the Court of Valdemar generally presented themselves at the private audiences.

These were held in the deceptively named "Lesser Audience Chamber." It might be "Lesser" in size, but it made up for that in opulence. No envoy of another monarch would feel himself or his office slighted here. The room was not unlike a jewel box, and the King, Prince, and any other royals as well as attending Heralds all wore formal Whites, with the blue velvet, cloth of silver, bronze fixtures and white marble making an appropriate setting.

Amily was just as glad that this only took place a few times a moon. This was the one part of the job of King's Own that her father had ever complained about, and she perfectly understood his feelings. Unlike the Court presentations, these audiences were nerve-racking. In many ways, this could be a prelude to a sort of combat. People often came in through those doors with *agendas*, generally secret agendas. Sometimes they also came burdened with orders, also secret. She always wished it was Mags that was here instead of her.

:Would it be a bad idea to ask Mags to wear a Guard uniform and stand in here with the others?: she asked Rolan. *:I mean, I know it's wrong to examine someone's thoughts without their knowledge or permission but—:*

:Hmm.: Rolan considered that. *:It is not as if he has not used his Gifts in that way before. And it is not as if people are not fully aware of the Gifts Heralds have before they set foot in this room. . . . :*

:And when Mags does that, he just . . . takes in what comes passively, it's

not as if he goes prying,: she continued, cheering up a bit. *:Rolan, if you think it would be a good idea, I'll put it to the others.:*

:I think it is worth considering.:

Well, that was both hopeful and frustrating. And . . . possibly another one of those cases where the Companions were just not going to offer advice. *Bah.*

As in the Greater Audience Chamber, the King and Prince sat side by side in nearly identical thrones, the Prince's being just a bit less elaborate than the King's. Nikolas stood behind the King's throne and to the right of it, Amily behind the Prince's and to the left. There were Guards all around the chamber; two at the door and one in each of the four corners of the room. Add to that Amily and her father were armed. This might be a place where important people were greeted . . . but that didn't mean precautions were going to be set aside.

Today's audiences had been less than exciting. A string of people—an ambassador, several highborn who were *leaving* Haven for the summer to make way for minor members of their extended families to come hunt for marriage alliances, and the Master of the Brewers and Vintner's Guild all turned up to exchange pleasantries, minor information too trivial for a Council Meeting, and make farewells. Kyril had always encouraged this sort of thing, as it enabled him to get to know members of his Court more personally than he would otherwise. The last of the morning was some priest or other—

"His Holiness, Theodor Kresh, High Priest of Sethor the Patriarch," announced the servant at the door, and striding in to pause as the double doors closed behind him was the fellow himself.

As priests went...he was "conservatively" dressed. His deep blue robes were of exceedingly fine material, but without ornamentation, although he did wear a heavy gold chain with an equally heavy gold medallion on it. He wore the hood of his robe back, although the four under-priests who had come with him wore theirs up. He carried a plain staff of black wood or wrought iron—it was hard for Amily to tell which—and he appeared to be of late middle age. He had hard features, deep-set eyes, and was partially bald; what there was of his hair was of a salt-and-pepper color. From the way he moved, and what could be seen of the arm that held the staff, he was in fantastic physical shape; she suspected that he could probably use that staff as a formidable weapon.

He paid absolutely no attention to her. This went beyond mere snubbing; when the Prince introduced them all he literally did not look at her, or acknowledge her presence.

Her father raised an eyebrow at her; she shook her head slightly. There was no point in making an issue of this, for all they knew, he had some sort of vow that kept him from even thinking about women. She'd never heard of Sethor the Patriarch—but it sounded as if this was one of those male-centric religions. Sometimes they were just fine. Sometimes they made her want to gag.

As if he were reading her mind, the King said, politely, "We have never before heard of Sethor the Patriarch, and there has never, to my knowledge, been a Temple to this god in Haven. I assume you are the first?"

Theodor bowed his head the slightest bit. "All this is true, your Majesty," he said, smoothly. He had a powerful, but cold and emotionless, voice. "My Order has only recently come into your land, last Harvest, in fact, and as is our way, we came to establish our first Temple in your capitol. We are shortly to open it to the public. We have, for some several moons now, been altering the building we purchased to suit our needs, and making much-needed repairs."

"Is there some public ceremony involved with this opening at which you would like a royal presence?" Kyril asked politely.

The Priest shook his head. "No, Majesty. We are a simple Order, and have few ceremonies. We prefer to confine our ceremonial and liturgical activities to our believers. We were fortunate to find a suitable sanctuary nearly ready to move into. The Sisters of Ardana were happy to sell us their building, and move themselves to another, more suited to their dwindling numbers. Perhaps you know the temple? As I said, it required some extensive repairs, minor alterations, and reconsecration to our purposes, but otherwise it was nearly perfect for us."

The King shook his head, but Amily *did* recognize that name; the Sisters of Ardana had once—as far back as *long* before Vanyel's time—been a large enough group of female votaries to require a truly substantial building. But over time, and as the neighborhood in which the Temple stood declined, their numbers thinned and dwindled. Now they were just a handful of old women, much too frail to do the needed maintenance on their building themselves, and who clearly did not have the financial means to hire someone else to do it for them.

"We found the Sisters a small farm, much more suited to their needs, on the outskirts of the city. Not so much a farm anymore, really; but there was a handsome floored barn that could be converted to a chapel, and enough land to give them ample room for gardens." The smooth, cold voice made it all sound perfectly reasonable, and exactly the sort of thing that surely the women would have welcomed. Amily could not find any fault with what he was saying, rationally speaking. Was it his inflection? The way he was saying this as if from the moment his group had entered the city it was a foregone conclusion that he would get whatever he wanted?

Well . . . all right, this god of his is titled "the Patriarch." So this religion is probably one of those that thinks that women should be properly subservient, give whatever a man asks for, and take what men are willing to give them. Irritating, to be sure, but unless they did something illegal—and she was rather sure, looking at that smug profile, this fellow knew Valdemaran law—it was their business and the business of the worshippers of this "Sethor the Patriarch" how they conducted their lives.

:We allow the Holderkin to live as they will,: Rolan pointed out. *:We can do no less for any other religion. "There is no One, True Way," Amily.:*

If she had been alone, she would have pulled a sour face at that. Hadn't that been drummed into her head from the time she could talk? It wasn't as if she was going to forget it. As it was she kept her expression as stony as that of the priest. *:I know. Unless he starts sacrificing virgins, scourging "harlots," or doing something equally illegal, he and his cult can do what they please. But I don't have to like it.:*

She resolved, however, to find out where the Sisters of Ardana had gone, and look in on them. Just to be sure they were all right, and that they hadn't been packed off to some ramshackle hovel with a leaky roof and rotted floors.

:The Temple roof leaked,: Rolan reminded her. *:And they had had to*

close off much of the building because they could not repair it . . . :

If she hadn't been standing here on her best behavior, she'd have rolled her eyes. *:You know very well what I mean.:*

:I'll find out where they've been relocated to,: Rolan replied. With the implication that she should remember what her *job* was, and stick to it.

She thought about making some sort of sharp answer, given that the Companion was playing "conscience" in the most patronizing manner possible, but then she reminded herself that this was relatively "new" to Rolan as well as to her. He hadn't had a female Chosen before. They didn't have *precisely* the sort of open, accessible communication he'd had with her father. And he surely knew just how badly she wanted to rattle that arrogant old Priest. He was just being cautious.

The King continued to make polite . . . but pointed . . . conversation. She could see what Kyril was doing; of course, the King had decades of practice at getting people to reveal far more than they thought they were revealing. Under the guise of idle interest, he was finding out just how big the group was, what their source of income was, and as much of their core beliefs as it was politic to discover. During all of this, she might have been part of the furnishings for all the attention the High Priest paid to her. It was *pointed.* The more she stood here, the more certain she became that this was not merely that he had some sort of vow against acknowledging the presence of a female. He was making it absolutely clear that she was utterly beneath his interest.

On the other hand . . . it might be irritating, but it means he's going to underestimate me.

That gave her a little more sense of satisfaction. *I think I'll see if Mags is willing to find out about these people for me.* If there was anything going on, she was sure Mags and his gang of streetwise children, or his system of informants, would ferret it out.

Finally the High Priest held up a hand to forestall any more questions. "I have taken up far too much of your time, Majesty," he said, still as smooth and cold as polished stone. "I will take my leave. We thank you for welcoming us so graciously to your land and your city."

And with that, he bowed himself out, leaving the room with his silent entourage for the entrance of the last of those scheduled for an audience today.

"Lord Semel Lional and family!" announced the page at the door, and suddenly the little Audience Chamber was . . . very full.

So full it took Amily a moment to sort everyone out, as Lord Lional made the introductions of his family to the King, the Prince, and by broad gestures, including Amily and her father as well. No snubbing here!

First, of course, Lord Lional; a handsome, vigorous man of late middle age, his hair still defiantly black, his eyes a warm brown, with a decided chin but a smiling mouth, a nose a little too big for perfection, and animated brows. Amily liked him immediately, and from the relaxed look of her father's eyes and shoulders, so did he. The King obviously knew him already, and it was clear he was delighted to see the man.

Lord Lional—indeed, his entire family—were dressed formally, in matching outfits made of excellent deep brown and cream linen, with ornamental embroidery and cutwork of deep golden yellow at the neckline and hems. Not in the first mode of fashion, the cut of the mens' tunics and the womens' gowns were almost a decade out of date. This made perfect sense, since Amily knew that Lord Lional had made a name for himself in the Northeast, far from Haven and the Court.

His wife, Lady Tyria, smiled often and warmly; she looked as if she might be distantly related to her husband—a cousin, perhaps—as they had similar features, although her nose was small and tip-tilted. Amily liked her just as much.

The four children all had raven hair and similar features, although it was a little difficult to see what the two youngest would grow to look like. Amily set them aside in her mind for the moment, and considered the two eldest.

The oldest boy—Hawken—was handsome enough to be popular with girls, but not so handsome that he was likely to be conceited. And, in fact, his expression suggested a personality much like his father's with just enough youthful rebellion to make him interesting. But the eldest girl!

Helane, was her name, and she was nothing short of stunning.

Everything about her was perfect—and it was none of that too-still, too-poised perfection of a girl who is *far* too aware of her beauty and reckoning to take advantage of it. She was animated; she was clearly excited to be here, a little intimidated at being in the presence of the King and Prince, but drinking in everything eagerly. As for her looks . . . Amily had rarely seen a face that could be described as "heart-shaped," but hers certainly was. Her complexion was flawless, her cheeks the exact color of wild rose petals, and her rosebud of a mouth a slightly deeper hue. Her eyes were huge, meltingly brown, and guileless. Her raven-wing hair had been done in a style Amily had never seen before—braided into a single fat plait down her back, but with a black and cream linen covering bound over and around it. The plait nearly reached her knees; unbound, her hair surely would pool on the floor at her feet. Amily was fascinated; how long did it take to brush out? To wash? To *dry*? That was probably the reason for the cover, to keep that mane as clean as possible.

And her body was neither thin nor plump, but once again, perfect for a girl who surely was athletic and active. Even her hands were perfect, graceful, long-fingered, each nail a perfectly polished pink.

The girl was called up to make her curtsey to the King; blushing, she did so, making a very good job of it, and staying down just long enough to make it clear that she was as graceful and poised as she was beautiful.

Truth to tell, she eclipsed the rest of her family; both Kyril and his son were giving her very appreciative looks, and Amily didn't blame them. For that matter, so was her father Nikolas!

I hope he's not getting ideas, she thought, more amused than anything else. *I would not appreciate having a stepmother younger than I am.*

It appeared that the two youngest children, a boy and a girl, were used to being cast in the shade by their enchanting older sister. They exchanged a slightly chagrined look. The boy shrugged, as if to say, *well what did you expect?* and the girl shook her head.

The oldest boy came up to make his bow, then the youngest siblings. Finally Amily learned the names of the youngest members of the family, Lirelle, and Loren.

"There is no need to wait on ceremony, Semel," the King said when all the introductions had been made. "We have not met in person before, but we have exchanged enough correspondence we certainly know one another well enough to dispense with such stiffness. Brand!" he called to the page at the door. "Bring the stools out so my guests can sit in comfort."

The page leapt to do so. There were square, padded stools set at intervals around the walls; they were seldom used, but it was clear that Kyril intended to have a good long chat with Lord Lional and his lady.

As they spoke, Amily quickly realized that Lord Lional was one of what Kyril called his "New Men." Like her father, and like Mags, the King had his own web of informants spread across the Kingdom; the main difference being that none of the correspondents were conducting their communications in secret. A highly prosperous tradesman here, a well placed highborn there, a Captain of the Guard, Bards, Healers . . . it all added up to a solid network of people who could be relied on to keep a finger on the pulse of the entire Kingdom. They all were in positions where they knew just about everything that was going on in their areas, and if they didn't know about something, they knew who to ask. The highborn among the "New Men" were not necessarily men who had newly been granted their titles and lands—although a fair number of them did fit that description. But they were all the King's age, or younger. "I have enough graybearded Councilors," he was fond of saying. "When it comes to eyes and ears, the younger, the better."

"How are we positioned at Halberd Hall?" the King asked immediately, once everyone had been settled in their seats. "Who have you left in charge?"

"My older brother is there. He knows as much as I know, and hears rather more," Semel said. "He——" He laughed a little. "—— he styles himself as *a country gent.* He wouldn't come to Court for any amount of money, and he never wanted the estate, only the managing of it. *Everyone* talks to him, and he talks to everyone. He's trusted by all to be fair and even-handed. I wouldn't make a move at the Hall without his advice—and a good dose of common sense: *now, you may be the Lord of Halberd Hall, but you're still my snot-nosed brother.* Nothing will get past him, and he will send me faithful reports. We're well served while I nose around for a husband for Helane and a wife for Hawken."

The King looked over his head to the two oldest siblings. "And what do you have to say about this?" he asked.

Hawken shrugged, and answered for both of them. "There's no one at home either of us are interested in. And . . . father promised us a mort of gatherings and fetes. Best we get at home is feasts where old men sleep off their roasts after, and country-dances and fairs." Helane nodded. The King was satisfied, and turned his attention back to Semel.

"You'll have a lot of arranging in front of you in the next few years. Aren't there four more at home?" Lady Tyria laughed, blushed, and nodded, and Amily was astonished. *What did she do, pop one out every year?* It was a rude thought, but there was no one to hear it but Rolan.

:Some women thrive on being mothers, I suppose.: But even Rolan sounded a little . . . dubious.

"You wrote and told me you had bought Count Renolf's town house?" Kyril continued, with a lifted brow. "I am glad to hear that

73

he has finally given up on living there alone, but—"

Semel sighed. "Yes. But. I thought I had given him plenty of time to move out, but it appears that the Count has . . . more possessions than he thought he did. He's still in the process of moving out. And that is what really brings me here."

Kyril broke out in a hearty laugh. "Don't tell me. You're all crammed into an inn, and you're hoping we can find room for you here in the Palace."

The hopeful looks on the faces of all six of them made Kyril laugh again. "Brand, fetch the Steward," he ordered. "And while you are out, send in some pages with refreshments." He turned to Nikolas. "You and Amily might as well get comfortable. Semel and I have a lot to catch up on."

It was well past lunch when his Lordship and family finally took their leave. The Steward did, indeed, have a vacant apartment in the Palace—not one that was very much sought after for permanent occupation as it was on the corner of the side of the building that got the least sun and most wind in winter, making it decidedly cold for six months of the year. But it had three small bedrooms, an unusual amount of storage room, and a small but adequate sitting room. The family accepted it with gratitude, and made arrangements to have all their belongings and some of their furnishings moved to it as soon as it could be managed. "The servants are taken care of at the townhouse," Semel said. "They are turning out to be extremely useful in getting the Count moved out."

:The Count has been living all alone in that place with just a cook,

a housekeeper, and his personal man. Small wonder he hasn't been moving quickly,: Rolan observed.

"The Palace servants will take care of everything you need," Kyril promised.

"It's just as well, it sounds as if there would be no room for them," Tyria laughed.

I'll need to let Lady Dia know about these people, she thought, as they continued talking. *For one thing, it is obvious that the King finds them useful, important, and agreeable. For another, someone is going to have to keep an eye on that eldest girl, or there could be a great deal of unruly head-butting among the young men.*

:That sounds like a task for the Queen's Handmaidens,: Roland observed.

:It certainly does,: she replied.

Well, this was turning out to be not quite so dull a session after all. She very much liked His Lordship and his Lady. The four children seemed very interesting . . . she hoped they weren't going to prove to be "interesting" in the sense of "attracted trouble," but they all seemed intelligent, and with any luck, whatever trouble they got themselves into they could also get themselves out of. She crossed two sets of fingers for luck on that thought, and settled in to listen carefully to what was shaping up to be a long conversation between Lord Semel and the King.

4

This would be an entire day spent as Harkon, which was unusual for Mags, but the things he needed to do today were going to send him all over the city, and dropping out of character would be ill-advised. He had to be very, very careful how and when he made his switches from one persona to the other, and those switches were best done when he *knew* there was no chance of anyone following him. By day, there was no guarantee. He knew what *he* would do if he was following someone, and those were tricks he might have a hard time sussing out, if the person tailing him was as good as *he* was. There was only one sure-fire way to avoid being followed; wait until the streets were clear enough that he could thin his shields and pick out the thoughts of anyone close enough to actually have eyes on him.

So, once he left Aunty Minda's, he headed to the spot where Coot ran the messenger service. Coot had taken down the shutter and opened the place up for the day; he had a loft over the stall where he slept. There had already been a nice little metal stove of the sort that Amily's protege Tuck had invented installed behind the counter, with a metal chimney to carry the smoke away. That had served the dual purpose of keeping the stallkeeper warm in winter and keeping his sausages hot. Now it made the stall cozy enough to sleep in comfortably even in the worst of winter. Coot was adding a second room on the back with Tuck's help, and paying him for the work, too; the big man might be a bit addled, but he was a genius with his hands. Last time Mags had checked, they'd put a pegged-wood floor, wall supports, and a roof extension in. Walls would be next, he supposed.

"Cap'n," Coot said respectfully, with a two-fingered salute.

"Got anythin' t'report?" Mags asked, leaning against the counter. Wordlessly, Coot handed over three or four sheets of paper folded over in thirds and sealed with a blob of wax with a sprig of dried herb in it. Anyone trying to tamper with the seal would certainly break the delicate bit of plant material. Mags nodded, and tucked the paper into the front of his tunic. "How's the buildin' comin'?" he continued.

Coot sighed. "Not as fast's I'd like."

Mags gave him a sidelong look. "A mort'f folk sleep out i' the yard or the roof or the like in summer. Ye got a roof—"

Coot reddened a little. "Aye but there be windows both sides." He jerked his chin at the taverns to either side of his stall. And for a moment Mags couldn't understand what his problem was.

Then it dawned on him. "So th'pup's a dog now, eh? What's 'er name?"

"Tilde." Coot reddened some more. Mags chuckled, feeling pleased. When he'd first started Aunty Minda's gang of littles, who would have thought that in so short a time, one of them would have found himself a girl?

"Watch out fer angry Pa, now," he replied. "Ye ain't gonna do me no good wi' yer head bust in."

"She ain't got no Pa, an' 'er Ma likes me. She's laundress over t' Tuck's place." Mags nodded with understanding. That would be how Coot met her, then, since he had to go over to escort poor Tuck back and forth from the job so Tuck didn't get lost. Tuck lived in what had been the stable of a large former brewery. The place was tenanted with laundresses, who rented one or more rooms to live in, and used what had been the brewing room as one communal laundry room.

Need to make some plans in case this turns out to be something more than two younglings in summer, he made a note to himself. But he didn't say anything of the kind to Coot. *I'll wait and see if* he *comes up with plans on his own. Though he's managed the second room well enough by himself* . . .

The runners from Minda's began straggling up at that point to take their places on the bench just under the counter, and an anxious-looking fellow who might well have been a shopowner on this street came hurrying up. "This is where I find a message-runner?" he asked, a little breathlessly.

Mags saluted Coot without another word and took his leave.

From here he went to visit several of his regular informants—all under the guise of errands run on behalf of the pawn shop. He left a handful of second- and third-rate gemstones at a jeweler, and was paid for them, and a quantity of the broken jewelry from which the gems had been pried at a silversmith. There it was carefully weighed and assayed before the smith paid him the value of it by weight. In both cases, notes were passed over along with the money.

At that point, he felt he deserved some lunch, and since he was near the river, he ambled over to a favorite stall of his for some fried fish, fried onions, and fried dough-balls, dished up with a hot sauce made with horseradish. This was *not* the sort of fare served up at the Collegium; served with a strong beer, it was food for a common worker. Maybe that was why he liked it.

He sat on a barrel by the stall in the sun, eating, watching boats come in to the docks and get unloaded, and felt pretty well contented with his day so far.

That contentment followed him as he made his way between two rows of warehouses toward his next destination, a brothel called "Boatman's Rest," another of his sources of information. The madame, an amusing old woman who claimed to have had five husbands and too many lovers to count, was as sharp as needle and never failed to deliver something useful. In the middle of the day these warehouses were packed with workers, so he kept his mental shields up tight.

The only warning he got was when he heard a scuffling of boots behind him.

He was hit from the rear by three men at once, all of them wielding heavy wooden cudgels.

One caught him across the ribs; his side exploded with pain, and he went down—but under control, shoulder-rolling to try and get out of the scrum and somewhere he could get his back up against a wall. His roll carried him as far as a stack of barrels, where he lurched to his feet again and pulled his sword just in time to parry a club coming down on his head. He made three slashing, sideways cuts with his sword to clear himself some space, and stood in a guarded crouch, facing his attackers.

There weren't three men. There were six. Six *at least*, there might have been more around the corner, in the narrow passage between buildings where they had been waiting to ambush him. He kept his expression blank, his side hurt in a way that told him his ribs were cracked, and it felt like his head had been hit, too, but he didn't intend to show them any sign of weakness.

For the moment, they seemed to be at an impasse. They must have expected the element of surprise to put him entirely at their mercy. He didn't straighten up; in this position his ribs didn't stab him with pain every time he breathed in. With two pain-free breaths he was able to put himself into the strange state of mind that the Sleepgivers did; where he would still *feel* the pain, but it wouldn't matter. It would be something he registered, but could ignore. That wouldn't last, of course, he was nowhere near as good as the Sleepgivers were, especially his cousin, but as long as he didn't take too much more damage, he would be all right.

He eyed the six surrounding him. They eyed him back. None of them were wearing swords, but that didn't give him any feeling of confidence. Six men with heavy wooden clubs who knew what they were doing could easily overcome one with a sword.

Whoever sent them probably doesn't want to kill me. They want to send a message. Well, message received. Harkon had become a nuisance, and someone bigger than Dog-Billy or Hatchet wanted him to understand that his depredations had attracted the attention of someone who wanted him to stop.

Dallen had certainly found a way to alert the Watch by now, and just as certainly he was on his way here. And it wasn't all that far from the docks to the inn where Dallen idled his time while Mags was being Harkon. But to have a Companion charge into this mob would certainly destroy the Harkon persona, so unless Mags was literally about to die, Dallen was not going to come dashing to the rescue. Nor would Mags want him to.

They were all still staring at one another; they were breathing heavily, but Mags was keeping himself as steady and calm as possible under the circumstances. Getting through this with minimal injury—until the Watch arrived—would take everything he had. Mags took the opportunity to slowly inch his free hand toward his dagger and ease it out of the sheathe. He thought about going for a throwing knife—but none of these brutes had brought a blade, and the last thing he wanted to do was supply them with one.

Just as he got the dagger securely in his hand, they decided to make a move. That was when he realized that not only had they not made any plans if their quarry was able to defend himself—they also must never have fought together. Ever.

They all came at him in a sort of abortive rush. Three of them managed to tangle each other up and actually went down in a heap. Of the other three, only one actually reached him before he was able to dodge to the side and knock over the barrels. That one hit him a glancing blow on his dagger arm, while he thwacked the thug in the temple with the flat of his blade, sending him reeling into the tumble of barrels.

That gave him the chance to get his back to the wall, and he scuttled back until his heels hit it. Besides covering his back, being at the wall gave him partial protection on the right and left, and that was a distinct relief.

Sudden movement in the periphery of his vision made him glance to the left and right before turning his attention back to the thugs who had ambushed him. The noise of the (fortunately empty) barrels tumbling to the ground had brought men out of the warehouses; as he warily eyed his opponents, and they got themselves sorted out and on their feet again, more and more men came out. Soon both ends of the street were blocked with groups of workers. He knew better than to assume they were on his side, however. As far as these fellows were concerned, he was a roughly dressed, heavily armed stranger, and his attackers were roughly dressed thuggish strangers with clubs. Just because it was six-to-one, that didn't mean he was in the right and they were in the wrong. For all *they* knew he'd done something heinous and was getting his just deserts. Basically, they had come out to make sure there was nothing going on that involved where they worked, who they worked for, or anyone they knew. Now that they were aware none of the three conditions held, they were settling down for the free entertainment of a fight, at least until and unless the Watch showed up to break it up.

One of the thugs lunged at him; this time he grabbed the man's wrist as the club came down, and *pulled,* letting the man's own momentum smack him headfirst into the wall, while another tried to take advantage of the fact that he was tangled up with the first thug. He *almost* got away unscathed, but a lucky hit on his already cracked ribs made him see stars for a moment, and took his breath away. He gritted his teeth and snarled at the same time, though, to keep from demonstrating any weakness.

It helped that they still were showing no signs of organization. And now there were only five of them; the one that had hit the wall was showing no signs of moving any time soon; he was sprawled bonelessly with his face mushed against the wall and the street, lying in what would have been an excruciatingly uncomfortable pose if he'd been conscious.

His neck's gonna be killin' him when he wakes up . . .

"I say we rush 'im!" growled one of the five left.

"Oh aye, cuz that worked *so* well th' last three times!" another snapped back. "Spread out, ye idjuts. We gotta get them stickers away from 'im fust!"

Oh hell. Now they're working together.

And that might have signaled the moment when he was going to have to resign himself to a nasty beating, except that from his left, one man shouted angrily, "Hey! *I know that bastid!* 'E's th' one been messin' wi' me sister!"

Evidently the fellow's mates knew exactly what the speaker was talking about, because there was a roar of outrage that was echoed by the mob on Mags' right.

Now the thugs looked startled . . . and alarmed. They made some abortive movements as if they were going to try to escape.

But it was too late. *"Git 'em!"* someone shouted, and the mobs on either side charged toward the middle, snatching up whatever they could use as a weapon as they avalanched toward Mags' attackers.

He just squeezed himself flat against the wall and stayed out of the way. The five thugs went down fast, and there was a lot of kicking and pummeling going on. Once or twice he got hit by accident, but for the most part, the men in this mob were intent on battering the thugs who were on the ground. So he just wedged himself against the wall, held his ribs and tried not to breathe heavily. His "detachment" had worn off with that second hit to his ribs.

By the time the Watch arrived—which was not too much later—there were only two of the thugs still standing, and they were in bad shape. This lot of the Watch didn't know Mags; all they saw was one slightly battered, heavily armed man who appeared to be the bone of contention of the scrum, so they collared him first.

He allowed himself to be collared; the one thing you didn't do when the Watch decided to grab you was to argue. But one of the warehouse workers (who was unarmed, having waded in with nothing more than his formidable fists) spoke up in his defense. "Har! Carter! He ain't th' bastid ye want. Them lot there jumped 'im! 'E was just 'fendin' 'imself."

Now, Mags knew very well that there had been no witnesses when he'd been ambushed. That had been the point of coming at him here, obviously, so he could be beaten and left in the street with no witnesses. But he wasn't about to argue if the man chose to volunteer himself as his advocate, so when "Carter" turned his red-eyed gaze on the captive Mags, and growled. "Zat true?" Mags just nodded.

"An' *thet* bastid's th' un what's bin messin' wi' me sister!" chimed in the worker who'd been the cause of the mobs descending in the first place. He pointed with indignation at an unconscious bullyboy whose face was so battered it was unlikely his own mother would recognize him.

Evidently this story was also well known to the Watch. The frowning faces turned away from Mags to regard the pile of unconscious and half-conscious thugs with acute distaste and disapproval.

"Ye willin' t'press charges?" Carter asked Mags.

"Hell yes," Mags said, fervently.

The Watch trussed up the thugs, recruited a cart from one of the warehouses, loaded their "prizes" into it—ignoring the moans and yelps as they tossed the thugs in without any care for possible injuries—and the entire parade of Watch, cart, thugs, willing witnesses, and Mags headed for the Watch station.

About two candlemarks later, Mags emerged alone. It had only taken about one candlemark for him and the "witnesses" to make their statements. The rest of the time had been taken up with getting names and addresses, and for the Watch to fetch a Healer from some distance away to come see to him. The Healer also tended to the thugs, although that had mostly been to look them over, pronounce "they'll live," and splint a couple broken bones. Mags, on the other hand, as the injured and aggrieved party, was looked over carefully with an eye to possible concussion, and had his ribs bound up as skillfully as anyone up at the Collegia could do.

:Where are you?: he asked Dallen, as he gingerly made his way toward the inn where his disguises were kept.

:Back at the inn. If you'd been—:

:In any danger, I know, you would have rescued me. And I'd have been mad at myself for losin' all the work I put into Harkon.:

:So let's be glad that I've arranged for Nikolas to bring a set of your Whites to Flora's.:

Mags sighed with relief. Flora, the titular madame of "Flora's," would help him out of his disguise and into his Whites, then smuggle him out again through one of the exits she used when gentlemen wanted their visits to her girls to be utterly confidential. And Harkon was a known patron of the place, and since he had no known female relatives, it would not be at all out of character for him to look for some female cosseting at the brothel. Not everything Flora provided had to do with sex.

In fact, the door-guard summoned one of the House servants as soon as he realized Harkon was in rather battered condition. That servant deposited him in an empty parlor and returned with Flora herself, and two of her girls, one of which was in a very racy version of Healer's Greens. The neckline was cut practically down to her navel, and the robes were slit up to the waist on both sides.

This was Cilla, the House Healer. She actually *was* a Healer; there were three brothels in Haven that had House Healers that Mags knew of, but Cilla was the only one of the three who also served as one of the House girls. Mags didn't ask why, and she had never volunteered the information; he didn't reckon it was any of his business, and since *none* of Flora's girls worked under duress, he knew it had to be because she wanted to, and that was all that mattered.

"What on earth did you do to yourself, boy?" Flora scolded, as the three of them helped him get stiffly to his feet, and led him down a hall to what turned out to be a lovely, warm bathing room. It was very welcome; the Watch Healer hadn't really cleaned up anything but his cuts before taping his ribs and sending him on his way.

"Didn't do it to m'self," he said, as they undressed him, untaped him, and got him into a bath so hot it was just short of painful. He hissed as the water hit his bruises and relaxed while they washed up his face and got the blood out of his hair. "Seems some'un didn't like m'methods of business, and set six bully-boys on me."

"Six!" Flora exclaimed. "Surely not—"

"They was carryin' clubs," Mags pointed out. "Still wouldn't hev got off this easy 'cept—" he chuckled, and explained.

A candlemark later, he was clean, his cuts were sealed, his bruises faded to a pale green, and his ribs, while still sore, were about two weeks-worth healed more than they'd been when he walked in. He was also in his Whites, and the servant was conducting him down a tunnel that looked nothing at all like a tunnel—it was beautifully polished wood, floor, ceiling, and walls, and lit by lanterns with topaz glass shades. "Where are we goin'?" he asked the servant, with mild curiosity.

"The White Horse Tavern," the servant replied. "This is how all our hot meals are brought over. We could hardly carry them through the streets, and Madame Flora prefers not to have more than a minimal kitchen. She says the smell of cooking food is vulgar, and the lingering aroma of cooked food is distasteful. And if this tunnel serves some of our patrons who would rather not be seen entering and leaving by the front door, you won't find any of us naming names."

"Right-oh," Mags said genially. The White Horse Tavern was perfect; he could stop there long enough for a good stiff drink to take the edge off the pain of his ribs and wait for Dallen to spirit his way into the stables, then leave as if he'd been there all along.

:As if you couldn't find out those names if you wanted to from Flora,: Dallen snickered.

:How far away are you?: Mags asked.

:I'm already there. There are pears, and a very nice stableboy who is feeding them to me. Take your time.:

:Reckon I'll have dinner, then,: he decided. *:Amily's eatin' with the Court, an' I don't fancy fightin' my way through the younglings and then tryin' t' get myself sittin' on a bench at the Collegium.:* Sitting in a quiet corner of the comfortable inn room, being brought his food by the smiling serving maid, his Whites getting him immediate attention, was much more attractive than fighting his way through a lot of rambunctious Trainees who would pay as much attention to his presence as they would a bench. Less; they could sit on the bench.

:Good idea,: Dallen replied. *:Send me out some pocket pies.:*

Amily saw the lights burning in the sitting room from a good distance, and smiled as she hurried her steps along the garden path. She had been hoping this wouldn't be one of the nights "Harkon" spent down at the pawn shop until nearly midnight. She wanted badly to talk to Mags about Lord Semel and his family—and about that disturbing priest of "Sethor the Patriach"—and to find out if he had heard anything about the Sisters of Ardana. While the former Temple of Ardana hadn't been precisely *in* Harkon's neighborhood, it had been only a few streets away. If there was any gossip about them, he'd have picked it up by now.

"You're back!" she heard from the sitting room as soon as she entered the door. "Good, I hope you didn't have to foil any assassinations tonight."

"Only one near-one, but not of the King," she said, coming in to find him sprawled in a slightly odd, stiff position in the most heavily padded of the chairs. *Did he have to go roof-running today or tonight? I wonder if he sprained a shoulder. Well, he'll tell me.* "There is a new young beauty at the Court, and if evil looks had been daggers tonight, she'd have been slashed to ribbons."

She filled him in on Lord Semel ("Yes, he's one of Kyril's unofficial field agents, Nikolas has shown me some of his reports" she confirmed when he looked alert and inquisitive at the name) and the entire brood. "Helane is the one causing all the clucking in the henhouse at the moment," she continued. "I've put Lady Dia on to her; we need some notion of her brains and personality. If she's the kind to meddle just for the mischief of it, we'll having young highborn lads meeting each other for dawn duels over the right to escort her in to supper. But if she's clever . . . and willing . . . we might be able to make use of those brains so she doesn't get into mischief out of pure boredom. She doesn't fit the Queen's Handmaidens, since with a title *and* property *and* the King's favor on her family, she doesn't need the organization to help her along. But she could still be useful in the same ways that Lydia's friends were."

"I'll have to introduce myself to Hawken then," Mags replied with a sigh. "If he was just anyone, we could probably afford to let him sink or swim on his own, but as the son of someone who's got Kyril's ear, I need to make sure he doesn't get in with the wrong crowd. *You* know what I mean."

Amily nodded; it wasn't that the young men of the Court were treacherous or dangerous, at least not the ones here now, it was that they were *young men.* And in every group of young men there were always those who were inclined to push limits and get into trouble.

And every time there was a group of young men like that, there was always another group of people inclined to exploit and prey on them. Blackmail being only one of a number of unsavory possibilities.

Amily told him about the Priest of Sethor the Patriarch. He made a face as she finished. "Reckon I think I know some of what they're preachin', by second-hand. Hard t'keep a eye on 'em though, without we get someone inta the flock. You want me t'do that?"

"Not yet," she said, wishing she had a *reason* to ask him to, aside from *I don't like him and I don't like the way he treats women.* "Are there any rumors about the group he displaced?"

He shook his head. "There wouldn't be, though, would there? A bunch of old women in a temple that's goin' t'seed wouldn't have anythin' worth stealin', and that's about the only way I'd'a heard anything about 'em."

"Oh, bother." She moved to sit on the arm of the chair and leaned over to hug him, and he . . . winced.

"Sorry, love," he apologized immediately. "I got crosswise of a buncha bully-boys an' got m'ribs cracked for interferin' with their masters' business."

"What?" she exclaimed, drawing back immediately lest she cause him any more trouble. "Are you—did you see a Healer? Why did—what happened?"

"Saw Flora's House Healer, got tended nicer'n I would'a got up here," he chuckled. She laughed with him, knowing exactly what he meant. When Flora's House Healer tended someone, they were cosseted, and cooed over and made much of, where if he'd come up to Healer's Collegium to get tended, he'd have gotten scolded for getting into a common street brawl and told he was an idiot, and strapped up brusquely. "By way of gettin' me out without the disgrace of seein' a Herald comin' outa Flora's, they showed me the tunnel t'the White Horse, an' that's where I got dinner."

She snorted. "As if there have never been Heralds in Flora's before!"

"Well, not in Whites, 'less there'd been somethin' that needed investigatin'." He shrugged, very slightly. "Anyway, that's what's what. *Good* news is, that lot'll get shipped out t'do road work someplace far, far away. All their master's'll know is they got arrested, just like Dog-Billy an' Hatchet an' that lot. Likely they'll think twice 'bout comin' after me, maybe even give over usin' younglings in their gangs."

She sighed; this was not the first time he'd returned injured, but it was the first that involved broken bones. "Father never used to come home beaten up," she said aloud, and only after the words came out of her mouth did she realize it sounded like a rebuke. She flushed and was trying to think of some way to soften that, but Mags was already answering.

"Actually, he prolly *did*, he just didn't let you know about it," Mags replied with blunt honesty. "Just like he didn't let you know more'n a quarter of the stuff he was doin', so you wouldn't be afeared for 'im."

Then he stopped, and bit his lip, looking shamefaced for having said that. They stared at each other in acute discomfort for a while. "I didn't mean—" they both said at the same time, and stopped.

"We're Heralds," she finally said, breaking the uncomfortable silence. "Whatever we do, the job comes with risks, and we both know that, and we both know there's no way to avoid them."

He nodded slowly. "We can't help the job. But we can help each other."

The tension drained out of the air, and she smiled at him. "Let me start by helping you out of that chair." She got up, and as she did, her foot hit something smallish, pale, and flat and sent it across the room.

"What's that?" he asked, as she chased after it and picked it up. It seemed to be a letter, on the crudest grade of paper, and sealed with a greasy blob of candle wax. She frowned at it, unable to think who at the Court or Collegium would have used paper of this sort to send *her* a message. And why not just tell her? Unless it was some anonymous tattling.

I hope we don't have any small-minded tattletales among the new Trainees. Surely someone in the Court would use old palimpsest for sending an anonymous bleat . . .

"Message?" Mags asked.

"I'll find out in a moment. Someone must have left it here when we were gone, or shoved it under the door." She opened it.

You can't even do the job you're supposed to, your father has to keep picking up after you. Why don't you just die so he can do it properly?

It was "written" in careful block letters, inscribed between three sets of three ruled lines, so there wasn't even "handwriting" to tell who could have written it. She swore and started to throw it into the fire, but Mags got it away from her before she could.

He read it and his face flushed with anger. She took it out of his hands. "It's just anonymous dirt. Put it where it belongs." She tossed it on the fire.

He gave her an odd look. "Have you gotten more of these things?" he asked.

"About a half a dozen all told. I showed the first one to Father, who said if that was the worst I got, I should count myself lucky." She grimaced. "I hate to think of the sort of things *he* got over the years, if that's true."

"It probably is." Mags glowered at where the orange and black ghost of the paper was dancing on top of the logs.

"Well, that was another thing I never knew, and if he didn't let it bother him, I see no reason to let it bother me," she said stoutly. "I just didn't see any reason to take up your time with this . . . infantile bullying."

"You'd'a rather he'd told you, at least when you was old enough to take it all right, wouldn't you?" he asked, with one hand on her shoulder.

". . . I suppose so," she admitted.

"And I'd rather you'd told me. And now you have. An' maybe 'tween the two of us, we can figger out where they're comin' from." A small, tight smile crossed his face. "Chances are, it's a coward with plenty t'hide. They don't take bein' exposed well."

"All right," she agreed with spirit. "I have, and we'll try. And if we can't figure out who it is?"

"Hm?" he replied.

"We'll make him *insane* with frustration by being stubbornly happy."

5

The next day, although there was usually a lesser Council meeting scheduled, there was so little to discuss that the King postponed it in favor of a meeting with the Exchequer, the Seneschal, and the Master of the Treasury. "Just building plans," he told Amily at their usual breakfast meeting. "We're going to spend the entire morning trying to change each others' minds. If you have something to do, go and do it."

Mags was in his persona of himself, Herald Mags, attending courtroom cases down in Haven, so she had the morning to herself. *As if that is even possible for a Herald,* she thought in the next moment. Because when it came right down to it, "having the morning to herself" didn't mean she could go curl up with a book, it meant she could go take care of other tasks that did not involve attending on the King. After intercepting Lady Dia before she went to her kennels and filling her in on the newcomers—Helane, in particular—it occurred to her that this was the ideal time to discover if she could track down where the Sisters of Ardana were now living.

Of course, she *could* run all over the Collegia and the various places where Records were kept in the Palace . . .

Or she could go straight to the one creature that probably knew who would know.

:Rolan, who would know where the Sisters moved?: She waited, while Rolan thought about that.

:The Exchequer, the Seneschal, and the Master of the Treasury, who are all in that meeting. You could also try down in Haven, and the Lord Mayor's various record offices, or even one of the messenger services, like Mags' little lot of runners. But since they might either need *a Healer or* have *a Healer, I would try the Chronicler of Healer's before I went trudging all over the city. The Healers have to keep careful track of where people live, if they are sent for in an emergency.:*

She grinned. Rolan had come through for her yet again. She trotted over to Healers' Collegium and took the stairs two at a time, hoping to find the Chronicler in the little office just inside the Archives. Fortunately the Archives were over the Trainees' rooms, rather than the part of Healers that housed the Infirmary and patients' rooms. The scents over there were not always pleasant.

The Chronicler was not a Healer herself since there was no need to have someone who was a Healer merely in charge of records. So the thin, earnest-looking woman who looked up at Amily as she tapped on the doorframe was wearing a plain, practical gown of brown linen. Her office was almost painfully neat; Amily repressed a sigh, wishing *she* was that organized.

"Can I help you, Herald?" the woman said, looking oddly hopeful.

"I think you can, Chronicler," Amily replied, giving the woman her proper title, which made her eyes light up a little. "Would you by any chance have a record of where the Sisters of Ardana were moved to?"

The woman blinked at her thoughtfully for a moment. "Why yes," she said, finally. "I believe we do. We just finished updating the Haven maps a fortnight ago."

Actually *finding* the location in question required leaving the office and having a look through a ponderous volume kept near the door. This proved to be an insanely detailed map of Haven and the Hill, with every building noted. "Ah, here we are," the woman proclaimed after a moment. She tilted the book so that Amily could see the page, which turned out to be a map of a small area of houses with as much as an acre of land attached. The Chronicler tapped her finger at a spot on the page, where whatever had been written there had been scraped off, and *Sis. Ardan.* written in its place. It appeared to be outside the city walls, which, if it *had* been a farm, made sense.

Amily memorized the location, thanked the Chronicler profusely (which made her go pink with pleasure), and headed to the stable to get Rolan.

:I don't imagine that she gets to interact with Heralds all that much, and far less does she get thanked by one,: Rolan observed, as she saddled and bridled him.

:Probably not. And that explains the blush.: Strange to think that someone who worked, and presumably lived, not all that far from Herald's Collegium saw so little of Heralds.

This was going to be a very different set of neighborhoods than she usually rode through; this was not one of the main thoroughfares. Once she was down off the Hill, she and Rolan took a side street, and from the Hill to the city walls they passed along quiet, narrow streets paved in cobblestones, with neighborhoods with few craftsmen of the sort that had to maintain a large shop or works. Instead, most of the buildings were residences, with the occasional small shop on the ground floor that served the neighborhood, the occasional small craftsman or woman who only needed a single room to ply his or her trade.

:Didn't this area burn about fifty years ago?: she asked Rolan, as it dawned on her that the buildings here were both oddly new for anything inside the walls, and made of fire-resistant brick and stone, with slate roofs.

:It did; in fact, the fire that spread through here was the reason for the ban on thatched roofs. Many of the wealthy and highborn hoped to annex this area to the Hill, but the King decreed that those who had lived here had first priority on rebuilding here.: Rolan tossed his head. *:There had been rumors that the fire had been started by someone who wanted to do just that. The King quelled those rumors nicely.:*

I wouldn't mind living here, she thought, *If I weren't a Herald, that is.* Although there were people about, the streets were mostly empty, curtains fluttering in the light breeze at open windows in the upper stories. The only cart on the street was the milk-wagon, making morning deliveries before it got too warm.

The city walls—walls that had once enclosed all of Haven, not just a third of it—loomed up at the end of the street. She passed through a very small gate in the walls, which took her out into another residential district, this one with houses boasting plots of land large enough to garden. The houses here were mixed in age; you could tell which one was the original farmhouse that had stood here, until its lands were divided up to allow for more houses to be built. Prosperous people lived here—not *rich*, but with a good enough income to have a house all to themselves, and three or four servants. Clerks and craftsmen who made things for those who *were* rich, men who were no longer farmers, but landowners, who paid other men to do their farming for them.

Gradually these plots became large enough to supply vegetables for a market-garden; the houses were smaller, more modest—except for the occasional old farmstead, like a hen among chicks. And that was where she found the new Temple of the Sisters of Ardana.

It was obvious that this had once been the house of an ample farm; this was no mere cottage, it was a three-story structure of whitewashed plaster and black beams, at least three hundred years old, roofed with thatch—thatch which would never have been allowed inside the city because of the risk of fire. At the rear was a second building too grand to be called a mere "barn;" it was identical to the house, save only that the windows in it had clearly been recently converted into glass windows from the sort of half-doors horses or milk-cows could use to observe the outside world from the comfort of their stalls. Then there were some sheds, and a third building that looked like a minature of the bigger one. A guesthouse, perhaps, but when this had been a farm, it had probably served to house the farmhands.

There was not an ell of ground wasted on mere grass; herbs filled the beds where flowers might have been at one of the prosperous craftman's houses, and the rest of the land was occupied with a pen for goats with long silky hair, a henhouse, several beehives, and vegetable gardens.

As she and Rolan rode up to the front door of the house, the double doors of the former barn opened, and five or six elderly people filed out, escorted by two equally elderly women in gray robes. *The Sisters of Ardana, I presume*, she thought, as they all caught sight of her, and stopped, waiting for her to come to them. She looped the reins over the pommel of the saddle and dismounted, making her way toward them with Rolan coming along behind.

The eldest, and most erect of the two women stepped forward as she reached the group. "I am Mother Yllana of the Sisters of Ardana," she said, in an authoritative, but not unfriendly, tone. "How may we help you, Herald?"

"It's the other way around," Amily replied cheerfully. "I found out that you'd been moved, and I came to find out if you had settled in satisfactorily, and if there was anything you needed."

Mother Yllana looked as if she wanted to think about what she was going to say, but one of her congregants was not nearly so restrained.

"It's not satisfactory, Herald, it's not satisfactory at all," said a little bird of a woman in a black gown, with a tilt of her head and a look in her eye that said she meant to put her two coppers-worth in before anyone had a chance to stop her. "We have to come *all* the way down from above Tanner's, and it's *not* satisfactory at all, what with my knees, and Neldie's hip, and Thoma's back and all. It's a long, *long* way to come for them as don't have horses or carts to ride. But we do it once a fortnight, that we do, because we don't feel *comfortable,* don't feel *welcome* in what that stiff backed old crathur made of our old home, and just who *is* this Sethor, when it comes down to cases, anyway? Some god from outlandish parts none of *us* ever heard of! So we come here, and *very inconvenient it is,* too." Then she stood there looking at Amily, as if to say, *And what do you intend to do about it?*

"I see," Amily replied gravely, making no other statement. Rolan held his peace, while she considered the implications. Clearly this woman felt that the Crown was responsible for rectifying her grievance. And to a certain extent, the Crown might very well be. There were several things Amily would like to promise, but she wasn't going to commit or even comment until she knew whether they actually *could* be done. The bird-like woman stared at her unblinking for a few more moments, waiting to see if she was going to get an immediate answer, before accepting defeat. *"Very* inconvenient," she repeated, and then she and the other members of the Temple congregation made their way down to the road.

"I hope you won't mind Klera Coppersmith, Herald," said Mother Yllana, without any indication that she disapproved of the old woman's forthrightness.

"Not at all, she only spoke the truth. It *is* very inconvenient for them, I can see that, and very unfair to make them come all this way." Amily cast her eyes over the house and former barn again. "Still, this does seem to be a better situation for the Sisters. From what I was given to understand, your former Temple was in poor repair, uncomfortable, and unsuited to you and the Sisters, given your age and lack of income."

There. Let's see what she has to say about that.

"Well, it is a better situation for us here," Mother Yllana admitted, reluctantly. "We have room for a goat herd, and beehives, and our own garden, and a flock of chickens. We haven't had to spend a copper on food. There's space for each of us to have her own little room, all together, and it doesn't feel at night as if we're a dozen little lost souls at the bottom of a great cavern. We even have income now, yarn from our goats, and cheese, and honey. We're thinking of brewing mead. This place is easier for us to keep clean, and now we can afford a man to come and do repairs. . . ."

"But?" Amily prompted.

"But it's not convenient for the Temple to be set apart from the Chapter House; setting the Watches of the Night means one of us has to make her way in the dark—and in the winter, that is through the snow as well. And it's very hard on our congregants. And—" Her voice took on the tone of one who feels very much aggrieved. "—this is *not* what we agreed to in the first place!"

Aha— "Oh?" she replied. "What did you agree to?"

"I am quite certain in my mind that our agreement with those Priests of *Sethor*"—her tone said, though she did not, *whoever or whatever this "Sethor" is*—"was that they were to repair our home and make it possible for us to live comfortably in it until the last of us died. And only *then* were they to take it over. But that is *not* what happened."

"What exactly did happen?" Amily asked mildly, not allowing her expression to reveal that this was exactly what she had suspected all along.

"Well, we signed the papers, and expected workmen to turn up and begin the repairs. The workmen turned up all right, but with them were men with carts, who told us they had orders to move us." Mother Yllana clenched her hands in front of her, her chin set with what looked suspiciously like anger. "I objected of course, but the workmen said it was for our own good, because the damage to the roof was extensive, and they couldn't be responsible for our safety if we stayed. And *just* as the chief workman said that, a great piece of stone came dropping right down near us!"

:How . . . convenient,: said Rolan, echoing what Amily was thinking.

"After that, everyone was so nervous that we packed up and left that very day. The men with the carts even helped—and when we found we were being taken here, it seemed completely delightful. We thought, well, we'll have a pleasant fall here, and when winter comes we'll be back in our old home, and snug and warm and no longer drafty." Mother Yllana frowned. "But winter came . . . and there was no word on when we were to return. So I went myself to see what the delay was, and here were all these *men,* repainting, putting up the things of this *Sethor,* and generally acting as if it was *their* Temple now."

It was clear this unpleasant surprise was a wound that was still raw. The indignation in Mother Yllana's face was unmistakable, nor did Amily blame her. "I assume that you demanded to see the man in charge?" she asked.

"And I was *sloughed off* with some under-secretary, who presented me with contracts he *said* we had signed, and witnesses to swear to it! Except I have my wits, I do assure you and I had never signed *those* papers! Those papers said we had made an even exchange with the Sethor-priests, this farm for our old Temple." She shook her head, bitterly. "Of course, I know exactly what they did. They got us to sign something else entirely, and those clever, clever scribes of theirs used our signatures as patterns to forge signatures on the new documents. We didn't have seals, of course, who would have thought we'd need such a thing! And I could see how it would go—all those men, swearing that we had signed all the papers, and we had mistaken what we had signed, hinting that we were old and possibly losing our wits—"

"You could have brought it into the Courts and demanded the Truth Spell," Amily pointed out. "You still could."

But Mother Yllana shook her head. "They could claim immunity, by virtue of their religion. And we are not young, Herald. The strain on some of us would be hard, and for what? If I were not so angry at being deceived, I have to admit we got a decent bargain; this lovely little farm, so much better suited to our needs, for that drafty old ruin, falling down around our ears, and in a neighborhood that was not altogether . . . nice, anymore. No, I put it to the Sisters when I returned and explained what had happened, and we held a vote, and voted to make no fuss about it. We did have a man of law look over the deeds and the contract, and there is no deception in that we do own this place, without any question. It's just—"

"Being cheated," Amily suggested. "It's the principle. And by *priests.*"

"Exactly," Mother Yllana sighed. "And it's hard on what is left of Ardana's worshippers."

Amily took a deep breath. Now that she had a better idea of what was going on, she also had a better idea of what she could offer. "Do I have your permission to tell your story to the Prince?"

Mother Yllana's eyes widened. "Y-y-yes," she stammered, obviously taken aback. "I—never intended—"

"You have been wronged, it's in the Prince's hands to put some of it to rights," Amily replied firmly. *And it will do no harm at all to the Prince's reputation either.* "At the least, we can make it possible for your congregants to come here in ease and safety, and address the problem of the distance between the Chapter House and the Chapel." She smiled. "It shouldn't take much. Supplying you with a mule, a cart and a driver, and building a covered walkway should address both your problems. I'll suggest that to the Prince, if that meets with your approval."

:Good thinking,: Rolan told her, as they rode back up to the Palace. *:Now, walk me through your reasoning.:* Rolan did this a lot; he wanted her to articulate her logic to him before she had to defend it to the King—or anyone else for that matter.

:I can understand completely that they feel they were swindled, because they were. But it's also true that in most respects, where they are now is vastly superior to their old Temple. On the other hand they clearly wanted to avoid an actual confrontation with the Sethorites, if that's what they're called. And I don't blame them; the Sethorites are obviously too clever; the Sisters might end up losing the new Temple as well as the old.:

:Good analysis,: Rolan told her approvingly. *:Why the Prince and not the King?:*

:Because the King might feel he had to take official notice of it. The Prince can pass it off as charity to the Sisters.:

:Excellent. You're catching on to the nuances of this job. By the way, Prince Sedric is practicing with the Weaponsmaster. I told his Companion that you want to speak with him. I expect he'll be free about the time we get up there.:

In fact, as they rode up to the stable, Prince Sedric was waiting for them, lurking unobtrusively just inside the door. As he helped Amily unsaddle and rub Rolan down, Amily explained the situation.

"So I more or less promised them you'd give them a mule and a cart and arrange for a driver," she continued. "That solves the last of their problems, really, which is how to get their congregants down out of Haven to services."

The Prince nodded. Like his father, he was a handsome man in the conventional sense, made more handsome in her opinion by the lurking good humor in his eyes. "I think that's easily done out of my charity allowance, and I don't think we've ever gifted the Sisters of Ardana. I can have the Stablemaster find one of the stable hands that's getting on; it will make an easy job for him to retire into, and everyone will be happy. Good solution, Amily. I'll get it all in motion." His face darkened a little. "It doesn't speak well of the honor of those—what did you call them? Sethorites?"

Amily bit her lip. "I suspect from their point of view, they were perfectly honorable. They traded the Sisters a well-maintained property much more suited to them, and with enough land that they can be self-sufficient, for a place that was in considerable disrepair, in a poor neighborhood. The fact that they *tricked* the Sisters into it is probably of no importance to them, because . . . well, because I got the impression that they hold women to be only slightly more intelligent and important than a good breeding cow."

The Prince looked at her shrewdly. "Something like Holderkin, then?"

She shrugged. "That's my impression. But you were there, and maybe I am doing them a disservice."

The Prince shook his head. "No, my impression matches with yours. If we challenged them, they'd be astonished to learn we considered they had pulled a swindle. By their reasoning, they simply gave the simple-minded old things what they were too stupid to realize they needed."

Amily made a rude noise.

The Prince smiled and gave a last brush to Rolan's satiny coat. "We'll make it right without making a fuss. Perhaps the Sethorites may come to regret their swindle, once winter sets in. If I am remembering the Temple correctly, it's a vast barn that is impossible to keep heated. The Sisters will be sitting by their cozy fires, while the Sethorites will be piling on every robe they own, and wondering when spring will come."

Amily laughed. "From your mouth to the gods' own ears, my Prince," she said.

Of all of his personas, Mags enjoyed that of "Magnus, Lord Chipman's cousin" the most. But then, that was because most of the time Magnus didn't need to watch his back for enemies, unlike Harkon, and Magnus didn't have a job to do—Magnus had all the leisure that Harkon and Mags himself did not. Magnus was *everyone's* friend; he had just enough money to pay his own way, without having enough to make other young highborn men jealous of him. He was just high enough in rank that he was invited everywhere, and not so high that anyone needed to worry that he might be courting their company with an eye toward poaching an advantageous marriage out from under them. Magnus didn't have an enemy in the world. He knew how to get the Weaponsmaster to find you a time for a lesson, he knew enough about horses to give you good advice, and enough about weapons to keep you from being cheated. He played at dice and cards without betting more than he could afford to lose, and when he lost, he laughed. He knew *all* the best taverns in Haven, and which houses of pleasure would offer a good time without fleecing their customers in some way or other. He was the perfect boon companion.

And just now, he was, to his astonishment, watching a young girl who, by Amily's description must be Lirelle, Lord Lional's younger daughter, as she crouched in the bushes under a window, furiously taking notes in a bound journal. She thought she couldn't be seen, since she was between the wall and the ornamental bushes, but Mags was hyper-vigilant about movement where none should be, and he had spotted her fairly easily.

While this was rather irregular behavior, it wasn't as bad as it could have been, as the window in question did not lead into one of the many private apartments here at the Palace, but into a classroom—one of the ones at Herald's Collegium, to be precise.

He finally decided he had seen enough, and made his way between the wall of the Collegium and the bushes until he stood a few armlength's behind her. She was so intent on making notes she didn't even notice him until he cleared his throat.

She squeaked, started, and fell over.

"It's a great deal more comfortable inside than in the bushes, you know," he said, as she scrambled to her feet, flushing with mixed embarrassment and anger. "I know who you are—you're Lord Lional's younger daughter—so you might as well tell me what you were doing here." He winked at her. "Don't worry, I don't intend to tell anyone about this. I can't imagine you'd be making yourself so infernally uncomfortable if you didn't have a good reason."

The anger faded, and she gaped at him for a moment. "Here, come along with me, milady," he said, offering his hand. She took it, tentatively, ignoring the dead leaves clinging to her brown linen gown. "Let's go somewhere quiet. The library just off the Throne Room is generally empty this time of day, and cool. We can have a nice conversation uninterrupted. I'm Magnus, by the way. Lord Chipman's cousin."

"I'm Lirelle," she said, as they exited the bushes and she blushed as she looked down at her gown, realizing she probably looked like a hoyden. Mags looked politely away as she gave herself a hasty brushing, then led her into the Palace and straight to the Library.

As he had expected, the room was quite empty, except for one ancient gentleman, snoozing in the warm sunlight of one of the windows. Mags led the girl to a pair of chairs as far from the old fellow as possible, and waited for her to take her seat before taking his own. "Now, why, exactly, were you lurking outside a classroom?" he asked.

"It was a history lesson and I wanted to hear it," she told him. Now that he had a good look at her, he rather liked what he saw: a young girl with intelligent eyes, a face full of personality, and no sign of sulkiness. "My tutor back home is useless. He won't teach me *anything* worthwhile!" That *could* have sounded petulant. It didn't. It sounded plaintive.

"And what *does* he teach you?" Mags asked.

"Poetry. Religious texts, all full of stupid homilies about obedience.

Memorizing the family trees of the entire Kingdom. How to write letters. *Nothing* interesting or useful. We left him behind, but I'm horribly afraid they're going to send for him as soon as the house is ready—" She looked at him, and only now did she have a stormy expression of pure rebellion.

"You're right. Your tutor is an idiot. And I doubt that will be necessary," Mags replied, and smiled. "Any highborn youngster here at Court can take classes at any of the three Collegia, as well as with the Weaponsmaster."

"Anyone?" she breathed, as if she was afraid by saying it aloud, he'd deny it, or amend it with something that would mean *she* was excluded.

"Boys, girls, anyone," he promised. "I suppose even your lady-mother, if she were so inclined." He looked about for writing materials, and got himself quill, ink, and a piece of the palimpsest-vellum from the next table over. "I'll just write Lord Semel a note, shall I? And then your parents can arrange whatever you like. The tutor can remain where he is and torment your younger siblings."

He wrote out a brief, polite note, saying only that he had found Lirelle listening to a lesson and not specifying where or how, and wished to let his Lordship know that any or all of his sons and daughters could be enrolled in Collegium classes of their choice, and told him how that could be arranged. He ended it with "your humble servant," signed it with a flourish, and waved it in the air until it was dry. "Here," he said, handing it to Lirelle. "Before I seal it, I want to make sure I haven't said anything out-of-turn, as it were."

She read it over, as he waited, then handed it back to him with a pleased nod. He pulled off Magnus' seal-ring, and folded and sealed it on the spot, addressing the outside to "Lord Semel and

Lady Tyria." Then he handed it back to the girl.

"The sooner you give this to them, the sooner you'll find yourself in a class," he said, with a smile.

She snatched it from his hand, remembered herself and did a little curtsey, then dashed off. He smiled to himself, and got up to have a look for any of the others of the Lional brood.

Helane wasn't hard to find, and he very much doubted that *she* would be interested in classes . . . although you never knew. At the moment, there was a group playing bowls and pins in the garden, and she was the center of a knot of eager young men. And although he had been warned, Mags felt himself feeling a little stunned at her beauty. She really *was* something exceptional. And she wasn't that vacant sort of beauty, who has nothing about her that distinguishes her except that—she was animated, and evidently holding her own in teasing and clever conversation. Even *he* felt as if he was being drawn into her orbit, and had to remind himself that this was not what he was here for.

A better look around showed him a group of slightly younger men playing at dice, and one of them bore a strong family resemblance to Lirelle and the beauteous Helane. He sauntered over, was recognized, and invited to join. Since the stakes were low, he did. After a few throws, one of the lot thought to introduce him. "Magnus, this is Hawken; his family just arrived at Court. Hawken, this is Magnus, who knows where to find the best of everything at a price that won't make our fathers swear and threaten to cut off our pocket-money."

Magnus laughed, and gave Hawken a slight bow. Hawken, who seemed to have remained a spectator at the dice-game smiled, but with an inquisitive look. "The shallowness of my own purse has forced me to become something of an expert in the study," he said, with a faint hint of self-mockery.

Now he just needed to let things take their natural course. Sooner or later, this lot of lads were going to suggest a quick trip down to Flora's or one of the other houses of pleasure, and he wanted to see what Hawken's reaction to that was going to be. On the whole, this lot of young men were feckless; not ill-intentioned, but not reliable. And this trip would be to determine just how deep Hawken's pockets were, and how long his parental leash.

And right on schedule, as it became apparent that Hawken was not going to be one of the players, the suggestion came. Shortcuts of walking lanes between many of the manor houses on the Hill meant that Flora's and the Sickle Moon were both within walking distance, so off they went. Mags kept to the back of the group, and by dint of a few subtle signals, indicated to Hawken he should probably do the same.

"Where are we going?" Hawken said in an undertone, once the rest had gotten about five paces ahead of them.

"The Sickle Moon. It's a bawdy house, and I suspect my friends there are going to see how much of *their* pleasure they can get *you* to pay for," Mags replied, with a cynical chuckle. "It's what they always do, see how much of a coney they can make any fellow that's new to Court, figuring that even if his Papa is not indulgent, he'll still have a plump purse that his parents anticipate will last him for some moons."

Hawken licked his lips uneasily. "I . . . is my father likely to find out about this?"

"Not if you don't tell him," Mags chuckled. "But if the lads empty your purse for you, he'll find that out soon enough."

Mags could tell that Hawken was torn . . . on the one hand, women! On the other, the prospect that his new "friends" would impoverish him in a single afternoon.

And on the third hand . . . . *:I think our friend has little to no experience with the fair sex,:* Dallen observed, saying exactly what Mags was thinking.

:I suspect his father is the sort who would not take kindly to his offspring making free with the servants and the dairy-maids,: Mags agreed. *:I think I had better take matters into my own hands.:*

"To be honest, visiting a house in a crowd is not to my taste," he said, curling his lip a little. "I'll tell you what; let's you and I take this lane here—" He took Hawken's elbow, and guided him down a branching path that led between two manor walls, and quickly out of sight of the group. "For now, I know a very good inn with some outstanding entertainment. We'll enjoy ourselves for a couple of candlemarks, then wander back, and claim we thought *that* was where everyone was going once they return. Then I'll take you to Flora's myself, in a couple of nights." He winked at Hawken. "The ladies there know me very well. You *won't* get gutted, and you *will* get your money's worth."

:And you'll have a chance to get your usual report from Flora at the same time. Excellent plan,: said Dallen.

:Thank you, nothing like using the same trip to accomplish two things.:

"And you *aren't* planning on finding out how much I'm good for?" Hawken asked, with proper suspicion, now that he'd been warned.

Mags laughed aloud. "If you're *offering* out of gratitude, I won't say no," he assured the young man. "But I promise you, these are my regular haunts and I know exactly what my pockets will bear. Cousin Chipman doesn't coddle, but he doesn't keep me short, either."

"In that case, pray, lead on," Hawken said. "Where are we going?"

"A highly entertaining establishment that boasts an actual stage, and actual players. The beer and wine are a little overpriced, but that is made up for by virtue of the fact that the entertainment is free," Mags told him, as they came out from between the two walls onto one of the streets that was going to drop them onto the street of inns once they passed two more manors. "I think you'll be amused."

With Hawken's assurance that he'd told his parents that he was probably going to dine with friends, the two of them stayed down at the King's Helm until well after dinner, a dinner which Mags insisted on paying for, to cement his trustworthiness in Hawken's eyes. He considered taking Hawken on to Flora's that very night anyway, but decided against it. The young man was enjoying himself very much with the tamer entertainment of light comedies and good music he was getting. There was no point in overwhelming him.

And besides . . . I probably ought to find out just what his father would think of him going to a brothel. He might be fine with it, but I'd rather Magnus didn't make an enemy of the man if he's not.

:Want me to get Nikolas to find out?: Dallen asked *:I think he and Lord Semel and the King are all doing the "old crony" chat at the moment and now would be an ideal time.:*

:If it can be worked into the conversation, please. Don't bother to tell me

anything unless the answer is "no," and I'll assume if I don't hear anything, I can go ahead.:

He hadn't heard anything from Dallen by the time he and Hawken walked up through the gate to the Palace and were waved through by the Guards, who recognized "Magnus" on sight, and nodded when Hawken fumbled out the token that showed he lived at the Palace.

There were a lot of members of the Court strolling about in the illuminated gardens, and that was where Mags bid him farewell. "I am going to walk some of this wine off, not be tempted into drinking more," he told Hawken. "I have a lesson with the Weaponsmaster first thing in the morning, and I do *not* want to be feeling the effects of our evening when I meet up with him." And before Hawken could say anything, he sauntered off into the darkness, only doubling back and slipping into his own quarters when he was sure Hawken would not spot him.

There were lights burning in the sitting room, but he had already sensed that Amily was there, and not socializing—if the King's Own could *ever* be said to be "socializing"—with the Court.

"I found the Sisters of Ardana!" were the words Amily greeted him with as soon as he was in the door. "And I went down to talk to them, and discovered . . . quite a bit, actually. How are your ribs?"

He sat down gingerly beside her, and put his arm around her shoulders. "Lubricated and pains eased with a good bit of wine," he replied, and told her where he had been, and his encounter with two of the four offspring of Lord Semel. "That oldest girl . . ." he shook his head. "She ought to come with a sign about her neck warning the susceptible. I hope she's got a sensible head under that cascade of perfect hair. The oldest boy is suggestible, but not a total innocent. I warned him off of Danver Haylie's set, and we went and had innocent fun. And in a few days I'll take him to Flora's."

Her eyes sparkled with mischief. "Oh, you wicked corruptor of innocent youth!" she said.

"The youth in question was going to get corrupted sooner or later," he pointed out. "And your father, via Dallen, made sure *his* father isn't going to object. I'm just making sure he does it safely and within his means. So, what happened when you visited the Sisters of Ardana? And where are they now exactly?"

He found a comfortable position to ease his ribs—which were starting to ache a bit after all that walking—and listened to her carefully, frowning when she revealed just how the Sethorites had tricked the Sisters.

"It's a pretty legal question," he said at last, out of his experience of *far* too much time in the Haven Courts of Law. "They certainly were tricked. But I think you'd have a difficult time getting a judge to agree that they were *swindled*. The value of that farm seems to equal or better the value of the property and Temple. In fact, it could be said they are much better off now, and that the only people who've been discommoded are their congregants. Can *they* rightly be numbered among the Sisters? Legally, I don't think so."

She nodded. "That was the conclusion I came to, so I went to the Prince with a suggestion, and he took it. He's gifting the Sisters with a big cart, a driver, and a mule; he specified an enclosed cart, with benches that can be removed. So the congregants can come down to services twice a week, and the rest of the time the Sisters have the cart to haul what needs to be hauled."

"They can probably even arrange for the cart to be hired for a half day at a time when they don't need it," Mags observed. "That's more income. But to get back to what the Sethorites did— if this case were to come in front of me at the Law Court, I'd have to say they were even, even if I got the High Priest under Truth Spell—which I will bet any amount of money he would refuse to do—and proved they'd deliberately swindled the Sisters."

It was too warm for a fire, but Amily had clustered some candles on the hearth, so they not only gave off a pleasant light, the heat went straight up the chimney. The light from those candles illuminated Amily's sober expression. "The Weaponsmaster always says to pick the battles you can win," she observed pensively. "This really isn't one we could win."

He wasn't about to say anything as patronizing as "you're learning," but he was aware that this *was* "one of those lessons." Being King's Own meant having to figure out things like that. And she'd done so on her own, he was sure of that. The only thing that this conversation with him had *really* been about was just her confirming to herself that this had been the only way to proceed— and maybe getting reassurance from his answer.

"Got a question for you," he said. "Think we're spendin' too much time on Lord Semel's family?"

She shook her head immediately. "He's a friend of the King, a confidant of the King, and I suspect it's an open secret that he's been one of the King's informants in the area of his estate. Anyone that wants to influence the King through him will go *straight* for one of his children or his wife. His wife is probably well aware of just that, and is not going to be taken in, but the children are not. I'll talk to one of the Trainees about keeping an eye on Lirelle once she starts taking classes. If we can interest Loren in classes, all the better, that puts two of them in a place where we can keep track of them. If you've become Hawken's confidant, that settles that. That leaves Helane, who I know *nothing* about, and as we saw with Violetta, that can be dangerous—but I have Lady Dia alerted, and I'm talking with her tomorrow about Helane."

"So the short answer's no, we ain't spendin' too much time on 'em." He grinned. "A little prevention's gonna save us a whole lotta cure, I reckon."

"Me too," she said. "Now I think we can afford to spend some time on *us.*"

Amily was in Lady Dia's kennel—a two-story building easily as big as the stable, that held her beloved dogs. No smell of urine or droppings here; Dia had two servants assigned to the kennel so that nothing was allowed to remain longer than a candlemark, and generally not even that. Whelping and nesting boxes were kept full of fresh straw and the floor of each pen had a thick layer of sawdust. The place was as immaculate as the Companions' stable.

No one who *only* knew the elegant, fashionable, poised, and polished Lady Dia would ever have recognized the woman down on her knees in the straw, surrounded by a tumble of enormous puppies. Dia was wearing a pair of stained and maltreated leather trews, tucked into a pair of scuffed and patched boots, and a canvas smock that looked as if she had stolen it off the back of a ploughman, and her hair was up on the top of her head in a loose and messy knot.

The "Lady Dia" that the Court knew was a stunningly beautiful woman, with masses of dark hair, huge, melting brown eyes, the only person with a truly "heart-shaped" face Amily had ever known until she had seen Helane, and one who was never seen without every hair in place, eyes subtlety shadowed, cheeks charmingly blushed.

This Dia looked like one of her lesser servants—at least, until you got a glimpse of her face, which was still stunning, even without enhancement.

Although Dia was known in Court circles mostly for her "muff dogs," well-mannered and placid little lapdogs trained to remain obediently wherever their owners wanted them, such as in a muff to warm hands, or under skirts to warm feet, these puppies were the size of four adult muff-dogs put together. These were some of Dia's prized mastiffs, loyal, brave, and steady. And, when grown, they were big enough for a small child to ride. That made them formidable opponents that even an armed and armored man would hesitate to engage.

"How can you tell which ones will make the best protectors?" Amily asked, curiously.

"I have Nils test them for me. He's one of my trainers, but until he tests them, they won't have seen him before," Dia said, giving all the pups a quick rub or tussle before standing up and closing the door on the kennel. "That's critical; the tester has to have no preconceptions, and the pups have to react to a total stranger. He's tested this lot already. We have a system worked out, so I know the one with the blue collar there will be good for someone who has never seen a mastiff before, the ones with the green and red collars will need someone experienced but will make excellent protection dogs, the one with the yellow collar is shyer than the others, and would actually do well to guard Seth Maren's old mother once he's trained, and that one with the black collar is a loner, and would do just fine as a cattle guardian, with minimal human interaction."

Amily blinked. "Goodness. I didn't know you could tell *that* much, so young."

Dia rubbed her hands on the seat of her trews. "Oh, you'd be surprised. But you didn't come here to hear about puppies, and there's something I needed to tell you about anyway. Let's go up to the bower and we can talk while Miana helps me dress."

They walked out of the kennel and through an enclosed walkway that led them into a private entrance to the manor. The enormous manor house owned by Lord Jorthun, Lady Dia's husband, was nearly the size of the Palace, and probably had been one of the first manors built on the Hill. Of course it hadn't been this size when it had first been built, but neither had the Palace. Both had been torn down, rebuilt, and added to over the centuries. Lord Jorthun's family went all the way back to the Founding, in fact, although you would never know it to speak to him, since he never made any reference to that fact, but his family was just as old as the King's.

They took back stairs normally used by the servants to get to Lady Dia's rooms without accidentally bumping into someone who might take Dia for a particularly grubby lackey. Like most of the passages reserved for servants who, unlike Dia, had masters that would rather not have their underlings intrude on their awareness unless they were summoned, these stairs were steep, narrow, dark, and unornamented.

"Remind me to have those stairs lit," Dia grumbled a little. "I don't want anyone breaking her neck because she can't see where she's putting her feet."

They emerged into the first of an opulent set of rooms, blinking a little as the light struck their dark-accustomed eyes. The huge suite of rooms reserved for the wife of the ruling lord that Dia referred to as "the bower" had, in fact, always been called that. It was the size of many townhouses, had its own guest rooms and servants' rooms and even a small pantry and a rudimentary kitchen, should her ladyship suddenly turn hungry and demand a snack at an inconvenient hour. The bedroom was palatial—the bed was big enough to fit a family, curtained and canopied in green embroidered hangings that matched the curtains, piled with pillows, decked with a featherbed and green velvet-covered comforter. It looked like something fit for a forest goddess to sleep in.

"But I rarely sleep here unless I'm sick and I don't want to infect Steveral," Dia had confessed to Amily when she'd first married Jorthun. "The servants are appalled. Apparently sleeping in the same bed with one's husband is only for those who can't afford a second bed."

For the rest, there was relatively little furniture: a dressing-table, a stool, and a couch. The walls were lined with richly carved wardrobes, since, essentially, Dia used this room as a dressing-room and for storage for her gowns.

Once in the mostly unused bedroom where Miana was waiting, Dia unceremoniously began stripping to the skin with Miana helping. "I'll get to your young lady in a moment," Dia said, as Miana took the "working clothing" away to be dealt with; presumably washed or otherwise cleaned, since Miana had very firm notions on how her mistress's clothing should be maintained. Meanwhile, Dia slipped into linen bloomers and a chemise of cloth of so fine a weave it practically floated. "We've had the devil of a time collecting the evidence or getting anyone to admit they've been victimized, but there is an anonymous letter writer of a truly *vile* nature up here on the Hill. Steveral calls him a 'Poison Pen,' which is appropriate enough, considering how poisonous the letters he writes are. And I say 'he', although it could be a woman."

Amily sucked in her breath quickly. *Does that mean I'm not the only one—?* "What exactly are we talking about here?" she asked carefully.

Miana came back in with another chemise draped over her arm. Dia kept right on talking. "Anonymous letters, really vicious ones, and as far as I have been able to learn, all aimed at women. They're all on cheap, rough paper, and they're all very carefully printed by hand in a way that makes it impossible to recognize anyone's handwriting." This second chemise, this one with a froth of lace at the neck and wrists, went on over the first. "They run the gamut from insults and barbs aimed at a woman's appearance and age, to very pointed allusions to affairs being carried on, to direct attacks on her virtue, competence or intelligence. Honestly, it seems as if anything and everything is fair game for an attack, and those attacks are utterly ferocious, almost as if the letter writer had a personal vendetta against the victim."

Miana brought one of Dia's elaborately embroidered gowns out for approval, one of a deep wine-red with gold-colored braided trim, and on getting a nod, helped her mistress into it. "I'm not surprised no one has said anything about these letters, Herald Amily," the handmaid said, as Dia's head vanished under the folds of the gown. "I've seen the letters her ladyship has managed to collect, and I wouldn't want *anyone* to read what's in them, if they'd been addressed to me. And . . ." she hesitated a moment. "Well, I'm no Mind-healer obviously, but it seems to me that whoever is writing them is just not . . . sane."

"How are they being delivered?" Amily asked. "Is there any way we could set an ambush for him?"

"I don't think so," Dia replied, her head emerging from neck-opening of the gown. "They've arrived all manner of ways. Shoved under doors, tossed in open windows, found in a bouquet, left in a book, given to pages along with other messages and letters—trying to find the one who is delivering them is like trying to catch a ghost. And I agree with Miana. Whoever is writing these things is definitely not sane—and not sane in a really malevolent, stomach-churning way."

"But there's nothing to them, surely," Amily protested, as Miana began tightening laces, pulling on and tying false sleeves, and pulling the sleeves of the second chemise into attractive little puffs in all the right places.

"Unfortunately, all the ones I've been able to check on have been frighteningly accurate," Dia replied soberly. "So accurate that whoever is writing them *has* to have an information network just as good as my Handmaidens, because what I can verify is a perfect match for things I already knew. And that's another thing that has me worried. Usually this sort of vicious attack that is exclusively on women is perpetrated by a man—but what if it's one of the Handmaidens? What if we picked horribly, horribly wrong in one case?"

"Well . . . I don't know about that, but I can add to what *you* know.

I've gotten at least one letter from the same source, and maybe more," Amily confessed, as Dia sat on a stool and Miana began brushing out her hair, in preparation for turning it into a work of art. "I had thought that this was just random, anonymous cranks, but the last letter I got sounds exactly like the ones you've described."

"You?" Both Miana and Dia gave her a dumbfounded look. "What on earth could a Poison Pen have to say about *you*?" Dia added.

"That I can't do my job properly, and that I should go kill myself so my father can get Rolan back and go back to being King's Own," she replied, and saying the words out loud made them hurt all over again, but she firmed her chin and stiffened her spine and refused to let the hurt show.

Dia winced. "That's a low blow," she said. "But that does tell me that people *outside* the Court are getting them too—and where there's one, there's likely more than one. We're going to have to start looking at the Collegia for victims, too, both the teachers and the Trainees, and maybe even some of the Heralds who aren't teachers." She turned to Miana. "I think we need to speak to all the Handmaidens and become more active in collecting these things."

"And I think *I* should see if the Poison Pen is sending them to people outside the Court other than me," Amily told her friends. "Technically, after all, I am part of the Court."

"Hmm—" Dia said suddenly, getting a thoughtful look on her face. "*I* haven't gotten one. Have I?" She craned her head around to look at Miana, who shook her head.

"While we would probably protect you from actually *seeing* something that nasty, we would definitely have let you and his lordship know," Miana said firmly. "And if there had been more than one, well, then we would have kept them and shown them to his lordship."

"And since the letters have continued and no one is dead, I think it is safe to assume I have not gotten one. Steveral would have left no stone unturned to find the bastard sending them, and . . . well, let's just say there would probably have been a body found floating in the river. And *that* is interesting. We should find out if *only* those who live at the Palace and not in their own homes are the recipients of these charming missives." Now she raised an eyebrow at Amily, who nodded.

"Mags can do that," she affirmed. "Or Father. Or both."

They all fell silent while Miana finished putting Dia's hair into two elaborate, decorated braids, then wove the braids into a kind of crown over the top of her head. "I know it's just a nuisance right now," Dia finally said aloud. "But . . . I don't like the idea of someone with that filthy a mind running about loose among us. If that makes sense."

Amily nodded. "Those are words intended to *hurt*. Not just sting, but to wound, and wound deeply. That speaks of someone with a vendetta, and you never know who someone with a vendetta is going to pick on next."

"Especially if it's a woman," Dia added glumly.

Amily knew *exactly* what Dia meant by that. *It's difficult enough to be taken seriously as a woman, but if this Poison Pen is female, her mere existence will just give more ammunition to men who say women are petty, vindictive, emotional, and can't be trusted to make the smallest decision.*

"In that case, I'd better get back to the Palace, tell Father and maybe Mags about this, and get things underway," Amily said at last. "Oh, about Helane—"

"Sorted," said Dia, with a touch of relief. Probably her relief was that here, at least, she had something that was not in the least nebulous, and that she had well in hand. "I've arranged for Fayleen Asterhass to attend the ladies of the family for such things that the Palace servants can't handle, allowing them to send their own maidservants back to deal with matters at that manor they've acquired. If the beauteous Helane is a troublemaker in disguise, we'll know it soon enough for us to put a stop to it one way or another. Worst comes to worst, Kyril can tell his good friend Lional that his oldest daughter is not . . . quite . . . ready for the Court, and have her sent home. And if she's not a troublemaker, she's got a confidant in Fayleen that she can trust to steer her through the rough waters of the Court."

Now it was Amily's turn to sigh with relief. "I don't want a repetition of the Violetta Affair," she said, as she rose.

"No more do I, my dearest friend," Dia replied fervently, holding her face up for Miana to apply darkening powder to her eyelids. "No more do I."

Mags lounged casually against a tree trunk in the Knot Garden, and felt eyes upon him.

Now, since he was being Magnus, and not Harkon, this did not alarm him much. He had just seen to it that young Hawken had gotten an introduction to a group of young courtiers who were not as feckless as his first lot of acquaintances. Since these new acquaintances were a bit better off than that first lot, they were not going to be inclined to cultivate him as a ready source of money.

Mags was keeping an eye on the lot of well-dressed, athletic young men milling about a statue of a girl holding a bird in her hands. Animated conversation, which involved a lot of gesturing, and a bit of laughter reached him at his out-of-the-way perch. Things were going very well on that head; the new friends were organizing a ride out into the countryside, which evidently suited Hawken right down to the bone. Mags already knew that he had a horse, and a good one, currently stabled at the manor not all that far away, and by the look of him, Mags figured he was probably a cracking good rider. The old friends did *not* have horses, which excluded them from this excursion, which pleased Mags very much. It looked as if separating him from those who might have gotten him into trouble was going to be painless, even effortless.

As for the promised expedition to Flora's . . . Nikolas himself had let him know this morning that Lord Semel had laughed knowingly when Nikolas had made several hints that his eldest son might find "adventures" down in Haven. *"And good for him when he does,"* had been the reply. *"Better a transaction where everyone knows the rules of the game than getting into trouble with the greedy, or worse, the innocent."*

So that was sorted.

The only question was . . . why was someone staring a hole in his back? And who was it?

:Why don't you turn around and find out?: Dallen asked.

:Because, horse, I don't want whoever it is to know that I know he's staring at me. And yes, I know, I could use Mindspeech to find out, but I'd rather flush him the old-fashioned way, by making him approach—:

His thought was interrupted by someone clearing his throat at his elbow. Since the sound was a boyish soprano, Mags already had a good idea who it might be before he turned around.

"Heyla, youngling," he said lazily, as he eyed young Loren, who was looking up at him. Which was an unusual enough circumstance, since Mags was short by the standards of most of the young men of the Court. "Is there something you wish to say to me?"

Loren looked like a much younger, much shorter version of the handsome Hawken. So far the family resemblance among all of Lord Semel's offspring was uncanny.

"You're Magnus, right?" Loren asked. At Mags' nod, he jutted out his chin as if he expected to be told to go away at any moment. "You wrote that letter for my sister to my parents, right? About classes with the Collegia?"

"I did, indeed," Mags confirmed. "Were you interested in joining the classes as well?"

"No!" Loren blurted, then flushed, and amended. "Well, yes, maybe, but . . . that's not why I wanted to talk to you. Do you know a way of getting lessons with the Weaponsmaster?"

So that's *the way the wind blows! Well, let's see if I can't bribe him to get him into a place where one or more of the Trainees can befriend him.*

"If I do," Mags said, slowly, "Will you also attend classes? I can absolutely guarantee that they will be infinitely more interesting than anything your tutor was teaching you."

Loren sighed heavily. "If I have to—" he said reluctantly.

"You have to," Mags told him. "You can't just idle around the Court you know, like one of those empty-headed asses with nothing more to talk about than horses and cards." He nodded slightly at Hawken's group of *old* friends, who were making a nuisance of themselves over some of the young women who were clustered in a defensive group under a tree that had a ring-seat about its trunk, pretending to embroider. The ladies in question were very well aware that *these* fellows were second-rate at best, and were trying to ignore their not-terribly-clever overtures.

Loren sighed again. "That's what Father says," he admitted. "He says I should be doing something useful while I'm here, but he hasn't said what it is he thinks I should be doing. Hawken's going to inherit the title and the estate, though, and I—I just don't want to be hanging around trying to find some girl with money and connections to marry, when there's better things out there!"

"You have something in mind?" Mags prompted.

"Sure! I want to be the Lord Martial!" Loren looked so enthusiastic that Mags choked down his laughter and managed to keep a straight and sober face. "I want to join the Army and be an officer and work my way up to General, and win all my battles, and be a hero, and then the King will make me Lord Martial!"

Mags scratched the side of his chin. "You do know that you have to know the history of every battle Valdemar has ever fought in to do that, don't you?" he asked casually. "That's part of learning how to win all your battles."

Loren lost a little of his glow. "I do?"

"*And* you need to know the geography of the entire country so you know exactly what kind of terrain you might be fighting in." Mags looked up into the branches of the tree above his head as if they were the most fascinating thing he had ever seen. "Battles have been lost by not knowing every inch of the ground you're fighting on."

"Oh—" Loren said, looking crestfallen.

"And mathematics, because before you become a General, you'll be going up through the ranks of all the officer grades," Mags continued. "At that point, you're left to make most of the decisions yourself, and you'll be doing your *own* calculations for provisioning your men, and deciding how many miles they can march, whether a bridge can hold up under them . . . and all manner of things like that." He looked down at Loren again. "How many wagons would you need to carry the provisions for a month for a full company? And how many more would you need to carry the feed for the horses that pull them?"

"—ah." Loren coughed. "Maybe lessons are . . . a good idea."

"I would say so." Mags patted him on the back, in a brotherly fashion. "Now you just trot on back to your parents, and come back to me when you've got those lessons set up, so I know what your schedule will be and what group to ask the Weaponsmaster to put you in."

Loren shot off like a lightning bolt, leaving Mags to saunter off to talk to Dean Caelen about the two new "Blue" students he'd be getting. *If only everything was this easy . . . but then, I wouldn't have a job to do.*

6

: $\mathcal{M}$*ags. Mags. Mags.:*

In Mags' dream, he was standing on the top of the cliff at the Bastion. He knew, somehow, that he was completely alone, even though it was too dark to see anything. It wasn't winter; it was a windy summer night with a sickle moon high overhead, and his cloak billowed in the gusts, tugging at his shoulders.

:Mags. Mags. Mags.:

Even though he *knew* he was alone, someone was calling him, calling his name, over and over. It was . . . getting annoying. It was pleasant up here, and he just wanted to be left in peace. Who could be pestering him like this?

:Mags. Mags. Mags.:

Oh, of course! he thought. *It's Dallen . . .*

And with that, he woke up. He was in his comfortable bed, on his side, with Amily curled up against the small of his back.

Unfair. It was totally unfair to be nagged awake in the middle of a pleasant dream.

:All right, I'm awake,: he replied, shaking his head a little to get the fog out of it. He cracked his eyes open. It was still dark. This was absolutely, completely unfair. What was so urgent that he had to be roused before the sun was up? *:What's the problem?:*

:The Prince needs you. He's in the Lesser Audience Chamber.:

Oh. That put a different complexion on things entirely. It wasn't just Dallen being annoying. Of course, it was still *unfair,* but it was the normal sort of unfair that came with being a Herald. *Huh. Me, he wants, and not Amily. So it's somethin' for the King's Spy, not the King's Own . . .* That in itself was unusual. *:Tell 'im I'll be there soon as I'm decent.:*

He slipped out of bed without waking Amily, grabbed his clothing as he tiptoed out, and pulled on his Whites in the next room, so accustomed to the uniform now that he could get himself presentable by touch alone.

It wasn't even pre-dawn yet; the sky was still dark, without so much as a hint of light to the east. Whatever had prompted the Prince to get roused out of *his* bed this morning, it must have been urgent, but not an emergency. Urgent enough to drag the junior spy out, not urgent enough to drag Nikolas, or the King, or anyone else out. *I can live with that,* he thought, as he hurried through the shiver-cold and damp air to the Palace, taking the quickest route to the appointed room once he got inside the Palace. The corridors were dimly lit, and eerily quiet. Probably the only people awake besides himself and Sedric were the servants in the kitchens and the Guards on the rooms of the Royals.

Anyone who knew Palace protocol would have known that one of the Royals was in the Lesser Audience Chamber; there were two guards on it. The Seneschal or other officials only rated one guard, and obviously no one guarded an unused and empty room.

The two Guards stiffened as they heard footsteps approaching down the barely lit hall, and relaxed when he came into the light and they saw it was someone in Herald's Whites. "Herald Mags, summoned to the Prince," Mags said formally—because the Guards weren't stupid and *anyone* could purloin a set of Whites. The Prince would have told the Guards exactly which Herald he was expecting, obviously.

"You're expected, Herald," said the right-hand one, and opened the door to the Audience Chamber for him.

There were only a couple of lanterns lit, up near the thrones. Sedric was sitting on his throne rather than his father's, leaning forward, elbows on his knees, looking very much as if he had just tossed on the clothing that was closest to hand—a pair of old, worn breeches, a heavy canvas tunic with the sleeves cut off at the elbow, and slippers. Mags tried not to gawk; it was the first time he had ever seen Sedric in anything that was not Royal Whites.

The Prince was talking to someone who was no one Mags recognized from the back—a woman, by the sound of her voice. Though with her graying auburn hair cut short and wearing full leather armor, with some drapings that might have been meant to suggest a religious habit or robes, from the back it was almost impossible to tell what gender she was. Sedric's solemn expression turned to one of relief when he saw Mags enter the room.

"This is just the person to help you, Prioress," he said, as the woman turned to see who had come in. "Prioress, this is Herald Mags. Mags, this is the Prioress of the Temple of Betane of the Axe."

The woman had an interesting face; square, androgynous, with a firm chin and high cheekbones. She regarded Mags soberly.

Mags gave the Prioress a little salute. "I beg forgiveness, but—"

"You've never heard of us, and why should you have?" the Prioress interrupted. From the sound of things, she was used to interrupting people. Mags decided it wasn't rudeness, precisely, it was the habit of someone who needed to get straight to the point, and couldn't wait while other people dithered. "We keep to ourselves for the most part, and I wouldn't expect every Herald to know every god and sect worshipped in the city." She glanced at the Prince. "Shall I tell the tale, or will you, Highness?"

"It's your tale to tell, Prioress," the Prince demurred.

She cleared her throat. "Well, we're a martial order, obviously. We're all women. Most of us are former mercs, with a sprinkling of private bodyguards, some young girls who've petitioned to join as Novices, and a few Valdemaran retired Guard. We've been known to augment the Guard at need, but otherwise, the most action we see is when the local Watch needs a little heavy backup, and comes calling on us. As a martial order, though, we keep our skills in warcraft sharp, and a few times a year we go out of the city on a combination camping and training exercise. We close up the Temple sanctuary—not *close* it, as such, since we don't—or didn't—lock it, but we don't hold services. It's a good chance to give the Novices a taste of what real war is like, without taking them out to a battlefield. The only people left behind at the Temple are anyone sick or hurt, and a handful of the really elderly who just can't camp anymore. We've got a smaller private chapel they use when the Temple sanctuary is closed up. We were out on one of those exercises—the rest of the Order still is, in fact—when I got the overwhelming feeling I needed to get back."

"This has happened before?" Mags asked. "This premonition sort of thing, that is?"

The Prioress nodded. "It comes with the office of Prioress. Actually, I thought for sure it was because maybe someone back here had fallen gravely ill or even passed on, so I hurried and got here a few candlemarks ago, but when I arrived, there wasn't anything amiss. Wasn't that is, until I followed the feeling in my gut and went to the Sanctuary. It had been—" She paused for a moment, taking slow, deep breaths. Mags could practically *feel* the rage radiating from her for a moment, until she calmed herself. "Defaced is too mild a word for what I found. *Violated* is more like it. Vile, despicable things painted on the walls. Obscene, filthy things. Whoever did this had to have been deranged—"

"Just a moment," Mags interrupted her, following his *own* impulse. There was no reason to think that this was linked to the Poison Pen letters Amily had told him about last night, and yet— "Have you been getting similarly vile letters recently?"

The Prioress started a little, and looked at him askance. "We've always gotten what I call 'hate notes' from time to time. That's the nature of things for a martial female order, some people think we're unnatural. But yes, we have gotten a *lot* more, recently, all, as far as I can tell from the same source."

Mags held up his hand. "Hand-printed on rough, cheap paper, the letters formed in a block-style, so there is nothing in the way of a 'handwriting style' to distinguish them?"

The Prioress narrowed her eyes. "Yes. Exactly. Is there something going on?"

"Nothing Mags is at liberty to discuss just yet, Prioress," the Prince interrupted. "Mags, I would like you to go down into Haven with the Prioress; she's put the sanctuary off-limits to the rest of the order for now, so nothing will have been disturbed or changed. I want you to gather as much evidence as you can, then report to me what we need to clean the place up and set things to rights by sunset at the very latest."

The Prioress bowed to the Prince, looking both shocked and a little dazed. "Highness, I did not ask—"

"No, you did not, but it was well within your rights to," the Prince told her. "I want the rest of your people to return to their home and find it ready for them. If we can't make everything the way it was, the least we can do is erase what was done. As for *what* was done to you, I would like you to remain silent about it. Don't even tell the rest of the Order. We'll think of an excuse if we need to alter anything." He turned to Mags. "Make it happen, Herald."

Mags saluted, the first time he'd ever done such a thing, but it seemed appropriate. "It will be done, Highness. Prioress, will you need a mount to get back down the Hill?"

"I came on my horse, thank you," she said, still looking a little dazed.

"Then we'll go to the stables; soonest begun, soonest done," he replied, as the Prince made a little, impatient gesture, suggesting there was no point in standing on ceremony.

Mags took the hint, leading the way without pausing for the usual bows.

Dallen was waiting outside Companion's Stable, already saddled, bridled, and waiting, glowing in what was now pre-dawn light; there were always a couple of stablehands awake to take care of tacking up Companions who made it known that they were needed. One of them was still waiting next to Dallen, and went off to fetch the Prioress's mount. He came back with—as Mags had expected—a very fine chestnut warhorse. She had probably ordered it be left tied up but not untacked when she arrived, anticipating she'd either get an audience immediately, or be sent back down the Hill to return at a later time. The beast dwarfed Dallen; the Prioress was actually taller than Mags as well, so the two of them mounted side by side probably looked rather comical.

She looked down at Mags from her lofty perch, morning sun touching her hair and giving her the odd effect of a halo. "Did he really mean that, about having the Sanctuary cleaned up by sunset?" she asked. "I just came to report the crime, since I didn't want to take something like *that* to the Watch, but I didn't expect the Prince to shoulder responsibility for rectifying it."

"Every word," Mags assured her. "I assume there will also be some sort of ceremony you'll need to do as well?"

She nodded. "But that can't be done until the physical defilement is gone," she said, sounding hesitant.

There must be a lot of damage . . . well, the Prince as much as said I'll get all the resources I need to take care of the problem. Enough workmen can clean up anything. And enough money will buy their discretion. "Let's get on down there then," he replied cheerfully. Dallen moved off without his needing to give a signal. The warhorse snorted, and followed, easily overtaking Dallen and taking the lead.

* * *

Mags surveyed the desecrated sanctuary, taking it all in. As the Prioress had said, the effect was nothing short of appalling. "There's something to be said for simplicity," he said, finally. "No decorations means nothing to replace."

The sanctuary had, indeed, been very simple; no benches for sitting on, no pews, there wasn't even an altar. It had just been a single, large room with a window high in the wall to the east, and another matching it to the west. Hanging on the wall under the eastern window was an enormous axe, an implement so huge Mags wondered how it had been forged, and how on *earth* the Order had managed to get it hanging on the wall in the first place. Some sort of hoist to get it up, of course, but how to *hold* it up there? There was no sign that anyone had tried to take it down or deface it in any manner, but most of it was hanging high above the reach of most people. Maybe that was what had saved it from desecration.

The plain, whitewashed walls, however, were another matter altogether.

They had been covered in words and drawings in red paint, the color usually used to paint barns with. Pornographic, demented, childishly crude pictures of naked women doing obscene things to bound or otherwise humiliated men alternated with ranting, obscenity-laden scrawls. Some concerned what was going to happen to women who didn't "know their place." Others concentrated on defamatory language against the Order in particular and women who dared to "take the place of men" in general. A few were very graphic descriptions of what the writer thought women were "good for." And of course, given that, there were obscene suggestions of what the women of the Order were doing with each other. All of them were scrawled in slashing letters in that thick red paint, which had been dripped all over the stone floor. The floor would be easy to clean, it was the paint on the walls that was problematic. No matter how much scrubbing was done, the paint was still going to remain, and it would probably take new plaster to cover it up enough that the ghost of this insanity didn't bleed through.

Mags whistled through his teeth as he contemplated the mess. "Some of the members of our Order have not been . . . treated well by men," the Prioress said hesitantly.

Mags didn't see any reason not to be blunt. "You mean they've been abused in the past. You said a lot of them were mercenaries; I imagine that's not uncommon in some merc companies. I can see why you wouldn't want them exposed to this. This, *here*, where they are supposed to be safe? I'm sure they are tough, but coming on this unexpectedly—" He shook his head.

"Yes. Exactly. I didn't even want the elders looking at this." He actually heard her grinding her teeth.

He took a few slow breaths; the paint was fresh enough to smear, so it was still giving off fumes. *At least we can be grateful that whoever did this didn't decide to piss and shit all over the room, too.* Was it only one person? Or more than one? This things wouldn't take long to scrawl on the wall, and without knowing how long the perpetrator or perpetrators had been at this, there was no way of telling if there'd been more than one.

One would be safer, though. Two people can keep a secret, but only if one of them is dead, as they say. If the remaining members of the Order had taken to their beds at a virtuously early time, the miscreant would have had candlemarks to do this in.

"We'll fix this, Prioress," he said, finally. "It looks worse than it is. Is there any reason why the sanctuary was whitewashed?"

"It was cheap," she replied dryly. "And easy to maintain. We don't waste coppers on ornament, as you've noted. Why do you ask?"

"Any reason to object to repainting in red?" he asked.

She considered that for a moment. "Not that I can think of. Associated with war, is the color red. Might be fitting." She looked about, again, with a sickened expression on her face. "I can't imagine any way this could be scrubbed clean."

He nodded. "My thought exactly. And it would take new plaster to keep the color from coming through new coats of whitewash. All right then. Give me a minute."

Mags had the strongest Mindspeech of any living Herald, and at the moment, that Gift was exactly what was needed. He closed his eyes for a moment, sought out the Prince's mind, and made contact. It was a little like tapping someone on the shoulder, actually. *:Highness?:*

:Show me the damage, Mags.: The reply was immediate. Good, the Prince was probably still sitting alone where they'd left him, just waiting for Mags to report.

Mags let the Prince see what had been done, sensing fragments of the Prince's reaction as he went over every inch of the desecrated sanctuary. There was disgust, anger, and puzzlement, which had been Mag's reaction, too. Because this made no sense, the Order couldn't possibly have offended anyone *this* much, could they? From the solid look of the buildings, they'd been here for decades, maybe even a century or two. So why had this happened now?

:Not as bad as it could have been, then,: was the Prince's first open response. *:I was thinking broken statuary, smashed furniture, something more difficult to deal with than paint.:*

:That was my thought. Four men to clean the paint off the floor, another half dozen to paint the walls, using the scaffolds left over from finishing the roof of Herald's Collegium. Big brushes and a lot of red paint should take care of the walls. The Prioress approves the color.:

The Prince considered this. *:It'll be a bit dark when they're done. I'll send some lanterns and brackets down as well. Sketch as much as you can stomach, write down all the raving, and stay down there in charge. I'll be sending a crew I can trust to keep their mouths shut. Tell the Prioress that all anyone will know is that I decided since I had made a charity gift to the Sisters of Ardana that I'd make one to her Order as well and redecorated the Sanctuary under your direction while the Order was out on their exercise.:*

Mags nodded. It was a very good story, and no one was likely to challenge it. *:Very well, your Highness.:*

:I'll leave you to it then.:

Mags let the connection between them drop, and turned back to the Prioress. "There will be a crew that will keep their tongues in their heads down here within a candlemark," he told the woman, who had kept silent while he spoke to the Prince. "The Prince will let it be known that he decided to gift the Order by redecorating the sanctuary, and scheduled it with you to take place while most of them were out on that exercise in order to keep any disturbance to a minimum."

For the first time since he had met her, he saw her smile, slightly.

"He's going to make a good commander and tactician," she said with admiration.

Mags made a little grunt of a chuckle. "He already is," he replied. Then he made another circuit of the walls, copying down the scrawls and the disgusting drawings. "You know," he said, as he worked, "The paint's still shiny in places. This looks as if every bit of it was done last night, in silence, without disturbing anyone here. They certainly carried away anything that could have been considered as evidence."

The Prioress folded her arms and contemplated the walls. "All I can say is, thank the Goddess that everyone still here is too old and too crippled to be larking about like this all night. If they weren't, anyone who got wind of this would probably accuse *them* of doing this."

"Hmm-hmm," Mags agreed, and pointed at one of the inscriptions. "Along the lines of that nonsense there, about women cooped up together turning into man-devouring monsters?"

She nodded. "There was a lot of that sort of thing in the letters."

"I don't suppose you saved any of them, did you?" he asked, not really expecting an affirmative answer.

"Dear Goddess, no," she said, curling her lip. "I got rid of the trash as quickly as I could. Into the fire they went, before anyone but me got a chance to read them. As I said, there are those among us who have . . . raw nerves on certain subjects. I didn't want to take the chance of exposing them to something that would awaken old, bad memories." She bit her lip and turned to look him fully in the eyes. "Do you really think the letters and this are linked?"

"You said it yourself," he pointed out. "Expressing the same sentiments. If you get any more, save them and send them to me."

Anything more they might have discussed was interrupted by

the arrival of a wagon, loaded with sleepy workmen and women, paint, brushes, lanterns, brackets, and the scaffolding. And Mags settled down to a steady job of supervising the workers, while the Prioress kept an eye on her aged, but still curious, Sisters, until the inscriptions were covered up and the repainting reached the ceiling.

Mags was glad to get back up the Hill, change out of the Whites that had (inevitably) gotten spattered with red paint, stuff himself at dinner, and go to lie down on the bed he had been forced to abandon *far* too early in the morning. Amily was off somewhere, but he knew Dallen had kept Rolan appraised of what was going on, and Rolan had made sure she knew what he was doing.

He wasn't altogether sure what *she* was doing, but it was probably her usual duties. That would be at least one Council meeting today, and he was quite, quite certain that the activities of the Poison Pen—or Pens—were *not* going to be mentioned at the meeting. First of all, they had nothing linking the letters to the Court with the desecration of the Temple. Second of all, the Prioress herself, as well as the Prince, had asked that nothing be said. And he understood why. Only too well.

He was no empath, but it hadn't been hard to read the shame and the doubt in the Prioress's stiff manner. It didn't *matter* that no one in the Order of Betane had done anything to earn those disgusting scrawls. The fact that the desecration had happened in the first place was enough to shake the Prioress's faith, not in her Goddess, but in herself. Mags had seen it time and again, administering justice down in Haven. Stupid people never doubted themselves.

Intelligent ones, however, went straight to self-examination whenever anything bad happened. *Did I deserve this? Did I bring it on myself? Did I somehow do something that I shouldn't have?* Even though the sanctuary of Betane was now clean, painted, lit with beautiful brass lanterns, and looked *better* than it had before the insult, the Prioress would probably be on her knees all night in there. She'd *say* she was guarding it until the rest of the Order got back, but the real reason was because she was going to punish herself for "letting" it happen, and beg her Goddess's forgiveness for whatever imaginary fault had permitted an enemy to penetrate into the Order's heart.

I would love to get my hands on whoever did this. But he already knew that he could administer all the punishment in the world, and it would have no effect, because the ones who had done this were *stupid* people, who had absolutely no doubt that they were in the right. No matter what they were told, no matter how many times they got caught and punished, they would go straight out and do it again. They knew they were right, and nothing would shake that faith.

:I wish there was a plague that would target only stupid people,: he thought stormily. *:Life would be so much easier for all the people that were left.:*

"What are you thinking, frowning like that?" Amily said from the foot of the bed. "You look as if you're aching to get your hands on someone and beat some sense into him."

"If only it were that easy," he sighed, opening his eyes, and told her what had been going on since he'd left her this morning.

She pursed her lips, and rather than replying, went back into the sitting room. When she returned, she had a leather document case with her, and sat down next to him on the bed. "It looks to me as if we have something widespread and nasty on our hands," she said.

"Wait," he interrupted her. "Let me find my notes." The notebook, as he had thought, was under the bed where it had ended up after he'd thrown himself down onto it. She pulled a handful of what looked like letters printed on crude paper and handed them to him. He looked them over, frowning, while she perused his notes.

"Look at this," she said, pointing to one of the inscriptions he had carefully copied out. "I'm sure there is something with the exact phrasing in one of those letters."

"There is," he said, picking it out of the group. "And this one is similar. Here's one that's like the inscription I wrote on the next page." He looked up at her, and saw she was as troubled by this as he was. "Clearly, we have a problem. If it's a single person, how is it that he can deliver letters up here on the Hill, and yet be down in Haven to desecrate a Temple in the dead of night? If he lives on the Hill how would he have known that the Temple was going to be empty? And if he lives in Haven, how would he deliver letters up on the Hill?"

"And if it's more than one person, clearly they are working together. They're using the same phrasing, and they think *entirely* too much alike." She shivered. "I'm beginning to be glad you sleep with weapons at hand."

He glowered at the letters. "I think you should start. I'm not always here."

"I think I will," she replied. "Or . . . better still, maybe I should get one of Dia's mastiffs."

"That wouldn't be a bad idea. We've got the room. I'd feel better about you being alone here. Not"—he hastened to add—"that I think you are incapable of defending yourself. But you can't be awake all the time. And if you sleep too lightly you'll never get any rest."

"I'll talk to her about it tomorrow." She put the letters into the document case, and when he handed it to her, added the notebook. "And we should both see the King and the Prince and probably Father tomorrow at breakfast." Her eyes went distant for a moment. "Rolan's taking care of it."

"Most people have a personal secretary for such things," he said, his mouth quirking a little.

"Hush. He might 'hear' you. Besides, he's no good as a personal secretary, he can't write." She leaned over and kissed his nose. And then his mouth. And then they forgot about breakfast appointments and Poison Pen letters for a while.

:Time to wake UP!: Perhaps it had been the remark about being a personal secretary, but Rolan seemed to take great glee in booting Amily out of what had been a nice, peaceful rest. But as she levered herself up on one elbow, hair falling down over one eye, Mags groaned theatrically and batted at the air, as if trying to make something invisible go away. *Dallen isn't being any kinder to him, I see.*

"It won't work," she reminded him. "He's in your head, and you can't get rid of him that easily." She pushed the hair out of her eyes.

"Wretched horse," he grumbled, and blinked sleepily. "At least they woke us up with plenty of time to make ourselves presentable. Did I tell you what the Prince was wearing when I got rousted out of bed yesterday?"

"No," she replied, groping for her shift. She definitely remembered it going over *this* side of the bed last night . . . *ah, there it is.*

She laughed at his description as they both washed up and put on clean uniforms. It was still dark as they left their rooms for the Palace, document case in Amily's hand, heading for the Royal Suite.

The Guards posted here probably would have been demoted to cleaning boots if they *hadn't* known the King's Own on sight, so the moment Amily and Mags appeared at the end of the hall, one of the men on duty started opening the door for them. They went through, side by side, with nods to both Guards, and the door closed smoothly behind them.

Anyone who had been expecting decadent luxury in the Royal Suite would have been profoundly disappointed. The furnishings were the very best, and the tapestries warming the walls were works of pure art, but there was a definite patina of daily use on everything. In fact, the King hadn't changed a thing after he'd inherited the title and the rooms. The colors were all muted by age, leaving the visitor with the impression that these rooms were part of an extremely comfortable, wealthy, if old-fashioned, country estate.

The cool, damp, morning breeze came in the open windows; to take the chill out of it, a small fire burned cleanly on the hearth. The clever folding table that usually stood against the wall of the sitting room had been unfolded and set with breakfast dishes.

It was just the King and the Prince seated at the commodious table, eating breakfast this morning. The Queen was probably still abed; she was not a morning riser. Lydia was, but she was in the first months of her first pregnancy, and at the moment, she and breakfast were bitter enemies.

"Sit," Kyril said, gesturing with a fork. "We'll eat first. I'd rather not ruin my appetite with what you're going to show us."

Amily was in complete agreement with that sentiment. They joined the other two in making short work of the dishes that had been set before them.

Only when the servants had cleared everything away and left, did the King indicate that he was ready to hear what they had to say.

The Prince was silent through all of Mags' report, but questioned Amily closely about what Dia had told her concerning the letters she'd been given. They both pored over Mags' notes, and the letters, with no comments except to each other, for the better part of a candlemark.

Finally the King put all the documents back in the case with a sigh. "I wish I could say that this looks like nothing more dangerous than mean-spirited mischief," he said reluctantly.

"But it doesn't," Amily replied.

"No, it doesn't," the King agreed. "There is definitely malice there. And right now, it *looks* as if it is limited to attempts to—" He looked as if he was at a loss for words.

"Put uppity women in their place?" Amily suggested, delicately.

"A little more forceful than that," Kyril replied, steepling his hands together thoughtfully. "In fact . . . *intimidate*, would be closer to what I have in mind. Intimidate in the case of the Order of Betane, but *shame and intimidate* in the case of those letters. . . ."

"And denigrate," the Prince added. "Let's not forget that. This is someone who hates women."

"Could it be a single person at work here? We thought not, given that whoever it is would have to have access to and knowledge of both the Hill and Haven," Amily said, doubtfully.

"It's certainly possible," Sedric opined. "If Mags' little adventures with the Sleepgivers taught us anything, it's that it's not that hard for a stranger to walk around to deliver things around the Hill and have no one take notice, especially if it's something that looks innocuous, like messages. All you have to do is wear Palace livery. We've *tried* to keep better track of all the suits of livery, but . . . if someone purloined a set of livery out of the stores just long enough to make his deliveries, then put it back, no one would notice anything."

"So someone comes up with a delivery, slips off, borrows the livery, drops off messages, changes again, and goes back down into Haven and no one's the wiser?" Amily asked.

Sedric shrugged. "We tried locking this place up like a fortress after Mags was kidnapped. It lasted about a week before everyone up here was in revolt. It's just not going to happen. So, yes, it could be a single person."

"Uneducated?" Mags hazarded. But Amily shook her head.

"It's easy for an educated person to pass themselves off as uneducated, especially in writing," she said. "And a couple of the allusions in the letters, the ones describing the women the letters were sent to as Mantids and Aura Spiders, aren't the sort of thing most uneducated people would know about."

The creatures she was referring to were female insects that killed and ate their mates after mating with them.

"So, it must be someone educated." Mags tilted his head to the side, then frowned in thought. "That still doesn't narrow things down any."

No, it doesn't. It doesn't even eliminate one of the Order. I am sure there are educated women among them. The Prioress, for instance . . . and we have only her word about when *she came back to the Temple.*

"The letters, even the desecration, aren't the problem," Kyril said into the silence that followed Amily's statement. "The problem is . . . that he's gone from letters targeting individuals and delivered privately, to the very *public* desecration of a Temple."

"You think he's not getting enough entertainment by bullying individuals—" Mags said, hesitantly. "But the desecration wouldn't have been all that public. Hardly anyone uses the Temple except the Order—"

"Yes, but instead of individuals, who have been concealing their letters and their hurt or fear, he meant to show up an entire group at once, catching them off-guard." Kyril drummed his fingers on the table. "That's an escalation. He's not content merely knowing he must be causing distress, he has to be *sure* he is causing it by exposing an entire group of victims to his abuse at once."

Mags frowned. "So you think he's going to get more . . . active?"

"I'd bet on it," the King said grimly. "The more especially as the Prioress discovered the desecration too early, and you handled the cleanup so efficiently, Mags. The impact, the shock, the revulsion, the horror at having their sanctuary violated, that won't be present. Instead, the returning members of the Order will find the delightful surprise of their Temple newly redecorated and cleaned. Their reaction will not be what he wants."

Amily bit her lip at that. "Do you think he'll be watching?"

"Without a doubt. But unless Mags was willing to go down there and violate perfectly innocent peoples' minds by reading the thoughts of everyone close enough to see what happens when the Temple doors are flung open, there's no way of finding him." Kyril crushed her hopes of a simple solution with a single sentence.

"And that's assuming he hasn't already found out the Temple's been cleansed," Kyril pointed out. "I wouldn't bet on that. He's already proven himself to be very clever. Or she . . ."

So there it was, the thing that Dia, the Prioress, and Amily had all been dreading. The King had pointed out the possibility that this could be a woman, the horse was out of the barn and there would be no getting it back in again.

"It would be easier for a woman to move about the Hill," she said reluctantly.

"And much easier for one to enter the Temple," Sedric pointed out. Then he said the very thing Amily had been thinking. "We only have the Prioress's word as to *when* she returned, after all. By her own word, she didn't actually check with her underlings, she only assumed that because all was quiet, no one was ill or had died to account for her premonition. She could have desecrated the Temple herself."

"You don't really believe that, do you?" Mags asked, looking aghast.

"No, of course not," Kyril replied, dismissively. "She has nothing to gain by it, and honestly, even in Palace livery she's a very distinctive woman. Someone would remember her and ask what she was doing there. But if I can think of it, so can someone else if this becomes public."

"We can't let this become public," Sedric shook his head. "Even though I am sure that is what this lunatic wants. The damage would be considerable. Reputations ruined, that would just be the start of the havoc. People would be at each other's throats in no time. The Court would be in chaos."

They all sat staring at each other in glum silence for a long while. "I think we should warn other religious houses," Kyril said at last. "This might be the work of a fanatic believer."

"But that would only let the Poison Pen know his work had been effective," Mags objected. "I thought we didn't want to do that. And so far, everything says to me that this person is a woman-hater, not just a religious fanatic. Religion might be his excuse, but that's all it is, an excuse to terrify and abuse."

They all looked at Amily. She bit her lip. This was *exactly* the sort of decision the King's Own was supposed to make, but she was of two minds. "We can't *not* warn them," she said. "But Mags is right, do we want to reward whoever this is by letting them know they've made us scramble to undo what he did? If you warn every Temple and religious organization in Haven, it will be impossible to keep this quiet, and people *will* start pointing out that the Order is all female, and they *will* wonder if there is some hideously repressed maniac in their own ranks."

"A compromise," Sedric said finally, "We *discreetly* warn only those institutions that are exclusively female. There aren't that many of them, they are quite used to keeping secrets, and I think we can rely on their own good sense to see what this means if people start making unpleasant inferences."

Amily pondered that, as did the King. Evidently they came to the same conclusion, but the King spoke first. "It's not the best solution," he said, "But I believe it's the only thing we can safely do. At least for now."

7

The rest of the morning, Amily fulfilled her normal duties, while Mags carried very carefully worded messages by hand down to every exclusively female religious organization in Haven. In some places, he was met with bewilderment, as the women there simply could not comprehend why *anyone* would choose them for a target of such abuse. "We've harmed nothing and no one!" the High Priestess of Birana the Flower-Crowned exclaimed in dismay, fluttering her hands as if she could shoo the terrible idea away. "We are an order of peace and harmony! Why would—"

"Because whoever is doing this is clearly insane, my lady," Mags replied, trying his best not to feel impatient. "One cannot hope to fathom the mind of the insane. One can only do what one can to guard against him."

"But—what can we do?" she cried, baffled, fluttering even more. It was clear that his message had done nothing except to throw her into confusion—and who could blame her? The worst that the votaries of Birana had ever had to cope with before was a sudden killing frost that destroyed their blooming gardens.

And so that proved to be his most important task of the entire day; to come up with answers to that question. It was not that these women were stupid; on the contrary, some of them were so brilliant—like the Order of Saint Hitia, who had the biggest library in all of Haven and devoted themselves to scholarship—that they made him feel like an ignorant schoolboy. But they were not accustomed to turning their minds to the subject of self-defense. And the idea that anyone would hate them so much was utterly foreign to them.

To some, he suggested hiring guards, and pointed out that both the Order of Betane and the Swordsworn Sisters were perfectly willing to *be* hired and certainly had capable ladies who would not disturb their quiet and peace, nor be a temptation to Novices. To others, he suggested guard dogs. Some, so far as he could determine, merely needed to be very vigilant about keeping all the ways into and out of their cloisters firmly locked. The Order of Saint Hitia was like that; they had so many rare and valuable manuscripts that it was probably easier to get into the vaults of the King's Treasury than it was into their walled and barred bastion of learning.

He was very careful to make his statements about the Poison Pen impersonal, but some of the more worldly heads of these organizations saw through his ploys. "So, already there are some who are sure it is a woman, eh?" said the Abbess of Saint Hitia, startling him. She shrugged at his surprise and screwed her mouth up as if she was eating something sour. "Oh don't think we haven't

153

heard this before. Here, particularly, we get a lot of . . . vitriol. We're unnatural women, abandoning our proper places as wives and mothers of the race to go steep our unbalanced brains in learning we can't possibly understand. Sour old maids, hating the women who have what they can't, families and husbands. Twisted harridans, probably engaging in *unnatural behavior* behind our cloister walls. And there are a few of our sisters who are extremely fond of each other, but what of it? As if something that occurs *in nature* could possibly be unnatural . . . Oh yes, young man, I've heard it all. You're wise to keep this quiet, but if it continues, it won't be kept quiet for long."

"We'll keep it under as long as we can, Abbess," he replied.

"And that's what will confound this . . . *person* . . . whoever and whatever it is," she said, shrewdly. "This is the one thing that a sick mind like that cannot comprehend. This mad creature imagines that we'll begin fighting among ourselves, scrabbling to discover who it is and offering each other up to the cold knife of public opinion in order to spare ourselves. A creature like this cannot imagine that we will hold to our loyalties to one another—it thinks that all women are ready to turn on each other. Nor will it understand *your* willingness, up there in the Royal Seat, to protect us. And that may well be its undoing, but not before things get much, much worse."

Mags marveled at her intelligence, and hoped, as he left the Abbey, that she was wrong.

But he feared she was right.

* * *

One day passed, without incident. A second passed, and the members of the Order of Betane returned to find their Sanctuary redecorated. By all accounts they were delighted; they certainly sent a letter of great appreciation up to the Prince.

"They won't be so delighted when the Prioress calls the general meeting and tells them *why* we repainted," Mags said to Nikolas, when word had generally spread of the Prince's "generosity" and the Order's response.

"No, they won't, but our perpetrator didn't get any joy out of it, either. Did your boys see anything unusual?" Mags had sent a half dozen of his messenger-lads down to the Temple when the members of the Order returned, ordering them to watch for anyone who seemed angry or dismayed rather than surprised when the Sanctuary was opened for the Order to troop inside.

"Not a thing," Mags replied, and sighed. "If our madman was there, well, he or she either was out of sight of my lads, or else was very good at hiding his or her reactions."

"There must be something I'm missing here," Amily said, putting her head on the back of her chair and staring at the ceiling. "I've gone over these letters until I could recite them in my sleep. I keep getting the feeling there's another clue here, something these women have in common, but it's completely eluding me."

"Well, you know these women better than I do," Mags pointed out. "So, let's try this. I'll say who a letter was written to, and you say the first, worst thing that comes to your mind."

Amily couldn't imagine how that was supposed to help, but . . .

anything was worth trying at this point. "All right."

Mags picked up a letter from the pile, and read the name on the back. "Maegery Erenson."

Amily made a face. "Tease. Leads boys on, then moves on to another, then when the first one starts to lose interest, goes after him again."

"Lady Jemma Teal."

Now she rolled her eyes. "The letter writer doesn't know about *half* of the things she's doing under her husband's nose."

"Amber Larelen."

"Flirt. Terrible flirt. And *will not* leave the lads who are pledged to other girls alone."

Mags went down the list, putting the last of the letters on the pile. "I see the common denominator," he said. "Whether or not the letters actually accuse them of it, these are all extremely attractive women and girls who are . . . rather free in their ways, or at least give the impression that they are. Now, are there women in the Court who are, say, having affairs, who are *not* attractive?"

"I can name you half a dozen," Amily replied, and gave him a sharp look. "Some of them are just lonely, some of them have cold husbands and just need a little warmth, and for some, well what personal attraction can't get, money can purchase, after all. What are you getting at?"

"None of *them* are in this pile," he pointed out, patting the pile of letters.

"So?"

"If this was someone motivated merely by the fact that women were making free with their favors, or pretending to, it wouldn't matter if they were pretty or not." He shrugged. "I hate to point this out to you, but the person most likely to single out attractive women for spite is another woman."

"So what this means is that we need to look for a woman and give up on the notion that this is a misogynistic man?" she demanded, her voice a little shriller than she had intended it to be. And a good bit more accusatory. But . . . how could *he* suggest such a thing?

"No, it just means we can't *eliminate* a woman," Mags sighed. "A woman can be a woman-hater as much as a man."

There was a long and awkward silence. They had not quite had the start of a quarrel, but . . .

Before either of them could think of anything to say, a page tapped on the open door leading to the greenhouse. For one moment Amily had the wild idea that the page might have been given one of those wretched letters, and was delivering it to her—and all Mags would need to do would be to read the child's memory, and they'd have their culprit. Her heart was in her throat at the idea—because already she had nearly bitten Mags' head off, and if she could get angry with *Mags*, who hadn't actually said anything that was at all out of line, how much worse would it get if word of this crept out?

If only the gods had decided to take pity on them and delivered a lovely way to wrap things up and put a bow on them before anything unfortunate happened . . .

But alas, no. It was a sealed note on extremely expensive vellum, sealed with Lord Jorthun's crest. *"We have more letters for you. Would you care to join us for dinner?"* Amily read aloud.

Her heart sank at the idea of going over *more* of those horrible abusive letters. But Mags perked right up.

"Dinner with Steveral and Dia?" He licked his lips. "I wonder what they're servin'?"

"Dinner first. And we'll have a good wine to wash down the unpleasantness," said Lord Jorthun, as he stood to greet them when one of the servants ushered them into the library. "I refuse to face that trash again without fortification. Shall we dine like barbarians here, or in one of the dining rooms?"

Amily and Mags spoke at the same time. "Which do you prefer, sir," Amily asked, at the same time that Mags said, "Which is less work for the servants?"

Lord Jorthun looked at both of them with amusement, one of his heavy gray eyebrows raised slightly higher than the other. "Fortunately the answer to both your questions is 'here.'" He rang for a servant. "Terun, tell her ladyship we'll be eating dinner in the library, and let the housekeeper know as well."

Dinner and Dia arrived at the same time; to Mags' amusement, it appeared that Steveral had decided to copy the folding table from the Royal Suite with an addition; elegant folding chairs of an extremely cunning design.

The servants had the table set and the chairs arranged in no time. One of them remained behind to serve, while the rest left the quartet in peace.

Mags was utterly silent, the better to completely appreciate the food in front of him. After all those years of deprivation in the mines, whenever he was presented with an especially wonderful meal, it was a little like being transported to another world for him. For a while, there, *all* food had made him feel that way! Now it was only meals cooked by someone who was as much an artist in the kitchen as any master painter or carver that made him fall into appreciative silence and savor every tiny bite.

And Lord Jorthun's cook certainly deserved to be called an artist.

Dia, Amily, and Steveral kept up a steady stream of quiet conversation while he maintained his silence. Amily was used to this, but Dia and her husband kept glancing over at him as if they were uncertain about why he was so quiet. Finally Dia whispered something to Amily, who laughed, and said out loud, "It's quite all right. He's merely maintaining a respectful silence in the presence of greatness."

Jorthun burst out laughing, Dia smiled, and they left him alone for the rest of the meal.

When the dishes were taken away, the table and chairs put back into discreet storage in a nook behind a tapestry, Lord Jorthun indicated to the servant that they would pour their own wine, and they all settled in comfortably upholstered chairs around a low table. Steveral brought out a leather document case not unlike the one Amily had brought with her.

"Well," he said, taking out a handful of papers. "Here they are. The Handmaidens, once alerted, have been very busy on our behalf. They've rescued these things out of fires and waste-cans and have been very careful that they were not seen while doing so. Fortunately the ladies in question generally stormed out of the room immediately after disposing of this trash." He pulled out a few that had been torn to bits, and reassembled on a backing of very thin, very tough vellum, with paste.

"I shall let you peruse these first, while I look over your existing documents, then we can discuss things further," he said, reaching for Amily's document-case. Mags took about half of the letters, Amily the other half, and they exchanged them as they read them.

"Fundamentally the same," Amily said at last, tossing her handful of poison on the table on top of the existing documents. "All that ever changes is the name and the details of affairs, flirtations, or . . . hmm . . . how do I describe a girl deliberately trying to charm a boy that is already betrothed elsewhere?"

"Poaching?" Dia suggested, with an arched brow. Her pretty face was clouded with an expression of concern. "But you're right. There is a great deal of repetition, and particular phrases stand out. The Handmaidens tell me that for the most part, the targets of these letters are angry rather than upset, but that a lot of temper is stewing in the Court. They think their rivals, or the girls they've poached on, or the girls' mothers are responsible for the letters. So far there have not been any confrontations . . ."

Lord Jorthun passed his hand over his face. "You may take it from me, that will not last. I shall have to think of some way to prepare for this."

Dia pursed her lips. "My girls are telling me that not everyone is upset. Some of them are taking the letters as a sort of badge of triumph—they not only succeeded in their mischief, but they've made people take notice." She shook her head. "I can't say I understand that sort of thinking, but there it is."

"Ugh." Amily made a face. "That's just . . . bullying of another sort. Passive bullying."

"Indeed it is," Lord Jorthun said, and leaned over with his arms resting on his knees. "And since you bring up bullying, that is *precisely* what I am concerned about. Not about the way that some of these ladies bully one another, but something else entirely."

Mags scanned Steveral's face, and to his relief, saw that his mentor was taking this situation very seriously indeed. In the back of his mind, he'd been afraid that Lord Jorthun, with his decades in the service of gathering intelligence for his King, would consider all this a tempest in a teapot.

But it seemed he thought the situation was even more urgent than Mags did.

"The problem we have is these letters are only the ones we've seen," he pointed out. "The ones we haven't seen are likely to be the real poison. They've been sent to women and girls who are much more vulnerable and thus more likely to hide that they've been the recipients of so much vitriol. Like Violetta—"

Now he took another letter out of his document case, and handed it to Amily. She scanned it quickly, and went pale, then handed it to Mags.

And there, as if the letter writer had actually been present in the room, was every detail of Violetta's seduction by the late and unlamented Brand, the son of the equally late and unlamented Lord Kaltar. *"I know everything, not just this, you filthy slut,"* the letter finished. *"You seduced him, then had him killed. Aren't you ashamed to show your face? You should be locked up for the safety of every man in the Court, you shameless slut."*

Mags bit off an oath.

"How is this even possible?" he asked angrily. "No one knows what happened but Violetta, Amily, an' me!"

"It could be pure speculation, but it's startlingly accurate speculation, judging by the way you two reacted," Lord Jorthun replied. "Or . . . and this is what concerns me a great deal . . . it could be the result of someone with the Gift of Farsight. The kind that allows someone to look into the past."

Mags gaped at him. "You surely don' mean a Herald—"

"That's exactly what I *don't* mean," Steveral said dryly. "What, did you think that Gifts were exclusive to Heralds? Not a bit of it. Quite a few religions not only have people with Gifts, they seek them out. There are others who practice using their Gifts in other ways. Such things are not *common*, but really, my dear boy, the temperament to become a Herald is much, much rarer than Gifts are."

"You mean you've found folks hurtin' others with Gifts?" Mags could scarcely contain his outrage. The very idea revolted him.

But Lord Jorthun just shrugged. "Gifts are uncommon; many of them are probably undiscovered by the holders of them all their lives. Generally, when we discover people with Gifts who are misusing them, they are brought before a Healer with Mind-healing, and the thing is shut down so they can't use it again."

Amily nodded, as if this was already known to her, but Mags blinked in surprise and no little shock. "You kin *do* that?"

"We can," said Lord Jorthun. "But that's only if it's being used for mischief. If someone can turn his hand to making an honest living of a Gift, or help out his neighbors, there's no reason to interfere with that." He pulled at his chin a little in thought. "Oddly enough, Mindspeech has never turned up as a 'wild Gift.'"

"That'd be because it'd prolly drive the person that had it insane without they got a Companion to help 'em and Herald's Collegium to teach 'em to shield," Mags said, after a moment of thought. "I know I would've gone balmy if I hadn't."

"Very likely—and we're getting a bit far afield. Back to the subject. I knew as soon as I read the letter to Violetta that a great deal of what this Poison Pen is writing about could have been learned by someone with a Farseeing Gift of the sort that allows one to look into the past, as well as the present. And this is terrible, especially for the ladies concerned, but this is not what has me worried at the moment."

"Which is?" Amily asked, although Mags had a good idea of what he thought Lord Jorthun was going to say. That there was going to be an eruption of rage and vitriol in the middle of something important that would leave alliances in shards and send the Court a hundred feuds instead of just one.

"The point is, right now the Poison Pen is only using his knowledge and power to torment and shame. And yes, it is a terrible thing, and these poor women and girls certainly do not deserve any of this— and it is almost certainly going to cause an emotional lightning strike, probably in the middle of some crowded Court function, that is likely to leave everyone dazed and shocked. But the Poison Pen's fixation on the sins of women is working to our advantage."

"I can't see how—" Mags replied, doubting Lord Jorthun's intelligence for the first time, ever.

"Because as long as the Poison Pen is concerned with the morals of others, he's *not* turning that Gift to look for State Secrets." Jorthun sat back in his chair, and nodded at Mags' thunderstruck reaction. "So now you see why I am concerned. Deathly concerned. We need to ferret this creature out now, not just for the sake of those he's tormenting, but for the sake of the entire Kingdom."

"No pressure," Mags muttered under his breath. If there was a way to discover when someone was using a Gift other than Mindspeech, *he* certainly didn't know what it was.

"Is Violetta all right?" Amily asked. "Yes, I realize that the Poison Pen *could* do damage later, but I'm concerned with what he's doing *now!*"

"She was very shaken, but she had the wit to bring the letter straight to me. Her parents are back on their estate, and it's unlikely the Poison Pen will send anything there. He wants reactions he can see, here and now, and the one thing I've been told about Farsight is that it is *limited*. You have to actually know either the *place* you are trying to see, or the *people* you are trying to see," Jorthun replied, and waved at the pile of papers on the table, as Mags emptied his wine goblet. Right now, he felt strongly in need of it. "These letters didn't start to appear until after your wedding, and Violetta's parents were long gone by then."

"We sent her away to one of Jorthun's estates for a little rest in the country," Dia added. "And we're making sure she gets no letters or messages that have not been screened by our Seneschal there first. But Amily, like you, I am concerned for other vulnerable girls. I want this *stopped*, before someone is really hurt."

"What 'bout the Collegia?" Mags said out loud, as the thought came to him. The others all turned to look at him curiously. "If it's got down into Haven—and it has—no reason t'think it ain't got into the Collegia, too."

"It will be far easier to get the Trainees to cooperate than the girls of the Court," Amily pointed out. "They trust Heralds, and they'll trust we're going to do our damnedest to get to the bottom of this. Mags and I will tackle the Collegia."

"I'll continue having the Handmaidens work—and perhaps they can get some of these girls to confide in them," Dia said thoughtfully. "That *was* part of the purpose of forming the group after all, to have someone in place trustworthy enough that the highborn women of the Court would take them as confidants."

"And I will see where my investigative skills will lead me," Jorthun concluded. "One never knows what odd things lurk in peoples' backgrounds. If we are very, very fortunate, I will uncover a link that ties all these letters together, and we'll have our culprit. Rest assured, Mags, I'm going to make this my priority. Now—would you like some more of this excellent wine?"

Herald Caelen, Bard Lita, and the Dean of Healer's Collegium, Healer Devin, sat in the silence of Mags' sitting room and passed the unpleasant letters from hand to hand.

Devin, new to the position of Dean, looked shocked. He was only middle-aged, but the expression on his face made him look older, as if he had somehow been personally betrayed.

Lita looked angry; she was clearly doing her best not to throw the letters on the table, and if glares could convey heat, she'd have set the papers, and the table, on fire.

Mild-mannered Caelen merely looked disgusted. Then again, Heralds did tend to see people at their worst as well as their best, so perhaps he was not surprised.

When they had finished with the stack of letters, Caelen shoved them all into the document case. "Now you know why I figgered it would be better we meet here," Mags said. "I wanted ye all t'see 'em at once, and here ye kin say anything ye want." All three nodded. "What we'd like, is fer all of you to gather up the girls of yer Collegia, and put it to 'em, and see if they've been gettin' letters like this too. Teachers, too."

"I think they probably have," Lita replied, still livid. "It would account for some odd behavior on the part of some of my more promising Trainees." She glared at the stack of letters on the table, and Mags again almost expected them to burst into flames under the heat of her stare. Then she looked at the other two Deans. "I think we can all manage, not just to talk to our girls, we can get any of them who've gotten letters to talk to you. Would you rather speak to them singly, or in a group?"

"Whichever you think would make them the most forthcoming with us," Amily told them, after a glance at Mags. "I wonder if it wouldn't be easier for them in a group. Aren't they used to supporting each other?"

"In Healers' and Heralds' certainly," Caelen put in. "But Lita—"

"I've been making a point of cutting down on the emphasis on competition and emphasizing community instead," Lita replied. "We all saw what competition fostered. We ended up with morons who thought nothing of stealing the work of talented youngsters who didn't know any better."

They all nodded. No need to go into that again. The disgrace of Lena's father the *former* Master Bard Marchand—he'd had his title and membership in the Bardic Circle stripped from him—was something everyone remembered.

"Well then, talk to 'em, then bring 'em here," Mags told the three

Deans. "We'll make it all cozy like. We got our whole day cleared t'morrow, we kin get the next day, too, an' we're havin' tea an' cakes brought in."

"What's the best way to handle this, do you think?" Caelen asked the other two. "The boys will be curious about why only the girls are being taken off to be talked to."

Lita leaned back in her chair, and drummed her fingers on the arm of it. "Is there any reason to keep any of this a secret from them?" she asked the other two. Some of her hair had come loose from the knot she'd bundled it into; Mags noticed that there were a couple of new white hairs in it. *This's likely to give her a few more.*

"I can't actually think of a reason," Caelen said, at last.

"Nor I. In fact, I think keeping this a secret from them is going to ultimately be futile, and counterproductive," Devin said, sounding and looking much more sure of himself than before. "After all, this—Poison Pen, as you called him—his goal seems to be to divide people. If we make our Trainees in the three Collegia united, then there will be nothing he can do that will harm any of them."

"That is a *very* good point." Amily nodded, looking, if not happy, then less unhappy than she had been. "Well then; let's tell them what has happened at breakfast."

Caelen chuckled a little. "Good idea. No one skips breakfast. We'll just let people come in and not let anyone out until we're sure we have everyone. We'll be able to tell the teachers at the same time."

"There is a great deal to be said for *not* keeping secrets, at least among our Trainees," Devin observed serenely.

Lita snorted. "Yes," she observed dryly. "Because secrets don't stay secrets among the Trainees for long."

* * *

The only "casualties" among the Trainees were two very young Bardic students who had burst into tears when they realized they were not alone in being sent those hideous letters. Interestingly, there were only three girls in Healers' who had been so graced, perhaps because the Poison Pen considered Healing to be "womanly enough." *All* of the girls in Bardic had gotten at least one, and often more than one. And so had the girls in Heralds'.

After a swift consultation, a general holiday was declared; the boys were to do what they wished, the girls were asked to go fetch any letters they still had from their rooms. Amily and Mags would host the three girls from Healers and all the girls from Bardic in the morning, and the ones from Heralds' in the afternoon.

The sitting room was rather full, but the girls had no problem disposing themselves around the room, going so far as to fetch rugs and pillows from their own rooms to sit on. Every bit of flat space held a girl by the time they were done, and two senior girls from Bardic took it on themselves to distribute the tea and cakes. When everyone had settled, and the fresh lot of letters was in Mags' hands, he nodded to Amily. He had the distinct feeling that the girls would respond better to questions from her than from him.

"All right, the first thing I'd like to know is how *you* are all feeling about this," Amily asked. "Both before we spoke to you this morning, and after. And if you have any ideas."

Mags could tell which of the girls had been talking about this among themselves long before they'd had the morning revelations. They were mostly sitting together in knots, and exchanged glances, evidently picking one person in each little group to speak for them.

"Relieved, mostly," said a girl who looked as if she was probably going into full Scarlets soon. "I suppose we've all been talking about this among our particular friends, but the little groups each thought we were being picked on . . ." she flushed. ". . . I regret to say that my lot thought it was someone in the new Trainees with a particularly nasty mind having a rag on us."

"And we thought it was you!" blurted one of the youngest girls, then clapped her hands over her mouth. "I'm sorry—"

"Don't be," said the older one, with a toss of her head. "*Obviously* that's what this nasty-minded bastard wanted us all to think, so we'd be at each others' throats. Dean Melita is right. We *really* need to stop thinking of training as a competition. If we do that, we all win it, anyway."

The three girls from Healers' shrugged, looking wry, and perhaps just a *tiny* bit smug. "We started talking about it as soon as the first letter turned up," said the youngest of the three. "We made sure the whole Collegium knew about it. There's speculation—"

"Go on," Amily urged. "I want to hear *everything*, nothing is outside the realm of possibility."

"Well, Kerl thought it might be a patient, or a former patient, or the relative of someone we couldn't help." That came from one of the other two. "But it didn't seem as if any of the instructors or the other Healers had gotten anything of the sort, and surely if it was from a patient, *they* would have been getting letters before we were."

Mags nodded thoughtfully. These youngsters had good heads on their shoulders, and when presented with a problem, had not hesitated in tackling it. "We know now ain't none of the Healers nor Healing instructors got anythin'," he put in. "So reckon you're prolly right, but we'll still keep that as a possible."

"Dean Melita is talking to the instructors that got some in our Collegium," said the first Bardic Trainee who'd spoken. Her dark brows creased suddenly. "I wonder why *she* didn't get any?"

Another of the Bardic Trainees snorted. "That's not hard to guess. Anybody that knows *anything* about the Dean knows she would *never* keep anything like that a secret. And this slimy wretch's plan to make us miserable doesn't work unless we all think we're the only ones being hurt and are suspecting each other."

The first girl's expression lightened, and she even laughed a little. "Now that's one of the truest things you've ever said. The Dean would have gone storming straight to the King with the letter in hand—"

"The King already knows," Amily told them. "He's assigned me and Mags to deal with this as our first priority. But remember, outside this group and the Herald Trainees and your teachers, no one is to know. If the Poison Pen thinks his plan isn't working and stops sending letters, we don't know *what* he'll do next, and it might not be pretty."

They all nodded.

"Now, how are these letters coming to you?" Amily continued. "Dropped through open windows? Left in your books?"

"Nothing so complicated," said the first Healer Trainee who had spoken. "Each building has three baskets where you can leave notes for other people; one for each Collegium. Once a day servants come around, collect the notes in the baskets, and go about shoving them under our doors. All the Poison Pen letters have been glued shut with paste and a bit of waste paper. People do that all the time, and really, the only thing unusual about them was how poor the paper quality was."

"So anybody could've just dropped them letters into baskets at any of the Collegia?" Mags asked, and all the heads in the room nodded. *Well, at least I can talk to the servants that do the collecting, and get them to hold out those letters for me.*

"All right then," Amily said, taking charge of things again. "Mags, if you'll take notes—I'd like all of you to start remembering, if you can, what was in the letters you destroyed."

With a sigh, Mags got out his notebook. This was going to take a *lot* of whiles.

8

The Heraldic Trainees had, as anticipated, formed a united front after the breakfast meeting. So did the Bardic Trainees. The Healers had always been a close-knit bunch, so aside from every Senior Healer making sure none of the Trainee or junior women were being harassed, nothing much changed.

To Amily's relief, the current crop of female Heraldic Trainees turned out to be remarkably stable; and, in a pleasant change from years gone by, *every single one of them* had come from normal families who were thrilled that their daughter had been Chosen. Of course, sometimes the reason they'd been thrilled was the stipend the Crown paid to a family whose child was Chosen, and sometimes the reason was because it meant that was one less mouth to feed, or one less dower to provide, but at least there were no emotionally damaged girls among this lot. Nothing but girls who had known all their lives that times were hard, the family had to work together, and it was their job to bring more food in than they ate. Which meant when they had gotten Poison Pen missives, they'd laughed, or snarled, and chucked them in the fire.

Rolan had verified that with their Companions while the girls had been talking. This was a tough-minded bunch.

"Do you want us to keep a watch on the baskets?" one of the middle-range Trainees asked, quite intelligently, during a pause in questions. "Between all of us, I think we could probably do that."

Amily hesitated, and looked at Mags. He shrugged. They'd talked about doing just this, after they'd spoken with the Bardic Trainees, and the problem was, if the Poison Pen realized a watch had been put on the baskets, he'd probably just do something else—or find another way of delivering letters.

On the other hand, it would give these youngsters practice in putting a watch on something. "Talk with your teachers, have them show you how to do that," she said. "Share the duty with the boys; they'll probably be put out if you don't. Don't miss classes or skip anything. I'll talk with the Deans and make sure the baskets are only set out after breakfast and taken away before dinner." That would eliminate the potential problem of some of them deciding they had to watch overnight.

After that, Mags just continued to take notes as the ones who had been targeted told him what they remembered of their letters, while the girls ate cakes and drank tea, quite as calmly as Amily could ever have wished for. When she shooed them all out, the room felt wonderfully empty again.

"Next time, let's do this in the library," Mags suggested. "Or maybe some room in the Palace. I finally feel like I kin breathe again."

She nodded, and placed a couple of cushions and a rug back where they belonged, although the girls had been very good about cleaning up after themselves. They'd even carried away the teapots and baskets of mugs. There wasn't a crumb of cake left, of course.

"So?" she asked.

He shrugged. "Looks like for the Grays he pretty much concentrated on things like *you're not fit t'wear the uniform, your teachers won't tell you how stupid you are but I will,* an' stuff'n'nonsense like that. Either he didn't go snoopin' on their personal lives, or—huh—if Lord Jorthun is right, an' he's usin' some kind of Farsight, maybe he was afraid Trainees'd somehow pick 'im up."

"Is that possible?" she wondered aloud.

"Hell if I know. I didn' even know there was people with Gifts outside of the Collegia." He let out his breath in an annoyed puff.

"Neither did I," she confessed. "It's just not something that ever came up." She hesitated a moment. "What do you think the Trainees will do now?"

He managed a faint smile. "Other than watch the message baskets like cats at a mousehole, an' prolly alert the Poison Pen that *that* ain't gonna work? Go back t'normal. That's all of 'em, not just the Grays. All the young'uns wanted t'know was that we was takin' 'em serious, and we're lookin' into it. They see *you* takin' point on this one—an' you're *King's Own.* That lets 'em know we're takin' it very serious." She looked at him doubtfully, but he gave her more of a genuine smile. "Mebbe the Court thinks of you as somethin' else, but t'these Trainees, *you're* King's Own. They seen more'f you than they ever did of your Pa. They got no doubt of who's King's Own, and neither do their Companions."

She felt a surge of gratitude to all those serious-faced girls who'd squashed themselves into her sitting room. And along with that gratitude came another unexpected emotion. Confidence. For once she actually *felt* like the King's Own.

"Anything else we can do here?" she asked. He shook his head, and his stomach growled. She chuckled. "Well then, let's get some dinner, before you wither away."

Days passed, and Mags' assessment of the situation, at least so far as the Trainees were concerned, turned out to be completely accurate. If there was any unease, not one of them showed it. No one came running and demanding answers; no one came tattling on anyone else. A few more Poison Pen letters turned up, this time arriving from outside the Hill with the regular letters and messages, and were handed over without a demur. There were no protestations of innocence, no cries of indignation—well, except the indignation from those who had assigned themselves to watch over the message baskets, when it became clear that the Poison Pen wasn't going to go that route anymore.

Mags continued to lurk around the Court in his guise of Magnus, but other than noting the increasing tension, suspicion, and irritability among the Court ladies, he didn't get much for his pains but a great deal of gossip. At least he was able to assure himself that Hawken had settled into the middle of a group of solid, reliable young fellows, and that the two youngest of Lord Lional's children were engrossed in studies they appeared to find highly rewarding. Loren hadn't even plagued him for that introduction to the

Weaponsmaster, and as for Hawken, he didn't seem in any hurry to take Magnus up on his offer to take him to Flora's. So either he and his new friends had already gone down there themselves, which was likely enough, or he had enough to occupy his attention up here on the Hill. In either case, he was still friendly with Magnus, but it was obvious he preferred the company of the lads his own age.

Eh, I'm an old man, making myself ridiculous trying to keep up with the young dogs . . .

For his part, he was very glad that Coot was now in charge of the messengers, and he had a good solid network of his own keeping an eye on things down in Haven. Regular notes, so carefully printed out that Mags had to smile a little in sympathy for the effort it must have cost the lad, came up from Coot every other day, making sure he was kept apprised of everything the young man and his small army learned, and that all was well with Aunty Minda and the youngest of the gang.

At least there was no more nonsense from any of the other thief-masters. Evidently the second confrontation had convinced them that Harkon was not to be trifled with, and no matter how they felt about the littles that had escaped their clutches, they'd best stick to working with adult thieves if they knew what was good for them.

Mags managed to get down into Haven long enough to contact Teo and ask him to keep his ear to the ground for any rumors about the Order of Betane of the Axe and let the men at the pawn shop know immediately if he heard anything. In his own person, he paid a visit to the Prioress, but all she could tell him was that there had neither been more letters nor more outrages.

"But perhaps that has as much to do with our vigilance as

anything else," she had added, a little grimly.

And so matters stood, as true summer cast its own influence over the city and the Hill. Increasingly warm days either made tempers so much shorter he expected every day for a fight to break out among the women fanning themselves, or induced such languor that even speaking a cross word seemed too much of an effort.

Mags hoped for more of the latter . . . but feared the former.

"Fire! FIRE!"

The shouts and the sounds of the Collegium bells being rung in alarm jolted Mags out of an uneasy sleep. He leapt to his feet—it was easy enough, neither he nor Amily had been able to bear so much as a sheet on them, and he was wearing the thinnest sort of excuse for sleeping trews. He made sure the drawstring was tight, and ran for the open door to the bedroom. As he sprinted through it into the sitting room he could see the reflection of flames in the glass of the greenhouse beyond. He paused just long enough to thrust his feet into a pair of the ankle-length boots that were all that were comfortable in the heat, and ran outside.

Something was going up like an uncontrolled torch out there!

To his immense relief, it was immediately obvious that the fire was a small one, and confined to an area of the garden. But his relief soon gave way to dismay when he realized that the thing that was on fire was vaguely human-shaped.

What the hell . . . tell me it ain't . . .

:It's not alive, Mags,: Dallen said immediately. *:It never was alive. It's some sort of . . . object.:*

By the time he got to the source, the gardeners were already there, throwing buckets of water on what proved to be an effigy. It was human-shaped, indeed. And wearing a crude gown.

Mags cursed under his breath.

"Blast an' damn these young'uns!" the head Gardener snarled as he ran up to the group, lantern in hand—a lantern that was needed now that the fire was out. "Ain't they make enough work for us'n wi'out settin' fires t'poppets i'middle o' night?"

Now that he was able to see, Mags stepped forward to examine the thing. "'Ere now!" the Head Gardener objected. "Leave thet be! Happen summon oughta see 'bout it—"

"It's all right, Siman, I'm Herald Mags, and I'm the proper person to be seeing about it," Mags replied, being especially careful about his accent and speech, since he certainly wasn't wearing Whites. But a cultured accent, and the fact he knew the gardener's name should be enough to establish his credentials.

"Oh! Beggin' yer pardon, Herald," Siman said, immediately contrite. "What kin we do fer ye?"

"Uproot this wretched thing and help me get it back to my rooms before anyone else comes nosing about," Mags replied. "I don't think *too* many people heard the call of 'fire,' and I'd just as soon we didn't have a festival out here."

It took only one man to pull up the stake the effigy was tied to; it appeared that it had been planted in a newly turned and planted bed, and Siman was very put out about the damage to the tender plants. Mags left him and the other gardeners to do whatever they were going to do about the garden plot and directed his erstwhile assistant to help him get the effigy into the greenhouse. *Absolutely no point in checking that flowerbed for footprints,* he thought with annoyance. *It's been trampled all over by too many people at this point.* And there was no point in examining people for dirty shoes. Once *off* the flowerbed, the perpetrator of this "prank" would merely have to wipe his or her feet on the turfed paths, and there would go any evidence. And, of course, the turf would show no further footprints.

Amily waited until the gardener had left before coming out to the greenhouse with another lantern, barefoot, with her hair loose around her shoulders. "That was the fire?" she asked, as he bent over the half-burned effigy.

"Yes, and I don't think it's a Trainee prank," he replied, examining what was left of the thing. It was definitely supposed to be female; it had long hair made of yarn, big, pillowy breasts, and a tightly cinched-in waist. He thought there had probably been a face painted on it, but that part of the effigy was too badly burned to be sure in this light. It had been clad in a rudimentary sort of gown made of what appeared to be old bedsheets, but it had an improvised corselet made of some old black material tied tightly around the waist area to emphasize the size of the "breasts," so he doubted the fact that the gown was white signified anything. It was far more likely that the thing had been made of whatever came to hand.

"I can't see much in this light," he finally said. "We'll look at it again in the daytime."

Amily nodded, and led the way back into their bedroom.

"Is it—" she asked hesitantly, as he kicked off his half-boots and lay back down on the bed, wearily.

"Very likely," he replied, as she put the lamp out and settled in beside him. "The Trainees know better than to pull a trick like this right now, and there's no one in the Court who I think would be likely to think of it."

"There's no one in the Court who'd be willing to get up in the middle of the night in this heat just to engineer anything of the sort," she responded dryly. "And why would they? If it had been meant to represent someone, something about it would have been immediately unmistakable, and there's no one *I* know in the Court who's angry enough at women in general to go to all that effort."

He groaned, and let his accent slip. "An' a-course, everybody'll hev the same alibi, that they was sound asleep in their own beds. An' if they *weren't*, they sure as hell ain't gonna admit it, even iffen that'd be a alibi thet'd clear 'em."

"This place is too big, too open," Amily whispered, in what sounded a little like despair. "And all the freedom we enjoy here only makes it easier for *him* to get away with this!"

"I *ain't* gonna advise we put th' Hill down under guard," he said flatly. "We do thet, an' all we do's give the damn bully what 'e wants, and 'e wants us afeared, mostly of each other."

There was a long heavy silence between them.

"Go to sleep," Amily advised, at last. "Whatever clues there are will still be there in the morning. And at least the Poison Pen has aired his frustration at being balked in the least harmful way possible."

"I've performed an analysis of your Poison Pen letters," said Lord Jorthun, as they all lounged in a sort of gazebo on the top of one of the round towers that ornamented his manor. At three stories up, it caught every bit of blessed breeze, there was plenty of shade from a wide, round, conical roof, and there were reed screens that could be let down to further block the sun. It was probably the coolest spot on the Hill, and Mags and Amily were terribly grateful he'd invited them here. "I didn't bother to bring them; I just brought my notes. So . . ." He consulted a leather-bound notebook of his own. "There are a remarkably *few* number of letters that are direct attacks on specific women—I say remarkably few, because I happen to know of nearly every single illicit affair going on at Court, and believe me, they outnumber the actual letters by a factor of five. These are all nearly identical . . . a lot of vitriol, followed by a lovingly detailed description of the sort of divine retribution that will strike the sort of whore who pursues another woman's husband or betrothed."

"The divine retribution part is what's interesting, in a sick sort of way," Amily observed. "Is it specific enough to pinpoint a sect or a religion?"

"Sadly, no." Jorthun shook his head. "On to the more numerous sort. The majority of these are harangues against women engaging in 'unwomanly' behavior, mostly daring to take on a 'man's job' and take the food out of a man's mouth. That covers all of the Trainees, plus a lone Guard here at the Palace, and the scrawls on the walls of the sanctuary. I don't actually have most of those letters, since your Trainees generally pitched them in the fire, but Mags' interviews give me the general numbers." He tapped his pencil on the page. "Now, of the ones I *do* have, there is a religious tone to them as well. *Women are divinely appointed to be the servants of their men,* is the general gist of the message."

"Huh." Mags scratched his chin. "Hadn't noticed that."

"Neither had your Trainees. But the Prioress certainly did, and so did the female Guard. And unlike the 'retribution' letters, the ones on the walls and the one sent to the Guard combined equal parts vitriol and obscenity. The theme of the obscenity seems to have been along the lines of what I would call, *railings against the maneaters.*"

"Then our culprit seems far more likely to be a woman," said Amily uneasily. "And a particularly insane one at that. With a religious mania and a craving for other peoples' pain." She shudders. "Ugh. *And* a lot of nasty repressions."

"Possibly. But I am by no means weighed in that direction myself." Lord Jorthun consulted his notes. "Either our Poison Pen knows *far* more about the Hill than anyone other than myself, *and* knows quite a bit about at least one part of Haven, *or,* as I suggested before, he is using Farsight."

"But how would the Poison Pen know where and when t'look?" Mags asked. "Farsight gets kinda specific. I been asking. You either got to know *who* you're lookin' for, or you got to know the *place* where they're at."

"The Sanctuary of Betane would have presented no problem," Dia pointed out. "Everyone in that neighborhood knew the Sisters were going to be gone, and when they're *there,* the Sanctuary is wide open for anyone to walk in. So it wouldn't have been hard for someone with Farsight to spy to a certain extent on the Sisters, and to know when it was safe to desecrate the Sanctuary."

"And the Court?" Amily asked.

"Now . . . that suggests that he's using his Gift on particular people, rather than looking at places," Jorthun replied. "That would account for the fact that he's only catching a fraction of the bedroom-athletics that I know are going on."

"Interesting, but I don't see how that helps us," Amily said at last.

"Not directly, but every bit of information we have will build up a picture of the person we are pursuing. A Gift plus a religious mania suggests to me that this might be someone who was cast out of a religious order for zealotry." Jorthun raised his eyebrows significantly at Amily. "Contrary to what you might think, most religions do not care for zealots. They are not comfortable to the rest of the congregants. They demand too much. They don't understand compromise. And they are absolutely, *positively* certain that they and they alone grasp the One Truth—whatever that 'truth' may be—and everyone else is either ignorant or willfully blind." He closed his notebook. "It's something I can look for. Nikolas has his people doing the same."

"Mine ain't gonna be much help," Mags sighed. "But I've got Teo keepin' his eyes an' ears open."

"You seem very certain that the Poison Pen is literally watching us, or at least, some of us," Amily said, as the breeze made a faint whistling sound through the reed screens. "But the letters have stopped having any effect on the Collegia *and* he or she is having trouble getting them to the Trainees now. So . . . now what's going to happen?"

"Ah," Jorthun replied, looking troubled. "I don't know."

"Is there any chance she'll give up?" Dia asked her husband, hopefully. "After all, that's how one deters thieves. Nothing is burglar-proof, but you just try to make it so difficult the thieves move on to an easier target."

Jorthun shook his head. "In my experience, people like this don't follow the rules of rational behavior. They aren't afraid of retribution, because they believe their cloak of righteousness will protect them. So they never back down. They only escalate."

Mags sighed into the glum silence. "That's what I was afeared you'd say."

For the first time in days, Mags was getting the reports of his runners in person. It felt *normal,* and normal was something to be cherished, so cherish it he did, finishing the reports off with a general distribution of sausage-stuffed-in-a-bread-roll he'd picked up at a baker on the way. Then he just sat for a moment, enjoying his happy, healthy young'uns scampering off to their jobs or their schooling. It was good to have something reliably going well.

Then he went next door and took his place at the counter of the pawn-shop, waiting for Teo.

Nothing much had come of the burned effigy; Mags had gone all over it, but there hadn't been anything about it that hadn't been common as grass. The effigy itself was two hay-stuffed tubes of canvas tied in a cross-shape. Where the two tubes intersected, the crosswise one had been tied to form the "breasts," with the rest of it forming arms. The vertical tube had been tied to make a head and neck, then split to make legs. Mags had halfway expected some pubic horror at the split, but there was nothing there. A crude face with black-rimmed red eyes and a huge red mouth had been painted on the front of the head. What he had taken for yarn was actually light rope sewn to the head with a canvas needle and sailmaker thread. Which might have suggested the maker was a sailor, but Jorthun told him not to put too much emphasis on that. "The same thread and needle are used to sew the mouths of grain-sacks closed," his mentor advised. Which left him right back where he started. And the fact that the effigy had been *sewn* might have suggested a woman's hand, but the fact was, there were plenty of men who sewed in the course of their jobs.

The "gown" was no help either. Except that it wasn't white, as he'd thought. It was yellow, the yellow of very old linen sheets that had been used hardly, and washed but never bleached. The crude corset-belt was of more canvas, black this time. The "gown" was nothing more than a T-shape sewn of three rectangles of cloth—which could have suggested a man, but the stitches were neat and the neck, wrists, and bottom were hemmed, suggesting a woman.

Unless, of course, the gown had been in use as a sort of bedgown, and the Poison Pen had just bought it on the second-hand market.

They had quite a pile of evidence by this time. The only problem was that it led nowhere.

He had just about given up on seeing Teo, when the bell over the door jangled, and the man himself came in.

Now, there was a reason why Mags had waited to see Teo, and it had nothing to do with the fact that he liked the man—no, he'd been testing Teo, leaking certain things to him to see what came of them, and every single time, Teo had proven himself worthy of trust.

Lord Jorthun and Nikolas had already run their own checks on him, and Teo had emerged clean, or at least, as clean as anyone in his profession could be. There were some items of "excess force" bandied about in certain circles, and it could not be denied that there had been broken bones in Teo's vicinity—but those all dated from the time he'd been employed to keep order in a tavern, and given the clientele of that particular tavern, neither Jorthun nor Nikolas were inclined to hold this against the man.

So, it was time to take the final step.

"'Ello, ye old barstid," Mags said genially. "Wotcher got fer me?"

Teo's face broke out in a smile. "I was beginnin' t'wonder if the ol' man decided t' give ye a rise."

"Well," Mags said, pleased at such an apt opening. "Come back'o shop. There's somethin' to that notion. An' it means a bit of change fer you."

He unlocked the door that divided the shop itself from the counter and the part where real valuables were kept, and let Teo in. Now the man's scarred face was a mask of curiosity. "Change fer me? Harkon, I ain't quittin' ol' Derrel t' come work this shop! I ain't no good at figgerin', an' Derrel pays me good. I reckon—"

"Ye ain't gonna need t'quit," Mags interrupted him. "Fust, com git yer grub, cause I want ye inna good mood."

Mags waved at an upturned keg, the top softened with a folded rug, and a wooden trencher of bread, cheese, and more of the sausage rolls he'd bought that morning. Nothing loath, Teo tucked into them, as Mags pulled him a beer from another, full keg on one of the shelves full of things people had pawned. He handed Teo the mug, and let Teo eat in silence, until there was a tap on the rear door that was triple-padlocked, and which seldom was opened. He unlocked all three locks, and let the door swing wide.

Amily stood there in her working Whites, Rolan peering over her shoulder from the tiny yard behind her.

Teo gaped, mug halfway to his lips, forgotten.

Then, as if he had suddenly remembered long-forgotten manners, he scrambled to his feet, nearly upsetting the keg he was sitting on. "Milady Herald, m'um," he stammered, looking at his hands in the next moment, as if trying to figure out what he should do with the mug and cheese he was holding.

"Eh, don't stand on no ceremony, ye ol barstid," Mags said genially. "This's m'wife, Amily."

"So I am," Amily corroborated. She looked about herself. "What an extraordinary collection of things. . . ."

"But you—" spluttered Teo. "But she—"

"Aye, she's Willy th' Weasel's girl. An' Willy's a Herald, too," Mags continued, grinning at Teo's reaction. "Fer that matter, so'm I."

Now completely gobsmacked, Teo did the only thing he could do. He sat down heavily. "Kernos' Balls!" he managed, then reddened. "Beggin' yer pardon, milady—"

"I've heard worse. Usually from Mags, although my father once came out with a string of curses the like of which I'd never heard before. I had to look some of them up." She offered her hand to Teo. "I've heard a lot about you, and I am very happy to finally meet you."

He took it, gingerly, as if he was afraid he'd break or soil it. Then—because he was a great deal smarter than he looked, the truth suddenly dawned on him. "Kernos' Balls!" he said again. "I bin workin' fer th' bloody Heralds!"

"Got it in one," Mags replied, pleased. "An' that's the change I wanted ter talk t'ye about. Ye wanta keep doin' thet?"

"Uh—" Teo looked from Mags to Amily and back again. "Aye?"

"Thought ye'd say thet." Mags grinned even more broadly.

"Well, thet means a rise in yer pay."

Teo brightened. Then looked bewildered again. "Who knows all this?"

"Auntie Minda, an' the littles. They're *my* gang. Willy gots his own—Jem an' Eller an' Sam an' Luke what works 'ere. Others, too, but tha's the ones ye'd know." Mags told him.

"My father has his gang of fellows that do what you've been doing—tell him what's going on. Sometimes they look into things for him, and sometimes they help him. The littles can bring Harkon everything they hear, and it's quite a lot, but what they can't do is help him or look into things where only a man-grown can go," Amily said, in a completely matter-of-fact voice. Mags was very proud of her performance. She was handling this in exactly the right way, saying exactly the right things. "That's why Harkon decided to see if you'd work out. You're the first adult besides Minda he's trusted."

"Bloody hell . . ." Teo looked at his cheese as if he had no idea where it had come from, and took a bite of it. "T'think, all this time . . . I knew ye was a right'un, Harkon, but I didn' reck *how* much of a right'un ye was." He peered up at Mags. "I'm damn sure yer name ain't Harkon. So what *is* it?"

"Herald Mags." Mags wondered if he'd recognize it.

He did. "Oh aye, the feller what did that bit'a good work wi' that halfwit o'er where them gaggle'o washerwomen is." He nodded, as if satisfied. "Good piece'o work that was."

"Some day I'll tell ye th' rest of it," Mags chuckled. "Fer now, there's summat I want ye t'keep yer ear out for, special."

He went on to describe the letters sent by the Poison Pen. Teo listened with his brows creased, but shook his head doubtfully. "Ain't nothin' like that I heerd about," he replied. "An'—I dunno Hark—Mags—"

"Keep callin' me Harkon," Mags urged him. "I druther that other name was't put about."

"Aye, Harkon. Well, that ain't the sorta thing wimmin talks about wi' a man, ye ken. I dunno how I'd get wind of 't."

Mags just waved the objection off. "Mebbe now that ye know t'listen, ye'll hear summat. Now, 'bout that rise in pay. . . ."

Teo objected to the generous boost in what Mags was giving him, but they both knew it was objection for form's sake. The reality was his eyes lit up, and Mags could tell he was already calculating how soon he could move from his current garret room—freezing in winter and broiling in summer—to something a bit more comfortable.

"Now ye know," Mags concluded, when the appropriate posturing had concluded, "Rise in pay means when I needs backin' up, thet backup's you."

"Figgered," Teo replied, raising his mug in a half-toast and finishing the contents off. "How ye gonna lemme know?"

"I'll collect ye afore hand." Mags made to take Teo's mug, but Teo held his hand over the top of it.

"An' iffen ye get inter trouble when ye didn't reckon on needin' backin up?" Teo's right eyebrow rose.

Mags nodded at Rolan, whose head was still in the door, watching and listening with acute interest. "I got one'a those."

"Huh." Teo eyed the Companion, who eyed Teo right back. "Reckon that'd do."

There was a little more back-and-forth between the two of them, as Mags fully outlined what he needed from Teo, and Teo agreed to all of it.

Finally Teo heaved himself up off of his keg, and made an awkward little bow to the Amily. "Well. I still got m'other job," he said, with an apologetic grimace.

"And ye ain't gonna do me no good iffen ye lose it," Mags agreed. He held out his hand, and Teo clasped it. "Reckon we're gonna do some good work t'gether."

"Fr'm yer mouth t' Kernos' ear," Teo replied, and sketched a salute to Amily. "Please ter metcher, milady. I know m'way out."

And with that, he ushered himself out of the back room, through the locked door, into the main part of the shop. The bell over the door jangled, and he was gone.

"Thanks fer comin' by an' helpin' me out, love," Mags said, reaching for Amily, pulling her to him, and kissing her heartily.

"It was no problem, the King let me off this morning." She made a little shooing motion, and Rolan backed up so she could close the door. "Sometimes I really get . . . irritated that so many people think Father is still King's Own but there are times like this when it's helpful."

"Enjoy it while ye can, love." He realized what he had implied when her eyes widened, and shook his head. "Nah, think of all the Trainees, 'member what I tol' ye, thet to them, *you're* King's Own. It'll happen, soon or late. Yer Pa knows, an' he's steppin' back, little by little. 'Ventually, time'll come when he steps up, an' whoever 'tis'll be mad 'cause 'e ain't got you. Guarantee."

She didn't say anything; she just lifted up on her toes and kissed his cheek.

He smiled and was about to pull her closer, when—

:Chosen, I hate to break into this tender moment, but the Prince needs you.:

"Kernos' *Balls*!" Amily said.

9

The Abbess of the Sisters of Ardana sobbed on Amily's shoulder as they stood on the edge of the room that had been designated as the Scriptorium. Outside, goats bleated and a rooster crowed, oblivious to the havoc inside. Amily patted the Abbess's back soothingly, but Mags could tell from her own compressed lips and rigid back that she was furious.

Amily had every reason to be furious. She and the Abbess and Mags stood in the doorway of the ruins of the Scriptorium, a large, well-lit room in the old farmhouse that had once been the loom-room. It had been chosen for this important task because of its southern aspect, two fireplaces, and south-facing windows. Once chosen, the room had been converted into the spot where the real work of the Sisters of Ardana had been done: the study, translation, and copying of manuscripts.

Had been done. . . .

Because the room was . . . well, there was nothing left of it, or the work that had been going on inside it.

Manuscripts, both those being copied and the copies in progress, been torn into confetti, and lay like ankle-deep snow across the floor of the entire room. Inks and paints had been splashed over the floor, the walls, even the ceiling. Pens and brushes had been snapped in half, or in four pieces, and metal pen-nibs had been split. Desks had not just been overturned, they, and their matching copying-stools, had been broken into kindling. Even the thin curtains, intended to screen out glare and let in light, had been torn from the windows and slashed to bits.

And scrawled on the wall, in letters hatefully familiar to Mags' eyes, were three sentences. *Woe to the woman who is not content to be a humble handmaiden, but seeks to exalt herself in learning above her teachers. Woe to the woman who leaves her proper place in the home and fills her mind with things she cannot understand. She shall be cast down into the dust, and eat the bread of abasement moistened with the tears of bitterness.*

Well, there were tears all right. The Abbess wept for the manuscripts that had been entrusted to the Sisters to copy, and the destruction of what they had innocently thought was their inviolable home, as well as for all the work now lost. She cried for her Sisters, for all their work destroyed, for the fear she had seen in their eyes, for their faith in the goodness of people destroyed. And she shivered with terror at the realization that someone hated them this much.

She wasn't alone. Three of the Sisters had been sent to their beds by the Healer who had been summoned when the first of them fainted, prostrated with terror. The rest, except for the Sister in charge of the Scriptorium, huddled in the chapel, which evidently seemed to them like the only safe place in the entire property, in various states of weeping and nerves. Looking at them made Mags feel savage. If, at this moment, he could have gotten his hands on the perpetrator of this—vandalism was not a strong enough word—the vandal would be having a very bad time of it.

They had had no warning of this. Everyone in this neighborhood loved having them there. Their congregants had been thrilled with the cart to transport them all. There had even been two local girls who had expressed an interest in becoming Novices, the first in decades. The livestock were thriving, and they had not only resigned themselves to losing their old home, they had decided this one was far superior to it.

Last night they had all gone into their new chapel—the converted barn—for midnight services. But when they had risen from their knees to go back to their cells and their beds, they discovered that the sturdy doors had been locked, from the outside. There was no way to reach the lock from the inside.

They were trapped.

There was no way out, not for mostly elderly ladies encumbered by bulky robes; the only windows that could open were high in the walls, too high for any of them to reach, even standing on furniture, not to mention that they would have had to somehow pull themselves up, clamber over the sills, and let themselves down on the other side. There was no other door. To their dismay, the building seemed to have been constructed perfectly to hold them all prisoner once the doors were locked.

Which did bring up the question, so far as Mags was concerned:

ho, besides the Abbess, had a copy of the key?

They had tried calling for help, but the walls were thick, and people around them were asleep, and there was enough distance between them and the next house that their high voices just faded away. They were exhausted and in a panic by the time the carter hired to drive their little cart and tend their mules arrived, heard them calling exhaustedly for help and let them out. Frantic to discover what had been stolen—because the only reason they could imagine for someone to imprison them like that was that the perpetrator intended to take his leisurely time ransacking the place—they stumbled into the Abbey. Then the damage lay bare before them. When they got to the Scriptorium, to their horror, they uncovered what seemed to be the real purpose behind the destruction.

The carter, being a quick-witted fellow, had already summoned the Watch. The Watch summoned a Herald, and the Herald reported the vandalism directly to the Prince. And that was how Amily and Mags had gotten involved.

Go sort things, Amily mouthed at Mags over the Abbess's shoulder. Not at all unhappy about being dismissed, Mags left the hallway and his wife, and went out to join the Herald who'd first been summoned, and the Captain of the Watch.

By now they had been joined in the refectory, the room used for dining in most houses of religion, by the carter, Kyle Benson. Benson had taken charge of the rest of the servants and gone over the place room by room once the Watch and the Herald had gotten a good look at things, looking for items that might have been stolen. The Sisters had trusted him because the Prince had sent him, and had shown him where all the valuables were, "just in case." Their trust had not been misplaced.

". . . so nothing else is missing?" the Herald was saying as Mags approached.

"Nossir," Kyle replied. "Everythin's accounted for. Strongbox's locked, an' I took it to Sister Ivy, an' she unlocked it an' counted it. Siller vessels was where they shoulda been. It's all there." He was a big, stolid man, who spoke slowly and with deliberation, giving the impression he was stupid. He was anything but. "The whole place was overturned, like a tribe of imps went rampagin' through, but nothin' is missin'. Ruint', but not missin'. Most of the food's gonna need replacin'. Pantry an' stores was turned out an' broke into. It's all been bust open and strewed on the floor an' trampled. Fit for nought but pig food, so that's what Jem's been doin', shovelin' it up and takin' it out t'pigs. On'y thing they left alone was the Sisters' liddle rooms, like as not 'cause ain't nothin' in them but a clothes-chest an' a bed, an' that's soon put t'rights." He heaved an enormous sigh. "Who coulda done this? An' *why*? Them Sisters wouldn' offend a damn fly!"

Mags and the other Herald—another of the ones assigned permanently to the court system of Haven, a tough, balding old bird called Willowby—looked at each other and shrugged helplessly.

"I've got no notion, Benson," Herald Willowby replied. "And I hate to impose on your good nature, but have you *any* guess as to what foodstuffs were spoiled and how much? I don't think we'll get much sense out of Sister Rose. Last I saw she'd been crying so much she was hiccuping."

Kyle's mouth twitched, as if he almost was going to smile, but his own anger at the situation was preventing him from doing so. "Oh ye, seein' as I'm the one's been fetchin' it these sennights. I kin make out a list, an' I reckon it'll be close enough the Sisters will do fine until they're fit to look things over an' give ye somethin' more exact."

Mags clapped him on the shoulder. "Good man. Make out the list, get what help ye need—" He reached into his belt-pouch and handed over a handful of the coin-like bronze objects Heralds often used in place of actual money in situations like this. The "Herald's scrip" had no denominations, as they were used in cases when no one knew how much something was going to cost. Like now. In theory, it would have been ridiculously easy to abuse such a system. In practice, no one wanted a sharp-eyed Royal clerk to go over a list and the charges, and find himself hauled into a courtroom to justify his charges to a Herald armed with a Truth Spell.

"I'll see we ain't cheated, Herald Mags," Kyle said shrewdly. "Hell, most of this stuff, I'll get local, tell folks what happened, reckon we'll get a discount an mebbe some gifted. Got two lads I know with their own rigs nearby, we'll have the Sisters restocked by nightfall."

As he strode briskly out the door to get on the task, Mags gave Willowby a questioning glance.

"Got cleaning crews all over the place," Willowby said, sounding a little helpless. "The livestock, thank the gods, was left alone, and the barn and sheds are all right, and so is the guest-house. Cleaning crews were the only thing I could think to do. Captain March helped me with that, this is his jurisdiction. He brought me a little army of women with mops and buckets and brooms."

Watch Captain March, who looked like one of those fellows who had Watch blood on both sides of his family going back generations, shrugged. "Seemed to make the most sense. That place where they done their writin's though . . ." he shook his head. "Ain't nothin' there t'save. Best we kin do is scrub her out."

"Well, I've got a notion," Mags replied, glad to have *something* to contribute, at last. "Two, actually. Reckon I know how we can keep this from happening again, and who best to ask about *that* problem. I just need to find out if the Sister in charge of the copying's fit to talk."

A single set of footsteps behind him told him Amily had left the Abbess—

"I persuaded the Abbess to go to bed, and Healer Margeritte took her off with a potion guaranteed to make her sleep," Amily said. "And I heard that last, and that, at least, I can answer. Sister Thistle is in charge of the scriptorium, and she's angry, not frightened or in shock."

"Come introduce me afore I go ridin' off," Mags said, making a request of it rather than a demand. Amily's lips lost a little of that angry compression, and she nodded. The two of them went off to the chapel, where some of the Healer's assistants were coaxing exhausted Sisters, who had wept themselves into a near-stupor, back to bed to finally get some rest.

One of the ones doing the coaxing was Sister Thistle, a round, energetic woman, with a smooth cap of bright brown hair threaded with gray, who actually looked as if she had gotten some sleep last night.

"Sister Thistle, this is my husband Mags," Amily said, when the Sister's attention finally came around to them. "He wants to ask you a few questions."

"Certainly, anything I know, I'll gladly tell you. Would you be the same as Trainee Mags who was such a ball of fire on the Kirball field?" Sister Thistle asked, her intelligent brown eyes lighting up.

Mags blushed and ducked his head. "Aye, that'd be me," he replied.

A hint of a smile crossed the Sister's face. "You know, Herald, I imagine you think, or at least thought, a lot about Kirball. Of course the Heralds that invented it certainly told you that it was important preparation for real, genuine conflict, war, even. Right?"

"I'd agree with that, Sister," Mags said, wondering what her point was—because he was sure she had one. "In fact, we used it right here in Haven in some serious situations—"

"Oh, you'll get no argument about that from me," she agreed. "But I think there's something none of you considered, and that's the effect seeing you lot out there on the playing field has on us ordinary folk."

:I wonder where she's going with this?: Dallen said, poking his nose in through the chapel door, with Rolan beside him. *:It's interesting. She's clever. I don't think it's anything either of us would expect.:*

"What effect'd that be, Sister?" Mags asked politely. He was interested but—he wished this was another time. *I've got a pile of stuff t'do, an' I hope she's not gonna be all day about this.* He suppressed a sigh. That was the problem with really intelligent people; they got off on their tangents at even inappropriate times.

:Or maybe she's off on a tangent to avoid thinking about what was done to the Scriptorium,: Dallen pointed out.

:Aye . . . can't say I blame her.:

"Most people never see Heralds in combat," the little woman replied. "Let's face it, you wouldn't want them to. Yet Heralds are in some sense the backbone of our combat forces. With this

Kirball you've invented, people can see for themselves how you work together, and how you work with those who are not Gifted. Without even realizing it, they learn that *should* they find themselves in a situation where they must do exactly as you say, you have already given them a reason to trust you because they have seen for themselves what you can do."

"Huh!" Mags said in surprise, distracted for the moment by her observation. Then he regathered his wits. "Well, Sister, that ain't why I need to talk to ye. An' I really hate t'ask ye this but I wonder—I wonder how much ye can remember 'bout the work that was goin' on—"

"In the Scriptorium?" she interrupted him, her cheeks flushing and eyes flashing with anger, though it was anger she didn't turn on him. "Everything, Herald Mags. I was in charge of all the work we did there. Sister Aster was copying *Mantella's Herbal.* Sister Loveage was copying *Detailed Anatomy of the Chest.* Sister Basil was copying *The Mechanics of Mining*—"

"Wait—" Mags interrupted, confused. "I thought you were copying religious texts."

"Pifft." Sister Thistle waved her hand. "Stuff. Oh we can, and we have, particularly if there are illuminations that someone wants copied exactly, but what the Sisters of Ardana have always done is copy detailed drawings and diagrams that those fellows with the clever moveable type *can't* reproduce yet. We are not artists, although we learn all the techniques of artists, but we are *exact* copyists. And, of course, we have to know enough about the subject to know if an error has been introduced into the drawing we're expected to copy, and correct that error."

Suddenly the scrawls on the scriptorium wall made more sense. And they made him all the angrier.

"Well, can you give me a list?" he asked. "Can't replace the work that was done, but I maybe know someone who can replace what you was copying from. An' if he can't, he knows who can."

A flicker of hope passed over Sister Thistle's face. "Easily," she said, and pulled a pencil and a scrap of palimpsest out of her capacious pockets.

"I'll have fifteen of my best at Ardana's Temple in the time it takes them to gather their light kit and march there," the Prioress of Betane of the Axe said to Mags, when he had explained what had brought him there. "That will give us three shifts of five, which ought to be more than enough to handle anything that comes up."

But Mags had another idea. "Seven or eight of your seasoned Votaries and seven or eight of your Novices," he suggested. The Prioress ran her hand over her short-cropped blond hair and gave him a skeptical look. "Let me explain why. The Sisters of Ardana are peaceful scholars, and if you fill their guest-house with grim, seasoned soldiers, you'll only terrify them more. They'll assume you think they're under serious attack by thugs. They're mostly *old*, they've had a very bad shock, and their hearts can't take too many frights. But if you have some nice, young, cheerful girls about, and explain it as a chance to give them patrol training, they'll relax. They'll feel safe, because of the seasoned ones, but not knowing anything about the Order, they'll think you'd never take Novices where there was a chance someone would be hurt."

"Then they truly don't know us very well," the Prioress snorted, but she also smiled. "You're right, though, it would be ill-done if we only made matters worse by frightening them. I'll order the Novices on during the two daylight shifts where the old dears will see them, and save a full contingent of Votaries for the shift that runs dark to dark. Though I pledge you, Herald Mags, if any fool tries those tricks again, we'll treat him like the enemy he is."

"Leave enough left of the perpetrator to stand trial," was all Mags said, and went out to where one of the Novices was fussing over Dallen.

:She won't be that . . . extreme . . . if they catch someone,: Dallen said. *:She'd like to, but she won't.:*

:I figgered,: he replied. *:It's just the mad talking. She's a professional, through and through, and she won't let the mad do any acting, nor will she let any of the Sisters do anything like that either.:*

As they clopped their way down side-streets on their way to the main thoroughfare that ran up to the Hill, he *almost* Mindspoke Rolan directly to find out how Amily was faring.

:Don't,: Dallen advised. *:Rolan wouldn't say anything about it, but unless it's an emergency, it's protocol not to Mindspeak the King's Own's Companion directly. It's . . . well, it's just not done, it's as if you're going around behind Amily's back.:*

Huh. He learned something new every day. *:All right, then, I'll put in the extra and talk to her instead.:*

:She'd probably rather you did,: Dallen pointed out. *:She's been having a bad day, too. She could use some good news.:*

:You're probably right.: It took more effort to Mindspeak someone who didn't have the Gift herself, but then again, this *was* Amily, and

shouldn't he be willing to put in that extra effort for his own wife?

By the time he and Dallen arrived at Lord Jorthun's manse, he had enough information from Amily to give the Prince a good, solid report by Mindspeech—a report that Amily herself could not give, because she did *not* have Mindspeech. The Scriptorium was cleaned out and the graffiti removed from the walls. New copying desks and stools were coming from several other scholastic Orders who had extras; two sets had already arrived. Inks, paints, and paper supplies were on the way. Those who had been promised copies of the works in production had been notified of the loss of their books and were understanding—and horrified, more for the sake of the Sisters than their own losses. The kitchen had been cleaned out first thing, and enough food had been found between what Jem had been able to salvage and the produce of the hens and the garden that the Sisters had been all put to bed—except the Abbess and Sister Thistle—with a good, if odd, meal inside them. The Abbess was overseeing the cleaning and refurbishing of the rest of the Abbey, while Sister Thistle saw to the Scriptorium and kitchen and was helping Amily oversee the restocking of the pantry and larder. Mags had warned her that the Sisters of Betane were on the way, so Amily had left Thistle to that while she made sure the guest house—which, being untenanted and separate from the Abbey, had thankfully not been touched—was opened up, aired out, and ready.

By that point, he was raising his hand to knock on Jorthun's door, so he didn't get time for more than a fleeting *:Well done:* from Sedric. He waited for the doorman to answer, hoping that Sedric had meant that. This was all new ground to him and Amily both.

Problems and petty politics in the hinterlands, they could handle. Thieves, frauds and other criminals he knew well enough to predict their next moves—mostly, anyway. Information-gathering was second nature. Coping with the politics and jealousies and ambition in the Court was something they could do without really thinking about it.

But the kind of twisted mind that was pulling these outrages off . . . no. This should have been the territory of a Mind-healer, not him, and not Amily. *Outrages. Surely the Poison Pen and the ones that destroyed the Abbey can't be the same. It would have taken more than one person to create all the damage we saw there, wouldn't it?*

Better talk to Jorthun.

The servant at the door took one look at him, and ushered him, not only straight in, but straight to Jorthun's study, where his Lordship was seated behind a desk that was nearly a work of art, it was so beautifully and intricately carved with the crouching cats of the Jorthun arms. Steveral Lord Jorthun looked up from whatever it was he was reading, and the next thing Mags knew, he was sitting in a comfortable chair with a glass of brandywine in his hands. And he hadn't even said a word yet.

"Tell me everything," the man said, in the most commanding voice Mags had heard outside of the Prince and the King. Mags did exactly as he'd been ordered, a strict recitation of facts from the time the Prince had summoned him to the moment he'd knocked on the manse's door.

It took a while, with several interruptions for Steveral to question him more closely on several points. When Mags was done, his mentor and friend sat for several minutes with his hands steepled on his desk, staring at nothing, wrapped in intense thought. His face was very still . . . and only now, when it was not animated by any expression, did he show his age. *He's furious,* Mags thought, and felt Dallen's unspoken agreement. *But I'm not sure why.*

"Why did you come to me, Mags?" Jorthun said, breaking the silence so abruptly that Mags started.

Mags scratched his head. "I got a list," he replied, pulling the list of the lost full manuscripts being copied out of his belt pouch. "This is all the books they was copying. I figured if anyone would know if there was any other copies, either you would, or you'd know who would."

Jorthun accepted the list, and looked it over carefully. "Fortunately these are not so obscure that I'd need to send you to someone else. They are rare by virtue of needing to be hand-copied, but not impossible to obtain. In fact, I believe I have most of them, and I know where I can get the rest. I'll see that the Sisters get new copies to work from. It's the least I can do, seeing that I have made use of their services myself more than once."

Mags nodded his thanks. *:Dallen, let Rolan know so he can tell Amily so she can tell Sister Thistle.:* There, that was oblique enough it should be at least a nod to protocol.

:You're learning. Done.:

"The other reason . . . this business is . . ." he waved his hand vaguely. "It ain't what I know. It ain't what I'm good at. If I were to go at this the way I *want* to, I'd be spendin' all my time just sifting through everybody's heads, neighborhood by neighborhood, till I found the one that's been doing this. Or ones," he added. "If he had my Gifts, that's how my cousin Bey'd be doing it, and no regard for anyone's privacy. But I can't do that."

"No," Jorthun agreed. "You can't."

The King's first spymaster sat back in his chair and pinched the bridge of his nose between his thumb and forefinger. "I am out of my depth here too, Mags. This isn't the work of a sane person— or persons; I still haven't made up my mind if there is only one or several. The only time I ever needed to hunt someone this unhinged was when I tracked a man who murdered and mutilated over and over. That was in my first years as Kyril's agent, and the Watch was baffled, so Kyril sent me down to see what I could do."

There was a long silence. "Did you catch him?" Mags asked, finally.

Jorthun shook his head. "I never did. The murders just stopped. To this day, I don't know why. I am sure you have seen that I am angry; this is why. This reminds me too much of that occasion. A different sort of madness, but madness nevertheless. This is not a task for a spy, but the Watch and the Guard will be even more out of their depths than we are. So we must use the tools we have, cleverly."

"One or several?" Mags asked him. "Man or woman?"

Again, Jorthun shook his head. "The signs point to both. But I will tell you one thing—I was right in my prediction. Whoever this is, is getting bolder, and taking more risks for a greater reward."

"Reward." Mags mulled that over. "I reckon it's gotta be a reward, wreckin' all this stuff, gettin' people upset and makin' 'em hurt."

"It's a blow against the enemy, in a war decreed by the gods themselves," Jorthun agreed solemnly. "At least according to those disgusting scrawls on the walls and in the letters. If it is several, there is *one* mind behind it, directing all of it. *One* mind that is convinced that there is only one, true way and anything outside that is blasphemy. And this person will not stop until the war is over."

"Then we'd better catch 'em, 'cause it never will be, not by their lights," Mags replied, and angrily drank Jorthun's excellent brandy down in a single swallow.

Mags had all the books the Sisters needed in his saddlebags within a candlemark, and made his way back down to the Abbey. He had the feeling that Sister Thistle wasn't going to rest until she'd gotten everything set to rights in her little domain, and that included having copies of the work they had promised in her hands.

And he was right.

He found her, looking exhausted by all the work, putting the last touches on the newly installed copying desks, reproducing from memory the exact combination of inks, paints, pens, and brushes each of the other Sisters had been using for her own project. When he silently handed over the books to her, she lit up like the sun.

"I do not know how you managed that, Herald Mags, but I am inclined to see Blessed Ardana's hand on you in this," she said fervently, taking the pile of books from him and clutching them to her ample bosom. "I would never have known where to look for copies."

"Oh, I reckon ye would have, if ye'd had a bit of time t'think 'bout it. And mebbe some sleep," he told her.

"Oh, I got some sleep last night. While the others were cackling like a lot of frightened hens, I made a bed out of the kneeling cushions and got some rest." She raised an eyebrow at his surprise. "We were locked in, and it was obvious after the first candlemark of shouting that no one was going to let us out until Kyle arrived in the morning. There was nothing any of us could do until then. There was nothing we could do to stop whatever was going on, and there was no point in trying to imagine what was being done. I come from farm folk, Herald. We know when there's nothing to be done you might as well get some sleep, because when there *is* something to be done you're going to wish you'd had some."

As she spoke, she distributed the books over the various desks, making sure they all had a stock of the proper paper for the copying. When she was done, she sighed.

"At least these days we no longer have to copy the text, unless it's a religious manuscript," she told him. "We just do the pictures and illustrations on the right page, then take the book over to the printer with the pile of pages. Then the printer does the rest." She shook her head ruefully. "And now we'll have to do twice the work, replacing the ones that were destroyed."

"Damned unfair," Mags agreed, not knowing what else to say.

She pinched the bridge of her nose, as if she had a headache coming on. "I think I need something to eat. I hope there's something in the kitchen by now."

Mags' stomach growled, reminding him that he had gone on for a very long time with nothing but that glass of brandywine. *It's a wonder it didn't knock me out. Reckon I must've been so mad I just burned it off.* "I'll go with ye," he said. "If there ain't, me an' Dallen'll go find some pocket pies and bring a basket of 'em here."

But they found the kitchen completely restored, bread baking, soup cooking, and some of the women who'd come to clean serving the Abbey workers and their fellow cleaners, and what looked like two thirds of the Sisters of Betane. The little kitchen and attached refectory were quite crowded, but pleasantly so. It was a relief not to see any weeping women. Amily was there with the Abbess, talking quietly over soup and bread. Mags and Sister Thistle got bowls and bread and went to join them.

"I got replacements for all the books, and Sister Thistle checked 'em, and said they were the right ones with the right pictures," he told Amily and the Abbess, as both of them stopped talking and looked up at them.

Thistle nodded, pulling up a stool to the table. "Copy desks are in place, all the supplies arrived, we can start again tomorrow," she said. "I think we should. The sooner we can get our *work* back to normal, the sooner things will *feel* back to normal."

"I agree with you," the Abbess replied. Her eyes were still red, but she seemed to have gotten over her despair. "Herald Mags, I don't know how to thank you and Amily for—well—everything."

"It's our job, Abbess," Amily reminded her gently. "And let's not forget Herald Willowby and the Watch Captain."

The Abbess rubbed her red eyes. "I have not forgotten them. I am simply amazed by all of you. So resourceful . . . and so kind. And Herald Mags, *where* did you find that martial Order? Betane of the Ax? They are the answer to a prayer I had not even voiced! I will be able to go to sleep without feeling I need to get up every candlemark and make rounds to ensure everything is all right!"

"They got hit by whoever did this to you," Mags said grimly. "That's how I run across them in the first place. And that's why they was so willing to come on the trot. I got the notion they're really hoping whoever done this dares to come back on their watch."

The Abbess blinked in consternation, and looked as if she did not quite know what to say. "I suppose—" she began, then looked as if she had decided that the less she knew, the better off she was. "Well, I doubt that anyone will try *anything* with them here."

"That's the hope," Amily replied, and turned to Mags, changing the subject quickly. "It's hard to believe, but we've gotten everything cleaned up. It will take some time to replace everything, but the main thing is there's enough food now, and enough drawing supplies to start work again, and the rest will come in over the next sennight or so." She shook her head. "It's a good thing that the Sisters are . . . a fairly ascetic order. There was less to have to replace."

The Abbess chuckled sadly. "I never thought I would be *grateful* to be poor. But you're right, it means there is less to replace."

Mags raised an eyebrow. "Afore this is over, you ain't likely to be poor anymore," he pointed out. "You got all kinda folk helpin' now."

The Abbess flushed, and looked surprised for a moment, then, tentatively smiled. "Why—you're right! And here I am, weeping over what was lost, when indeed, it is only *things,* and so many people are coming to our rescue! I should be—well, not *rejoicing,* but I should stop feeling wretched and be *grateful.*"

"What you should be doing is getting some sleep," Thistle scolded. "It's what I intend to do as soon as this soup is inside me." When the Abbess looked uncertain, Thistle added, "There is nothing else you can do. We have our guardians, who are never going to let anything get past them. We've got enough food for days. We can go back to our work. The bees, the chickens, the goats, and the garden were untouched. In a few more days, given how many other Temples and Orders have leapt to help us, not to mention the Prince and the Heralds, you won't be able to tell anyone had troubled us. So! Get some sleep! I'll finish overseeing what's left today before I nap; remember, I was snoring on the floor of the chapel all night."

"Thank you, Sister Thistle," the Abbess said, gratefully. "You are absolutely right. I will turn my mind to gratitude, and the proper means of thanking everyone who has helped and is helping us."

She finished the last few spoonfuls of her soup, then, bidding Amily and Mags an absent "good night," although it was barely afternoon, she took her bowl and spoon to the sink and headed in the direction of the cells.

Thistle shook her head. "I've never seen her this . . . unsettled. Usually she's the one with a cool head in a crisis. Then again," she added thoughtfully, "the crisis has usually been something on the order of a leak in the roof. Still."

"First she got swindled by that double-crossing Priest," Mags said bluntly. "And she was swindled, no doubt about it. Even in rough shape, that Temple of yours was worth more than this farm. Then this. If I was her, I'd be rattled, too."

"Ah . . . yes." Thistle nodded shrewdly. "Well, sleep will help. So will concentrating on being grateful. She's good at gratitude."

"And you're not?" Amily asked, amused in spite of the situation.

"No, I'm not," Thistle replied frankly. "It makes me want to bite. That's why I'll never be an Abbess. And I think I'd better get back to overseeing things before I decide I should be grateful to Herald Mags and bite him."

With that, the little Sister nodded to both of them, got up and went off to the next job, as Amily suppressed giggles.

"Well," Mags said, weakly. "At least she warned me."

10

It had been a quiet day . . . and Mags was beginning to look upon quiet days with a suspicious eye. There had been no sign of the Poison Pen; no attempts at further vandalism at either the Abbey of Ardana or the Temple of Betane. No Poison Pen letters at all at the Collegia. Not even the ladies of the Court had gotten any for almost a sennight, and that made Mags uneasy on two counts. First, that if the Poison Pen wasn't making trouble up on the Hill or the other two places he'd hit, he was probably making trouble elsewhere, and second, that if he *wasn't* making trouble elsewhere, then trouble was bound to break out badly, and soon.

And if he ain't doin' somethin', then how can I catch him?

Lord Jorthun had not yet come up with anything substantial either. The King and the Prince were inclined to believe the creature had run its course, but Jorthun didn't believe that, and neither did Mags or Nikolas.

It had been one of Mags' days attending the Law Court, and that, too, had been a quiet one—a day when just his presence made people who might have been planning something dishonest change their minds and meekly take their losses. He had just finished his stint in the courtroom and was literally on his way out the door when one of the black-uniformed Servants of the Court waved to get his attention before he left.

"There's a Watch Captain to see you, Mags," the man said. "Captain March?"

"March?" for a moment Mags puzzled over the name—then he remembered, it was the Watch Captain who'd been so helpful with the Sisters of Ardana. "Oh, right. Where is he?"

"Waiting at the back." The Servant left to see to his own duties and Mags reversed himself and headed for the back entrance.

Sure enough, it was the same man, who greeted him with a little sketch of a salute. "Herald Mags. I wonder if you might help the Watch out?"

Without waiting for an answer, Captain March started walking. Mags fell in beside him, with Dallen trailing behind them both, reins looped up over his neck. "Given how helpful you was with the Sisters of Ardana, don't see how I can fail to," he replied. "What's the problem?"

"It's not mine, it's my brother's, he's got the district where the Sisters *were*," Captain March explained—which made Mags feel a tiny little jolt of *victory*, that he'd been able to peg the fact that March's family was multi-generational Watch. "He's a Captain too—it's the district our Pa has. Ned's got the Night Watch, Pa has the Day. Ned's the one with the problem."

Mags tried not to be impatient with the way the man was circling around the problem without actually getting to it. "I take it he doesn't actually know any Heralds to bring this to?" he asked.

But March shook his head. "No, not exactly. I mean, he don't know any Heralds, it's just that last night was the first time he put everything together." He took a deep breath. "Easier to show you. Ain't that far. And Ned's better at explaining things than I am."

March stopped at a vendor and bought them both a couple of pocket pies, while Mags took a moment to report back up the Hill by Mindspeech where he was going and what he was doing— however sketchy that was. Dallen begged for pies, and with a faint smile, March bought him a pair, too. They moved on, the men eating as they walked—Dallen had already inhaled his.

Shortly after that, they were at the Watch Station in a district that Mags had never been to before; it seemed to be an area with a lot of small craftsmen. Looming over it all was a Temple, a three-story-tall, simple, dignified structure that Mags realized with a start must be the former home of the Sisters of Ardana.

He examined it for a moment, finishing his luncheon, while March trudged stolidly along next to him. It looked austere enough to have been the home of scholars; nothing ornamental, just plain white stone, clean, simple lines and plenty of tall, narrow windows, with a tower rising a story above the rest at the front.

But that was not where they were going, and he followed March around a corner, taking him away from the building.

The Watch-house was easy enough to pick out among the rest of the buildings; all Watch-houses were built to the same plan; red brick, tile roof, square, with wooden-framed doors and windows.

Resting on a bench outside it was a man who clearly was related by blood to Captain March.

"Ned!" Captain March hailed the fellow, with a wave. "Brought Herald Mags, like I promised."

:This will be interesting. Two Captain Marches. How are you going to keep them straight in conversation?: Dallen asked, facetiously.

:Easy. I outrank 'em. So I call that one 'Ned' and t'other one 'Kay'.:

Mags held out his hand to the square-faced, sandy-haired fellow in a Watch uniform who leapt to his feet. "I understand you got a problem, Ned," he said without hesitation. "An' just call me Mags."

:See? Sorted.:

Ned March pumped Mags' hand vigorously in both of his. "Thankee kindly for takin' the time to come down here, He—Mags," he said. "I tell you, my granddad was Watch, and my Pa is Watch, an' Kay's Watch, and none of 'em never had a thing like this come up."

"So," Mags said, sitting down on the bench. "Let's hear it."

"We got—well, all I can call it is, break-in-and-smash." Ned ran his hand through his abundant hair. "I don't understand it. Somebody's breakin' into shops just to trash 'em out. Not one thing stole, an' it prolly doesn't take half a candlemark, but when they're done, place is a wreck."

"Huh." That sounded very like what had happened at the Abbey of Ardana. "Anythin' written on the walls? Anybody leave a note pinned to the door?"

But Ned shook his head. "Nothin'. Just break in the back way, wreck the place, an' leave."

Mags scratched his head. "Anybody got a feud goin'?" he asked, though he was pretty sure Ned had thought of that already. "There a new gang moved in?" That was always a possibility; the old threat of "nice little shop you got here, bet you wanna keep it nice" was something gangs would try any place they thought the Watch couldn't stop them.

"Nope and nope," Ned replied. "I thought of gangs first thing. Nothin'. I got ears in the streets, too, I'd'a heard. An' *nothin'* about any of the shops is the same!"

The last was said in tones of despair.

"'Cept one thing," said the elder March, quietly. "I'm tellin' you, Ned, that's got to be it."

"What does?" Mags asked, already sure he knew the answer.

"They're all run by women," Ned sighed.

It turned out there had been six of these break-ins. They all occurred in places where the shop owner lived elsewhere, and there was no one living above the shop, or behind it. There was never any indication that there might be trouble. The owner would lock up, just as she had every other day previously, and when she returned in the morning to open up, she would find the place in ruins. Goods would be piled in the center of the room and trampled, shelves pulled down, large items tipped over, and everything that was breakable would have been smashed to bits.

So far the victims had been a candle-maker, an herbalist—one who carried not only medicinal herbs, but culinary and fragrance items—a stationer, a leatherworker who made nearly everything *except* shoes and boots, a seller of yarns, cords and threads, and a blacksmith who made small items. The candle-maker had not fared too badly; she'd been able to sweep up and re-use practically everything, and only her time had been lost. The yarn-monger had recovered most of her stock, too; apparently taking the time to tangle everything into a giant ball of fiber had been a little too much for the vandal to attempt. And the blacksmith's goods had been unbreakable; the vandal had taken out his ire on her shelves and bins, reducing them to splinters, but fixing that was the matter of a day or so. But the leatherworker had found nearly everything spoiled with water or stained with lamp-oil, and the stationer had to replace everything, as did the herbalist.

None of the women knew each other, or were related in any way. They didn't have mutual friends. They *might* have shared customers, but none of the customers in the days previous to the break-ins had excited any alarm.

There was nothing to link them to the depredations of the Abbey of Ardana, or the Temple of Betane, much less to the Poison Pen's antics up on the Hill.

And yet . . . and yet . . .

The elder March nodded as Mags glanced at him. "Aye. You're gettin' the same feeling, ain't you?"

"They don't seem linked at all," Mags demurred.

"But yer gut tells you they are." Captain Kay March nodded. "So does mine."

:He's just referring to the Abbey, of course,: Dallen pointed out. *:Nobody knows about the Temple but you, the Prince, the Prioress, and the work crew. And he can't know about what's going on up on the Hill.:*

Nothing connected them. Except . . . one thing. They were all in the neighborhoods surrounding the Temple of Sethor the Patriarch.

:Still. What's the odds?: Mags replied, and turned his attention

back to Captain Ned. "I can't think of anything you haven't, but that don't mean I won't. Tell me about anything else that comes up. If I'm not at the East Beech Courthouse, a message left there'll reach me."

Captain Ned sighed, but didn't look particularly disappointed. "It was long odds you'd come up with anythin' Mags. 'Preciate you tryin'."

"I ain't givin' up," Mags pledged as he stood up. "Keep me informed. I'm gonna let 'em know about this up on the Hill."

"That's more'n I asked for, Mags. Thankee again." They all three shook hands solemnly, and Mags finally mounted up, and was off with a wave.

But not far.

:You're thinking what I'm thinking,: Dallen observed, as Mags turned his head in the direction of the Temple that now belonged to the followers of Sethor the Patriarch.

:Mebbe, mebbe not. One thing I do know, religious types are up at all hours, generally. Mebbe someone saw something. Mebbe one of 'em heard something from the people comin' here. They're smack in the middle of everything, an' it ain't goin' out of our way to pay 'em a visit.:

He left Dallen at the entrance—there didn't seem to be anyone prepared to "take charge" of the Companion, and Dallen was perfectly fine all on his own, although Mags could tell he was a bit miffed at not getting a proper reception. Then he just strolled in, hoping to poke around a bit, and talk to the underlings.

That, however, was exactly what he was not allowed to do. As soon as he set foot in the austere, white-stone antechamber to the sanctuary, he was spotted by a lesser priest, who hurried up to him. "Ah, Herald," the man said, deferentially, "Welcome to the Sanctuary of Sethor the Patriarch. Allow me to take you to the High Priest immediately; as it happens, your timing could not have been better, he has just finished afternoon services and is free."

"That's not necessary—" Mags protested.

"Oh I assure you, it is," the priest said, and would not hear otherwise. So Mags found himself escorted past all the acolytes and servants and other underlings he would very much have *liked* to speak to, and straight into the capacious office of the High Priest.

"Capacious" was indeed the right word for it. The office was the size of the Lesser Audience Chamber at the Palace, but sparsely furnished. The walls were the same plain, white stone as the antechamber, the Sanctuary, and the exterior. There was a single strip of blue carpet leading from the door to a desk at the back of the room, and two chairs, one behind the desk, and one in front of it. If the High Priest wanted the place to look austere, he was succeeding.

Nice an' cool in here, though. Damn comfortable in all this heat. Truth to tell at the moment he envied them this stone pile.

"Ah, good afternoon, Herald!" The High Priest was already standing when Mags entered, and Mags' immediate impression was of a hard, cold man, very erect in his blue robes. Deceptively simple, those robes were, but Mags, who was good friends with the now-Princess Lydia, had learned all about fabrics from her. And he could recognize, by the drape and the suppleness of those "simple" robes, that they probably cost more than double what the more elaborately embroidered vestments of some other clerics he knew cost.

As for the heavy gold chain and medallion around the High Priest's neck . . . it probably represented the combined wealth of a small town.

"I am Theodor Kresh, High Priest of Lord Sethor the Patriarch. And you are—?"

"Herald Pippin," Mags lied, knowing Pip would cover for him. He took extra pains with his pronunciation and accent. "I was just passing through this neighborhood and I thought I would pay my respects."

But the High Priest smiled thinly. "Oh, come now, Herald. We both know that Heralds are far too busy merely to *drop in and pay respects.* Let's not insult each other's intelligence, Herald Pippin. What brings you here?"

The High Priest gestured to the chair; it was a hard, unyielding, straight-backed thing. Mags took it. All right, the first bout had gone to Theodor Kresh. He would have to make sure he won all the rest.

"The local Watch consulted with me on a string of crimes in this neighborhood," he replied, with the strict truth. "I was hoping perhaps one of your underlings might have noticed something, since you men of the cloth are apt to be awake at all hours of the night, and certainly get to hear many things from your worshippers."

Kresh took his own chair, and steepled his fingers in front of his face, not quite hiding a faint smile. "Ah, I believe you are referring to those shops that were so peculiarly vandalized?"

Mags merely nodded.

"It is my personal belief that the women did it themselves," Kresh continued. "After all, if one is failing at running a business, and doesn't want anyone to know this, how better to get out from under the burden of the business *and* garner sympathy at the same time, than to destroy all one's stock and pin the blame on mysterious vandals?"

Mags was glad he had his best gambling-face on, since otherwise he might have tipped his hand with his reaction to such an outrageous statement.

"That's a theory I had not considered," he replied, again truthfully. "Do you really think it's possible? I am given to understand these depredations amounted to a considerable financial loss to these women."

"Which, thanks to all the well-meaning sympathy of their neighbors and the generosity of those around them, they have no doubt recouped," Kresh retorted, waving his hand as if it were a foregone conclusion. "As it should be. No woman should attempt to run a business. A woman's place is as the helpmeet and support of her husband or father. The God Sethor created them to serve, not push themselves forward. Now they can resume a woman's proper place, a little the poorer in worldly goods for it, but so much richer in spirit. They will be happier when they are in the position that God designed them for. Don't you agree?"

"Of course," Mags said, vaguely. "Nevertheless, this vandalism is a crime against *property*, and it has caused no end of inconvenience to the gentlemen who were expecting to be able to supply their needs from those shops. As such, we really should take them seriously and give it a thorough investigation. And if said investigation turns up the fact that your allegations are true, would that not be so much the better?"

The High Priest snorted a little, but admitted that might be the case. "Still, don't you think it is better for them to have their misplaced ambitions quashed all at once, rather than watching their business and the health of their souls perish little by little over the course of a year or more? This is kinder, not unlike the removal of a rotten tooth. Get it over with at once; one sharp pain, then all will be well."

"Still," Mags insisted. "These are crimes. We simply cannot allow them to go on, nor can we allow the perpetrators to go unpunished. The next things to be vandalized might belong to men—or religious orders."

"Well, of course you can't, Herald Pippin." Theodor Kresh responded immediately. "I never implied that you should. I am merely trying to point out that for every evil that befalls, some good can come out of it, and if that good in this case is that these women come to understand their proper place in the world, and that God has given them a *very* gentle chastisement at the hands of a criminal, then that is the best possible outcome." He huffed a little. "Of course you must pursue every possible path of investigation, and *of course* if we of Sethor hear of anything to assist you, we will inform you immediately."

It was a very uncomfortable interview, which in the end yielded no information whatsoever. Mags left the Temple feeling faintly dirty, and very much as if he had been jousting with an eel.

Nevertheless. . . .

:*I think I need to join that Temple,*: he told Dallen.

:*Hmm. I did notice that there seem to be an unusual number of street toughs among the devotees of this "Sethor,"*: Dallen replied, craning his head around to look at Mags with one blue eye.

:*All the more reason. But not as Harkon. I guess I am going to have to go invent someone else.*:

* * *

This was going to be a very hot summer, and the heat was not improving tempers up on the Hill. People were trying all manner of things to deal with the heat, and the most popular was the most dangerous.

The Terilee River that cut through the Palace grounds and ran down the Hill into Haven was *much* too fast to swim in safely until it widened and slowed outside the city boundary. Even the best swimmers could be caught unaware by the fast current, and it was a fight to get back to the bank. But the water was fresh, clean enough to drink, and cold—there were laws, strictly enforced, about running sewage pipes into it—and oh, so very tempting when the sun blazed down overhead.

Boats were fine for sculling about on the river, and there were plenty of them to be had, but evidently it was not enough for some people to row or sail, or sit on the riverbank and trail arms and legs in the current. Down below Haven, where the current slowed and the river widened, it was perfectly safe to swim, and people just couldn't understand (or pretended not to) why swimming was allowed there and not here. After far too many instances of chasing half-naked people out of the water, Prince Sedric threw up his hands and demanded that *someone* come up with a solution. "Something other than lining the bank with Guards," he said, crossly.

As Lirelle and Loren, Lord Semel's younger children had discovered, there was a subset of people at the Collegium (informally called the "Blues," since they were encouraged to wear a blue variation on the Trainee uniforms when attending classes), allowed to take whatever classes interested them. While most were the children of the courtiers, there were some from middling or outright impoverished backgrounds that had won a place here by virtue of their intelligence and talents. So while others, supposedly older and wiser, were debating things like fences and punishments for being rescued, *they* were working on the assumption that people were going to go right on trying to river-bathe, and probably do it at riskier times or places, so it would be better to just find a way to make river-bathing safer.

When one of their artificer instructors found out what they were up to, he set it to them as a class project, and presented the result to Sedric. Sedric was delighted, and ordered their clever plan constructed at once.

So now, on either side of the bridge crossing the river for several lengths, heavy, well-anchored ropes crossed the span, with floats at equal intervals. Hanging from these ropes down into the depths of the water were heavily weighted, coarse nets, with holes large enough for fish to fit through, but not people. There were half a dozen of these nets on either side of the bridge. At the banks between the nets were rafts or floating docks, providing safe exits and entrances to the water.

By common consent, ladies took the upstream side of the bridge, and men the downstream. Most of the female Trainees just went in wearing lightweight breeches cut off at the knee and shirts with the sleeves cut off, all out of the rag-bags, but ladies of the Court tended to concoct loose dresses that were more modest in theory, and absurd in practice. And most of these ladies didn't know how to swim, so the Trainees had to put up with helping them into the river, then haul them and all their dripping yards of fabric out onto the docks, and watch them clinging to the nets and shrieking nervously.

But at least it gave them something to do besides sit in the shade and fan themselves in a vain attempt to escape the heat, stew about the vicious letters they'd been sent, and engage in whispered gossip about who the sender probably was.

And after a few days, some of them had begun begging the Trainees to teach them to swim, which gave everyone something constructive instead of destructive to concentrate on.

Amily had escaped from the oppressive closeness of the Council Chamber and opted for a chance to cool off, instead of pick at a luncheon she was too hot to eat. Like the Trainees, she cut the arms and legs off some maltreated Whites, and joined them at the river. She found herself in the middle of an energetic pod of mixed Trainees, who had just helped the last of their swimming students out of the water. The ladies looked exhausted—which pleased Amily no end. That meant they'd probably find a cool spot and sleep the afternoon away. And *that* meant they wouldn't be brooding over imagined wrongs, or picking quarrels with people.

The current really *was* strong here; it was work to stay in between the ropes and their nets. She and the others splashed their way across and back about half a dozen times, then lined up like birds on a branch, arms draped over the downstream rope with their backs to it and letting the water push them into the net.

"Well," she said to the nearest. "You lot haven't brought me any reports, so I am assuming there is nothing *to* report. Am I right?"

The Trainee nearest her was wearing an excuse for a shirt in faded pink, so she assumed it was a Bardic Trainee. "Nothing to speak of," the girl said, as the one in faded gray on Amily's other side nodded. "A very few letters coming up from Haven in the regular mail, in proper envelopes sealed with a proper wafer, so there's nothing to pick them out from ordinary mail. He's learned, whoever he is."

"The letters are the same, except he seems to have figured out who's about to go into Whites or Scarlets," said the Heraldic Trainee. "Though maybe it's just that he's good at guessing ages and assumes the older you are the closer you are to getting promoted. Most of the letters, ours at least, are general pronouncements that we're going straight to some form of hell for daring to act like men, and a wish for us to fail and get sent away in disgrace."

The Bardic Trainee craned her neck to look around Amily at the Heraldic Trainee, her expression one of utter disbelief. "He actually said that to *your* lot?"

The Heraldic Trainee laughed. "I know, stupid, isn't it? He clearly has *no* idea how things work. I wonder if he just thinks Companions are fancy horses?"

"If he's that stupid, I wouldn't be at all surprised." She smiled. "I'll have to pass that on. It might make things a little better. Even if they aren't true, those letters still sting."

"Has anyone caught anyone lurking about?" Amily asked— without much hope.

"No, worse luck, which kind of speaks to the notion that he's living up here, doesn't it?" the Heraldic Trainee—Sara, that was her name, Amily remembered at last—said. "Which is not at all comforting."

"No, it's not," Amily agreed. *And they don't know the half of it.* All the Trainees knew was that there was a Poison Pen sending nasty letters about. They didn't know about the burning effigy. They didn't know about the outrages committed against the two Orders down in Haven. Or these new things that Mags was investigating, the vandalism of shops owned by women. *One bad actor? Two? More?* It hardly seemed possible that it could be a single person. It hardly seemed possible that it could be more than one. The messages were all so similar . . .

But there were no messages at all in the vandalized shops, she reminded herself. *So what does that mean?*

At least it was easier to think, here with the cool water holding her against the support of the net.

Sara began giggling. Amily looked over at her. "What?" she asked.

"Well, if he *is* up here, he won't be able to avoid seeing us all frolicking about in semi-undress in the water, showing all our curves for anyone to see," Sara replied, face full of amusement. "And if *that* doesn't send him off on a tirade, I don't know what will! We might start getting letters by the wheelbarrow full!"

"Which will give us a *much* better chance of catching him," agreed the Bardic Trainee with renewed enthusiasm. "Glory! When you think how nasty-minded he is, all of us flouncing around like watery floozies is going to make him pitch the most *enormous* fit!"

The Trainees nearest the three of them had been listening with interest, and seemed to think this would be a wonderful thing.

But Amily found herself suppressing alarm. Because she remembered what Jorthun had said about people of this sort always escalating, rather than backing down.

And she dreaded to think what form that escalation might take—given all this provocation. . . .

* * *

"Fire! *Fire!*"

Once again, Amily and Mags were awakened by frantic alarms—but this time, it wasn't just one voice, it was several, and there was real fear in the words.

Mags had taken to sleeping in something he could at least run out wearing, and with his soft half-boots right at the side of the bed. He was shod and out the door in a flash, and it was clear that *this* blaze was not a mere effigy. It was the size of a good-sized bonfire, and clearly intended to attract attention. Once again, it was in the middle of the gardens—but this time people were boiling out of all three Collegia and even the Palace to come and gape at it while the servants struggled to put it out.

That was when he got a flash of foreboding, and ran for Herald's Collegium.

Tried rather. By the time he fought his way through the mob and into the corridor of the classrooms, the damage had been done.

Someone had come through like a rampaging bull. The corridor was full of books, papers, even a couple of chairs—

Mags took it all in at a glance, and in that glance knew that this vandalism was fundamentally identical to what had happened down in Haven, in those shops.

And even as he thought that, he was running again, this time heading for Bardic; but some of the Heraldic Trainees had just discovered the mess in their Collegium, and now he had to fight to get through, as panicked Trainees struggled to get to their rooms, thinking that the demon of destruction had surely been *there* as well.

The scene was the same at Bardic, and the people who had seen him fighting his way through the crowds, and had either assumed *he* was the troublemaker, or was chasing the miscreant, stumbled into the corridor next to him and started clamoring about the damage there—

He abandoned them and sprinted for Healer's. But there, at last, he found that people with a level head had anticipated trouble at the first cry of *Fire.* He found adult Healers with staves and grim looks on their faces posted at every entrance, including the entrance into the greenhouse. No one had seen anything, but then, it would not have been at all difficult for the vandal to spot people standing in the doorways, guarding them. It seemed the hunt was over, and the fox had escaped again.

"It looks like a pile of rags," Mags said dubiously, as he poked at the pile of burned fabric with a stick. The reason it had been so difficult to put out was because every stitch of the clothing in that pile had been soaked in oil.

"It does," Amily agreed. Primed, perhaps, by the conversation in the river this afternoon, she had recognized immediately what had been burned. "I would bet any amount of money, though, that what was in that pile were the river-bathing outfits people have rescued out of the rag-bag."

He looked mystified, but of course he would; he hadn't been up on the Hill of late until after sunset, and left right after breakfast. He knew nothing about the new sport of river-swimming. She explained it all to him as he listened, brows creased. She saw understanding light up his eyes as she described the abbreviated costumes the Trainees were wearing to swim.

"Don't tell me—when people are done they go hang them out on a line in the laundry-garden, and fetch them in the morning?" he guessed.

She nodded. "It would be child's play to gather up as many as the vandal wanted, dump oil on them, and set them on fire."

He cursed. "The bastard foxed us again. An' *nobody* but the Healers have got alibis. Most of the Hill was runnin' around like chickens last night."

She sighed. "And he wins again."

"Or she," Mags reminded her grimly. "Or she."

11

A day. Three. A sennight. A fortnight. And still nothing had happened up on the Hill, except that the weather had grown hotter, and courtiers had settled into new configurations of trust, or rather, lack of it. But people were minding their manners, at least to the extent of not fighting openly, possibly because it was too hot to fight openly. Instead, they were figuratively walking on eggshells around each other, and gathering in tight little cliques.

This had *not* discouraged the female Trainees from river-bathing; if anything, it made them more defiant, and their bathing-costumes more abbreviated. The ladies of the Court, however, were more mixed in their reactions. Some had decided to shy away from river-bathing altogether, some only did so at dusk, when the near-dark preserved some of their modesty, and some had joined the female Trainees in their defiance, concocting similar "bathing outfits" of lightweight breeches and shirts.

Down in Haven, Mags had investigated three more shop break-ins, to no end. All three had been accomplished in the dead of night, there were no witnesses, of course, and no reports of any disturbance in the night. As with the first six, the owners of the shops turned up to open them, and discovered the destruction.

By this point the reports of the vandalism of the shops had come to the attention of the Lesser Council, and Mags was asked to report on it all. It felt very odd indeed, to be standing in front of a table full of important people and giving a report, when one of those people happened to be his own wife.

It was the first time he'd ever been before either of the Councils; he wouldn't have known this was the Lesser Council had not half the seats at this horseshoe-shaped table been empty. And he would not have known who was missing had Nikolas not told him beforehand.

The Lord Martial was not here; this sort of business internal to Haven was not in his purview. The same held for the Seneschal. Several of the Guildmasters were not here either, though if it had been Mags, *he* would have been, and he considered them very foolish for thinking that this sort of thing could not happen to one of the members of *their* Guilds. None of the heads of the Bardic, Heraldic, or Healers' Circles were here; Bardic didn't care, Healers' was not involved, and the Heralds were already represented well enough by Amily and her father. The Lord Mayor of Haven was not here either; things had not yet gotten to the point where he felt he needed to make an appearance at the table; he was trusting to the Watch, the Heralds, and the King to see that he didn't.

So although some of the owners of the vandalized shops were in other Guilds entirely, everyone had agreed to have their interests represented by the heads of the Mercantile Guilds.

The Council Chamber was a bit dim, as white curtains had been drawn over the windows to reflect as much heat outward as possible. As with most of the Palace, the walls and floor were polished wood, and behind the King was a tapestry of an enormous map of Valdemar. It was embroidered, rather than woven, so at least changes to that map were slightly easier to make than having to reweave entire sections of it.

Mags stood in the center of the horseshoe, all eyes on him as he made his report. Never had he been so careful with his words and his diction as he was now. None of these people knew him; they'd weigh the importance of what he said in part by how he sounded. He had thought he would be nervous, facing such an audience, but he hadn't been. If anything, he'd been gratified that they had simply listened, attentively, and had not pelted him with questions.

". . . we're all at our wits' end down there," he concluded. "The Watch has put on extra patrollers, but they can't hire just *anyone* for the job, people's backgrounds have to be investigated, and they've got to be doubled up with a Watchman with experience, so that's been going slow."

"Could we send some Guard down to patrol as well?" Amily asked.

"We could, and we should," the King said immediately, much to the relief of the representatives of the Mercantile Guilds.

"If you'll allow, Majesty," Sedric said, before his father could add anything to that. "Lydia and I have decided we are going to assist those whose stocks were destroyed out of our household budget. She told me this morning that she would *much* rather have a prosperous herbalist or apothecary than a new gown."

The two representatives of the Mercantile Guilds looked very gratified. The King smiled, and Mags knew what he was thinking—first, that Sedric was going to make an excellent King, and second, that he and Lydia were going to purchase themselves a great deal of good will with actions like this. That boded well for their reign, when they came to take the Crown.

Which's about the only thing good comin' out of all of this. The owner of the third shop—a glassmaker—had been so emotionally shattered—not unlike the fragile contents of her shop—that she had cried on his shoulder until she needed a Healer, and he couldn't blame her.

He was somewhat impatient to get all this over with; he'd established a new persona of an out-of-work common laborer, and had just joined the general worshippers of Sethor. He was hoping for some sort of lead out of the place, since it was certainly a gathering place for malcontents. The persona was an easy one to stay in; he said nothing, but listened a lot, with an air of respect and agreement, and did his best to impersonate a man who was a natural follower.

"Thank you, Herald Mags," the King said, as if sensing his impatience, although he was *sure* he had given no sign of it. "Now, I believe our next order of business, at the request of the Lord Mayor, is to bring in watering carts to dampen down the streets and ease some of the heat?"

Mags didn't wait to hear anything else. He bowed himself out, and headed for the stables, where Dallen was waiting, already saddled. If he got down to the inn quickly enough, he could change into Geb Lackland, and be at the Temple in time for the noon distribution of bread for men out of work. Only men were allowed to collect said charity, though, unless the acolytes distributing the bread happened to know that any women who turned up were collecting on behalf of a sick or injured husband, father, or brother. It was a great opportunity to grumble a little, and listen a lot.

Within moments, he was in the saddle and riding out of the Gates, with a friendly, commiserating nod at the Guards there. At least in this heat, Heraldic Whites were cool. The dark blue uniforms of the Guard must have been pure torture to wear.

Very careful monitoring of surface thoughts had told him that his ruse was holding. And maybe, just maybe, since he had begun laying hints that he'd been out of work long enough he'd be open to doing just about anything, it would be a chance to worm his way deeper into the workings of the Temple. Probably the Sethorites had nothing to do with the Poison Pen up here on the Hill. But the shops? So far as he was concerned, they were his primary suspects, given what he'd been hearing from them for the past several days. Maybe it wasn't being done "officially," but he'd be willing to bet that at least the lower tier of the priests knew about it and were winking at it.

:Too bad that Teo is busy,: Dallen observed as they headed down the Hill. *:He'd be very convincing.:*

:Iffen he could keep a straight face,: Mags replied, remembering how Teo had reacted only a few short sennights ago to that lot of louts in the tavern who had been spouting the same sort of garbage, just more crudely.

:Hmm. Good point.: Dallen adroitly avoided a child who ran after

an escaping kitten right under his nose. :*I know why you want to go down there, though, and it has nothing to do with working your way into the hearts of those Sethorite idiots.*:

:*Oh? Really? Why'm I goin', then?*:

Dallen heaved an enormous sigh. :*It's the coolest place outside of the river. And I wish I could sneak my way in there myself.*:

:*Well, don' give away my secret,*: he replied. :*Or every Herald in Haven'll be puttin' on old trews an' canvas shirts an' pretendin' t' hate wimmen. Even the wimmen.*:

I think this may be the coolest place outside of the river, Amily thought, as she lounged in a springy chair made of woven reeds, and waited for the last of the Handmaidens to arrive. They were meeting in that lovely, shaded gazebo on top of one of the round towers on Lord Jorthun's manse; the stately house was at the top of the Hill, and the gazebo was three stories above that, so it caught every little breeze. Since the last time she'd been up here, the gazebo had been furnished with reed screens that could be let down on all four sides, so no matter where the sun was, the inside was completely shaded. There were plenty more of those woven-reed chairs, as well as linen-covered cushions. There was a servant stationed up here whose only job was to periodically wet down the reed screen on the windward side of the gazebo, so that the breeze coming through was cooled even further. Quite frankly, Amily would have been just as pleased to conduct all of her business up here and not leave until fall.

With no one to see them, the Handmaidens had all stripped down to their shifts, and Amily did not blame them one little bit.

She'd have done the same, had her linen Whites been any heavier. As it was, she had the sleeves rolled up and her boots off.

When the last of them had settled, and fans had been handed round to augment the breeze, Amily spoke. "All right, ladies. Is there anything new since your last report? Besides the heat, that is."

"I think the heat is the only thing that's prevented a murder or two," replied Keleste, a deceptively frail girl who could best men twice her size in the Weaponsmaster's lessons. "If I could distill the venom down there"—she pointed her fan at the distant Palace—"I could poison the entire Kingdom."

Solemn nods all around. "The heat's keeping people from *acting*, but it hasn't kept them from *talking*," agreed Joya, a little dark-eyed, fox-faced girl. "When our ladies aren't trying to nap through the heat, they are gathering in cliques and gossiping. We've all been comparing notes. Aside from personal enmities that existed before all this started, it seems the majority of them have settled on a handful of suspects. I know of two in particular. Lady Herra and Lady Amberly."

Amily nodded. That was to be expected. Both ladies were unmarried, had lived at Court most of their lives, had been spinsters the entire time and showed no interest in acquiring husbands.

They had enough money to live independently, and at some point both of them must have done *something* to earn themselves permanent lodging in the Palace, otherwise they wouldn't be here.

Perhaps they are distant relations of the Queen. They are in her Court, after all. Amily was a bit vague about the Queen's Court; it wasn't anything she had ever had much to do with. The Queen was as private a person as a Royal could be, and had never, to Amily's knowledge, meddled in politics. Most, if not all, of her ladies were personal friends or relations, who also had reputations for staying out of politics.

I imagine that makes things rather restful for Kyril, Amily thought, *knowing his beloved will only tender advice that has no private agenda.*

:It was the choice she made when they married,: Rolan informed her, as one by one the Handmaidens chimed in with what their particular ladies had said about Lady Herra and Lady Amberly. *:She's been giving Lydia some very good advice on that head, since they are both ordinary women, not highborn, wedded to someone who is both Royal and a Herald.:*

Amily made a mental note to see Lydia more often after this. If being a Herald married to a Herald was hard, how much more difficult was it to be someone who was *not* a Herald but was wedded to one?

She bent her mind back to the business of listening to the Handmaidens. Lady Herra had been rather waspish about the river-bathing, and the costumes (or rather, the lack thereof). She was already known for her deadly barbs before this; she had a sharp wit and an equally sharp tongue and knew how to use both to effect. Now the resentment of those who were not nearly so clever had an outlet. "*Sour spinster,* they're saying, and *something deeply wrong there,* as if not being married means you've probably got a rotten brain," Joya continued. "And part of it may be to get back at her for all the stones she's cast in the past, but some of it is making more reasonable people nod and look thoughtful."

Lady Amberly, on the other hand was distinctly unfeminine, to the point of wearing breeches as often as she wore skirts or gowns, and there had been dark whispers about her before this. "Well, you know they're saying she's *shaych*, though she's never so much as flirted with a chambermaid," observed Keleste. "But what that has to do with hating women, I haven't the slightest. I should think it would mean the very opposite if it was true, and if it isn't, why should being mannish make you despise women enough to send them into hysterics?" She shrugged eloquently. "Not that any of this makes sense. People are afraid. *Someone* knows their secrets, they don't know who it is, and they are desperate to find out and hush her up. It's all stabs in the dark, and I suppose we should be glad no one's bled from them yet."

"You're right, both of you," Amily told them. Knowing that even if the whispers about either of the ladies in question had been true—which they weren't, as Amily knew from her father—that shouldn't have made them candidates for the Poison Pen. After all, if Lady Herra had something to say to someone, she came right out and *said* it, in as public a place as possible. She would be the very last person in all of Haven to confine herself to writing nasty letters, meant only for the eyes of one.

And as for Lady Amberly, while she was standoffish, and far more interested in horses than in people, there was nothing to suggest the religious fanaticism the Poison Pen displayed, much less the vitriolic hatred of her own sex.

"Anyone else?" Amily asked. The rest offered up their gleanings of the gossip. It wasn't much. Just four more names came up as suspects, including Helane and Lirelle, Lord Lional's girl-children, for no better reason but that half the women down at the Court were inflamed with jealousy, and their excuse was, "Well, none of this was happening before *they* came."

Which was selective memory, as Amily herself knew very well. She'd gotten letters, and probably so had they, in the sennights before the arrival of Lord Lional and his family.

"And do any of you think any of the Court is to blame?" she asked. It was a calculated risk; although Dia and Steveral were ninety percent certain that none of the Handmaidens was the Poison Pen—there was still that ten percent. *But if one of them is our culprit, now would be the chance for her to cast doubt on someone else.*

One and all, they shook their heads. "Not the ladies we serve, anyway," said Joya. "And not their husbands. And . . . all right, maybe I am being extremely naive, but as horrid as those letters are, it takes a kind of mature immaturity to write something like that, don't you think?"

Amily shook her head. "I'm not sure what you're saying."

"I don't think anyone younger than us would be able to write something like that," Joya explained. "Oh, I don't mean they couldn't write obscenity, because they certainly can, but there's a *feeling* to those letters I can't quite explain. The sentiments are pathetically childish. But the mind expressing them is mature; it's been holding in these grievances for a long, long time, and now it's letting loose. I think it must take *decades* for that kind of hatred to settle in and fester into something that could create those letters."

They all fanned themselves, attentive, but silent, while Amily thought that over. "I'd tend to agree with you," she said, finally. "But I can't think of *anyone* in the Court who fits that picture." She looked around her, and the Handmaidens all shook their heads.

After a little more talk, she left the Handmaidens enjoying their relatively cool, idle hour, and headed back to the Collegium. And it was only when she got there, and caught sight of a tall, thin girl in what could have been a Trainee uniform—except that it was blue, not gray, green, or rust-colored—that she remembered there was a group up here on the Hill that she knew little to nothing about.

The so-called "Blues."

:Rolan?: she thought, as she altered her steps to the Seneschal's office. *:Tell me about the Blues. I know I was one myself, technically, but I never wore the uniform, and the only people I ever socialized with were Lydia's crowd.:*

:There are three sorts of Blues,: Rolan reminded her. *:The first sort are the children of people here at Court—like Loren and Lirelle, Lord Lional's children. And like you. The second sort are the children of courtiers and the wealthy who live on the Hill, but not at the Palace. Lydia was one of those, if you'll recall, as were many of your friends. The third sort are the "Blue Scholars." They are extremely intelligent young people who have earned the right to study here. Some are supported by their parents, but those who are from poorer families are often sponsored by religious groups, and there are the "King's Scholars," who've been supported by the Crown for two hundred years, at least, if not more.:*

:Thanks, Rolan,: she said gratefully. Well, these were certainly dark horses, at least to her. She didn't *think* any of them could be the Poison Pen but . . .

. . . *sponsored by a strict religious group . . . suddenly exposed to how things are at the Court and Collegia . . . and learned enough to cite those mythological man-eaters . . . could one of them have just snapped and broken out in a rash of religious mania?*

It seemed unlikely, but at this point, she had to consider the possibility and eliminate it.

The question was, how?

:And where are they living? That would answer some questions.:

:Raise more questions than answer them, I'm afraid,: Rolan replied regretfully, as she reached the relative coolness of the Palace, and ducked inside with a sigh of relief. *:Some live in the Palace with their families. Some live on the Hill with their families. Some are boarded with the families of Blues they have become friends with on the Hill. Some live in some of the nearby Temples. And some have been put up in otherwise unused servants' quarters in the Palace. There's two living in Mags' old room at the Companion's Stable right now, in fact.:*

Some were living in Temple quarters? That sounded like a prime environment to develop religious mania . . .

Except she couldn't think of a single Temple or other religious housing near the Hill that held any sect that would hold the sort of vitriolic abhorrence of women that was expressed in those letters.

:Who would know where they all live?: she asked, although she was pretty certain she knew the answer.

:Actually it's probably not the Seneschal,: Rolan corrected. *:But the Seneschal will know who knows.:*

She managed to intercept that harried individual just as he was leaving his office. "I'm sorry, I wouldn't ask you this if it weren't important," she apologized, "But who has the list of the Blues, who they are, and where they live?"

"Royal Housekeeper," the Seneschal said, and hurried off without waiting for her thanks.

The Housekeeper had an office as well, in the basement of the Palace, and it was with profound relief that Amily descended the stairs into the *real* cool. The basement might not be very pleasant in the winter, but right now . . .

I've got to figure out a way I can spend more time here.

Amily found her in her office, as expected, and she was not nearly so harried as the Seneschal. But she had a small army of maids and pages under her, and seldom had to leave her office except on her rounds of inspection. It was the first time in a long time that Amily had needed to come talk to her about anything, but remarkably, the woman remembered her.

She was a tall, thin, stern-looking lady who habitually wore black gowns with snowy white trimming, and the heavy ring of keys to everything in the Palace that needed to be locked up jangling at her belt. But she smiled faintly when Amily tapped hesitantly on her doorframe, and gestured her in.

"Well, little Amily, you have come up in the world since I saw you last," she said, sounding pleased, and not at all as if she was trying to make it a veiled insult. "And I am more than happy to see you so well settled with your young man. What can I do for the King's Own, my dear?"

:What does she know?: she asked Rolan.

:Everything. She has to. She's one of your father's people.:

That made things easier. "Well, you know I'm helping Mags and Father try to find this . . ."

"Wretched letter-writer," the Housekeeper interrupted. "Yes, he told me, I'm in his circle of informants."

Perfect. "I'm more or less in charge of weeding out the people who live or move about in and around the Palace. So I need the list of the Blues, who they are, and where they are lodging."

Now the Housekeeper smiled broadly, and with great satisfaction, like someone who has done a job before anyone even knew it was going to need doing. "I thought someone might. I made a copy. Here you are." And with that, she handed over a neatly folded, thin stack of papers. "I'm sure you haven't considered the servants, but I have. Nikolas asked if I could think of anyone among the servants who could be responsible, and honestly, I can't. They've all been here . . . three or four years at the very least, and those who have little seniority are all young under-servants. The letters didn't start until this summer, and I cannot imagine why any of them would suddenly break out in a flurry of acidic letter writing. Not to mention, I absolutely assure you, they simply do not have the *time* to have written all those letters, delivered them, and still gotten their duties completed."

Amily nodded; the Palace servants were treated well, paid well, and certainly not overworked—but the sheer volume of letters sent and delivered would have meant that a servant would have been sitting up past his or her bedtime for hours several nights in a fortnight. The Housekeeper, and their fellow-servants, would absolutely have noticed someone showing signs of that sort of exhaustion.

"As for the Blues, they are all youngsters. The missives he showed me left me with the impression that the writer is an adult."

Well, that was two observations from two separate people, Joya and the Housekeeper, coming to the same conclusion. "You're probably right—but that's not the only reason I want to check on them. What if this creature has been sending *them* those horrible letters? If they are anything like the Trainees, they are going to assume that *they* are the only ones being singled out, and will have no idea how much of this poison has been strewed around the Hill. And they'll hide the fact that they are getting these things, because they won't want anyone to know."

"In that case, I am sure you will think of a way to find out. I'd appreciate it if you can solve this nonsense as soon as possible. It's not only creating a great deal of unrest, but it has the potential to turn deadly." The Housekeeper gave her a fixed look, as if to be certain that Amily was taking her seriously.

Startled, Amily just nodded. "Thank you, Mrs. Pellam. I'm doubly glad to discover you're someone I can rely on."

That last brought a gratified smile to the Housekeeper's face, and on that note, Amily hurried off, reading down the list, and noting where each student was quartered.

I need someone who can keep an eye on them from inside, but who? All *her* friends in the Blues were long since grown and most were married. None of them had had younger siblings who might be students now, and their children were toddlers at best.

Of course. Lirelle. Mags had said the girl was smart, smart enough to have figured out within days of arriving that there were classes in those three Collegium buildings that she could eavesdrop on. And she was sensible; sensible enough to know that even if she was caught listening to classes, there wasn't much anyone would say to her except "don't do that." *And she probably figured out she could go right back to listening in as soon as she found a more secure hiding place.*

So, smart and sensible, and new enough here she hadn't gotten sucked into any cliques yet.

:*Rolan, get Dallen to have Mags talk to me, would you, please?*:
:*Of course.*:

She glanced around and spotted a handy bench, and sat down on it, taking her time reading over the list. As she had thought, the Blues that were boarding in nearby Priories and Abbeys, Monasteries, Convents, and Temples, were all in what she would have been willing to *swear* were "safe" places. All of these particular houses of religion were the sort that concentrated on good works, scholarship, and prayer, or any combination of the three, and had she shown the Poison Pen letters to the heads of any of those particular institutions, they'd have gone livid, and possibly forgotten their vows of peace, at least temporarily.

:How can I serve ye, milady?: The familiar Mindvoice sounded like Mags' real voice, but it seemed to be coming from between her ears and had a slight echo to it.

:I need an ally in the Blues; they are the only group we're not watching on the Hill. Do you think Lirelle, Lord Lional's daughter, would work? Papa has the Housekeeper with an eye on the servants, by the way.:

She ran her eye down the next page of the list while he thought. *:Aye. I think she'd do. So does Dallen.:*

That settled it, then. But Mags had something more to say. *:Get her brother, too. And afore ye do, get their schedules and go to the Weaponsmaster and have 'em both set up with lessons. I promised—or Magnus promised— Loren'd get 'em and you might as well get the girl started, too. If she don't like 'em, she can quit, and tell her so.:*

:Thank you, love!: she thought affectionately.

Well, the likeliest place for the girl to be at this moment was, in fact, in a class. And just as she realized that, she turned a page in the list of Blues and discovered that the hyper-efficient Housekeeper had already appended the schedules of all of them.

No wonder Papa has her as an agent! She saw that Lirelle was indeed in a class, and had a long break afterward. Perfect.

She got in place just outside the class in History that Lirelle was taking just in time for class change. Lirelle was one of the last to leave, and was chattering away at high speed to a Herald Trainee when Amily intercepted her.

"Lirelle, would you mind talking with me a moment?" she said— although the conversation abruptly stopped when both girls realized there was a Herald at the classroom door looking right at them.

"Absolutely, Herald," Lirelle said, although Amily could tell the girl hadn't recognized her.

"That's the King's Own, dolt!" her friend hissed at her, and Lirelle's eyes widened, and she glanced at her friend for further help.

But her friend just shrugged. "I'll see you later, Liri," she said, and scuttled off.

Amily nodded in a friendly fashion, and said, with a little hand gesture, "Shall we walk?" Lirelle just nodded dumbly, and followed where she led.

The most private place she could think of where they stood no chance of being overheard or interrupted was her own quarters, so that was where they went. "Take a seat anywhere, but I'd suggest the floor," Amily said, folding her legs under her and sitting down on a floor cushion. "It's coolest down here."

"All right," Lirelle agreed, and did so (a little stiffly), setting her books down beside her. She clasped her hands in her lap and fixed her eyes on Amily, looking more than a bit apprehensive.

:I like her: said Rolan, abruptly.

"I wonder if you know about the unpleasant letters people have been getting?" asked Amily, throwing caution to the wind and jumping right into the subject.

Lirelle made a face. "Ugh. Yes. I got two. Helane has gotten lots. Not so many lately, though. Why? Have you caught whoever has been doing it?"

"Not yet," Amily admitted. "In fact, the problem is, we really don't know where to start."

Relaxing now, Lirelle nodded. "Aye, I can see that. I mean, she could be *anybody*, from one of those nasty old cats in Court to . . . I don't know . . . anyone, I guess."

"You said *she*," Amily pointed out, her pulse quickening to think that this child might have information no one else did.

"Oh, did I?" Lirelle shrugged. "I guess . . . I guess I've just thought it was a *she* because of the letters. It could be a man, I suppose. . . ."

"Ah, well," Amily made sure her disappointment didn't show on her face. "It's just because we have no idea who it is that we're trying to keep an eye on everyone. But one group we don't have someone watching is the Blues. The fact is, I don't really know anything about any of them except the ones that are in the Court."

"Oh! And you want me to!" Lirelle perked right up at that, which was a relief, because she *could* have been indignant about Amily wanting her to spy, so to speak, on her friends. "I can do that, I don't mind a bit. I can tell you, though, I don't think any of them are your trickster."

"Why is that?" Amily asked curiously.

"The only reason we're all in the Blues is because we want to *learn things*. Even the ones from Court." She grinned unexpectedly. "Even Loren, now that he's started. So I don't know how any of us would have the time to write all the letters *and* run around delivering them and still keep up with classes. Did you ever think how much work it is to print them out the way they are? So there's nothing of someone's handwriting to tell who wrote it? That's the sort of thing a copyist learns to do, you have to take a lot of pains over it, and it takes time. A couple of the ones Helane got were three pages long!" Lirelle shook her head. "It's not easy, and it's not quick, and it's not the kind of thing we have time for. Especially when we'd *much* rather spend our free time in the river."

"So would I," Amily sighed. "What can you tell me about them, then? Here's the list."

She handed over the Housekeeper's list of the Blues, and Lirelle summed each of them up in a sentence or two, while Amily took notes.

Then she stopped, abruptly. Amily looked up to see that she was frowning over the paper. "Is something wrong?" she asked. "Do you think—"

Lirelle sucked her lower lip. "No, no, Katlie couldn't have written things like that to save her life. I doubt she knows what half the bad words mean. But . . . there's something about her that isn't right. At least *I* think so, though nobody's said anything, so maybe she's just like that. Still—you said you wanted my impressions—"

"And I do," Amily insisted. "So what is it that she's like?"

"Nervy," Lirelle said succinctly. "Like a rabbit that's being chased. It's much more than just shy. Starts when you talk to her, keeps to herself, and sometimes I get the feeling when I'm speaking to her that if I made a sudden move, she'd break and run." She sucked on her lower lip again. "Now that you make me think about these things, she's got a look of being hounded or bullied, but I will swear to you, if she is, it's not by one of us."

"Keep an especially attentive eye on her for me, will you?" Amily asked, not liking the sound of that at all.

"I will. I should have been, anyway, since no one else seems to," Lirelle replied decisively.

"Good, and thank you." Amily smiled at her, and she blushed. "Now, as a bit of a reward, I've been asked to get you and your brother Loren into classes with the Weaponsmaster." She leafed through the pages of the schedules. "Now, how would you like to see him just after your Map class? That should give you enough time for a quick splash in the river before supper."

Lirelle's face lit up like the sun.

12

Lirelle was rewarded, but if some of the rest of the Blues had known who to "blame" for the changes they suddenly got in their lives, they probably would have cursed Amily's name.

The problem was, with no way in place to keep track of their comings and goings, it was obvious that the authorities just couldn't keep on allowing people to parade in and out of the Gates based on the fact that the Guards all knew them.

So things changed, almost immediately. It was just a good thing that the Palace had its own metalworkers right on the grounds in their own shop, next to the blacksmith. It made doing things much quicker.

So now those who were boarding outside the Palace grounds were required to keep a *new,* named and numbered little brass pass-tag on them at all times, and to check in with the Gate Guards every time they entered and left. There was some grumbling from the Guards about all the lists and paperwork, but Amily had expected that.

And really, after that mess with the Sleepgivers, they surely must have realized we were being too slack when it came to the Blues and eventually things would have to change.

With the new system explained to all shifts of the Gate Guards, Amily went on to the next tedious step. She made visits in person to every one of the religious orders that were boarding Blues, and made the heads of those establishments aware of some of what was going on and why the students needed to have an eye on them. "It's not that we suspect them," she explained over and over, "It's that we're afraid that now that we've stopped the letters going to the Trainees, some of the independent students might start getting them."

That explanation passed muster—because, of course, it was entirely true, even if it wasn't the whole truth. She got promises from all of these heads of Orders that they'd make sure *their* charges had a discreet eye on them.

As for the ones that boarded up at the Palace, there was some shuffling of servants' rooms, and within a day the Blues there all ended up in a set of rooms next to the Handmaidens. Anything that went on after hours, those sharp girls would catch in a heartbeat. No one complained, at least not in her hearing. Then again, the Handmaidens were an extremely convivial lot, and she'd asked them to make themselves congenial to the Blues, so . . .

So there are likely to be a few late-night bread-and-jam feasts for a while. No one is going to complain after that.

All this had to be sandwiched in around her other duties, but at least there were people taking charge of some things without her supervision. All three Collegia had established a night-watch on each dormitory floor. This probably discouraged some bed-hopping among the older Trainees, but Amily knew from Rolan that most of them were going to go take their partners out to Companions' Field instead. That was fine with her. More than fine, actually; with the Companions out there keeping track, at least the next time trouble broke out on the Hill, the ones in the Field would be oblivious to it and not rushing about, and the Companions could establish their alibis. Right now, Amily would have given almost anything to have a nice long list of people on the Hill with solid alibis.

Finally Amily was able to settle back to her regular duties—somewhat curtailed regular duties, since absolutely no one was willing to sit through any sort of meeting in the afternoon heat.

Oh, the heat. She couldn't remember a worse summer. During the worst hours, Mags had told her, nothing stirred down in Haven, and even the most ambitious stopped for a nap in the coolest places they could find. Those who shivered in damp cellar rooms three seasons of the year suddenly had cause to be grateful for the cool, and anyone who had such a room soon found himself with many, many friends. Aunty Minda let the littles spread their blankets in the cellars of their own home and the pawn shop, until temperatures dropped enough to go back to work.

She would have envied Mags his stints at the Sethorites' Temple (which he carefully timed for the hottest parts of the day), except that she had the river, and she wondered how anyone had ever managed a summer this hot before the ropes-and-nets had been thought of.

That was where she was now, arms draped over the rope and letting the current hold her against the net, wearing an enormous hat to keep the exposed parts of her from getting sunburned. It was *just* cold enough to keep her from falling asleep, although she had a shrewd notion that if nothing came up after she left the river, that was exactly what was going to happen to her. She didn't envy poor Lydia *at all.* To be pregnant in this heat . . . *when I do that, I am going to have better timing,* she decided. Then blinked at herself, because she had used the word "when" rather than the "if" she'd been saying to herself all this time.

Well, this is not *the time to think about that,* she reminded herself, and with that, reached over and grabbed the upstream rope, hauling herself hand over hand to the bank. Her spot on the rope was quickly taken by someone else.

Some people brought towels with them; she didn't bother. She knew she'd be bone dry by the time she reached her quarters, and she didn't particularly *care* who saw her in cut-off breeches, a shirt with the sleeves rolled up and tacked in place, and sandals. So what if she was the King's Own? A little slovenliness was hardly going to damage the dignity of the office, especially since she couldn't be told from the Trainees at any distance. And as for the Poison Pen, well, if he was watching her, he was welcome to rail at her for being some sort of harlot all he wanted. In this heat, she very much doubted that any man would look at her with lust. *Unless it's lust for my cooler clothing and my hat.*

Sure enough, by the time she reached the shelter of her own door, her bathing gear was dry enough to fold up and leave on a stool for tomorrow, and her hair dry enough to comb out. She put on a clean shift and braided her hair in a single tail down her back.

And now for the part of the day I have not been looking forward to . . .

The Poison Pen letters had slowed, but not stopped. They were all coming from down in Haven, paid for and dropped off one at a time at post-locations all over the city. They were still printed on that same, coarse, cheap paper, but were enclosed in an ordinary-looking outer sheet and sealed with proper wafers, so it was impossible to pick them out from the regular correspondence. At least no more were being slipped under doors or dropped in through windows, so the vigilance of all of her careful watchers had paid off somewhat.

Amily picked up the first from the pile, frowning. It was directed to one of the Bardic Trainees who had gotten ones like this before— a general wish that she would fail spectacularly and become a disgrace and an embarrassment to her entire family. Since pigs would fly before that happened, the Trainee in question usually found these little notes hilariously funny. The next few were more like that, directed to the Healer, Bardic, and Herald Trainees most likely to graduate to full status some time before the end of summer.

Then came an entire bouquet of stink-blossoms for the lovely Helane, rescued from the fire by her little sister Lirelle and delivered directly to Amily. *:Oh my . . . :* Rolan said, "reading" the letters through her eyes. *:All that is lacking is the obscene pictures illustrating the acts described. Whatever occasioned all of that, pray?:*

:According to the Handmaidens, there are at least five young men who are betrothed—actually betrothed, and not just in some stage of prebetrothal negotiation between two families—who are bringing Helane gifts and flowers. Hence the obscenity. Evidently our ugly friend is convinced that those gifts are payment for a lot more than a smile or permission to sit beside her.:

Rolan considered that for a moment. *:And of course, that explains* *the various punishments in the afterlife they are consigning Helane to. How did she take this?:*

:Bravely, actually. Lirelle says that she's frightened, but determined not to show it, and determined not to allow these filthy things to drive her into seclusion.:

Lirelle had gotten a lot more detailed than that, describing how her sister had burst into tears, then exclaimed, "I've done *nothing* wrong, and I'm not going to act as if I have!"

And Amily supposed that technically, she was correct, although she probably could be doing more to discourage those young men now that she knew they were betrothed to other girls. But on the other hand, *she* wasn't the one who was betrothed; technically it was up to the young men in question to behave themselves. Or at least *tell* Helane about the fact that they were not free. She supposed that for someone who had been living in a rustic environment, with no one marriageable anywhere near enough to engage in pre-courtship, all the games and flirtations of Court must be very exciting. *And betrothals are broken all the time, if the parents decide there's a better offer out there.* She recalled one poor young man several years ago who had barely gotten settled and used to a girl before his father broke the thing off and flung another girl at him. So, really, Helane had done nothing at all wrong except, perhaps to accept the gifts. Then again, it depended on what the gifts were. A pretty ribbon was a serious present to a girl living down in Haven—to someone here at Court, it meant no more than a flower.

At least there were no more alarms in the night . . .

There was another sealed message on the bottom of the stack, and Amily frowned at it. She didn't remember that one being there when she'd left for the river . . . but it was on creamy parchment, and sealed with the Royal Seal, so she relaxed, and opened it.

As you know, there is a yearly reception scheduled just before Midsummer for the heads of all the religious houses in the City, the letter read, in Kyril's distinctive, angular handwriting. *Despite the plague of letters—in fact, in part because of it, I am determined that we will hold this event as we always have.*

Amily felt her jaw drop open a little. Surely the King wasn't serious!

:Oh dear. This seems ill-advised.:

But it appeared that he was. Quite serious.

The Council officially knows nothing about the outrages up on the Hill, they are only officially aware of the vandalized shops down in Haven. I am certain that at least some of them have friends or relations who have been so graced with the Poison Pen letters, and for all I know, some of the female Councilors themselves have gotten letters, but they have said nothing at all to me, and I think it is important that we keep up the appearance that all is normal. It is only a single night, and it is a small gathering by Court standards. None of the Court are invited. So I think we can manage to pull this off without anything untoward occurring. And more to the point, I think we must. We cannot let this unknown madman or madwoman dictate our actions.

In principle, Amily agreed with him. But in practice?

This is going to be a nightmare.

There was more. *Please meet with me at mid-afternoon; we will assemble in my suite and move somewhere private and cool from there. With everyone drowsing away the heat, no one will notice that we are having a private meeting.*

Mid-afternoon—was now. She sighed. So much for that nap.

* * *

"This is going to be a nightmare," Nikolas said, flatly.

He, too, had gotten one of Kyril's notes, and the first thing he had done when he'd read it was to gather up Amily, wake Sedric from his nap, and bring them all together at the King's Suite. From there they moved to a little unlighted cubby of a room in the basement of the Palace, just under the Royal Quarters. Her father had the forethought to bring candles and a striker with him, and set them in two sconces, one on either side of the door.

At least it was cool down here. They were all sitting on storage chests, which was a very peculiar sight to say the least. They were very stout, very heavy storage chests, with formidable locks, and she couldn't help wondering what was in them. *Heirloom weapons, perhaps?*

:Amily, I'll tell you later. For now you do have a meeting.:

Amily wrenched her wandering thoughts back to the conversation.

"I told him, Niko. I told him, myself. This is a *stupid* idea." Sedric crossed his arms over his chest, still a little sleepy-eyed. "Father, I love you, and if I didn't love you so much, I would just wash my hands of this and let you do it."

"It's not a publicly known gathering," the King replied, not at all put out by his son's rebuke. "But I can promise you that if we *don't* have it, some very prominent people in Haven will be wondering why, and from wondering to themselves, they will probably start wondering out loud. Right now, we're managing to keep the Poison Pen quiet. Cancel the reception, and that won't be possible anymore, and sure as I am King, *someone* will link the shop-wrecker with the letters up here. Amily, what is the word down in the city?"

"So far, the vandalized shops are all people know about," Amily said, slowly. "Mags has *all* his children listening for just the sorts of rumors we could expect if more got out, and so far there's nothing. Even what happened to the Sisters of Ardana hasn't been linked to the shops, and absolutely nothing about what happened at the Temple of Betane has gotten bruited about."

"There, you see?" Kyril hit the top of the chest beside his leg. "So far, no one has been putting two and two together. But if we cancel this reception, they might start to. Especially if some of the Councilors start to talk."

"I still think it's insane," Nikolas replied, making no attempt to hide his exasperation. "But I can see I can't talk you out of this. If we hadn't thoroughly vetted all the Palace servants during the Sleepgiver debacle, I'd have insisted that we put them all to the Truth Spell."

"At least that much good came out of that five-year mess," Amily pointed out. "We can at least be certain of the servants and the Guard."

Sedric just threw up his hands. "If you are going to insist on going through with this despite our council, then Amily and Mags and I will have to see what we can do to make sure our guests don't find obscene notes under their napkins."

"Or worse," Nikolas said, grimly. "Obscene notes are the least of my concerns. Jorthun says—" But then he stopped and shook his head. "Never mind. We'll just have to do our best to see that nothing happens."

The reception was the last thing on Amily's mind as she headed for her rooms. It had been another long, long day, and it wasn't over yet. It wasn't only the amorous who were heading out to Companion's Field at night; it was stuffy, humid and hot tonight. There were plenty of Trainees who were having trouble sleeping in the heat, and were taking bedding out to bunk down under the trees where the ground always stayed cool. And how could she blame them? She couldn't exactly confine them to their rooms on the basis of a burned effigy and a bonfire of clothing rescued from the rag-bag. Rolan told her that the Companions had divided them all up, and were keeping a sharp watch on them. Even the foals had their assigned Trainees to watch, and if it meant the Companions were drowsing all day in the heat after being up all night, so be it. Rolan assured her they didn't mind.

She doubted that last statement, but if the Companions were choosing to sacrifice their sleep, she wasn't going to discourage them. It meant one less thing she needed to worry about.

But Mags had gotten in early from down in Haven—there was something going on at the Sethorite Temple tonight that was not open to mere plain worshippers—and she was hoping that nothing was going to interrupt a quiet evening together.

"Amily!" came an urgent call out of the darkness, utterly shattering that hope with the anxiety that was in Lirelle's voice. "I've been looking for you since just after supper!"

Since she, her father, the King, and the Prince had all been stuffed in that storage room together until supper, and after supper she had been consulting with a couple of the Handmaidens, that was not a surprise. "What's wrong, Liri?" she asked, stopping where she was on the garden path, right next to a lantern. She peered into the darkness, but couldn't see anything.

"It's Katlie," Lirelle said, finally coming into the light from one of the lanterns in the garden. Her young face was a mask of worry. "She hasn't come in, she's not in her room, she's not in any of the libraries, and no one's seen her since before lunch! She should be in her room!"

"You're sure?" Amilie asked.

"I've asked *everyone*, even some of the servants. The last anyone saw her was before lunch. Kaven said he saw her then, she looked really pale and sick, and he asked her if she was all right. She said it was just the heat and he shouldn't worry about her and just walked away."

:I'm telling Mags,: Rolan said immediately. *:It could be nothing, but we can't take that chance. She might be ill, and have fainted somewhere on the grounds. Or it could be . . . she's been getting Poison Pen letters and she hasn't been laughing them off.:*

That was exactly what Amily was afraid of. *:Tell everyone,:* she corrected. *:Tell Mags to coordinate searchers. I'm going to go check the Gate Guard, in case she decided to run away, or go down into Haven, or something. Maybe someone invited her to stay the night in a cooler room.:* "Lirelle, come with me, please," she said aloud. "I may need you to introduce me to your fellow Blues."

She half-ran to the nearest Gate; Lirelle sprinted along beside her. By the time they reached the official Gate to the Palace, Rolan thundered up to join them, his mere presence adding importance to their questions. The Guard looked a little startled to see them. "Sir, have you seen Katlie Gardener?" she asked as Rolan pawed the ground a little, his silver hooves shining in the lantern-light. "Did she go down into Haven?" *Please let her have gone down with friends, maybe someone from one of the Orders . . .* With so many of the religious houses being constructed entirely of stone, like the Sethorite Temple, they were ever so much cooler, and if Katlie hadn't been feeling well, perhaps someone had invited her down to sleep overnight where she would be more comfortable.

The Guard checked his book—*thank the gods we started these checks before this!*—and shook his head with regret. "She's not in my book. Perhaps she went out by one of the other three gates?" There was a postern gate usually used only by Heralds, plus a pair of gates big enough to allow in delivery wagons, and if Katlie had left to go anywhere but the manors on the Hill one of those would have been more likely for her to take. Amily nodded, put both hands on Rolan's back, and vaulted herself up into place. She held out her hand to Lirelle, who looked at it as if she had no idea what it was.

"Put your foot on mine, take my hand, and I'll pull you up behind," she said trying not to show any impatience. "I don't want to have to come looking for you after I check the gates."

Lirelle did as she had been told, and in a moment Amily had her perched securely behind. "Put both your arms around my waist and hang on," she ordered, and the second Lirelle was secure, Rolan launched himself toward the postern gate, which was the nearest. They pounded through the patches of light defined by lanterns amid the darkness, and Amily cursed herself for not getting to the Blues sooner.

Her heart was already sinking, and it just went lower and lower as checking the other three gates gave the same result. With one small difference. The Guard at the third gate said that he often saw her out at night, walking about alone. "She tried to leave from here two nights ago, and I thought she just looked . . . wrong, Herald. Strained.

Nervy. So I lied, and told her no one her age was allowed off the grounds after dark without leave from a teacher. Did I do right?"

"I think you must have," Amily told him. *And we'll have to make that a rule now, dammit.* Without prompting, Rolan turned back toward the Palace. As soon as she got within sight of Healer's Collegium, it was clear Mags had already been working. There was a crowd of people milling about in a group in the herb garden, most of them with torches. Mags and Dallen as well as several other Heralds were with them. She and Rolan galloped up to them, but before she could ask anything, one of the Handmaidens, Joya, held out a sheaf of far-too-familiar papers to her, wearing a grim expression. "I searched her room on Mags' orders," Joya said, as Amily slid off Rolan and accepted them. "And I found these."

"You're going to fail and disgrace your family." "You deserve to fail, and the gods will see to it." "How dare you think you can be as good as a boy?" The letters were all short, and all abusive. *"You stole the place that should have gone to a smart young man."* Perhaps those had not affected her as much as the Poison Pen had wanted, because there were only a few in that vein.

But he clearly found a theme that produced the reaction he wanted. *"You're ugly, fat, and horrible, no wonder you are here, no man would have you."* There were many, many like that, asking her if she was really a boy pretending to be a girl, if her parents had sent her away because they couldn't bear to look at her, and enumerating in detail everything that was physically "wrong" with her. *"You can't be a proper woman and you can't do what a man can do, give it all up, fat girl."*

Amily felt sick, but there was worse to come. Because now that he had Katlie's attention, he had her exactly where he wanted her.

"You should throw yourself off a tower, and rid the world of a useless blob." "Kill yourself so no one ever has to look at your fat face again." "Take poison, and give someone who deserves it a chance."

Wordlessly, she passed the letters to Lirelle, who read them with horror, as she turned back to Mags. "Mags, can you tell how long she's been getting these . . . things?" she asked.

"Prolly since the letters started," he said. "An' I don't think they've let up—"

"But why didn't she *tell* us?" Lirelle wailed, looking as if she felt she was somehow personally responsible. "Why didn't she show them to us after you Heralds told us all about them?"

"Because," Joya replied, her dark eyes clouded with thought—or memory. "When you are being endlessly persecuted and bullied, that is the last thing you want to do. At least, that's how some people react. She probably thought it was one of you, didn't know who to trust, and like a wounded wild animal, she was afraid to show her wounds because she feared you would all turn on her."

"But—" Lirelle said, anguished. "We'd never—"

Mags impulsively reached out and put his arm around her to give her a quick hug. "It takes a real strong mind, an' someone who's perfectly sure of themselves t' hold out against that kinda bullying," he said. "Now, enough of that. Spread out, people; there's enough of us to search the grounds, an' the Companions have got the Field. Go in groups of two or three, but not more. We don't wanta scare her, in case all she's done was go for a walk. Tell 'er—" His brow crinkled as he tried to think of something.

"I know!" Amily said. "Tell her that Lirelle is missing and we're looking for her. Lirelle, if we find her, your story is that you went looking for a Healer for a headache potion, took it and fell asleep in the examination room. Everyone, go!"

People quickly sorted themselves in groups of two and three, and dispersed. "That's everybody sensible I want out lookin'," Mags said to her. "Some last-year Trainees, all the Heralds, an' some of the steadier servants. Should we be lookin' too?"

"No," Amily told him. "Someone needs to be here. We're central to everything. And . . ." She felt her mouth go dry. "I think we should go get a Healer. Just in case."

"Aight," Mags agreed. "I'll git one."

Amily looked like a ghost. Beside her, the girl Lirelle looked like another. Mags sympathized; Amily had told the poor girl to keep an eye on this Katlie, and now she felt as if she had failed both Amily and her fellow student.

He'd had a horrible feeling ever since he'd heard about this; was *this* what Lord Jorthun had been worrying about? *:Among other possibilities, I'm sure,:* Dallen replied grimly, as Mags kept his shields very tenuous, and "listened" to all the searchers out there. Amily was right. Of all of the people up here on the Hill, he, with his impressive Gift of Mindspeech, was the best suited to keep track of all the searchers, human and Companion alike, and coordinate . . . whatever needed to be coordinated.

But it seemed utterly wrong to just be standing here in the dark garden, waiting and doing nothing.

:Is anyone down by the River-Gate?: he broadcast to Heralds, Trainees, and Companions.

:I am,: came the immediate reply. *:Companion Seraf. The River-Gate was open last I saw, and I think the Guard forgot to close it again. People were rowing about earlier, and wanted to go down to Haven by way of the rapids.:*

The River-Gate was not a "gate" as such; it was a sort of portcullis in the arched opening that let the river flow through the wall about the Palace. Some of the more daring boaters liked "shooting the rapids," and in a boat, it really wasn't all that hazardous by day. By night . . . that was another story. It probably shouldn't have been left open this late—

But Mags' thoughts were shattered by a sharp mental cry.

:I see her!: called Seraf. Then came an anguished mental cry. *:No! No! She's thrown herself in the water! I'm going after her!:*

Mags and Dallen didn't hesitate and neither did the Healer standing beside them. The second he offered his hand to the Healer, the man was up behind and clinging on for dear life as Dallen leapt into action. As images came from Seraf, they headed for the postern-gate at top speed, Dallen as sure-footed in the darkness as if it was broad daylight.

Seraf had managed to catch the girl's collar in her teeth and was holding Katlie's head up out of the churning water with every iota of her strength. But they were out past the walls now, and down into the tumbling rapids that sent the river swiftly down into Haven, and the poor Companion wasn't even trying to fight the current, when it was all she could do to keep Katlie from drowning and herself off the rocks. What wasn't hazardous in a shallow boat was punishing to the flesh and blood body of the Companion. All Mags was getting were flashes of foaming water, glimpses of the bank, and the terrible strain of keeping the girl's head from going under.

At least this time it's not the dead of winter. . . .

They shot out the postern-gate and pounded for the river. Mags hardly noticed the Healer's desperate grasp on his waist as he strained his ears for the sound of running water, and his eyes for a flash of white ahead.

There! There was the river!

They surged forward, and now Mags had that peculiar . . . mental snap that he had learned from his contact with the Sleepgivers and his cousin's mind. *Everything* except the task at hand receded into the depths of his thoughts; emotion was gone, replace by a cool calculation that took in every bit of information and made constantly changing plans based on what he saw. Thank the gods, there was a path along the riverbank that allowed Dallen to stretch himself out and run as fast as ever he had in all his life. And there— ahead in the water, there was that flash of white!

The water was not as fast as Dallen; they caught up to the Companion Seraf, then passed her. Getting ahead of the pair until Mags thought they'd come to the right spot to intercept, they stopped just long enough to drop the Healer on the bank before Dallen turned on his heels and plunged them both into the churning, cold water.

:Hurry . . . : That was all Seraf could manage; Mags felt her fading strength and desperation in her Mindvoice.

But he and Dallen were fresh . . . and they'd done this before.

:There they are!: They crossed in front of Seraf; as the mare's chest and shoulder ran into them, Mags scooped the unconscious girl up by the waist and pulled her up in front of him, draping her over his shoulder. Dallen turned in front of the mare. *:Grab my tail!:* he

ordered, and Seraf reached out, exhausted, closing her teeth on the hair, just missing the bone.

Now it was all on Dallen; Mags hung on to the saddle and the girl, grimly, while Dallen worked with the current to get to the bank, the Healer keeping pace with them on foot. And by this time, they were down in Haven proper, and people had begun to notice the Healer running along the bank, and then the unusual objects in the water. Soon there was an entire crowd running along with the Healer, cheering them on.

Then one of them had the wit to run downstream and throw in a rope.

Dallen's teeth closed on it as they passed, Mags let go of the saddle long enough to get the end and get three turns of it around the pommel, and with a team of townsfolk hauling, they got the last few armlengths to the bank.

Then stumbling up the bank, Seraf clinging on to Dallen's tail for dear life. Flashes of torch and lantern light. Hands everywhere, grabbing the saddle, the girth, even his legs, pulling. Hands reaching for Seraf, hands tangled in her mane, hauling her up by anything they could get hold of.

Then they were up the bank, and there were more hands guiding both Companions to get to the safety of the road. Light, lots of it, and people bringing blankets and torches and brandy. The Healer and two helpers took Katlie from Mags; he slid off of Dallen's saddle, as the Healer took her aside and got to work on her. People closed around, holding lanterns so the Healer could see, but blocking Mags' view.

And a moment later, he heard the sound he had feared he

wouldn't—Katlie coughing and gasping, and then throwing up all the river water she'd swallowed.

And *now* it hit him, the insanity of what he'd done, the chill from the river. He started shivering, then shaking uncontrollably, as much in reaction and exhaustion as from cold. The hot night air, that had been so oppressive, felt like a welcome embrace.

Now it was the turn of Mags and Dallen and Seraf to be surrounded, swathed in blankets, and pelted with questions. He managed to gather his wits. He had to be careful what he said. Truth, but not too much; truth was easier to keep straight than a lie.

"Student at the Collegium," he said, in answer to the question of who she was. "Poor girl hasn't been sleeping well, and we think she went for a walk along the river alone, hoping to cool off."

"Half the town's been a-doin' that," someone observed with sympathy. "Wha' happen?"

"I don't know for certain," he said truthfully, then accepted a brandy and downed it. "But I imagine she forgot how swift the current is up there, and perhaps went to bathe her head or her feet. All it takes is one little slip—" He shook his head. "You know, you tell younglings that it's dangerous, and they nod their heads and—"

"And ye might as well be talkin' t' th' air," replied a knowing voice out of the crowd. "I tell me damn boy all th' time, an' 'e lissens t'me about as much as if I was speakin' Karsite."

Mags took a long, deep breath, and looked around at the faces surrounding him, letting his shields down a little. It appeared this was going well, friendly, concerned faces, friendly, concerned thoughts. The Poison Pen wasn't among them. He didn't know whether to be glad of that or annoyed. "Anyway, it was near

Companion's Field, and Seraf here saw her go in. If it hadn't been for *her*, we'd be pulling a body out of the river, and that's a fact." On the one hand . . . if the Poison Pen had been lurking, watching, he'd have been able to identify the bastard. By mental "picture," at least. On the other hand . . . what if Jorthun was right, and the bastard was Gifted? *I don't have the strength to get into a mental wrestling match right now.*

His little speech was enough to distract the crowd, who surrounded Seraf, offering her bread, pears, brandy, anything they could think of. The quicker-witted, at least those who knew something of horses, began giving her a brisk rub-down with some of those blankets. Seraf wearily accepted a pear, then another, and began to revive. Dallen roused himself to beg and was fed as well.

The sounds from where the Healer was working on Katlie were encouraging enough that Mags sagged against Dallen's side, all the energy that fear and nerves had given him running out of him. Dallen let his head droop with weariness . . . but he was not too weary to refuse those juicy pears people kept giving him and Seraf.

The crowd's curiosity had been momentarily assuaged, and they stopped pelting him with questions and started passing what he had told them to the newcomers who were arriving, and gaining a little in importance as they did so. Mags let them do his work for him, as the uniform dried on his back and he started to feel all the aches and strains of the rescue.

His mind just went blank for a little while, as all the things that *might* have gone wrong washed over him, and he dealt with the aftermath. And then, after what seemed like a very, very long time, the rescue party from the Collegia arrived.

The crowd parted to let them in, and Mags could finally see how the girl was doing. Katlie was lying on a blanket, head propped up on another, folded blanket, looking a little like a half-drowned mouse. The Healer had outdone himself. Katlie was conscious and dazed, and Mags suspected he was making sure she *stayed* dazed so she didn't say anything. The rescue party had brought a small cart with them; while the onlookers carefully lit them up with their lanterns, the rescuers loaded the girl and her Healer up, and off they clattered, back up the Hill, with some of the party lighting the way ahead.

Mags looked over at Seraf. *:Got enough strength back to make it, or d'ye want us t'stay with ye until ye do?:*

Seraf raised her head, her mane and forelock still wet and dripping a little. *:I think I can, if you'll come with me.:*

Mags got the feeling she didn't mean *him*.

His guess was confirmed when she continued, *:I hope I didn't damage your tail, Dallen.:*

:It's only hair,: Dallen said gallantly. *:It will grow back. I'd have sacrificed my whole tail to help you.:*

"Welp," Mags said aloud. "I think I'm gonna catch that cart, if you two'll be all right."

:We'll be fine,: Dallen replied. But he was looking at Seraf as he said it.

Mags chuckled wearily, and trudged after the cart.

"What a night," Amily said, wearily, helping Mags out of his uniform. "I think we can save our uniforms, but those boots are a lost cause. And I can't believe it's not even midnight yet."

They had gone straight to their room, with Mags politely brushing off any congratulations. Morning was going to come too soon, and they were both exhausted, him physically, her emotionally.

"It's not?" he replied in surprise. He stripped out of his breeches and tossed them on the pile of clothing that was *definitely* going to need some attention. "I'd'a thought it was near dawn. Gimme them breeches, eh?"

She handed him the soft breeches he slept in, and stripped down herself, pulling on her sleep shift. She ached as if she had been beaten, and knew he must be feeling even worse. The two of them dropped into the bed and she exerted herself just enough to blow out the candle before rolling over to kiss him.

"I managed to round up everyone and convinced them that Katlie had told you and the Healer that she'd just gone out for a walk to clear her head, bent over the water to bathe her face, slipped and fell in," she said into the darkness. "That story was genius."

"Thanks." He chuckled a little. "Lirelle think the same thing?"

"No, I told her the truth." She had known she was going to need at least one ally who was also a friend of the girl, and had bet that Lirelle would rise to the occasion. She had. "As soon as Katlie is out of the Healers' hands, Lirelle is going to be right with her until we figure out what to do with her. . . ." She bit her lip. "Mags, what *are* we going to do with her?"

"Nothin' fer now," he said, pulling her into his arms, and cradling her. "Right now, we're gonna sleep."

13

Amily fumbled for her lightweight shirt, and pulled it on over her head. It was still dark outside. She was getting a little tired of being awakened at dawn. *Was it only a few weeks ago that I actually resented Father taking over so much of my place as King's Own?* Now all Amily could feel was gratitude. If it had not been for her father's help this morning . . .

I don't remember things being this frantic when he was King's Own . . . at this rate I'm going to need three of me.

Mags had jolted awake the moment she moved this morning, and she had moved in response to a light tapping on the inner door to their rooms. It had been her father, with the gray light of dawn barely lightening the sky above the trees of Companion's Field. She and Mags had taken turns telling him what had happened last night, and when he was certain he had all the details—and she had given him that stack of vile letters—he had gone off to give the

King and the Prince a better report than Mags had been able to do by Mindspeech last night. "I'll play King's Own this morning, Amily," he said, before she could even ask. "You can serve better figuring out what to do with that poor child. I haven't a clue."

Then he'd kissed her on the cheek, and gone, leaving her awash with relief. And scrambling for her clothes.

"I've got cold fruit pocket pies, and I can make tea if you want to have breakfast here," she said to Mags, as he rummaged for a uniform that wasn't stained green with river-weeds and river-water.

"That would be excellent," he replied, having found trews, shirt, and tunic, and now looking for replacements for his ruined boots.

She hurried into the rest of one of her "working" uniforms, and put a kettle on over the little fire, and unlocked the sealed box where they kept food secure from insects and vermin. There were four pies there, more than enough to hold both of them over until they could get something more substantial.

The sun was just barely up when they took the seldom-used inner door of their rooms into Healer's Collegium and the House of Healing, and went in search of Katlie Gardener.

That is, Amily was *going* to search, but Mags headed straight down the hall, and Amily followed, wishing enviously that she had a *useful* form of Mindspeech. Rolan was silent this morning. Then again, Rolan might still be asleep. Mags, however, could look for Katlie's familiar mind and follow it to where she was. They ended up outside a door in a white-painted, white-tiled corridor lined with doors spaced so closely together that it was obvious the rooms were very small. Then again, how big did they have to be to house a single patient?

Mags tapped on the door, and opened it before anyone could answer. Amily followed him in.

There was a bed, little bedside table, and a single chair. The chair actually looked more comfortable than the bed, which was a good thing, since Lirelle was curled up asleep in it.

Katlie's pale, round face stared at them from the bed. It looked as if she had not gotten much sleep last night; there were huge, dark rings under her bloodshot eyes. "I—I am sorry—" she began, in a voice hoarse from crying, coughing, or both.

"Hush," Amily said, sitting down on the end of the bed. "The only thing we are annoyed with you about is that you didn't *say* something about those horrid letters after we told all of you that other people were getting them. If you had, we'd have made sure you didn't get any more, and we'd have made sure you knew that there is absolutely nothing in them that is even remotely true and everyone here knows that except, it seems, you. Katlie, *you* are the victim here, and the only person we are angry with is the vile beast that was persecuting you."

The poor girl burst into tears, which woke up Lirelle, who fumbled her way to her friend and began awkwardly patting her back. She looked about as awkward as Amily felt, not knowing quite what to do, or what to say, and helplessly trying to get her to drink a glass of water.

Between the two of them, they got Katlie calmed down again, although Amily had the feeling she'd break out in weeping again at the least provocation. And she had *no* idea what she was going to do with the girl . . .

She turned toward the door, to consult with Mags, only to discover that Mags was gone. *Bother* . . . she thought with exasperation.

It appeared that while she and Lirelle were doing their best to calm and comfort Katlie, Mags had slipped out. Amily didn't blame him, but . . . it seemed unfair for him to just *leave* her here like this.

Fortunately, right after they got Katlie calmed down again, one of the Healers came in to check on her.

"Ah, Herald," the Healer said, quite as if she expected strange people to be in one of her patients' rooms at odd hours. "If you'll move off the bed—thank you," she appended, as Amily hastily got out of the way.

But this seemed like a good time to get Lirelle out of there. *I know she feels guilty about not stopping Katlie, but there's no point having her falling asleep on her feet.* "You go get some sleep," Amily told Lirelle—then had an afterthought. "Wait a moment," she added, and rummaged in her belt pouch for a pencil and a bit of paper. She scribbled a note to Lady Tyria about how Lirelle had been very helpful all night, and she very much appreciated her calm and good sense. "Here, give this to your lady-mother. I don't want you in trouble."

"Oh, I won't be," Lirelle replied, but took it anyway. "Mother has a rule about everyone telling people where they are going. I told her my friend was missing and I was going to be with you before I ran out to look for you. Then after we all got back, I went back to our rooms. She was still awake, so I made sure it was all right to stay with Katlie."

Out of the corner of her eye, Amily saw Katlie's face suddenly suffused with surprise and gratitude to hear herself called Lirelle's friend. But at the moment, Amily was feeling no little amount of gratitude herself. "You—" she said, pointing a finger "—are entirely too sensible for your age. You and I are going to have a very long talk when I am done with Katlie. Also . . ." she scribbled another note ". . . give this to whichever Dean is in charge of you, I'm excusing you from classes today."

"Oh thank the gods," Lirelle groaned, finally sounding like a normal girl. "I don't think I could add two numbers together and get the same answer twice right now."

"Deliver your notes. Go to bed. Then to the river when it gets hot if you're too warm to sleep. Then back to bed until dinner. You and I are having dinner together; I'll come to the suite to fetch you." Amily stated this in tones that would allow no argument, but it didn't look as if Lirelle was inclined to give her one. She pocketed the two notes and slipped out the door while the Healer was still performing a complicated series of checks on Katlie.

"You are an extremely lucky girl, young lady," the Healer said, finally, and sighed as Katlie cringed. "I am not going to berate you. I understand exactly why you felt as you did. But I *am* going to ask you to start believing in what real people, not anonymous bullies, are saying to you and about you. You owe the Healers, Herald Mags, Companions Dallen and Seraf, and your friend Lirelle that much. Understood?"

"Yes'm," Katlie whispered.

"All right then. I, or someone else, will be back later with your breakfast. We expect you to eat it." The Healer got up and left, but not without a significant glance at Amily.

Amily took the chair that Lirelle had vacated, and sat down in it. *Great, I'm supposed to start . . . making her feel better. And I have no idea how to do that. I'm a Herald, not a Mind-Healer!* "Let's start with something simple," she said, finally. "Where are you from?"

"You'd not know it," Katlie whispered, shrinking into herself visibly.

Amily smiled, thinking of all those maps she had memorized. "Try me."

Bit by bit, she pried Katlie's story out of her. Her father and mother were smallholders, but their farm was in an area of poor soil, where every vegetable had to be coaxed to grow. She was the eldest of five living children—with the implication that several more children had died in infancy. She had been *no* good at farming, hopeless at spinning, knitting, sewing, or weaving, could not tell one plant from another, did not have enough beauty to make a good marriage without some sort of useful village talents, and until the village schoolmistress—who was a Priestess of Rimon—had discovered a gift for mathematics and mechanics in her, her parents had despaired, for they had no idea what they were going to do with her.

She had thought she might—do something at the Temple of Rimon. Learn some useful skill, something practical, like building, or repairing things. To her shock, she had been sent to Haven as a King's Scholar, the first one *anyone* had ever heard of in all of the half dozen villages she was familiar with. Her parents were proud, but desperate. It was very clear to Amily as the girl spoke that they had filled her with the fear of failure even as they praised her and sent her on her way.

". . . and every time I gots a letter, it felt like me brain was goin' to pieces," she said, clearly about to burst into tears again. "The letters'd say I'm goin' ravin' mad, an' I thunk it was so. An'—I cain't. I cain't fail. I druther die! I—"

Amily seized both her hands, and gave them a little shake. "You are *not* going to fail!" she replied, trying to sound firm, but not scolding. "There is nothing wrong with your brain, and your teachers have all told me what a fine scholar you are." That was a little bit of a fib; Amily hadn't actually spoken to the girl's teachers yet, but it was pretty obvious that this was a young creature that would keep throwing herself at a fence until she got over it, so she probably *was* doing well. "There is a vicious bully out there somewhere," she continued, waving her free hand vaguely at the door. "We don't know who he is, or where he is, but he gets great pleasure by hiding in shadows and tormenting people. He works at them until he finds their weak spot, and then he *jabs* and *jabs* and *jabs* at it until they bleed. He found yours, and that is what he did."

She went on in that vein for quite some time, trying to convince the girl, and feeling as if she was beating her head against a wall. And then came a savior.

The door opened without anyone knocking, and there was one of the Sisters of Betane of the Ax standing there in her full armed and tabarded glory. "Forgive my interruptin', Herald," the young woman said, looking every inch the Holy Warrior. "But that's exactly what this poisonous serpent does, all right."

Amily glanced over at Katlie, who was staring at the Sister with nothing less than instant hero-worship in her eyes. The Sister smiled. "I'm Acolyte Asha, and I can see you recognize my tabard, don't you?"

"You're from th' Temple of Betane!" Katlie breathed. "Yer what fought off them raiders whut tried t' overrun us twa yearn agone!"

"So we are. Or at least, another of our Temple Sisterhoods

is responsible for fighting for you." Now the Sister—or rather Acolyte—lowered herself down to sit on the foot of Katlie's bed. Gingerly, and with much creaking of leather armor. "And my Prioress sent me here to talk to you the instant she heard about what sad straits you are in."

"Me? Why?" Katlie's eyes had gone very round indeed. And Amily was just as interested to hear the reason this warrior had turned up as Katlie was. . . .

"Several reasons. First—" Asha held up one finger. "—you've been made a victim of the same serpent that tried to desecrate our Temple here in Haven, and for that reason, the Prioress has taken an interest in you. Second, we're sibling-sects with the Temples of Rimon, and your Priestess would want us to look out for you. And third, we want to take you under our wing for a bit, where that sick . . ." Asha struggled with her words, then got her anger under control. ". . . sick, cowardly bully will not dare come at you again. And there's a fourth." Now she eyed Katlie with a raised brow. "Young lady, you've been half-starved on little but bread and porridge most of your life, your health was poor because of it to begin with, and now you spend entirely too much time indoors bent over books."

Katlie blinked. "But—"

"Ah-ah! But me no buts," Asha interrupted. "You will ruin that fine mind if you don't also make your body strong. So you're coming with me as soon as the Healers give you leave. The books will still be here when you get back to them. We'll put pink in those cheeks, and lean muscles in those arms and legs, and you can come back in the fall fit to tackle your studies instead of feeling half-sick and always tired. Because you *do*, don't you?"

Katlie's mouth had fallen open at that. "Yes—but—how did you—"

"Pish, it's written in the rings under your eyes, your ashy skin, and the trembling of your fingers," Asha said, as if it were of no matter at all. "And don't you worry about your parents. You're *still* a King's Scholar. You'll just be getting a different set of lessons for a while. If they send you messages, you'll get them. If they ask after you, the Heralds will tell them you're making them proud." Asha stood up. "Understood?"

"Yes'm," Katlie said obediently. But there was relief there. Perhaps the relief that someone *else* was going to take charge of her, and tell her what to do for a while? *Perhaps we assume too much of the Blues; assume they are as self-reliant as adults. I'd better talk to the Deans about this.*

"Now, are you safe for the Herald and me to leave by yourself? Eat a good breakfast? Not do yourself any more mischief?" Asha demanded. "Promise me you'll do as the Healer tells you, and wait for me to come fetch you."

Katlie nodded. "Promise, on Rimon's Tree," she said, her pinched, round face looking very earnest.

Asha ruffled her dark hair. "Good enough for me. I'm thinking the Healers will let you go tomorrow. I'll make all the arrangements and I'll see you in the morning." Now Asha looked at Amily. "Care to come with me, King's Own?"

"Certainly," Amily replied, so relieved to be rid of this problem for which she had no solution, she'd have swum the river uphill if Asha had asked her to. The Acolyte went out the door first, and held it for Amily.

Asha looked back at Katlie just before she closed it. "You remember that promise now," she said with a smile.

"Yes'm," Katlie said obediently.

The door closed, and Asha motioned for Amily to remain quiet as they started back down the hall. Once they were well out of Katlie's hearing, even if she'd had the ears of an owl, Asha winked. "Herald Mags sent me," she said, "Or rather, it went a little like this. Mags headed for our Priory, and meanwhile Rolan was lurking outside Katlie's window and telling him everything that was going on in there with you and the other young wench. So by the time he and Dallen got down to our place, he knew all about the girl; he and the Prioress palavered, I got sent for, and he told me what I was to do on the way up."

:I'm sorry I didn't tell you sooner,: Rolan said contritely. *:But I was rather busy being an accurate relay.:*

For a moment, Amily was angry. They could have *said* something—couldn't they?

But maybe not. When she used her particular form of Mindspeech, she had to lie flat in a bed or supported in a chair and not do anything. Mags had been riding furiously down into Haven—he had to have been to have gotten down there and back so quickly—and maybe he just couldn't juggle listening to Rolan *and* riding like that *and* filling her in at the same time.

I'm tired, I'm already hot and it's just past breakfast, I'm hungry again, and I'm frustrated and I really need to watch my temper.

"How much of what you told her was true?" Amily asked instead, holding the door at the end of the hall open for her. It was one of the ones that came out into the herb garden.

"Thankee. Most of it. The only shading of truth is that Herald Mags came directly to us and asked for help, rather than the Prioress volunteering it." They both went out into the sun-drenched garden, and Amily sighed at the heat. "You'll have to ask him yourself why he immediately thought of us, but I'm glad he did." She pointed. "There he is now, waiting to take me back down."

Amily caught sight of him, still on Dallen, waiting in the shade. "I have an idea. I'm starving. I know he's starving. I bet you're starving. Let's beg some breakfast and take it somewhere cool to eat."

"I do like the way you Heralds think," Asha responded, as Rolan ambled up to join them.

Cold fruit juice, a basket of fruit, cheese, fresh bread, and butter made a more than adequate second breakfast. They took it to the grotto that Amily, Mags, Lena, and Bear used to share back when they were all Trainees. It was not just cooler than the air in the garden, it was actually comfortably cool there, and at this time of the morning there was no one using it. They spread their bounty out on the moss, and set to.

"How did you manage to think—" Amily began, looking at Mags.

"I didn't. Dallen did. He said *what that girl needs is a spine, and mebbe there's one for her at the Temple of Betane*. And I didn' even have t'think twice 'bout it." Mags shoved half a slice of buttered bread into his mouth. "For once the damn horse volunteered somethin' useful."

From outside the grotto there came an indignant snort.

"It's a good plan," Asha agrees. "We'll put her with our Novices, but keep the exercises simple and easy until she builds up some strength. And—believe it or not, we may be a martial order, but we don't neglect the mind. What is it she's here for?"

"Math. Artificing. That's as much as I know," said Amily. "I gather she's something fairly special along those lines."

Asha ate a plum, neatly, with a care for the juice. "Hrrm. Not something we meddle in, usually, but I'll talk to the Prioress about it. We'll find something." Then she got a sudden look of inspiration on her face. "Oh, wait, I know! Maps. Maps and navigation. Mapping requires all manner of calculations, and doing dead reckoning by sun and stars is an art form." Her face cleared. "That'll keep her busy enough until we can send her back up here again. And who knows, it may come in useful for her at some point."

Amily pinched the bridge of her nose, trying to stave off a headache. "I wish it was as easy to figure out who this vile letter-writing creature is. I'm not sure it will be safe to bring her back here until we have."

"I wouldn't worry about that," Asha replied with a dry laugh. "When we're done installing that spine, if she gets another letter, she'll either laugh it off or use it for target practice."

By noon, it was almost unbearably hot, and to cap it all off, there was a storm threatening. People were snapping at each other; the only reason fistfights didn't break out a time or two was probably because it was too hot to fight.

Those who had no reason to fight with each other were indulging in gossip that was actually malicious, and a lot of it centered around the water-rescue. Even those who knew nothing much about last night's near-tragedy knew that *something* in the way of an accident had happened last night, and they were perfectly happy to make up whatever gained them a lot of attention. Rumors were flying all over the Hill; even being told that it was nothing more salacious than a Blue student falling into the river didn't stop people from concocting the most ridiculous stories.

Or rather, they were stories that in other circumstances would have been taken as ridiculous, but with people sniping at each other, they became one more weapon in the ongoing gossip-battles.

Stories that one unspecified young lady, outraged over the fact that her betrothed was paying too much attention to another unspecified young lady (but everyone knew Helane was the one meant) had gotten into a hair-pulling fight on the riverbank, and one or the other had gone in and had to be rescued. Or stories that an *older* lady, having grown tired of her husband's philandering ways, had confronted him and been pushed in.

These, of course, were piled on top of stories that had nothing whatsoever to do with what happened last night, just the usual vicious gossip that seemed to be echoing the Poison Pen. It was as if the horrible things in those letters had taken on a life of their own and were infecting everyone at Court.

Helane put on her prettiest gown and showed herself all over the Palace and grounds to shame those who were saying she was the one in the House of Healing, and to put the lie to the story she had been in an undignified fight. Mags thought all the better of her for that.

Still, by suppertime, everyone was on edge, and Mags had to reinforce his shields just to keep all the anger-edged thoughts from scratching their way in to him. He was probably much too silent during dinner, and he could tell that Amily thought he was being quiet because of something she'd done—or hadn't done—and *she* wanted to snap at him for it and he wanted to snap at her that he was just hot and tired and sick and tired of this Poison Pen business. But with every passing moment, it was getting harder and harder to keep from lashing out at something or someone, and she was the nearest. He had to keep batting down angry thoughts. They both managed to stop themselves from having an outright fight right there in the Dining Hall, and walked back to their quarters in complete silence.

Mags was seething. At Amily, and at himself. He *should* have been able to figure out more by now! But in order to do that, he'd have to use Mindspeech in a way he didn't feel was right.

Worse than that, if people found out about what he'd done, they'd never trust a Herald with Mindspeech ever again.

As for Amily, he was pretty sure Amily was wondering why he hadn't done anything by now, and blamed him for the fact this had gone on so long that poor Katlie had almost killed herself. And that was *totally* unfair. She should know better, since her father was King's Own *and* the King's spy! *I'll bet* he *never went poking around in random peoples' heads because he could!*

He could just feel the irrational anger building up in him, like it had back when he was still a Trainee and Amily wasn't able to walk and he still hadn't known where the Sleepgivers were coming from or why they wanted him or even their name. It felt as if he had hot coals lodged in his gut. If it hadn't been threatening to storm, he might have been able to throw himself into the river to swim, or race Dallen around the Kirball field, but it was, and that would be stupid and he just . . . wanted . . . something . . . to hit . . .

He was all wrapped up in his thoughts when, half way back to their rooms, the storm didn't just break overhead, it *shattered*.

A bolt of lightning arced down and literally exploded a tree just inside the fence of Companion's Field, and the thunder that accompanied it deafened him for a moment. Then the sky opened up and rain pounded down on them. Not like "rain" at all, like standing under a waterfall.

Without even thinking about it, they grabbed for each others' hands, and ran as best they could the remaining distance to their rooms. He got his hand on the door to the greenhouse by virtue of longer reach; he wrenched it open, and they both tumbled inside, panting, ending up sitting on the floor of the greenhouse, staring out at a downpour so heavy he couldn't see more than an arm's-length past the door. Anything further than that was just vague blurs.

They sat there, wordlessly, until Mags could finally hear again. He cleared his throat. "Got my ears back. You?"

She nodded. Slowly they both got to their feet and went inside, shivering, because the temperature had not just dropped, it had plummeted.

"I think I might have to build up the fire," Amily said, and laughed. "And for the second night in a row, you're a wet mess."

"So are you," he replied, with a slow smile. "Think we can save our boots this time?"

"Probably." She shivered. "I want dry things. And as long as this is coming down, there's going to be nothing moving outside."

They got changed into their night-clothes, and rather than

building up the fire, just got a blanket and bundled together in bed to watch the storm through the bedroom window. It showed no signs of tapering off any time soon. All the tension between them seemed to have evaporated with that lightning-strike. Mags wasn't sure how long it was after it got dark that he found himself falling asleep, but after the last two days . . . *I've earned it* . . . And that was his last thought until morning.

The morning dawned bright and fresh and blessedly cool. Since for once they had gotten to sleep *early*, and since for once there had been no tearing emergencies to wake them in the middle of the night, they woke up naturally, about dawn. Mags lay quietly, listening to birds caroling, reveling in the fact that he wasn't covered in sweat.

:Temper back under control?: Dallen asked.

:That why you didn't nag at me last night, nag?: he replied, feeling much more like himself.

:You'd have needed stronger shields than you have to keep out all the garbage flying through the mental air last night,: Dallen replied. *:You're not an empath, but when rage and hate are that strong all around you, something's going to get through. It was bad enough before the storm broke that the Healers and Heralds barricaded themselves together in their Collegia and put up group shields. There is a lot of ill-will up here right now, and all I can say is it's a good thing it's only affecting the Court. And mostly only affecting women. Women don't generally duel each other.:*

:Might be better if they did,: he replied. *:Let out some of that crazy if they poked each other.:*

"Talking to Dallen?" Amily asked. "Rolan and I have an idea."

"And what idea'd that be?" he said, rolling over on his side to look into her face.

"We haven't checked on the Sisters of Ardana since they got vandalized, and I want to see if they've had any more trouble down there. If we get breakfast in a hurry, we'll be in time for their open services, and I've never been." She wrinkled her nose as he made a face. "What? I feel like I need a nice big dose of virtue to wash out all the dreck from last night."

"Then we'll go," he said, glad enough to give in to her whim to make up for all the nasty thoughts he'd had about her last night.

The ride down was . . . idyllic, was the only word that seemed to fit. The torrential rain had washed everything clean, the road was clear of even a hint of debris. There was that exploded tree in Companion's Field, of course, and probably more downed trees and limbs, but out here there was no sign of last night's destruction. Haven was awake, people eager to get out and *do* things while the air was cool after the heat and lethargy of the last sennight or more. They actually caught up with and overtook the cart carrying Ardana's worshippers to the new venue; the driver recognized them as they passed and waved; they waved back.

The service was nothing like what Mags had expected. He had anticipated a lot of talking; prayers, homilies, at least one sermon and probably more, based on what he'd been enduring at the Temple of Sethor all this time. But once the little chapel filled— not just with the old devotees and the Sisters themselves, but with additions to the flock in the form of what must be their neighbors and some of the Sworn of Betane, Mags was treated to something that was incredibly peaceful.

There was a lot of music. Hymns, which seemed to take the place of prayers and which he *much* preferred, even if he and Amily were the only ones not singing. Interspersed with the hymns were musical interludes performed by two of the Sisters, one on a small organ, the other on an enormous harp, the biggest such instrument he had ever seen. Evidently they were all supposed to meditate on the lesson in the hymn they'd all just sung during these interludes. The music was simple, the words straightforward, and even though this was nothing like a Bardic performance, Mags found himself enjoying it a great deal more than he had thought possible.

After they had gone through this for about a candlemark, the Abbess mounted the pulpit and Mags braced himself, for this was the moment when the High Priest of Sethor would harangue his congregation for what always seemed like forever, and left him with a throbbing headache.

But instead of a harangue, the Abbess cleared her throat gently and began. "Perhaps it may seem odd that I, a member of a celibate and chaste Order, should speak on the subject of marriage and family. But we Sisters are as married to the Order as you good people are married to each other, and we consider ourselves a true family. And—" her eyes twinkled with amusement "—trust me, my dear friends, the road of our family can be, at times, as rocky as yours might be. So if you will forgive my boldness, let me talk about the marriage that is the true partnership of equals, and the family that gives each member that greatest of gifts, respect."

The homily was all about husbands and wives, brothers and sisters, respecting each other and each doing the job he or she does best without getting into a competition over it—"Neither a competition in boasting nor one in complaining," said the Abbess with another twinkle. "And always keeping in mind that as hard as your job is, your partner has one that matches it. Not at that instant, perhaps, but in another candlemark, or a day, or a sennight, your partner's job will be harder than yours, while you appear to be at leisure."

Her words painted a picture—perhaps a touch idyllic, but what was the matter with that?—of the sort of family Mags had seen in Lydia's and Amily's and that, until now, he had not realized he longed after. When the Abbess finished and stepped down from the pulpit, he found himself with a strange ache in his throat, and the feeling that he had seen something he wanted with all his heart that just . . . might . . . be within his grasp.

Then there was more music, and the ceremony came to an end. *No wonder them folks was willin' to come all the way down here for this,* he thought to himself, as Amily got up to intercept the Abbess before she retreated back into the main building. *An' no wonder these local folks have been comin'.* And for a moment he wondered if he had arranged to send Katlie to the wrong people—

:No, you didn't,: Dallen replied firmly. *:The Sisters are excellent women, but they would only succeed in comforting, not strengthening. They don't understand how someone can have the kind of low opinion of herself that Katlie does. Sister Thistle would . . . well she is absolutely the wrong person to deal with someone like that girl. We made the right choice.:*

Mags saw that Amily had succeeded in intercepting the Abbess and Sister Thistle; Mags headed in their direction, but found himself being accosted by an old couple who looked absolutely determined to speak with him.

Well, Amily don't need my help . . . With a smile he turned to the old man and nodded. Taking that as encouragement, the old gentleman tucked his wife's hand in the crook of his arm and smiled back. "We're told, Meya and me, that you're responsible for our cart, Herald," the old fellow said. "And if that's so, then we'd like to thank you ourselves, and if it's not, we'd like you to carry our thanks to the Herald that *is*."

"That would be me, Amily, an' the Prince," Mags said truthfully. "We had the ideer, the Prince made it happen."

The man and his wife beamed. "We went to *one* service at the old place, where they have that Sethoras or whatever his name is," said the old man. "Or, I did. *Meya* was made not welcome, but told me to go anyway and see what's what, and a nastier, more hateful lot of so-called holy men, I never saw." He looked as if he would have liked to spit, but was too polite. "It was all *women must submit* and *women are not fit,* more trash like that. Ugh. We were ever so glad to come up here to our dear Sisters again, thanks to the Prince, you, and Herald Amily."

Mags was properly modest, and thanked them; they thanked him and the Prince and Amily a few more times, then realized that the wagon was probably waiting for them and hurried off. Mags waited politely for Amily to disengage herself from the Abbess before joining her.

"You look like you got some good news," he said. "Which I'd like to hear, good news bein' in short supply lately."

"Come on then, we should be getting back up the Hill," she replied. "The guards that the Prioress sent here are certainly keeping things quiet. Having them here makes the Sisters feel secure, and the Abbess tells me they are back to their old selves. Not only are all the old adherents coming down, but as you saw the neighbors have decided to join, too. *And* there are three new Novices, the first in ages. Sister Thistle tells me that they are slowly replacing the manuscript copies that were destroyed, but work is going faster than it did back at the old Abbey because it's so much more comfortable here."

They had reached the Companions by that point, and Mags raised an eyebrow. "Really? They ain't bakin' in the heat?"

Amily shrugged. "Maybe not. I know that great stone building stays cool, but cold fingers have trouble drawing."

They mounted up, and the Companions ambled out onto the road again. Mags told her what the old couple had said to him.

"The Prince will be pleased," she observed. "But . . . ugh. That matches with everything you've seen there. I wish they would fail miserably, and I would *love* to discover one of them is our Poison Pen."

Mags sighed. He couldn't blame her. But he had been haunting the place for sennights now, and so far . . . while there might be— probably was—a link to the vandalized shops, not by any stretch of the imagination could he come up with one to the Poison Pen. "Those toughs down in Haven I told you about were saying the same things *before* the High Priest opened up the Temple. And we're still lookin' at the same problem we had afore; with everyone we got watchin' now, an' the Guards on alert, how could someone from down in Haven be getting up the Hill to wreak havoc?"

"Isn't that just the question." She bit her lip. "It would actually be easier for someone on the Hill to have vandalized the Abbey and the Priory than someone from Haven to have gotten on the Hill. I think I dislike logic and facts. A lot."

At the moment, Mags was inclined to agree with her.

14

The gazebo was now the place of choice for Mags, Amily, Jorthun, Nikolas, and sometimes Dia to meet. It would be impossible for an outsider to overhear them talking. Even if Mags and Amily were followed, there was no way anyone could get near the thing. Jorthun had *never* brought an outsider up here, so even if the Poison Pen was a Farseer . . . he'd never be able to Farsee inside the gazebo.

And that was the current topic of interest. "He or she has to be a Farseer," said Mags. "There ain't no other explanation 'bout how that Poison Pen bastard knowd how what was diggin' under Katlie's skin and concentrated on it." He scratched his head. "I'd give a lot t'know how whoever it was aimed in on Katlie, though."

There was no need for a servant to wet down the reed screens that had been let down around all four walls of the gazebo today. It was hot, yes, but not the punishing heat that had clamped down over all of Haven before the great thunderstorm. The breeze that filtered through the walls of the gazebo was adequate to keep them all comfortable. And not for the first time, Mags admired the sheer efficiency of Lord Jorthun's household. For this delicate structure to survive the storm, someone must have come up here before it broke, disassembled it and stored it somewhere safe, then put it all back up again the next morning.

Lord Jorthun looked at him from across the gazebo. "Oh," he said, calmly. "It's a *he*. I'll stake my reputation on it."

Nikolas raised an eyebrow. "I've seldom known you to be mistaken, but how can you be so sure the Poison Pen is a man? Aren't women usually the ones—" He caught sight of his daughter glaring at him, coughed, and didn't finish the sentence.

"It didn't take long to deduce," Lord Jorthun said smoothly. "If the Poison Pen was a woman, why attack the Sisters of Ardana? They are a chaste and celibate order and after no one's man. They are taking no man's job, or at least, they are taking no job that a woman with conventional ideas of men's and women's roles would consider to be a 'job.'"

Amily's brow wrinkled. "I'm not following."

"It is exceptionally clear that the Poison Pen has rigid notions of what the roles of men and women should be. Fiddling about making pretty drawings is not the sort of thing a manly man does, not in the eyes of a woman." Jorthun massaged his right temple a little. "And that was the key, right there. There was absolutely no reason to attack the Sisters of Ardana on either the grounds of being man-stealing hussies, or stealing men's jobs."

"So?" Amily asked. Mags was pretty sure Amily's eyes were

lighting up, but she was trying to hide her enthusiasm. He knew why. She *hated* the idea that the Poison Pen could be a woman. And it irked her that he refused to leave the idea that it could be a woman out of his calculations. Such as they were. So far . . . he was coming up blank, except that he was fairly sure that *someone* who was a Sethorite was behind the shop vandalizing.

"Only a man with a vendetta against women who step out of their destined places as wives and mothers would see the Sisters of Ardana as a worthy target. The Sisters of Betane of the Axe, yes, a woman would view them as being utterly unwomanly, but the Sisters of Ardana? Never." Jorthun nodded decisively. "There they were, doing what old women should do; get out of the way, tend bees, and paint pretty pictures."

" "Wouldn't a woman be just as inclined to see them as being unwomanly because they do all that studying? Competing with men intellectually?" Nikolas asked skeptically.

"In my experience, no, a woman would not consider that competition, and as for the studying in and of itself? In that sort of woman's mind, as long as the Sisters weren't trying to corrupt younger women into their intellectual lifestyle—and remember, at that point they had no new younger Novices—what they did with their time until they died would be of no consequence." Mags was a little startled. He'd rarely heard Jorthun wax so eloquent on anything. "But to a man with rigid ideas about the proper place of women? To a man like that, no matter her age, any woman who steps out of the proper sphere must be beaten back into her place. And no woman should presume to display her intellect, for the sphere of intellect is the domain of men, only."

"But . . . what about the shops?" Mags ventured.

"At the moment, I am sure that the one vandalizing the shops in Haven is entirely separate from both the Poison Pen and the vandalizing of the Sisters of Ardana and the Temple of Betane." Jorthun paused to collect his thoughts. "The incidents may be—I will go so far as to say *are probably*—connected, but it is two different individuals or even groups. Had it been the same, the Poison Pen could not have resisted leaving written messages, but all he has left is wreckage."

Mags let out his breath at that. "I couldn't see a connection," he confessed.

"Oh I am sure there is a *connection*, and I am exceedingly suspicious that the connection is the Sethorites, but the where and how of putting it all together." Jorthun's brow furrowed. "However . . . you mentioned a Farseer and I am totally in agreement with you. It would explain how someone in Haven—in the Sethorites, even— could know what to put in those letters, who to send them to, and when to send them."

"Katlie—" Mags ventured.

"Nothing we need to concern ourselves with now. She's protected from the Poison Pen by the best people possible. There will be time enough for discovering how he managed to find Katlie to target her after we've caught him." Jorthun's mouth thinned into a hard line. "It's tempting to concentrate on her, but at this point, she's inconsequential to catching him, because I will not use her as bait. She's too fragile."

Mags heard that with relief, although Nikolas frowned a little. Then again, Nikolas hadn't seen the poor girl when he'd pulled her out of the water and handed her over to the Healers. And he hadn't talked to her, or seen her when Amily was trying to talk to her.

He knew exactly why Nikolas wanted to do that. And he honestly didn't blame his mentor a bit for considering the idea. He also knew if Nikolas saw Katlie, he'd put the notion right out of his mind. *It's a lot easier to think of using someone when you haven't looked into their eyes.*

"But that brings me to what I was thinking, when Mags insisted the Poison Pen must be a Farseer," Lord Jorthun continued. "Is there any way a Farseer can be kept from seeing what is transpiring up here on the Hill? Or at least prevented from seeing inside the walls around the Palace grounds?"

"No," said Amily and Nikolas together, in tones of deep regret.

"Yes," said Mags at the same time.

The silence in the gazebo at that was so profound that every bit of breeze whistling in the reed blinds seemed overly loud. Everyone stared at him. "Maybe," he amended. "I'm not sure. But I think . . . a definite maybe."

Nikolas continued to stare at him, but then narrowed his eyes speculatively. "Are you thinking of—"

"Aye," Mags said, nodding, anticipating where his mentor's thoughts were going. "That . . . thing that's connected to the stone in the middle of the table in that room in the basement of the Palace. The one I . . . uh . . . *talked to* when I was a Trainee and Amily was taken by the Sleepgivers, except we didn't know that was what they were called. The thing that makes powers stronger."

"Thing?" said Amily, bewildered.

"Go on," urged Lord Jorthun, leaning forward.

"And what makes you think it will be able to block Farseeing?"

Nikolas probed, as Amily looked from one to the other of them, even more bewildered. *Did I never tell her about that? Maybe I forgot . . . oops.*

"I think it's worth waking it up again to see if it can help. It's blocked things in the past, like the interference of the Sleepgivers' amulets with protections on the Palace. It might be able to block Farseeing." It was a gamble, he knew, but it was a gamble in which there was nothing to lose. It didn't harm him to talk to the stone, or library, or whatever it was. And the worst it would tell him was that it couldn't do that.

And I can't believe I didn't think of this until today. Was this another manifestation of that odd inability to think of the old magic of Vanyel's time except as something in the past?

So think about it as a Mindmagic thing.

"The thing is . . ." he continued, still pondering out loud. "There might be other consequences. It might block Farseeing *out* of the area, too. So people up here wouldn't be able to Farsee down in Haven."

"It's worth it," Nikolas replied, grimly. "We can always send our Farseers to the other side of the Palace Walls. Or keep one or two here, and send the rest to lodge with Lydia's uncle until this is over. I don't want any more girls bullied into throwing themselves into the river, or off the top of a building, or hanging themselves."

Well, good, Mags thought. *I believe he's given up on using anyone as bait.*

Nikolas turned to Lord Jorthun. "You warned us, and you were right. You were completely right about him escalating things, Steveral. I am sure that it is the fact that we thwarted him from getting letters to his victims as easily as he once could that made him concentrate on Katlie Gardener. We were lucky once, thanks to quick thinking by Lirelle, Amily, and Mags. We may not be so lucky a second time."

"But Nikolas, if we do this, if we block Farseeing up here at the Palace and he *is* a Farseer, this will only frustrate him further, and he *definitely* will escalate," Lord Jorthun warned. "If his intelligence is cut off, he may actually become frantic with rage, and more dangerous, not less."

The four of them exchanged long looks. It was obvious to Mags that Lord Jorthun and Nikolas were both weighing all their options. Amily was just anxious, and he didn't blame her at all. They'd already had such a close call with Katlie . . . when the Poison Pen escalated, what would he escalate *to*? How much worse could things get? Was it possible even the Royal Family could be threatened?

"Well, nothing else has worked," Nikolas said at last. "And we've learned next to nothing about him. *If* this works, and the letters stop, or at least become more general, we'll know for certain he *is* a Farseer and he's not on the Hill."

"Well," Amily said slowly. "One thing at a time. First Mags has to find out if this can be done. If it can't, we've lost nothing. And maybe this stone can tell him something else he might try instead. If it can be done, and we do it, and the Poison Pen *isn't* a Farseer, or *is* on the Hill, the letters will remain the same, and we'll not have harmed anything."

"All good points," Lord Jorthun replied, nodding his silver head gravely.

"The question is," she continued. "If the letters don't change, how can we tell where and what he is or isn't? How will we know if he's on the Hill, or if he's getting his information by some means other than Farsight?"

"I'll think about that," Nikolas said slowly. "But . . . I do have one idea. The people here up on the Hill have been subject to quite a bit of persecution at this point. It might be worth it to gather everyone together and have the King explain what has been happening. Just . . . get it all out into the open, as we did with the Trainees. And at that point . . ." he paused. "You know, people who have been subject to an ongoing campaign of bullying and harassment are very likely to think very differently about Mags using his Mindspeech powers freely among them than, say, people who have not been subjected to the same treatment down in Haven."

"As in . . . they might could give me permission to go all open and just start sifting through their heads?" Mags asked. "It'd be all right to do that?" He blinked and thought about that. *:Dallen?:*

:If they give permission, it's ethical. And anyone who doesn't give permission could be considered a suspect. So . . . it's really a winning situation no matter what.:

"I think your Companion is probably suggesting that anyone who objects is going to become an object of suspicion," Jorthun said shrewdly.

"Aye." He smirked. He couldn't help it. "There's no win there for 'im, if he *is* on the Hill, is there? Either I find 'im, or he refuses, an' everyone figgers who it is. That's a lotta highborn who have a lotta connections who can make life pretty miserable for someone that don't cooperate."

"Or the King could politely suggest that anyone who doesn't wish to cooperate should relocate. Far, far away. The Border, perhaps, or if they have estates, their own estates," Nikolas pointed out. "Anyone who did would *always* be under suspicion, there would probably be a great deal of money spent making sure he lost every ally and friend he had, and so far as he would be concerned, his reign of terror would be over since he would be under watch constantly. I would make certain of that, personally."

His elation faded when he thought about unintended consequences. And of all people, he knew personally all about unintended consequences. He also knew all about people being perfectly willing to accuse others when they only had a corner of a story. "But what if someone's innocent, at least of this, an' doesn't want me pokin' about in his head for whatever reason?"

Nikolas gave a helpless shrug. "We're speculating—"

"Well, *somebody'd* better speculate what t'do t'make sure nobody that ain't the Poison Pen gets hurt just 'cause 'e don't want me in his head!" Mags retorted, his cheeks getting a little red with anger.

There were plenty of people ready to point fingers at me when there was a Foresight vision of a foreigner, the King, and a lot of blood. The unspoken accusations had driven him out of the Collegium to hide in the streets of Haven, and had made him try to drive away Dallen. . . .

Amily snapped her fingers. "Simple enough. I have a much better idea than running nets through peoples' heads and getting more trash than treasure. We use the Truth Spell. We ask very direct questions that can't be evaded. No poking about in peoples' heads at all. In fact, we could do *that* with every single one of us that can do Truth Spell, rather than have Mags rummage all by himself. That would take far less time, and people are familiar with the Truth Spell. They know we'll only ask questions about the Poison Pen and nothing else. They know they won't have to worry about Mags discovering embarrassing things, or secrets that aren't theirs to share."

Mags sighed with relief. "An' I could just open up an' *listen* close for as long as it took to either find 'im, or figger out he weren't on the Hill. Passive listenin', like I do all the time." He felt much easier about having all the Heralds involved in this rather than just him. After all, leaving aside the fact that he was having serious ethical problems with ruthlessly going through peoples' heads, he was *supposed* to be blending in with the rest of the Heralds, not standing out!

"He could run, of course . . . which would paint a target on him," Amily observed, clearly feeling pleased, as well she should, for being the one to come up with a good solution. "In fact, that would solve all our problems in one go. There is not a single person in the Court, on the Palace staff, or at the Collegia who should be unwilling to face a Truth Spell."

"That brings us back to what we do if Mags' plan to block Farseeing off the Hill actually works," said Nikolas. "And we have cut off his information."

Jorthun took a long, deep breath. "Then—I repeat, we could turn him from something nasty to something potentially lethal."

Nikolas pondered that for a while. "If you'd had this opportunity with your multiple murderer, Steveral, what would you have done?"

"Taken it, of course." Jorthun's mouth thinned again. "I have to remind myself, we are talking about the Hill, not Haven. There are Heralds, Guards a-plenty, and your spies and my spies. There is far more protection for the people up here than I could have dreamed of for those poor girls in Haven. Still. I just want you to be aware of what we might be getting into." Lord Jorthun closed his eyes, and for once . . . Mags was aware of his age. "I will be advising the

King of as much, but I expect him to tell you to go ahead."

"Aight then." Mags got up from the far-too-comfortable woven chair. "Dallen an' me better get back to the Palace. That rock ain't the easiest thing t'palaver with. I need to get my head set for talkin' to it."

The King had, of course, given the order for Mags to go and "talk to the rock." Prince Sedric had volunteered to stay with him—but he was just going to talk to the thing this time, not join with it and try to do a mental search of all of Haven. He opened the door into the stairway going down into that basement corridor, and lit his way down the darkened stairs with a little lantern he had brought with him. *Well . . . there's one thing to be grateful for. It's nice and cool down here.*

Although it was not as *punishingly* hot as it had been before the rain, it was still summer, and it was still quite warm by midday. As a precaution, the room with the stone was kept locked now that people knew it wasn't just an odd, ornamental object, but he'd been given a key to keep, and he unlocked the door now. *Any* room in the basement of the Palace was pleasant, but for Mags, this room was a haven. Not only was it cool, it was shielded somehow, in a way that kept stray nattering thoughts out, but let him selectively get anything he wanted to read from the minds outside. He could easily talk to Nikolas and Dallen, for instance, but all the mental chatter of the surface thoughts of several dozen Trainees was kept out. The result was a mental "quiet" he found very restful.

He hung up the lantern on a hook at the door, and closed the door behind himself. Nothing had changed. This was still a small room, only big enough to hold a round table with padded benches all around it, that seemed to have a globe made of crystal embedded in it. But he knew from past experience that if he tried to move that globe, he'd be unable to. In fact, somehow that ornament was fused to the top of a rock column that, from his vague understanding, ran all the way down to the bedrock of the earth beneath the Palace. How had anyone done that? *Who* had done that? He had no idea.

Magic. The old magic, the magic of Herald-Mages, the magic that had—he thought, everyone thought—died with Vanyel. But it hadn't. It was just kept outside of Valdemar's Borders. This crystal globe was somehow connected to that. How, Mags had no idea, and the globe, or the presence living in the globe, was unable or unwilling to explain. Still, this was the one place in all of Haven where it was possible to think and talk about magic with a clear mind. So making people forget about magic surely had something to do with that.

He knew from past experience that he didn't have to gaze into the ball or touch it to connect to the presence in it. The past sennights had been stressful enough that instead of leaning over the table and the strange crystalline "ball" embedded in the center of it, he arranged himself in a kind of semi-curl on the seat that encircled the table. He was just short enough to do so comfortably. Then he closed his eyes, and reached for a "presence" that was now fairly familiar.

And there it was, just as it had been when he left it last, as if no time had passed. Then again, he had no idea whether the thing even noticed the passage of time. It wasn't quite a "person." And it wasn't a "thing." It was something in between.

:*Hello,*: he said. :*I have come to ask some questions.*:

He sensed it focusing on him. *I am here to answer questions,* the presence replied. *Please ask.*

:*Is it possible to block Farseeing? Can you tell me how, if it is? Can you do it?*:

Well . . . he knew a moment later that perhaps he should have asked a more specific set of questions. Because his mind was *flooded* with information.

It was not unlike the time he had taken the Sleepgiver drug, the one that was supposed to wake up all his hereditary memories and turn him into a Sleepgiver himself. The information poured over him in a flood—but having gone through this once, he knew now that he needed to relax and ride on the top of the flood.

:*I'll remember what you don't,*: Dallen promised, at some remote distance. He acknowledged that and thanked Dallen without words, and let the knowledge swirl through him. How Farseeing worked. What could be wrong when it didn't. How to fix it. In fact, as far as he could tell, the stone was feeding him with more information about Farsight than most Farseers knew!

But although this was something like the experience he had—suffered—under the Sleepgiver drug, it was nothing like the ruthless pounding he had taken then. This was a flood, but a slow flood. Like the river once it got down into Haven, spread out into a broader channel, and slowed, rather than how it was when it tumbled down the Hill. Impossible to resist, but it didn't threaten to drown him.

And finally, he realized that in all of that was the information, that yes, Farsight could be blocked. And how to do it. And how the stone could help show someone who was a Farseer—as Mags really was not—how to do so.

Because, it turned out, Farseers could themselves block Farsight, in the same way that Mindspeakers could block Mindspeech.

:Well,: Dallen said in surprise. *:That's entirely new to me.:*

It didn't have to be a Herald, the stone let him know. The stone would work with anyone Mags vouched for to boost him—or her.

:You trust me that much?:

You trust me *that much.*

That answer left him a bit . . . dazed.

And, finally, the stone gave him the answer he was really hoping for. *I can also do this myself. It will not upset the balance. It is merely adding to the shields that are already protecting the . . .* And here, Mags got a confused impression of what the stone thought the Palace and the Collegia were. There was no corresponding equivalent in his head. Home/teaching place/place of power/center of the web *(what web?)*/sanctuary. All these things, and more, shades and subtleties he couldn't quite grasp.

But that was all right, the point was that the boundary that the stone recognized was essentially the wall around the entire complex. That was where the shields were.

It will not be permanent, the stone warned. *That would upset the balance.*

:That's fine,: Mags assured it. *:How long can you do this?:*

Indefinitely. But it will upset the balance if it goes on for a year.

:That's fine,: he repeated. *:Our problem'll be solved long afore that. I'll come tell you as soon as it's safe to stop blocking anyone who wants to poke around up here. Do it.:*

He couldn't tell any difference at all, but the stone said, *Done. Is there more knowledge you need?*

:I don't suppose you can figger out anything about our Poison Pen problem?:

he asked tentatively. Because if the stone could do this much—
what else was it capable of? And how could it hurt to ask?

Let me look, said the stone, and now he had the disconcerting
sensation of someone riffling through *his* head for a moment.

There is no exact replica of this situation in the history I hold, the stone
said. *Please come and inform me when you have a solution so I may add it to
my knowledge.*

:I will,: he promised, and then the presence in the stone was gone
from inside his head, just like that. He sensed that it was still there,
poised within the stone like a flower preserved in amber, serene,
and unemotional.

He reached for Nikolas's mind, finding it child's play to touch it
down here. *:Nikolas, the stone is blocking Farsight around the Hill. Or at
least it says it is. You oughta check.:*

:I'm going to find a Farseer now,: Nikolas replied. *:Stay where you are
until I have an answer, would you?:*

Well, right now, lying on this comfortable bench, in the silence
and the cool, there was nothing he would rather do. *:Gladly,:* he
replied, and allowed himself to doze.

"So," said Amily, with one eyebrow arched, intercepting Mags
as he came up from the basement. "How did things go with the
talking stone?"

"Yer Pa says it's blockin' Farsight all right. Up here, cain't see out,
out there cain't see in." He ran an anxious hand through his hair.
"Did I really not tell ye that much about it?"

"You told me some," she admitted. "Just . . . not enough, I suppose.

So I was a bit startled by what you and Father were talking about."

"Well, no time like the present," he agreed. "Come on down an' I'll show it to ye."

He turned around and led the way back down the stairs, with cool air wafting around them, as if the building was breathing. There were no lights down here, but then, she supposed they really shouldn't keep unattended candles burning in a place hardly anyone ever came. This looked to be a very, very old part of the complex; she couldn't quite tell if this corridor lay under the Palace, or the Herald's wing.

He stopped at a door, inserted a key, and unlocked it. He held up his lantern so that the light fell on the only furnishings in the room, a round table surrounded with padded benches, with what appeared to be a crystal globe set in the top.

"That's it?" she said, doubtfully.

"That's it. Ain't much t'look at. But it'll make *your* Gift stronger, it'll make any Herald's Gift stronger. This's 'bout the only place I ever found where I could talk about magic, an' not have t'fight t'do it." He raised an eyebrow of his own as she turned to look at him with astonishment.

"I remember!" she exclaimed. "I remember Lena telling me how hard it was for you three to talk about magic when you were Trainees and those men that were supposed to be envoys turned up!"

"Aye," he replied, nodding. "But here, we kin. Ain't like tryin' t'push the words through treacle t'do it. There's this . . ." he shrugged. "It's a thing, in the stone. It ain't alive, an' it ain't dead. It ain't like nothin' I ever run into, afore, or since. We all *think* it's tied into what keeps magic outa Valdemar. It's runnin' some kinda protections on the Hill. For some reason I cain't figger, it'll talk t'me. An' it knows a hella lot."

"So that was what you meant when you said you were going to ask it about blocking Farseeing!" she exclaimed.

"'Xactly," he agreed. "Now, you wanta sit down an' try an' talk to it yerself, or, shall we get upstairs again?"

She contemplated the shining globe for a moment. "Maybe later, when we aren't up to our necks in other things."

"Well, that'll be never," he said wryly, but closed and locked the door.

They went back upstairs, and were enveloped in heat. "What now?" she asked.

"Well, now I go talk to the best Farseer in the Heralds, and tell 'er what the rock tol' me," he replied, taking and squeezing her hand. "Feel like bein' bored, ye kin come along."

"I'm King's Own. The more I learn about other people's Gifts, the better," she replied.

It wasn't quite as boring as Mags had threatened, although she did lose the thread of conversation a time or two, since what Mags had learned from the stone covered a great deal more than just how to block Farsight. But Herald Lora certainly was appreciative of the information, even effusive. And she came away with a much greater understanding of what a Farseer could and could not do.

"I wanted to talk to you about something else," she said, when Herald Lora had gone, and they were alone. "About what Jorthun said—that if this worked—"

"He's gonna escalate." Mags nodded.

"Do you think there is any chance that Lydia might be in danger?"

she asked urgently. "I didn't want to say anything around Father and Jorthun, or they might have decided *not* to let you act. I talked to Lydia myself, and she's absolutely adamant that we do everything we can to stop this fiend, especially after what he did to Katlie. But if you think she's at any risk, I'll persuade her to go somewhere else for her confinement. Now, while she can still travel."

Mags sucked on his lower lip and considered her words thoughtfully. "Well," he said, "Le's look at this the way Lord Jorthun put it. Would ye say so far as ev'body outside the family's concerned, Lydia's a real womanly woman?"

Amily giggled a little, her ears going red. "Well, she's certainly . . . uh . . . doing her dynastic duty."

"An' she does all sorta good works, while Sedric goes out and Princes about. So, honest an' true, I'd'a have t'say *you're* in more danger than Lydia or th' Queen." He eyed her with a touch of worry. "But mebbe he ain't seen ye actually doin' things."

She snorted. "If he's been watching me, he's been seeing Father acting as King's Own, not me."

He relaxed a trifle. "Aight then. 'E ain't gonna like female Heralds, but you're jest one of a bunch. But I wantcha to watch yer back. I'm gonna be down in Haven; I wanta see if there's any sign anybody in th' Sethorites is havin' a major fit."

"We both think it's the Sethorites, don't we," she said, slowly. "Why are Father and Lord Jorthun resisting?"

" 'Cause it's too easy an answer," he snorted. "An' when hev our answers ever been easy?"

"Never." She sighed, stood on tiptoe and kissed him. "I need to go do some things for that blasted fete that the King wants to hold for all the High Priests and Abbesses and Grand Whatevers. You keep yourself safe. If you get even a *hint* there might be trouble, take Teo."

"I will," he promised, and kissed her back. She stood in the door of the Collegium and watched him swing up on Dallen, trot off to the Gate, and head down into Haven.

15

Locking any Farseers out of being able to view the Palace complex did change one thing. Not a single letter arrived from the Poison Pen by means of being pushed under a door or thrown through a window. Letters delivered by that means had already been cut off to the Collegia; now not even the ladies of the Court nor the Blues were getting them.

They were still arriving by regular post, although there were not as many of them. Now what *that* meant, not even Lord Jorthun could deduce. "If he were using his Farsight to avoid being caught in the act, he would still be able to do so within the Palace shields," his Lordship had pointed out. "So the only thing safe to assume is that he is, for some reason, prevented from delivering anything by hand."

"And that could just be the increased vigilance, and nothing more," Nikolas had agreed. Which left them with putting everyone on the Hill to Truth Spell; Nikolas had consulted with everyone who could invoke it, and no one objected to anything but the amount of time it was going to take, and that was more of a complaint than an objection.

"But not until after the Evening of Concordance," the King had insisted—which was the rather ostentatious name for that annual (dull!) fete at which he hosted the heads of every religious organization, major and minor, in Haven. The one Amily and Nikolas, and even Prince Sedric, really wished he was *not* going to hold, and which he was insisting on anyway.

Mags, declaring that there was absolutely nothing he could contribute to the evening until the Concordance itself, was spending most of his time down in Haven, sniffing around the skirts of the Sethorites, still not able to get past the Outer Temple where anyone could go. Even women, although such were few and far between, and in Mags' estimation more timid than rabbits, were allowed that far. But he was determined to keep grinding at it, telling Amily that they probably wouldn't take him seriously without steady persistence. And he might even have been right.

Or he might have been doing his level best to avoid the stew of nerves that everyone involved with the preparations was in. Including her.

She really could not blame him. While in the absence of the frequent letters things were calming down a little among the courtiers, and the three Collegia had gotten practically back to normal, those who were aware of the whole of the situation were on edge, fully expecting some fresh outrage to erupt at the Concordance. What better place to arrange an outburst than there? There would be roughly three dozen dignified ecclesiastics there, easy to shock, and some of them would be women—the Poison Pen's particular victims.

But the afternoon of the Concordance, she found herself without anything to actually *do*. There were going to be people watching the food and its accoutrements from the moment it entered the kitchen to the moment it entered the dignified mouths for which it was destined. There were going to be people watching the dignitaries themselves. There were going to be people in the gardens, *all* the gardens, and all over the grounds, making sure no one burned any more effigies. The Companions were going to be patrolling Companions' Field, and the Trainees of all three Collegia and the Blues had been given notice that after supper there was to be *no* straying out of their buildings (or in the case of the Blues, their rooms) the entire night. The penalty for doing so would be to be forbidden to attend the Midsummer Fair, the Harvest Fair, *and* the Midwinter Fair in Haven. Missing one would have been bad enough, but all three? The thought instilled enough horror in every single one of the Trainees that Amily and Nikolas were satisfied there would be no straying. Not after supper, anyway. A gentle hint was dropped that no one would be penalized for entertaining guests overnight, so long as they arrived at their destination within the candlemark after supper that had been appointed for everyone to get into place.

Amily had the distinct feeling that this would be used as an excuse to hold several parties, but that was none of her affair.

:Ah but you won't be one of the long-suffering Trainees who is trying to sleep next-door to a room full of rambunctious younglings,: Rolan pointed out.

:And I will *have my hands full making sure an obscene note about the*

Votaries of Betane doesn't flutter out of someone's napkin,: she responded. *:The Heralds and Healers and Bards who teach these youngsters can surely figure out some way to keep them from disturbing others for one single night.*

It was still too early to dress for the Concordance, so she headed for Companion's Field, and Rolan. She hadn't gotten much chance to physically *be* with him for the last several days—he was always "with" her, of course, but she missed grooming him, missed the comfort of his physical *solidity.*

:And I will never, ever turn down a brushing,: she heard teasingly. *:Bring that nice boar-bristle one I like so much, and meet me at the bent elm.:* One of the trees in the Field not far from the stables had a low branch coming off a fork very near to the ground that had been bent some immense time in the past, so that it formed a sort of sitting bench before shooting straight up again. Amily went to Rolan's stall, got the brush he wanted from his gear-bag hanging on the post nearest the stall door, and went looking for him.

She understood at once why he wanted her to come to that particular spot. The temperature was considerably cooler here, possibly because of a spring nearby that ran into the river. He was waiting patiently for her, standing hip-shot, right by the sitting-branch. Which would, of course, allow her to reach his back in much greater comfort by standing on it.

"You think of everything," she said fondly.

He switched his tail. *:Of course I do. It's my job.:*

She felt all her tense muscles relax. Of course, she knew she would tense up all over again as soon as she left the Field, but at the moment, everything that *could* be taken care of had been. There was nothing she could do right now that would make any difference, so she might as well just . . . not think about it until supper.

Another way in which brushing a horse was very different from brushing a Companion—a poor horse would be pestered with flies. There wasn't a fly to be seen in the area around Rolan. In fact, the only signs of life were a few sparrows in the tree above her head, sleepily drowsing in the heat and occasionally letting out a soft chirp.

:Mags does that much better than you do,: Rolan observed, as she began giving him a good, firm brushing. He must have been having a dust-bath; she was brushing out clouds of the stuff from his coat. No wonder he wanted her to groom him.

"Let things go, you mean?" she asked, leaning into the strokes. Rolan always looked *good,* but a proper brushing would make him shine like satin. "I think it's something he got from Bey, or that bout with the Sleepgiver drug. I expect assassins spend a lot of time waiting, and it's easier if you just learn how to relax and not think about much while you're waiting, I suppose."

:I could ask Dallen, but you're probably right. A valuable lesson, but an unpleasantly harsh way to learn it.: He moved a little, so she didn't have to, bringing his haunches into reach.

"It strikes me that almost everything a Sleepgiver learns is by a harsh method," she mused. "I hope Bey can change that a bit for the better."

She still was more than a bit nonplussed by the Sleepgivers. She *liked* Bey; he was an incredibly personable fellow. It was unnerving to think that the charming young man who had helped end his own people's pursuit of Mags, and who had shared their fight, their hardship and their friendship, was also the sort of cold-blooded killer that the rest of the Sleepgivers were. She just didn't want to believe it. And yet, all the evidence pointed to him being exactly that, when the circumstances called for it.

:That young man has an uncommonly strong will, and an uncommon amount of cunning. If anyone can, he can.: Rolan leaned a little into the brush strokes. And then, because he had certainly sensed her unease at thinking for too long about Bey, he changed the subject. *:Don't forget to save the mane and tail hair for Mags.:*

"As if I would forget," she scoffed, thinking of all the lovely little gifts Mags had made over the years with braided Companion hair. "I wish I could do this all night instead of going to that wretched Concordance. What do *you* think of all this?"

The lovely thing about being linked so closely with your Companion was that you could abruptly change the subject of conversation yourself without anyone getting confused. *:That if all these letters and vandalism were not harming people, it would be funny.:* Rolan confessed. *:When you think of how some of those people who've behaved badly behind closed doors and pretended they were as holy as a Sister of Ardana in public are stewing about how their secrets are coming out, it's quite comical. But people are being badly hurt by this. Poor Katlie might be the one that was driven all the way to desperation, but there were plenty of others whose health and emotions were badly battered. Not to mention what was done to the Abbey of Ardana and the Temple of Betane.:*

Amily nodded, as Rolan turned so she could work on his other side. *:What would you have said if we'd asked you?:*

:Well, until Katlie, I would have advised, counter to Jorthun, that we should just let the Poison Pen wear himself out sending letters. In fact, now that Katlie is safe, I would have advised the same. Eventually even the most hysterical

ladies in the Court are going to get tired of it. No physical harm is being done, and I think you have found everyone likely to be emotionally harmed. I would drop the Farseeing Shield, be rid of the extra watchers, let him do his worst, and let him discover that he's accomplished absolutely nothing.:

She nodded; much as everything in her screamed to *do something* about all of this, sometimes the best thing to do was not to react at all. Wasn't that what she was doing when people snubbed her in favor of her father? Eventually it would just become too much work to go around her, especially when Nikolas took on tasks that would take him outside of Haven, and they *had* to acknowledge that *she* was King's Own. But why had Rolan not advised this in the first place, while they had all been discussing this?

:Because now that I think about it, it is obvious to me that this man has an agenda that he is cloaking with his Poison Pen letters. And because Jorthun is right; rather than giving up, whether we oppose him or not, he is going to escalate. I believe he is no longer getting the thrill he used to get from sending the letters and tormenting women with them. I think there is grave danger here, because I believe he has a greater goal in mind, and we have no idea what it is . . .: He turned his head, and regarded her soberly with one blue eye. *:I think that he was surprised by the fact that except in the Court, rather than being driven apart by his actions, we are pulling together, women and men. We are better off forcing his hand, making him reveal his true goal before he is ready. If we allow him to work at his own speed, and strike when he has everything in place . . . I don't know what he intends to do, but I suspect it would be quite bad for the Kingdom. What happens here at Court can have repercussions all the way to the Borders.:*

"So we're doing the right thing." She made it a statement, not a question.

:So I believe.:

Well, will wonders never cease. Clear, concise advice. From a Companion.
She would have smiled, if the discussion hadn't been so serious.

"All right then. The next time we gather, I'll tell them what you
said."

Rolan nodded, then turned the nod into a vigorous headshake.
:And until then—yes. Right there. Harder. Ahhhhh.:

Amily and Mags usually used their wedding outfits as Formal
Whites, but even though they'd been married in the summer, it
hadn't been as hot as this. The Concordance was being held in the
Greater Audience Chamber, every window and door that *could* be
opened, *had* been opened, and the number of candles burning was
the absolute minimum to avoid adding yet more heat, but it was
still too warm for anything that elaborate or heavy. In heat like this,
Amily didn't even want to *look* at a corset, much less wear one.

So Amily had improvised. She'd had the Seamstress make a shirt
and divided skirt of the lightest linen possible, and a laced-up tunic
of the same fine white canvas that painters used for portraits, but
brushed all over until it had a nap a little like short velvet, and
she'd asked for blue and silver trim anywhere blue and silver trim
could be put. In daylight, it would be obvious that the materials
were . . . not the sort of thing that Formal Whites were generally
made of. But by this dim candlelight the effect was actually opulent.
Lydia—who wisely was skipping this dreadful thing—had loaned
Amily her personal maid, so her hair had been piled up on the top
of her head, held in place by clever braiding and silver ribbons

and an absolute minimum of hair pins, so her head was cool and comfortable. Or, at least, her neck wasn't drenched in sweat under the heavy fall of her hair.

She waited unobtrusively near one of the windows as the guests began to arrive, and were announced and taken to greet the King. Her father was in *her* place, as they had arranged beforehand. The guests were, of course, all of the religious leaders in Haven, mingled with the members of the Greater and Lesser Council, all three Deans, a couple of very senior Healers, and some carefully selected courtiers. Amily was rather pleased to discover that two of them were Lord Lional and Lady Tyria.

Slowly, over the course of a candlemark, the guests presented themselves, until the last of them had arrived and the serving of wine and refreshments could begin. At least the room was not over-full; it could easily hold three times as many people as it did now. And at least there was nothing, other than the candles, creating more heat. She remained by the window, enjoying the breeze wafting through her light clothing, waiting while the guests sorted themselves into groups. The various ecclesiastical dignitaries actually created quite a festive air, in their embroidered robes and sacred accessories.

Many of these religious leaders were elderly. Beyond merely "elderly" . . . to put it kindly many were aged long past the time when a secular person would have stepped down from an important office and enjoyed a well-earned rest. Some of them were a bit feeble in the wits. Hence, the Senior Healers, keeping an eye on things and making sure none of them over-exerted themselves, although for one or two, "over-exertion" could have been a bout of coughing that wasn't stopped quickly enough. Quite a few of these worthies were entirely unaware of anything that had been happening up here on the Hill since—well, since Mags came as a Trainee. So they were all serenely certain that her father, and not she, was King's Own, which was why he, and not she, was at the King's side. "Let's not confuse any of them," her father had said. "Or rather, let's not add confusion to any befuddlement they are already living with. They know me as King's Own, so let's give them that point of familiarity."

And tonight, truth to be told she was perfectly willing to let them think that. Especially since, once all the formalities were concluded, it was pretty obvious by the anxious attendants some of these poor old dears had at their elbows, that her father had been right. It wouldn't have been at all fair to *them* to upset the pattern they already knew. *Just give them a pleasant night out, the knowledge that the King knows and values their service to their gods.*

A little quartet of Bards was playing unobjectionable music in the corner—and, she was quite sure, exerting their Bardic Gifts to keep everyone cheerful and disinclined to argue. She began to breathe a little easier. This just might come off without a slip. But she crossed her fingers for luck as she thought that.

It certainly helped that the refreshments were all light, delicious, and nothing that might overtax old stomachs. And the wine had been chosen very carefully; there was nothing about it to say that it was not one of the finest vintages that the Palace cellars boasted— which it was—but the alcohol content was so low it probably could have been given safely to a toddler.

Time for me to make my rounds, and find a group to settle in with until someone tells me to move on. That was the plan, anyway. In theory, tonight she was no one of importance—so she should, if she could, stick close the Prioress of Betane and the Abbess of Ardana, just in case something erupted that was meant to disgrace them.

Circulating among the (mostly seated) guests, she was pleased to see, off in the northern corner near one of the open windows, were people she would be perfectly happy to sit with and talk to as well as her two targets. The Abbess of the Sisters of Ardana, the Prioress of Betane of the Ax, Lady Dia, Lord Jorthun, one of those senior Healers, one of the Bardic instructors, and, leaning casually a little way away from them all with his back to the wall, Mags. He was obviously not part of the group, and obviously did not want to be included in the conversation.

:I'll move on once you've settled,: she heard in her head, and nodded just enough for him to see.

Now she was perfectly free to sit down with the others, and she did. There was literally nothing she could do using her Gift here. There were no pet animals around as the King had specifically asked that muff-dogs be left behind, and the Palace cats were vigilant and aggressive when it came to rodents. So the best thing she could do was converse and keep an eye on the Abbess and the Prioress.

And . . . feel out Lady Tyria about her daughter, young Lirelle. More than ever, Amily was determined to recruit her. Violetta was a help, but nowhere near as steady and intelligent as Lirelle had already proven herself to be.

". . . and we are anxious, since these are the first Novices we have had in a very long time, and they are *quite* young, to ensure they get the best education possible," Abbess Reed was saying as Amily nodded to everyone in the group before taking her seat and accepting a glass of white wine.

:That's the damned thing 'bout bein' a Herald,: she heard. *:Not a drop of red wine for us, 'less we're alone in our rooms.:*

She smothered a nervous giggle, but the joke made her feel a little more relaxed.

"Even if that causes them to leave the Sisterhood?" asked Lady Tyria, curiously. "Because education might do that. Broadening a youngster's mind often enough makes him want to broaden his experience. Or hers."

"Oh certainly! We don't want anyone in the Sisterhood who is not completely sure that this is where she wants to be!" No one could have doubted the Abbess's sincerity, and the Prioress of Betane of the Ax nodded hearty agreement.

"We do *something* of the same, but in the direction of physical training," the Prioress said. "We want to make sure our younger Novices know damned good and well that serving Betane is not all parading about in handsome armor. That's why we take them rough camping several times a year, and make sure everyone takes a turn at chopping firewood and scrubbing floors."

"Abbess, if I might recommend something? You might consider creating an actual school," the Bard suggested. "Not for the very young, but for those who have shown talents along the line of the ones the Sisters already use. There are always places for good copyists, and many might prefer girls to boys."

"Oh, that sounds like a *quite* good idea, thank you!" the Abbess beamed. "I'll take it up with the Sisters, but I think Thistle might welcome the chance to teach willing pupils, and it would give the new Novices some company. I always worry about the young being taught alone. Isolation is all very well when you're *our* age but the young need the company of others." She blushed a little. "And if anything is likely to sway their determination to join a chaste and celibate order, it will be hearing other young women chattering about their swains. I would rather they found it out that way than provide the fodder for a tragic Bardic ballad."

The Bard chuckled. "Except that I cannot picture you, Abbess Reed, holding a girl to her vows against her will."

"Well, of course we wouldn't, but you never know what is going to flit through the minds of some of these girls, and I'd rather have things done tidily, and not with attendant scandal." Her cheeks flushed a little pinker. "If anything is far, far worse than providing fodder for a tragic Bardic ballad, it is providing fodder for a farce, and worse than that, is providing fodder for a naughty joke."

Everyone laughed gently at this, and Mags moved away under the cover of the laughter.

"If Lirelle were not so happy here in the Blues, I'd consider sending her to you," Lady Tyria said, with a twinkle in her eyes, that suggested she was about to make a joke of her own. "I might anyway. Her handwriting is atrocious."

"Her handwriting is not that bad," the Bard objected. "She's in one of my classes and her copying is quite competent, thoroughly legible. You must have been looking at her notes. She's always trying to take down every little thing we say, and not the gist. I should get one of the older girls to show her tricks of note-taking."

"I will take your word for it, Bard," Lady Tyria replied, with a gracious nod. "You certainly have far more experience in teaching than I."

"I suppose you're wanting her to take all the usual sorts of things," Amily put in, deciding now was as good a time as any to see if Lady Tyria was determined that her younger daughter follow the usual path of the highborn daughter. "Penmanship, the art of letter writing, courtly graces, dancing—"

But Lady Tyria laughed. "Oh good gracious, not at all! No, Lirelle is taking whatever she wants to take, which seems to be heavily weighted toward history at the moment. She has a good mind, and Semel and I are disinclined to thwart it. Not—" she added, making an amused face "—that she'd let us. She'd find a way around us, somehow."

Hmm, like she did when you first got here, I'll wager. But Amily was not about to let on that she knew that story. It was, after all, potentially embarrassing for Lady Tyria, and Amily wanted to keep on the Lady's good side.

"Oh yes, the big, pleading eyes, trembling lower lip, and the *oh please, please Mother dear, Father dear,*" said Lady Dia, doing a stellar imitation of just that, while everyone laughed. "I know I got my way with my father often enough with that ploy. Mother, however, required a very good reason before *she* would give in. She knew me far too well by my way of thinking. Then, of course, I grew up, and realized she'd been wise, not a tyrant."

Lady Tyria shook her head. "Oh yes. Not Lirelle, though. That was Helane. 'Oh *please*, mother, may I have the same dancing tutor as Arielle Enton?' and 'Oh mother, I *must* have Master Bretan, he's the only one who knows the proper etiquette for the Court at Haven.' Mind you, the governess we have for the younger ones was not up to teaching her, but nothing would do for her but the most fashionable of tutors."

"Expensive," the Abbess said, shrewdly.

"Fortunately we could bear the expense, and she certainly applied herself with a vengeance. But I am happy she is here, and if there is anything she feels she needs to learn, she can take it in a proper class, with others around her." There was something a little—off—about the way Lady Tyria was speaking. Amily didn't allow her face to slip into a frown, but . . . there was something that was dark lurking just under the surface.

"All those tutors, running in and out of your house," said the Prioress of Betane, dryly. "It must have been like a farce. The second act would be one of them trying to woo your eldest, while a second drinks all the wine and a third one gets a dairy-maid in the family way."

Lady Tyria's expression darkened, and she lowered her voice, after a swift glance around to see that none of the other ecclesiastics was near. "I would not speak of this to anyone but all of you—Abbess, and Prioress, you have had your own set of troubles, I know from Semel, and I feel I can trust you. There . . . was a situation. Or a potential situation, at any rate. And it was not at all farce-like. We were just lucky that Helane was too young to really understand what was going on at the time."

"Well, that sounds serious," the Prioress said, tilting her head to the side. "I gather it involved one of those tutors?"

"It did," Lady Tyria nodded. "Helane was only ten at the time and we had engaged a particular music tutor she was especially enamored of—all her friends, it seemed, were taking lessons from him. He did come highly recommended, and I had no hesitation in offering him a position tutoring Helane, even though he was a good deal younger than most of the gentlemen we had hired to teach her. A music tutor—*not* a Bard, I hasten to add," she said with a glance at the Bard. "I will admit he was a competent musician, and he must have been a very good teacher as well, since both Helane and Lirelle learned enough from him to proceed on the lute on their own. But he was relatively young—in his twenties or so—and quite handsome. The little girls loved him because he treated them all as if he was a Court Musician and they were the ladies of the manor, complete with love-songs composed in their honor. I thought it was quite clever of him as it certainly got their attention, and I didn't have a second thought about it. Until, that is, Lirelle and Helane both came to me—Lirelle dragging her older sister by the hand."

She paused, and cast another look around to be sure that there was no one else within hearing distance. All of Amily's instincts for *trouble* rose up, and warned her. This was going to be important. She didn't know why, but it was. "I am very fortunate that my children are not afraid to tell me things. Helane was only reluctant at first because she was terribly embarrassed, but Lirelle convinced her to come speak to me in private. And . . . I won't go into details, but there was some potentially inappropriate behavior going on. It had not proceeded very far, but at the very least, this young man was exhibiting very poor judgment when it came to how he acted with Helane. I spoke to some of the other mothers immediately, and they confronted their own girls, and from that we knew that this was not a momentary lapse, this was a pattern. And what is a farce, with a young lady old enough to be married, and quick-witted enough to turn inappropriate behavior back on the young man in such a way that he never attempts it again, is something else entirely when used on a child, who does not know better, and does not know how to extract herself from a situation that is . . . uncomfortable."

While Lady Tyria was speaking, Amily felt herself growing more and more horrified by what she was hinting at. And looking around the group, it was clear that they were just as horrified—except for the Prioress of Betane, whose stormy brow suggested that the young man in question would have been teaching lessons in singing soprano if *she* had gotten hold of him. *This is definitely important. And it explains a lot about Lirelle.*

The worst of the story now out, Lady Tyria relaxed a trifle, and her expression cleared. "Nothing had happened to Helane—yet— that could not be soothed away, fortunately. And of course we dismissed him immediately. When he called on me to ask why we would no longer require his services, and I told him in the bluntest of language why, he attempted to make excuses, but quite frankly, they rang false. And I didn't like the sly look in his eyes when he made them, as if he fully expected to pull the wool over my eyes because he was a charming, intelligent man, and I was just a stupid woman." She shrugged. "He probably came to me because I was the one that started the investigation, and he thought if he talked me around, he'd get a reprieve and we'd all take him back."

"Well, I must play advocate for the demon in all fairness," said the Abbess. "It *is* possible that his intentions were innocent. And you could have called a Herald to invoke the Truth Spell on him. Why didn't you do that? Then there would have been no doubt."

"Ah!" Lady Tyria raised a finger. "There, we are ahead of you, because some of the families who had engaged him did indeed wonder about that. So one of the other parents *did* suggest that, as a condition of being taken back into service. It wouldn't even have been difficult, we knew there was a Herald due within a few days, and it would have given him the opportunity to clear his name. Rather than face the Truth Spell, he vanished. Completely disappeared. There was not a trace of him, in the town or outside it, and he left no clue as to where he intended to go."

"Hrm," the Abbess said, then nodded. "That's almost a confession in and of itself."

"Well," Amily felt forced to say, as they all turned to look at her. "If you *had* called in a Herald, and he'd admitted he had . . . improper intentions toward the girls under it, you do realize that the Herald would have to have him arrested and brought up on charges, don't you? That sort of thing is very much against the law. The fact that he vanished the way he did also suggests he knew, not only that it was improper, but that it was illegal."

One of the Healer-teachers looked at her with a bit of surprise. "Is it? But what about people like the Holderkin, who marry off their girls at about that age?"

Amily didn't have to answer that one. Herald Lora, who had been part of this group, but silent, answered for her. "If I had my way, they wouldn't be allowed to," she growled. "But that's their religion and their custom, the parents are agreed, and the girls aren't *un*willing, so—" she shrugged, "—but molesting an innocent child against her will and the will of her parents, that's lawbreaking." Her eyes gleamed. "And if it was me that found it out, he'd be slapped into a gaol so fast he'd have thought he'd been Fetched there."

"A man like that is dangerous," the Prioress snarled, looking every inch the aroused warrior. "He might do anything."

"So he might," the Bard agreed. "Anyone that preys on children is not to be trusted in any capacity whatsoever."

"Some people would hold that women and girl-children are men's to do what they like with," said the Prioress of Betane, her eyes smoldering with anger. "And even that the girls were at fault in the first place."

That was too much; never mind that she was supposed to be a Herald, and be as impartial as possible. She couldn't be impartial on this. "So they might," Amily snapped. "And those people are not fit to live."

The Bard nodded, followed by the others. "I agree, Herald Amily. However, that is not up to us. All we can do is place them where they cannot threaten the wellbeing of children, *if* they are caught meddling in that way with children. We cannot rule someone's thoughts. If they leave children alone, we cannot do anything about what they think or say. That is what the law allows us. We may not agree with that, but it is the law, and we are law abiding people."

"Oh, I know, I know," she grumbled. "So we are. But in this case, I don't have to like it."

"True enough. Of course," he added, "Given the circumstances, there is nothing in the law that says we cannot mock them unmercifully for their opinions." His eyes twinkled. "In as public and comedic a manner as possible, which will make others think twice about holding that opinion, lest they, too, find themselves the subject of mockery. There it is, you see. Sometimes the most effective weapon is words."

Amily gave him a little bow, which he returned. "I acknowledge the wisdom of someone who is obviously better at thinking clearly in an emotional situation than I am," she said, and he returned her bow, and then asked Lady Tyria what her daughter Helane was currently interested in studying—if anything.

:You probably didn't notice, but the High Priest of the Sethorites was standin' just on the other side of the pillar behind you, listenin' to every bit of that,: Mags said, startling her so much at his unexpected contact that she nearly jumped.

:I didn't,: she thought hard.

:Well, he just walked away. An' I can't read anythin' off him, not without crackin' into private thoughts. There's nothin' in the way of surface thinkin', just a smooth shell. There's plenty of people that got that sort of thing natural—it comes with concentratin' hard on somethin'. Or it might be somethin' to do with Sethor. Or for all I know, he's got a Gift. I can't tell.: She could hear the frustration in the way his thoughts had slipped into a more common sort of speech. And she didn't blame him. He'd been trying to get closer to the High Priest and the upper echelon of the Sethorites for weeks now, and here the High Priest was . . . and he couldn't get anything without moving into the unethical.

:And now he's taking his leave of the King,: Mags sighed. *:I'd give a lot to know what he thought of all of that. He surely was paying close attention to it.:*

:I would, too,: she replied, and then was distracted as both the Prioress and the Abbess rose. As she looked around, it appeared that all the other ecclesiastics in the room were getting ready to leave as well. *Oh, of course,* she realized. *They all have some sort of service at midnight that they have to observe.*

Mags must have realized the same thing, or heard her thoughts.

He appeared from deeper in the room and strolled over to her as she and the others bid farewell to the Abbess and the Prioress. "If you like, we can escort you to your transportation," he offered, smiling, but his eyes serious.

With a little flicker of a glance, both the ladies indicated they knew exactly why he was making the offer. So far there had been no outrages, not even any inconveniences—but after being victimized, both of them were wary. "We'd appreciate it," the Prioress said. "Older eyes are none too good on dark paths. My warhorse is down at the stable, and I believe there are carriages for everyone else that are supposed to be there."

"Then let's go enjoy the night air on our way," Mags said smoothly. "Ah! Here's your husband, Lady Tyria. I assume it's safe to leave you in his hands. Abbess, Prioress, shall we?"

He gestured, and the ladies preceded him to the line of their fellows to bid farewell to the King.

:You didn't mean that about Lady Tyria being safe in her husband's hands entirely in jest did you?: she asked.

:No. Not entirely.: And with that, she had to be content.

16

After all the tension of the previous evening, they were not entirely surprised to be awakened by screams the next morning.

Mags shot out of bed, as if he had been propelled by an artificer's spring. The sheet and blanket came with him, and he flung them on the floor, and grabbed for his clothing. Without even thinking, he was running with his shirt in one hand, his belt and boots in the other, and by the time he reached the greenhouse door, he had all of them on. Amily followed more slowly, but he knew she wasn't far behind him.

He burst through the door and paused for just a moment, orienting himself. It wasn't at all difficult to tell where the screams were coming from—

Not only was the screaming *still* going on, if anything, the shrieks were rising in pitch and hysteria.

The Formal Garden.

It would have been shortest to cut through the Palace, but with someone—no, several someones—screaming in terror out there, Mags wasn't interested in testing the reactions of however-many now alert Guards lay between him and the other side of the Palace. So he surged forward in a dead run, planning to take the long way—or started to—

He hadn't gone more than a few running steps when Dallen came thundering up beside him, and slowed only long enough to allow him to get two handfuls of mane and haul himself up onto the Companion's back. Then they were back at full speed, racing to the Formal Gardens so fast that they were actually the first to reach the scene of carnage.

He went light-headed with relief when he realized that the body wasn't a *human* body.

One of the little muff-dogs had been pinned to the dial of the sundial, splayed out ritualistically. There wasn't a lot of blood, because the poor little thing had obviously been viciously battered to death, from the way its limbs looked. A knife driven through a letter on that all-too-familiar coarse paper held it to the pathetic little corpse on the face of the sundial; the gnomon had been broken off at the base and lay in the gravel next to the dial.

Gravel. Won't hold footprints. This whole area is gravel, plenty of gravel paths in and out. Nothing to find there.

Dallen shoved his body between the three young ladies and one old one who were standing there in various attitudes of horror. Mags slid down from Dallen's back, gathered them all up in his arms, and ushered them to one of the stone benches far enough away that they would be out of the way. As soon as he touched them, two of them burst out into terrified weeping, one (the old lady) grabbed his arm and clung to it as if she was afraid she would fall down at any moment, and the third went stark white and looked as if she was about to faint.

He got them as far as the bench when the first Guard pelted in, running as hard as she could; providentially, it was a woman. She came to a halt next to him, rather than next to the sundial. "Let me," she said, as soon as she got close enough to be heard over the crying. "I can handle them. The rest of my shift is on the way."

Since he was entirely sure he *couldn't*, he gladly passed them over.

He turned just in time for Amily to gallop up on Rolan. She slid off her Companion's back at the sundial, and Rolan carefully made a second screen of himself to keep people in the Palace who were now looking out the windows from seeing anything.

"Well," she said, calmly. "There's our outbreak. Would you call this an escalation?"

He joined her and looked down at the poor, pathetic, innocent little victim. "I'd say so. This time he actually killed something. And it's not as if he didn't have opportunities to do that at the Abbey of Ardana. There were all manner of livestock animals there, if he'd wanted to make that sort of statement."

She nodded slowly, and they both examined the area without touching anything.

The dog had been splayed out, belly up, in an X shape. It appeared boneless, which suggested that all of its bones had actually been shattered. Mags found himself hoping that the first blow had killed the poor thing, since . . . the amount of pain it would have been in . . .

"I think he killed it with a blow to the head, then did the rest," Amily continued, a little pale, but otherwise showing no sign of being disturbed. Then again . . . she was used to dead things now as much as most soldiers. "That makes sense, he would have wanted to kill it quickly, so it couldn't alert anyone by crying in pain or yapping in fear. He wanted to make a statement, he didn't want to get caught."

"When do you think it happened? While the Concordance was going on?" Mags asked.

By this time more people were piling in. Nikolas ran up, without Companion, but at this point one more would have been one too many. More Guards. A Healer! The Greens were a welcome sight against the dark blue of the Guard uniforms.

Mags reached through the crowd and got the Healer's elbow before the man could be diverted to the women—who, after all, were only frightened and upset, and didn't actually *need* a Healer. The Healer could deal with them *after* he told Mags, Amily, and Nikolas what they needed to know.

"How long ago did this dog die?" he asked, before the Healer could say anything.

The Healer looked startled for a moment, but then nodded, understanding why Mags had asked. "That's a good question. Has anyone touched it?" the Healer asked. Mags shook his head "no." "All right then, give me a moment."

The ginger-haired Healer held his hand over the corpse, not quite touching it. He frowned as he concentrated. Finally he pulled his hand away. "Not less than four candlemarks ago, not more than six candlemarks ago." He looked expectantly at Mags, who nodded.

"After the Concordance, about the time pretty much everybody was in bed, and the kitchen folks hadn't got up yet. Thenkee, sir," he observed. The Healer took that as his signal to go to the four ladies, and eased his way back through the crowd.

"Don't touch that—" he warned someone, who was reaching for the knife-handle. "Not until Herald Kerit gets here." At almost the same time, he was casting his mind about for the "feel" of Kerit, who was one of the teachers at the Collegium. *I hope he's already awake and I don't—there he is—*

:Kerit—we've got something nasty for you in the Formal Garden,: he Sent.

Kerit's Mindvoice was sluggish; he was not a graceful waker. *:Ugh. Was that the screaming? Is someone dead?:*

*:Some*thing.*:* Better to warn him so he wasn't startled. *:Our nasty friend left one of his letters pinned by a knife to a muff-dog.:*

:Oh gods . . . is there a Healer there? I'm going to need one or I'm going to throw up all over the evidence.: Poor Kerit. Aside from Mindspeech, his Gift was to touch things and read their past. Normally he didn't have to read anything dead. Normally he didn't have to deal with anything this evil.

:Yes, there's a Healer here. Sorry, old man, but we have to have anything we can get from this. We've got precious little on our nasty friend as it is.:

:I know, I know. I'm on my way.: Satisfied that Kerit would turn up reasonably soon. Mags turned to one of the Guards and asked him to make sure the Healer stayed.

Just after the Healer had turned his charges over to a pair of servants and had returned to Mags' side, Kerit turned up on the trot, looking like he'd slept in his uniform. But then, he always looked like he slept in his uniform, and his head of unkempt brown hair always looked like an unmade bed. He eased his way through the growing crowd of the curious and got to the sundial. His face turned green when he saw what it was he was supposed to be "reading."

Mags didn't even have to prompt the Healer. The Healer touched Kerit's elbow, and his face went back to merely pale.

"I don't think you need to touch the dog," Amily suggested, helpfully. "Just the knife and the letter."

Kerit gave him a grateful glance as Mags nodded agreement. Gingerly he reached out, touched the hilt of the knife, and closed his eyes.

He opened them almost immediately, to Mags' profound disappointment. "Brand new. Kept in the dark, brought here in the dark and used in the dark. Whoever did this knew about my particular Gift."

Damn! "What about the letter?" Mags suggested. "He won't have been able to write *that* in the dark."

Kerit nodded, and took a corner of the letter in his thumb and forefinger, being careful not to touch the dead dog. Then he swore, and let go of it. "This bastard is too clever to live," he snarled. "He did the very *opposite* with the letter. He passed it around to so many people that I can't read anything but a crowd of hands."

Mags wanted very much to do more than swear, but he didn't. "Thanks, Kerit. Go with the Healer and get your insides settled. We can take it from here."

Nodding, Kerit did just that, looking relieved to have his part in this over so quickly.

While the Guards kept the ever-growing crowd of curious courtiers and servants at bay, Mags and Amily lifted the sad little corpse, knife, letter, and all from the sundial. Gardeners who had been waiting at the edge of the crowd swooped in and carried the sundial itself off, stopping long enough to pick up the gnomon before they hustled it away to be stored somewhere out of sight.

Nikolas intercepted them before they got too far. :*I'm sending the sundial to Steveral,*: he told Mags. As soon as the first set were out of the way, another trio of gardeners swooped in with an ornamental statue of a dog. Which seemed in rather poor taste to Mags, but maybe whoever's dog it turned out to be would decide it was meant to be a memorial. The gardeners with the sundial dutifully headed in the direction of Lord Jorthun's manor-house.

Meanwhile Mags bundled the dog, letter, and knife in a piece of canvas that the gardeners had brought with them. "Now where?" asked Amily. Already there were frantic calls of dogs' names coming from the open windows of the Courtiers' part of the Palace, as word spread as every woman who had a muff dog and couldn't immediately locate it went slightly insane looking for it.

Mags jerked his head at the Palace. "I don't want to be anywhere near any of that," he said. "Lord Jorthun. There's no point in looking for any clues here; the demon that did this is too clever by half. This gravel around the sundial is not going to hold any footprints, there wasn't any dew last night to show prints. He picked exactly the right place for his little statement." He let out his breath in an angry sigh. "Nikolas sent the gardeners ahead with the sundial, we might as well take the rest of it, too. Maybe Jorthun can make something out of this."

Amily nodded. "Dia is going to be furious."

Mags rather thought she was going to be a lot more than furious.

"The gods help this bastard if Dia gets him before the Guard does. They'll be burying him in a comfit-box."

After informing the Prince of what had happened, Mags and Amily arrived at a workroom just off the kennel at Lord Jorthun's manor house, shortly after the sundial had been delivered to the same place. By that time Nikolas had been there, with the poor dead dog, for about a quarter candlemark. Mags' prediction about Dia's reaction was right. She was far, far more than merely furious. When they arrived she was still examining the poor little body minutely, bent over it with a lens. Finally she stood up straight, and looked at them, then shook her head. "She was killed instantly with a blow to the head, then . . . beaten until every single bone was in fragments," she said, in an ice-cold voice, only her eyes betraying her rage. "I can't tell which dog she was, and anything that identified her has been taken away. We'll just have to wait until someone can't find her little bitch. And I don't want to be the person that tells the owner."

"I will," Mags said, not relishing the task.

"No, you won't," Nikolas contradicted him. "I will. I want your face kept out of this as much as possible. It's bad enough that you took over the investigation this morning, but that could be explained by virtue of the fact that you were the first Herald on the scene. But no more. So far he has only gone after women, and has been very careful about choosing those who can't or won't fight back."

"Except the Votaries of Betane," Mags reminded him.

"Who were far from Haven at the time he struck," Jorthun

341

countered. "He's taking more risks now. He could easily have been caught last night. He tried to drive a young girl to suicide, and he's actually killed a dog with his own hands. He's getting bolder, and quite frankly he might well think he's invincible—or invincible enough."

"That's my thought," Nikolas said, in complete agreement. "I don't want to give him another target. And remember, it probably *won't* be you. It will probably be Amily."

Since Jorthun was nodding at that, Mags kept his mouth shut. Besides, he really did not want to have to deal with another weeping woman today, and . . . the owner was going to weep. They might be fashionable, but the muff-dogs were also endearing. Women openly adored them, and he'd seen plenty of men take the little things on their laps when the lady-owner wasn't around.

"Kerit said the knife was brand new, and kept in the dark until it was used," he told them all. "And that the letter had been passed around so many hands that it was impossible to tell anything about it."

"So he knows, not only about Gifts, but about some fairly obscure ones." Jorthun picked up the letter, and looked it over. *"Death to the vain, and vainglorious. Death to she who treads on the backs of men. Death to she who deceives her masters. Death to she who spurns the worthy and breaks their spirits. Death, disgrace, and degradation to the harlot and whore.* Well, that's rather specific, don't you think?"

"It sounds like someone who's been jilted—perhaps? Or passed over, or completely overlooked," Nikolas observed. "Also, put together with someone who knows about quite obscure Gifts and how to befuddle them, I'd say we are dealing with a man of some education."

"Highborn?" Dia asked.

"No way to tell," her husband admitted. "But my instincts say no." His brow furrowed. "It might be my snobbishness speaking, but I just can't see anyone highborn using some of the obscenities that have been in the past letters and painted in the Temple of Betane and the Scriptorium of Ardana."

"But why kill the dog?" Mags asked.

"Not prepared to do anything to a human being yet, but needing to kill something to make his point, perhaps?" replied Jorthun. "Or just as his anger built to the bursting point, he came across the dog?"

"Well . . . if someone was observing the Court from outside, it would be reasonable for him to assume that *every* woman has one of these little dogs," Nikolas pointed out. "They're certainly ubiquitous, and they're so good-natured, they'll go to anyone who pets them. If he wants to terrify and upset every woman in the court, killing one of the dogs in that particularly brutal fashion will certainly do that. The Healers will be making up soothing teas by the gallon today."

"So basically," Mags said, thinking out loud, as Amily, white-lipped with fury, helped Dia wrap the little thing in a kind of shroud, "it probably didn't matter who owned it, just that *only* women own these things, so it became a target."

Dia took the shrouded dog off somewhere; probably to have one of her kennel-men dispose of it properly.

When she returned, Jorthun summoned them all with a crook of his finger, leading them out of the kennel, across the yard, and into the manor. The great library was nearest the entrance to the yard, so that was where he led them, taking the dagger and letter with him. He summoned a servant and ordered food and cold herbal tea. Suddenly reminded that he hadn't eaten since they'd been awakened that morning, Mags' stomach growled, and so did Nikolas's, to the latter's profound embarrassment.

"I can't be entirely sure," Jorthun continued, after they had all seated themselves, "But I don't think he *came here* intending to kill a dog. You know how the little things are; they're very well trained. If they need to relieve themselves, they find a door and let themselves out. I suspect the poor thing was just at the wrong place at the wrong time, he saw it, he was furious, and he met the dog with blind, bestial assault. I fancy that sundial was the real reason the man was there."

"The gardeners have complained about the little messes the dogs leave in the gardens that they have to clean up first thing in the morning so often that the Head Gardener hired three new boys just to deal with it," Nikolas observed. "I think you're right. And there is a dog-and-cat door not far from that spot. But why the sundial?"

"Because of the inscription on that sundial," Jorthun told him. "Did you never read it?"

Both Mags and Nikolas shook their heads.

"Sweet her allure, by nature born. Crave the rose, and brave the thorn."

"Oh," said Mags.

"Exactly," replied Jorthun grimly. "Exactly. If we don't get to the bottom of this, there will be murder done."

The dog's owner had been discovered. She was heartbroken—so much so that she and her husband were packing up to leave for the country, and the estate of one of their relatives. Just as they had thought, the little thing had let itself out in the middle of the night by the dog-and-cat door by the sundial, the door it always used.

I'm just as glad, at this point, Amily had thought, Nikolas relayed the information to Mags. *That's one more innocent out of here until we can find this bastard.*

Dia had said that when she came back, she was going to give the lady another puppy, one as unlike the previous dog as possible.

That's an excellent idea, and very generous of Dia, Amily mused, thinking about the situation as her hand fell on the door-handle. *But I'd rather the Court was deserted right now.* It wouldn't be, of course. The Poison Pen letters were drying up. And even the most persecuted of the women would probably rather be scalped than be idling her time somewhere in the countryside, with no gossip, no intrigues, no one to watch, no one to be watched by. *Maybe* the four who'd seen the murdered dog would leave, but the rest? In three days they'd forget whose dog it was, and in a sennight they'd forget that anything had happened except something vaguely disturbing where that new statue was. In a fortnight they wouldn't remember the statue was new.

Mags was closeted with Lord Jorthun and Nikolas; there was nothing she could contribute to that. Amily had just finished making a detailed report to the King and the Prince on behalf of all of them, and now she stood in the doorway of one of the doors into the Collegium gardens, just watching. This was the middle of the afternoon, and there should have been Trainees and some courtiers soaking in the river; instead, there were only a handful, and most of them were the lads. The gardens were usually bedecked with courtiers in every spot of shade at this hour, but the lawns and gardens were nearly empty. After a moment she spotted a couple of Trainees nervously crossing from Herald's Collegium to Bardic.

I need to talk to the Deans, she decided. *All together, I think.* And sighed. *This is like trying to herd fish. It's probably going to take all afternoon to round all three of them up and get them sitting down in one place.*

It looked as if she was right as she headed into Herald's Collegium. When she looked for Dean Caelen he was not in his office, no one had seen where he had gone, and her heart sank a little.

All right then. Bardic next. And if I can't find Lita, I'll see if Rolan can find them all for me. But when she arrived at Dean Lita's office, she found not only Caelen, but the Dean of Healer's Collegium, Healer Devin, as well.

"Oh thank goodness," she said, as Lita moved a pile of music from a chair so she could sit with them. She took her seat, and felt herself relaxing a bit. Lita's office was . . . wonderful. Big and airy and she had the door open so a good breeze was sweeping through. Things felt *normal* in here, in a way they had not since the Poison Pen letters began. Unfortunately, she was going to ruin that. "I wanted to talk to you all about what happened this morning."

"We know most of it. So do all the Trainees and teachers. The Trainees are terrified," Lita said grimly. She glanced out the window at the river. The empty lawn spoke volumes.

"They should be, I won't lie to you," Amily replied, just as grimly. "I think you should issue orders that no one goes anywhere alone. Pairs are good, trios and larger are better. And I think we should allow them to go armed with knives, at least—I can't think of any Trainees in any of the Collegia right this moment who hasn't had basic knife training by now."

The three Deans looked at each other. "I think you're right," said Caelen, "But we'll check our records to be sure. I don't think it would do any harm to have them carry wooden training swords or Kirball sticks either. Most of them have had stick or staff training as well."

"Both good ideas." She nodded. "Have you got any more? Have you planned to change anything?"

"We're suspending outside watches at night," Caelen told her. "While I don't think this madman would be bold enough to try to take one of the Trainees on watch duty, I don't want to take a chance on it. And only the most senior Trainees are going to be mounting watches in the corridors at night. Sedric sent me word he's bringing in more Guard; it's summer, so they can camp when the barracks fills up. I was wondering if we ought to ask the Companions to patrol the grounds at night as well—"

"A fine idea, except that a bright white horse that very nearly glows is going to be pretty conspicuous," Amily pointed out. "I asked Rolan about that, and he made that same point. He said we should leave the patrolling on the Palace and Collegium grounds to the Guard, and I think he's right and told the King as much. The Companions will just make sure no one sneaks in by way of the Field."

They sat and stared at each other for a moment. Amily was feeling exhausted. *This is taking more out of me than anything other than a real fight,* she decided.

"The devil of it is, there really isn't a great deal we can do, is there?" asked Lita.

"Not really. Just make sure the Trainees stay safe. Hopefully get their self-confidence back to where they can act normally, but *not* get them over-confident so that they stop taking precautions," she advised.

Caelen snorted. "They're younglings," he pointed out. "Overconfidence is part of being young."

She held up her hands, helplessly. "You three are the Deans. I'll leave it all up to you."

"At least we have something we can actually do, now," Devin, the Dean of Healer's, observed dispassionately. "That's better than sitting about on our hands."

"And on that note—on to my next errand." Amily got up, bade each of them farewell individually, and headed for Lord Jorthun's manor again. This time to a meeting of Dia and all the Handmaidens.

They could not all fit in the gazebo, so they were all waiting for her in what Dia called her "solar"—a room that got *all* the sunlight in the winter—but in summer was heavily shaded. Thanks to the many windows, it also had a bit of breeze as well. The rugs had been taken up, so the bare stone floor was exposed, and looked cool and exceptionally inviting. Most of the Handmaidens had their shoes off, and were resting their bare feet on it.

They all looked up at her entrance—and to her surprise, they were all smiling.

"What's going on?" she asked suspiciously.

Dia waved her to a chair where there was already a glass of fruit-infused water waiting for her. "We have good news for you for a change," she said. "We've persuaded about half of the ladies of the court to take self-defense lessons with the Weaponsmaster. Most of them are the ones in the most danger, the younger set."

She sat down in the proffered chair abruptly. "*How* did you manage that?" She simply could not imagine anything of the sort happening. And in this heat!

"Because I announced that *I* am taking them," Dia said serenely. "Suddenly they are fashionable."

Amily rolled her eyes. She could just imagine what *that* was going to mean. Ladies descending on the local metalsmiths demanding jeweled daggers . . .

"Joya is helping by designing special fighting sticks for me to sport, beside my dagger, of course. And thick heels will be coming into fashion, thanks to me," Dia continued. Amily did not trust her serene expression, not one bit. Dia was out for blood—and Amily knew very well that she didn't actually *need* self-defense lessons. "I've designed an outfit to practice in that will probably be copied within two days."

"Please tell me that Steveral got you to promise you wouldn't go out looking for the Poison Pen yourself," she begged. Because she had a notion that if Lord Jorthun had forgotten to get that promise . . .

Dia's eyes darkened, and she frowned a little. "Yes, I promised. In fact, I promised before he even asked me. I would *love* to encounter this bastard and show him what it feels like to be beaten to death, but . . . I'm practical enough to know that is *not* how it would likely go. Besides, we still have no idea where to look for him."

"All right then," Amily said, and leaned forward in her chair. "Let's figure out what *we* can do to teach these ladies how to protect themselves. Or at least, hold off trouble until help can arrive."

"Screaming lessons are a good way to start," Joya said, unexpectedly.

"So they are," Amily encouraged. "Tell me more."

* * *

"Today turned out to be more productive than I thought it would be," Amily told Mags, as they walked back from dinner together. They had met right outside the dining hall, and the talk inside had been too loud, shrill, and nervous for them to actually converse.

"I'll just say today didn't turn out as bad as it coulda—" he began, and stared across the lawn at two figures, one tall, one short, who were making their way toward them at a very determined pace.

By the clothing, they were highborn. As they neared, Amily recognized them. Hawken and Loren, Lord Lional's sons.

But Mags spoke first. "Heyla milords, kin we help ye?"

He was using his most uncultured voice. It took a moment for Amily to remember *why.* They *both* knew Mags, not as Herald Mags, but as "Magnus" the cousin of old Lord Chipman. Fortunately it was twilight, and dark enough to obscure Mags' features. And fortunately neither lad had seen him often as Magnus, nor for very long.

"There's something going on," said Hawken. "Something more than just a dog being killed. The girls were terrified all morning until someone came and said there were going to be special classes just for the Court Ladies with the Weaponsmaster, and they couldn't get up there to the salle fast enough. We need to know what's going on. *Please.* If—if it's what I think it might be, it may be important."

Mags and Amily exchanged startled looks. Well . . . this was interesting.

"Iffen we tell ye, ye gotta tell us *why* it be so all-fired important," Mags told them, and crossed his arms over his chest, and looked down at them with authority. He managed the "with authority" part pretty well. Amily was impressed.

Even in the dim light, Amily could see Hawken's jaw working. "I'd say it's none of your business. And I'd say it's not my secret to share. But—you're Heralds. And one of you's the King's Own. And . . ." She watched his shoulders sag as he gave in. "All right. It's two things. First of all—there was this music tutor, back when Helane and I were younger . . ."

Quickly, he repeated what Lady Tyria had said the night before, during the Concordance. Amily and Mags nodded along, as if they hadn't heard it before. But *then*—

"Helane and I are really close," he said. "She tells me everything. And she's told me things about the man that she's never told Mother. He didn't just *try* to fondle her. He actually did manage a little bit before Lirelle came in and interrupted him. I guess Lirelle figured out something wasn't quite right, because she stayed there until the lesson was over. Problem was, he caught Helane before she left, and he told her that his father was a priest, and had a *lot* of power. And I don't mean he knew people, I mean according to Jared, the tutor, his father could call on his god to do just about whatever he wanted. He told her he'd make sure that if she told Mother and Father, and if she didn't do *exactly* what she was told, that God would send monsters to kill us all, and carry her off. He got pretty deep in his descriptions, too. Helane woke up screaming from nightmares for a couple years after that."

Amily's fists clenched involuntarily. "I take it she told *you* because she hadn't promised not to?"

Hawken nodded, as his little brother stood by, wide-eyed. "She made me promise not to tell them either. Lirelle told, but she didn't hear the threats, so she just told about the fondling. He thought she hadn't seen, but she had. So he never got a second chance. He got dismissed, and Father made sure he wasn't allowed near the house after that. And Helane didn't go out until after he'd killed himself."

"He—wait, what?" Mags said sharply. "That ain't what yer Ma said last night!"

It was Hawken's turn to shrug. "She don't know. We didn't tell her. We figured she'd feel bad about it and he didn't deserve anybody's pity. I found him—well, I wasn't supposed to be there, Kend Millerson and Dal Bakerson and me were going . . . ah . . . looking for bird's nests. Anyway we found him. And instead of fetching the town constable, we fetched the Guard so nobody in the town'd know. But I told Helane so she wouldn't be afraid of Jared anymore. And now she's scared. She's scared that Jared's priest-father's found her, and he's sent his demons to kill that dog as a warning. The letters she got were all about wicked women leading good men to their deaths, and corrupt girls tempting men who couldn't resist. She didn't think much about Jared, until the dog was killed, but now she's sure it's demons."

Amily and Mags exchanged startled looks. Because there it was. The missing link between the Temple of Sethor and the Poison Pen letters up on the Hill. Mags clapped Hawken on the shoulder. "Ye done th' right thin' t'tell us. Now I want ye both t'swear ye ain't gonna let yer sisters outa yer sight."

Hawken and Loren looked at each other, then back to Mags, and both nodded quickly. "Do we tell Mother and Father?" Loren asked in a very small voice.

"Not yet. I can tell you one thing, though," Amily replied,

her voice hard. "It's not demons. It's just a man. And a man is something we can catch and punish, and we will."

"Now ye git back t'yer Ma an' Pa," Mags told the boys. "We got people we gotta talk to."

They both ducked their heads, as if they couldn't quite make up their minds whether or not they should bow, and turned and headed back toward the Palace. Mags looked at Amily.

"Jorthun," they both said at the same time.

:Just let us jump the fence and we'll be there in a moment, if you don't mind riding bareback,: Rolan said.

:I'd rather you hurried,: replied Amily.

Less than a candlemark later they were telling Dia and Steveral what the boys had told them. They'd interrupted dinner. Lord Jorthun didn't look as though he cared—though he'd sent a servant for wine and two more wine-cups.

When they were finished, Lord Jorthun's eyes darkened with thought. "I need to send some letters," he said, finally. "So far . . . the Poison Pen has done nothing more than harass and terrify people, and kill one small dog. In the eyes of the law, that's not a great deal. And it appears he is a priest, a man of great secular and sacred power. It will be our word against his, and we might not be allowed to use the Truth Spell against him. If we are to put an end to what he's doing, we are going to have to tread carefully and make sure we have absolute proof. So I am going to need to send some letters."

Mags nodded, and Amily bit back her disappointment. But he was right, absolutely right. They couldn't just barge into the Sethorite's Temple and demand to know which of them was Jared's father. First they had to figure out which of them was—and it was entirely possible the man wasn't even a priest anymore. He was certainly hiding his identity.

"Meanwhile," Mags finished. "*I* need to talk to some people." He smiled grimly. "At least now we're moving."

17

"*Promise me that if you need help, you'll bring Teo along.*" That's what
Amily had said, and he had promised. Well, he was going to
try, although . . . well, he hoped there was a way to do this without
Teo losing his job.

This time of the night Teo would be either home or at his favorite
tavern. Mags tried the tavern first with no luck, so he headed for
the goldsmith's shop.

Luck was with him. The wind was blowing away from the
tannery district tonight. He wasn't going to have to battle his way
through eye-watering stink.

Never one to miss an opportunity to get as much out of his
employees as he could, Teo's employer, the moneylender Bren
Kriss, rented Teo the smaller of the two rooms above the shop.
Teo got a good deal on it with the understanding that if Teo heard
anything in the shop below, he was to deal with it.

Mags got to the back of the goldsmith shop down the alley, and across a tiny yard with an outhouse in it and not much else. Good thing there was moonlight; he didn't have too much trouble picking his way down the alley and across the tiny yard. Teo had a separate entrance from his employer, a staircase going up the outside in the back, and Kriss kept everything about his shop and home in good repair, unlike a lot of the buildings around here. Mags took the staircase, noting that it didn't even creak, then paused at the door before knocking, and listened hard. There were no windows on this side of the room, but there was a thin line of dim light under the door. And if Teo happened to be entertaining someone else, Mags was going to go this alone.

But Mags heard nothing except a metallic clinking, interrupted with an occasional soft thud, just like someone putting a full pottery mug down on a wooden table. *He's eatin' soup and drinkin' a beer, I reckon.* That meant Teo was alone. So he knocked.

He heard the scrape of chair or stool legs on a wooden floor, then a couple of footsteps. "Whozere?" Teo said quietly, a note of suspicion in his voice.

"'Sme. Harkon." Mags spoke just as quietly.

The door opened immediately, and Teo grabbed him by the elbow and pulled him inside, closing the door behind him after a quick look around to make sure there was no one else out there.

The light inside was very dim indeed, and not surprising, since Teo was using some form of a dark lantern, one that made the candle stub he was burning dimmer rather than brighter. After a moment, Mags figured out why—this was to save his night-sight. The tiny room didn't hold much, but it was scrupulously clean, and curtains made of feed-sacks covered both windows, allowing in air while keeping out most of the bugs.

"Ye wouldn' come here this time'a night without it bein' important," Teo said, his back to the door. Mags edged aside so he could get back to his stool; there was just barely enough room in here for Teo's pallet on the floor, the table cobbled together of odd bits of wood, the stool, and the two of them. Mags leaned back against the door.

"Finish yer supper," he said. "I kin talk while you eat."

He explained what had been happening up on the Hill, to the Sisters of Ardana and the Sworn of Betane, and the female shopkeepers down in Haven, while Teo ate and listened with his brows furrowed with concentration. "Well," Teo said between bites. "Tha's a mess."

Mags nodded. "We figgered all of 'em was the same people, but we couldn't link 'em till tonight. Then we found out 'bout somethin' what happened t'one of the Court gals when she was a mite."

When Mags explained what Hawken had told him, Teo's brows furrowed with more than concentration. "And you reckon these Sethorites got that priest among 'em, an' he's coverin' up thet he wants t'get revenge on this liddle gal by goin' ater everyone up there?" Teo hazarded, which, in spite of the seriousness of the situation, made Mags rejoice inwardly. He'd picked the right man in Teo Lendsler.

"Well, none of this was happenin' until thet gal an' her fambly got here," Mags pointed out. "An' Sethorites been here 'bout half a year. Aye, I reckon this all *started* 'cause'a thet, but there's gotta be more *to* it. An' I bin sniffin' round the Sethorite Temple fer a good bit, an' I ain't got no hint they's doin' anythin', an' I got no ideer who's the boss. But I gotta find out, so I'm gonna pull th' trap-door on whut I got set up, tonight an' see iffen anythin's standin' on it. An' I need ye with me."

"This could take a while," Teo said, worriedly. "Days, mebbe. I got *my* boss t'think 'bout."

"Ye trust 'im?" Mags asked.

Teo looked at him startled, with his mug halfway to his mouth. "Serious?"

"Damn serious. Ye trust 'im?"

Teo put his mug down and scratched his head. "Well . . . reckon I do. Ain't never done me wrong. 'E trusts *me* t'watch over th' shop. Why?"

"'Cause we're gonna tell 'im what I am, an thet ye work fer me." This was a desperate, maybe stupid ploy, but Mags trusted Teo's instincts, and as Teo had said, he might need Teo's full help for several days. Several years ago he would *never* have revealed himself to a stranger like this unless there was no other choice. Even a year ago he would have hesitated. But he had gotten a good feel for this, and a good sense of the kind of man Teo was, and he thought this was worth taking the chance.

:Besides, you can always make him think it was a dream,: Dallen said cynically.

:Shut up, horse. It'll have to be pretty damn dire before I meddle with a man's memory.:

Teo's eyes bulged for a moment, but he didn't object.

"Boss still awake?" Mags asked.

"Aye, an' 'e'll still be i'shop, doin' books," Teo replied.

"Good. Thet means I kin prove it t'him same as I did t'you." Mags pushed away from the door, and opened it, walking softly down the stairs into the night, until he reached the ground. He heard the creak of the door above him and the soft steps of Teo following.

There was a second door back here, with a little stone sill and a substantial wooden frame, which Teo rapped on. "Mas' Kriss?" Teo said softly. " 'Tis Teo."

The door opened quickly, and an old man looked out, peering suspiciously at Mags. "What is this? Th' money's gone. I take it out of shop every night—"

"We know that, Mas' Kriss," Teo said patiently. "This's somethin' else. This's a friend'a mine. We gotta talk t'yer. 'Simportant."

At this moment, Dallen eased his way into the tiny yard behind the building. In a case of exquisite timing, the moon came from behind a cloud and moonlight struck the Companion and made him as luminous as a horse carved of pearl. This was not something Bren Kriss could ignore.

And in fact, his eyes practically popped out of his head. "Tha's a Companion!" he rasped. "Whut th' *hell*, Teo Lendsler?"

"Aye, tha's a Companion," Mags said, speaking up for the first time. "An' I'm a Herald. An' Teo's bin workin' fer me on th' side. Tha's part'a what we gotta talk ter yer about."

Of all of the reactions Mags had anticipated, the one he got was one he never would have expected.

Bren Kriss began to laugh. A choked snicker at first, as he crammed his fist into his mouth to keep from laughing hard enough to alert the neighbors. Then a wheezing guffaw. Then torrents and gales of helpless, repressed laughter as he slapped both hands against his mouth to hold the sound in, tears pouring down his face.

Mags looked at Teo. Teo shrugged. Dallen move closer and snorted.

Kriss kept laughing.

The old man finally gestured at the two of them, beckoning them in. "I'd invite th' nag in, but 'e ain't gonna fit," the old man managed, still chortling.

Dallen looked at them with ears perked forward in interest, and for once he didn't take offence at being called a "nag." *. :I assume you won't need me anymore?:*

:Reckon not,: Mags said.

:Right then. Off I go. Call if you need me.: He trotted off into the moonlight, making no more sound on the ground than the moonlight did.

How does he do that?

Mags followed Teo into the building, and once he was inside, Teo closed the door, his face a veritable mask of confusion.

The old man was already sitting in what looked like a very comfortable chair, behind a table and facing the door, still wheezing with laughter, as he indicated they should take two of the stools nearby on the other side of the table. Meanwhile, he snatched up a rag and mopped at his eyes. "Oh, hells. Oh bloody hells. I ain't had a laugh like that in . . . well, I cain't 'member. Yer a Herald. An' iffen yer creepin' 'round Haven lookin' like a bullyboy, I reckon yer gotta be workin' fer Willy th' Weasel, which also happens t'be Herald Niko. Aye?"

Now both of them were staring at the old man in confusion. And then it dawned on Mags what the explanation—and the hilarity—was about. And it was his turn to burst out into guffaws. "Oh—my bloody lord," he gasped, in between peals of laughter. "*You work fer Nikolas!* All this time, Teo's bin workin' fer me on th' side, an' *you* been workin' fer Nikolas, an' not one on the three of us figgered thet out!"

It was hilarious. It was a farce. And things could not have worked out better if he'd tried. No wonder Bren Kriss was one of the few honest moneylenders in this part of the city; he'd have his fingers on the pulse of the entire network of moneylenders and he could tell Nikolas just about everything Nikolas wanted to know about finances in Haven. *Where* the money went and *who* it went to and *what* it was buying was information that could be more valuable than gems to Nikolas.

"Aye, thet I do," Bren Kriss said, proudly. "Twenny yearn, iffen it's a day." He dipped water from a pottery jar on the table into mugs and passed it round to the two of them. Teo's face had lost its look of confusion, and Mags had finally got himself under control. "So, my lad Teo here's bin workin' fer ye on the side like. On'y tonight somethin' bad's come up, an' ye need 'im fer more'n a couple candlemarks, aye?"

"That's about the tale," Mags replied, unspeakably grateful that he wasn't going to have to go through a long explanation, and then persuade Kriss on top of that.

"I don' need t' know no more'n thet. An' if Niko *wants* me t'know more'n thet, he'll tell me." Kriss waved off any other talk. "You jest use that there Mindy-speak an' tell 'im I'll need t'borrow some of 'is muscle t'take Teo's place fer a while, startin' tonight."

The *look* he leveled on Mags made it very clear that he meant *right now.* Which Mags didn't mind a bit. After all, a moneylender had *money,* and thieves go where the money is. It was only fair; if he was going to take Kriss's protection away, he should make sure there was an alternate in place.

He closed his eyes for a moment to concentrate.

When he opened them again, Teo was looking at him curiously, Kriss with expectation. "'E says," Mags said ruefully. "Thet 'e cain't believe it took't me this long t'find out."

That sent Kriss off into laughter again, which Mags could scarcely blame him for. He had a very unique laugh, odd enough to finally put a smile on Mags' chagrined face. "Whut else?" Kriss asked, wiping his eyes again.

"'E'll send a lad over in a candlemark, a new feller i' Guard whut 'e's feelin' out fer 'nother set'a eyes an' ears. 'E ain't a good 'nuff play-actor yet t' be in shop, but long as 'e keeps 'is mouth shet, should be all right. Reckon thet'll do?" Mags asked anxiously. "'E kin cover fer Teo t'night, an' arter thet, Niko'll figger somethin'."

"Iffen Niko sends 'im, 'e'll do," the old man replied. "Now, off wi' th' pair of ye. Whatever 'tis that got ye out this late, gotta be bad 'nuff ye should get *to* it."

"Yessir," Mags said obediently. They got up, opened the door behind them, and left, and heard the lock slide home on the door once they were outside.

"Well," Mags said, looking at Teo in the moonlight. "Ready t' see whut we kin see?"

"Aye," said Teo.

The Sethorite Temple—or at least the area that the Novices referred to as the "Fellowship Hall"—was a nightly gathering place for men like that set of rowdies Mags and Teo had heard spouting off about women.

Had it only been a couple of fortnights ago? It seemed an age.

Since it was open all day and all night, that it was a gathering-point was hardly unexpected. When you were a poor working man, if you had a family, they were all crowded into a single room and if you were single, you shared a room with at least three others; here at least you had space, and you were out of the weather. When you were a poor working man, you took every bit of free food you could get. Here there was free heavily watered, sour wine—though it was more like faintly wine-flavored water—and there was bread and drippings, also free. As much as you cared to eat and drink; no one seemed to be keeping track of how much anyone took.

They entered the Fellowship Hall, which looked not unlike the Dining Hall at the Collegium, except with stone walls instead of wood. Like the Dining Hall, it was packed with wooden benches and trestle tables, with the food and drink being served at the back. Mags got some of both, as did Teo, and he led his friend to one of the tables at the front of the room, where Novices sat, mingling with men who were known to them. Mags had been setting this up for sennights now, and he was ready to see what he could catch with the right bait.

"Ah, Pakler," said one of the Novices. "We didn't see you today. Or indeed, for several days."

"Tha's cause I got work, sor," Mags said, with a little duck of his head and tugging on his hair since he didn't have a hat to doff. "I got me some *connections* up to Palace, an I bin' doin' a sight'uv fetchin' an' carryin'."

Well, that got the interest, not only of the Novice that had recognized him, but two more down the table. "Indeed?" the Novice said smoothly. "Why the need for extra porters up at the Palace? I would have thought they would have more than enough servants."

Mags shrugged. "Highborn movin' out," he said. "Dunno why. Too many of 'em fer them up-nosed servants uv their'n t'do all the totin', so they hired from town." He took a bite of the bread—which he suspected was half flour and half sawdust—and washed it down with the sour watered wine. "M'second cousin on Pa's side's a potboy i' one uv th' kitchens. 'E put me wise to't t'when they was takin' lads at th' gate. I wuz there, afore dawn, you bet!"

It was true enough. There *had* been temporary hiring at the front gate for people to load up the belongings of the courtiers that were fleeing the Poison Pen. Of course, the one place no thief in his right mind would attempt would be the Palace in broad daylight, with Heralds and Companions all over, so it was a good bet only the honest were applying for the work.

"And what have you been seeing of the Palace?" the Novice asked smoothly, with *just* the right amount of indifference. *Oh, he's good.*

"They got me hoppin' all *over,*" Mags asserted, boastfully. "T'other lads they got, they ain't *pushin'* it like I be. I mean ter get all the work there is up there. I be in ever' place but where the Royals be, afore day's over." Then he made a face. "Work ain't bad, 'cept fer the wimmen. Them highborn wimmen, they's needin' some proper men t'show'em their place, I reckon. Niver seen sech a lotta yammerin' hens i' m'life. Aye, Teo?"

Teo grunted, and continued slowly eating his bread.

"Got Teo up there yestiday, but 'e left it."

"Cain't abide pushy bitches," Teo muttered.

"Fascinating," said the Novice, and turned to the other two. They got their hooded heads together for as long as it took Mags and Teo to finish their first pieces of bread and start on a second. Then one of the Novices got up and left, while the first one turned back to Mags and Teo and—with a much friendlier demeanor— engaged them in a conversation about the highborn women they had encountered.

Mags did the best performance he could manage of a fellow who was just bright enough—and just enough in need of money—to put up silently with slightly hysterical highborn women who were fussing all over their belongings and making impossible demands of the porters. But of course, a true Sethorite—which he was supposed to be, after all—would have been seething inside at how the women were ordering him about, when *he* should have been telling them to *sit down, shut up, and it'll get done when it gets done.* So he put in some asides about that, and about how the weak-spined highborn should be doing more to teach their women their proper place.

And, of course, as the Novice drew him out further, he waxed eloquent on how vain and empty-headed they were, how flighty, how hysterical, how they all seemed to be in fear of some unnamed *thing* haunting the Palace. He even named a couple of names, knowing that would only help him to be more convincing.

He and Teo had finished their bread and were drinking the last of their wine when the missing Novice returned. But instead of sitting down, he gestured to Mags. "We believe, Brother Pakler, that you may be ready for the next stage in your service to Sethor. Will you come with me?"

Mags glanced over at Teo. The Novice followed his glance, and smiled sympathetically. "Alas, Brother Teo. We have room only for one recruit at this time. Would you care to wait for Brother Pakler here, or in the Sanctuary?"

"Sanct'ary," grunted Teo. "But might come back here iffen it takes too long."

The Novice actually chuckled. "There is only so long that a red-blooded man can spend on his knees, indeed. Come, Brother Pakler."

Mags followed the Novice deeper into the Temple, past the Sanctuary, down a long corridor with a lot of little closed doors on it, and to a small, bare stone room, where one of the priests waited, sitting behind a table. Not a high ranking one, which was a little disappointing, but Mags covered his disappointment easily. There was no place to sit, so he stood, as the Novice closed the door to the room and stood a little aside. Once again, he bobbed his head, a bit deeper this time, and tugged the front of his hair. "Sor," he said, humbly. "Ye reckon Sethor's gotta use fer me?"

"Aye, Brother Pakler, the Great God has, this very night." The priest regarded him steadily, out of deceptively mild eyes. "There are women in this town, stealing the bread from the mouths of men and their families."

"Aye, sor, there are," Mags agreed resentfully. "Not me, s'much," he added. "Ain't no fool bitch kin lift an' tote like a man. But plenny other stuff they be doin' thet a *man* should."

"It is the mission of certain chosen among the followers of the Great God to deliver unto them proper chastisement, so that they will give over their vainglory and the aping of their betters, and return to the proper place of women as helpmeets and followers," the priest continued. "Tonight, we have chosen you for a trial of your faith in the deliverance of that justice to one such harlot. Should you successfully complete your mission, you will be rewarded, and not only by the Grace of Sethor, but in silver." Mags started, and the priest smiled at his reaction. "And should you complete this mission *well*, there will be greater things in store for you."

The start of surprise had been entirely natural. The last thing that Mags expected was to discover that the Sethorites were so bold as to arrange the vandalism like *this*. He'd thought they were using their own people, not recruiting outside their ranks. He had to simultaneously repress his excitement and his fear.

"Sor, yessor," Mags repeated, bobbing. "I'll do m'best, sor."

"Good. Do you know Goose Lane?" the priest asked, watching him closely.

Have I given myself away? He strove to look eager and earnest. "Aye, sor. It be comin' off Goldoak Street, almost t'Balcher's tavern."

"So it is. And do you know the herb shop across from Gerand's 'Pothercary?" the priest continued.

Mags furrowed his brow. *Best not to act as if I know every nook and corner of Haven.* "I know 'Pothecary. Reckon I kin find 'er."

"Excellent. Then this is your mission." The priest leaned foward on the table, and the hood of his robe fell back, revealing an uncomfortably intense man with chin-length hair and a beard that looked scraggly, even though it was neatly trimmed. "You will enter that herb shop. You will destroy everything in it. You will return here. All without being detected." The priest smiled thinly. "Do not concern yourself over being detected from within. The whore that owns it, and steals bread from the mouth of Gerand, sleeps elsewhere, and it is only locked, not guarded."

Well, of course it ain't guarded. Goose Lane's a good neighborhood, an' it's patrolled by the Watch.

Now, Goose Lane was *outside* the area where the previous shops had been vandalized. *They're moving further afield. Not good.* "I kin do thet, sor," he promised, though inwardly he was sick at the idea that he was about to wreck another woman's livelihood.

But there it was. Proof positive that it *was* the Sethorites behind the trail of destruction. Now if he could just find the one orchestrating things up at the Palace! *They said there's better things if I pull this off. Maybe it will have something to do with that.*

"Well, go tell your friend he's free to go home, or stay and wait for you. Then get on with it, Brother Pakler." The priest jerked his head, and Mags took that as the signal to leave. He followed the Novice back out as far as the Sanctuary, where Teo was dutifully occupying a pew, and miraculously not falling asleep. The Novice tapped Teo on the shoulder, and he followed them both to the Fellowship Hall.

"I gots a job I gotta do fer Sethor," Mags told Teo. "I dunno 'ow long I'll be."

Teo grunted. "I don' mind waitin'." He looked around, and noticed a few men dozing, stretched out on the benches against the walls. "Likely I kin catch a nap."

The Novice smiled. That seemed to be the right answer. "All right, Brother Pakler. On your way. Don't make your friend wait too long."

Aha. Now I see why he let Teo stay. Using that as a way to get me to move faster. Mags nodded, and headed out the door at a trot.

The streets were lit brightly by the moonlight—moonlight which would also reveal him, and would have been a problem for anyone but Mags. Mindful of the fact that whoever was behind this might just have Farsight, and might just be watching, Mags took himself into the alleys, and once he got to Goldenoak Street, took to the roofs. It would do him absolutely *no* harm with these people if they knew he knew the thief's high road.

He found the herb shop easily enough, and dropped down off its roof into the tiny alley behind it. The lock was nothing to someone of his skills; he easily forced the door with almost no noise. And once inside—well, it was an herbalist. The fastest way to wreck it was to throw everything off the shelves into the middle of the room and grind it all to powder under his boots.

Because it was an herb shop, the counter was right at the door; you came in, said what you wanted and how much, and the herb-woman measured it out for you into small paper packets. It was heartbreaking how easy it was, and how little time it took, to turn a prosperous shop with excellent stock into a worthless, empty store. A candlemark, a candlemark and a half at most.

Then he was back out, up and over the roofs again, dropping down into an alley far from Goose Lane, after making sure there were no telltale bits of dried leaves or stem clinging to him. The Watch came along just as he started his stroll back. They eyed him but he looked them in the face, and gave them that nod-bow, and they moved on, satisfied he was no threat to anyone.

:Dallen,: he said, as he walked at the sober pace a tired man returning home from a hard day's work might take. *:I won't be coming home tonight, and probably not for several nights. Tell Rolan to tell Amily. I'll*

talk to her myself once I've got a place to sleep and some privacy. And tell her to make sure that herbalist gets help from the Prince and Princess.:

:Done,: said Dallen. *:I've been keeping Nikolas apprised as well.:*

That left him only to get back to the Temple without calling attention to himself. The best way to do that was to walk as he was doing, head down, shoulders slumped, looking like a man who only wanted to get to a bit of soup and a bed. And every time he came across members of the Watch, he would look up, meet their eyes, nod-bow, and move along. The fastest way to draw the attention of the Watch to yourself was to look uneasy around them.

He was met at the entrance by the Novice, who clapped him on the back, confirming his suspicion that he had been watched with Farsight. How else would they have known he was coming, or when he would arrive? "Well done, Brother Pakler," the Novice said, cheerfully. "Well done indeed! Precept Darent would like to have a word with you again before you go talk to your friend."

"Yes, sor," Mags said, and followed the Novice back to the office. It was, indeed, the same office, and the same intent man behind the same table.

This time there was a chair waiting for him, and Mags dropped heavily into it with a mumble of gratitude. "Brother Pakler," the Precept said, both hands clasped in front of him on the table. "You showed a remarkable set of skills tonight. We were impressed."

All right. How to act? Be impressed and afraid that they kin see me, or act as if I knew they could all along? I don't wanta oversell this . . .

Settle for being unsettled. "Ye saw me?" Now with a touch of suspicion. "How? I didn't see none uv ye!"

The Precept chuckled. "Well, the God grants us the ability to do many things, Brother Pakler. We need not be present to oversee our Brethren."

That's all but admitting to Farsight. And it's as much warning as anything else. But they can't be watching everyone all the time, or they'd have more Farseers than all the Temples and such in Haven put together, and that ain't likely. Mags switched back to being unsettled. "Aye, sor," he mumbled.

Now the Precept leaned over his hands, staring at Mags intently. Suddenly Mags knew what the Precept's eyes reminded him of. There was a highborn, Lord Kallian, who'd lost an eye, and rather than covering it over with a patch like a sensible person would, he'd had a very expensive replacement made of glass. It unnerved so many people with its cold, inhuman gaze that finally he'd discarded it and gone back to the patch.

"Now, we have a few questions," the Precept continued. "We would like to know how you came by the skill of roof-walking. You appear very . . . practiced."

"Learnt it as a little, sor," Mags said. "M'sibs an' me, we useta roof-run alla time when we was littles. Safer nor bein' on street; them carters, they don' look out fer kids, neither do them highborns when they's in a hurry. On street, ye kin get snatched up, too. Cooler t'sleep on th' roof in summer. Faster t'get almost anywheres is t'go by roof." He scratched at his head, and looked rueful. "I bain't a big man, sor. Still safer b'night nor bein' on street. Less'n m'frien' Teo's wit' me."

"So it is," the Precept chuckled. He lowered his lids over those uncanny eyes. "And that accounts for you wanting him to stay. Being none too stout myself, you have my sympathy, Brother Pakler. And that clears away a question I had."

He didn't *ask* that question, but Mags could imagine what it was. Whether or not he'd gotten those skills as a thief. *I wonder what he would have said if I'd claimed to be one?* It occurred to him that such an answer would not necessarily mean rejection—just an offer of a different sort of "job" altogether.

"Now." The Precept leaned over his hands again, fixing Mags with a piercing stare. "Are you a true son of Sethor, Brother Pakler? Are you prepared to take His cause to the heart of the corruption in this land?"

Mags decided that bewilderment was the best reaction here. "I ain't sure whatcha mean, sor," he said, scratching his head again. "But what'er Sethor wants, I reckon I'll do 'er. Sethor bin good t'me. Right good. Reckon I kin pay thet back."

"Very good." The Precept sat back in his chair. "You may go and tell your friend that he can go home without you. You will be moving into one of the Novitiate cells here in the Temple. You have no family, so you have only yourself to provide for, which makes you an ideal candidate for service."

"Ye don' mean me t'be no Novice, sor!" Mags said in alarm. "I bain't that smart!"

The Precept laughed heartily. "Of course not. You will eat and sleep with the Novices, but tomorrow you may well meet one of your fellow Soldiers of Sethor, who are quite different from Novices, with fewer restrictions on their behavior. Sethor will be seeing to all your needs from now on. We will supply you with shelter, food, and clothing. We will require your faith, and your labor. You will be one of us, Brother Pakler."

"Aye, sor," he said obediently, although his mind was reeling. He hoped that Teo was smart enough to know what he should do from the few clues he was going to give the man. "I'll go tell Teo now." He smiled uncertainly at the Precept. "Reckon he'll wish't it were him."

The Precept nodded his acceptance; the Novice opened the door and let him out, then followed him. Mags hadn't expected anything else.

In the Fellowship Hall they found Teo sitting on the edge of a group of men that were airing their grievances against women under the direction of another Novice, from the bits that Mags caught as he and the Novice walked up to them. Teo looked up before they got to the group, got up, and left them.

"Teo!" Mags said, sounding nervous and excited (he hoped). "They're takin' me in! They got work fer me. I got grub, bed, duds, ever'thin'! I gotta stay here but that ain't no thin'!"

Teo's face transformed into a mask of pure envy. "Wish't I got thet," he said, with jealousy tinging his speech. "Hellfires, yer gonna sleep cool, an' ev'thin'!"

The Novice laughed, and clapped Teo on the shoulder. "Keep coming and showing your faith, Brother Teo, and one day we may take you into our secular fellowship as well. But go on home now—stop by the food table and tell them that Novice Tomson authorized you to take home a blessing-basket. If we are going to deprive you of the company of your friend for a while, the least we can do is feed your body as well as your soul."

Teo's face lit up. "Thenkee sor!" he said, and clasped Mags shoulders. "Ye do good, Pakler. Ye put in good word fer me."

Mags slapped him on the back. "Damn if I don'," he promised. "Now git, so's ye kin git some sleep."

Teo hurried off to the food table. As the Novice let Mags back toward the cells, he saw Teo talking to the Novice in charge of the food. The man left and returned quickly bearing a covered basked that looked quite heavy, which he put into Teo's hands.

At that point they left the Fellowship Hall, and Mags didn't see what happened next.

Mags lay back on a very comfortable bed by the standards of Harkon and Pakler, with his hands under his head. This was a real bed, rope-strung and all, with a good tufted wool mattress and real sheets, blanket, and pillow. He was clean—and very glad that his "disguise" of Pakler was far less than Harkon required, or it wouldn't have lasted past the extremely thorough bath he'd been told to take. He was wearing brand new clothing—just for sleeping, he'd been told—a set of light trews and a sleeveless jerkin that had been cut out of extremely worn sheets, and expertly sewn together. The very sort of sheets that effigy that had been burned had been made of. . . .

He had two more sets of common clothing, also clean, waiting for him, and several changes of breeks. And new, canvas boots. "Sethor requires cleanliness, Brother Pakler," the Novice had said, in a voice that told Mags that there would be no arguments accepted. Not that he intended to argue. If anything, he was grateful. All the sweating he'd done tonight as he ran over the roofs and wrecked that shop had made herb-dust stick to him all over, and until that bath, he'd been intolerably itchy.

Once clean, with his new possessions in hand, and his few

personal belongings piled on top of the new clothing, he'd been shown to one of the cells—which turned out to be what lay behind the doors in the corridor. As he had expected, they were small, narrow rooms, with a bed, a table, and a small chest where he was told to put his things.

Then the Novice had bid him good night, and shut the door, leaving him in darkness. Not total darkness; there was a slit window just at the ceiling, presumably to let in fresh air, and which now let in moonlight, but there wasn't enough light to do more than grope his way to the bed and lie down on it.

He was just composing himself to try to talk to Nikolas, when his father-in-law's mind touched his instead. *:Mags?:*

:Aye. I'm alone, and kin talk.:

:Teo came and reported to Kriss. Kriss wrote it all down and sent my man from the Guards back to me with the report.:

Mags smiled a little into the dark, but was careful to make it no more than the smile of a simple man who has found himself in sudden comfort. Just in case someone was still watching. Then he turned over on his side and tucked his arm around his head. *:That Teo's as smart as I hoped. Aight. Here's what happened.:* He told Nikolas everything, as concisely as possible. Not that there was much to tell, except that *now* they knew for certain that the vandalism of womens' shops had been done—or at least, hired done—by the Sethorites. And he had more evidence that someone, or more than one person, was using Farsight.

:I'm followin' through,: he finished. *:This's every bit as good a foot in as I'd hoped.:*

:It's more than I hoped for,: Nikolas said. *:I'll make a report to the King.:*

And there it was. No, "be carefuls," no orders to stay in touch via some agent or other, just the plain acknowledgement, in what Nikolas did *not* say, that Nikolas was certain of Mags' competence and was going to leave him alone to work the job. Mags felt a little thrill of accomplishment.

:Thankee, Nikolas.: The "presence" that was Nikolas faded from his mind, and he turned his concentration to the harder task of talking to Amily.

:Hey, love,: he sent her.

Mags! he "saw" in her mind. And then a waft of emotion poured over him. He was no empath, but he felt it dimly anyway, perhaps because of their emotional bond, or maybe it was all in his head, just because he knew her so well. But he didn't think so; it was compounded of worry and pride, love and frustration. He fully understood the frustration. She felt like she was doing nothing.

:We need you there, *'cause the only person who can properly protect Helane is you,:* he reminded her. *:If we put a guard on the girl, an' he's got someone with eyes on her, we'll alert the Poison Pen. If we send her away, we know for sure he'll find out. But you kin be her friend. An' you know what t'look fer. An' most of all, you got little spies all* over *the Palace. Somethin's not right, all them muff-dogs'll know.:*

He sensed that she was thinking, hard. *:I wish their quarters were bigger. We could use one of those mastiffs Dia raises.:* Then he *felt* an idea hit her. *:I wonder if she breeds a smaller dog that just alerts, rather than attacks? I'll ask her . . .:*

:Leavin' all that in your hands, love. You'll know best what t'do when you take the lay'a the land. Tell yer Pa I said so, too. Wish I was up there, but at least I ain't far.:

More love. And a sense of amusement. *:And at least you're not a hostage. Goodnight!:*

He pushed his face into the pillow so his grin wouldn't show. *Heh. At least I ain't a hostage . . .*

18

Mags sat patiently in another small, bare room. He'd dressed in his "new" clothing—which was clearly used, but much better and cleaner than anything Pakler had ever worn, and breakfasted in a smaller hall with the Novices, the Precepts, and a half dozen men who were dressed as he was. *The "Soldiers of Sethor?" Probably.* He took careful note of his surroundings, without seeming to. This, at least, was something he had a great deal of practice in. He did have to wonder at the Sisters of Ardana; they were supposed to be an entirely peaceful Order, but he'd seen keeps that were less like fortresses than this. Take this room; stone all around, except for three windows high up on the wall, with decorative iron grates over them. Decorative, yes, but still, they were *iron grates.* But maybe the Sisters had bought this place from another dying religion, as they in turn had been bought out.

He made no conversation, and no one made any with him;

everyone seemed very intent on their own food and their own business. Then when he was done, he was sent by one of the Novices he had been eating with to this little room, with a couple of stone seats in it. He took one, and waited.

If he had been the same stolid character he was pretending to be, waiting wouldn't bother him, so he didn't let a bit of impatience show. Someone like Pakler would be used to waiting on other people's leisure. In fact, that was half of what poor people did, when it came right down to it; if you had no steady job, you did a lot of waiting.

Eventually a new Novice came in, and took the other stone seat. This was a tall, thin, blond one, with the same hard—say it, *fanatical*—eyes as all the rest. "Well, Pakler, are you still prepared to serve the God in whatever capacity he calls you to?" the robed man asked.

"Aye, sor." Mags bobbed his head earnestly. To Pakler, who was at the very bottom of the social scale, everyone was "sir." And he would bow and scrape to whoever had marginally better clothing, just in case.

"Are you prepared to take your instructions by Mindspeech?" The Novice raised an eyebrow. Mags did not have to conceal his shock. Thank goodness. Because this was a real shock and not at all anything he had expected. *Mindspeech? They've got Mindspeech too?* Never had he heard of anyone but a Herald with Mindspeech.

Then the impact of that shook him, and he clamped a shield down hastily around his inner thoughts. Oh, it was a damn good thing that Dallen had drilled him in every sort of thing that Mindspeech could do, because if he had to hide his identity from another Mindspeaker this could get . . . interesting.

He let careful things leak. Slow, methodical thoughts. Puzzlement. That should be the chief one. A little fear, because someone like Pakler was a little afraid of anything new.

"Mindspeech?" he said, sounding like a man who was sorely puzzled, and letting more fuzzy impressions of puzzlement and worry drift over the top of his mental shield. "That be like them Heralds, with talkin' in yer head, belike? But I thunk—on'y Heralds could do thet."

The Novice smiled. *Is he a Mindspeaker? No . . . no, Or I'd already be beaten within an inch of my life. Or, more likely, beaten to death. Would they dare to kill a Herald? They might.* It was a big step from killing a dog to killing a man, but on the other hand, if they knew he was a Herald, that might send them over the edge enough to do just that. "The God gives us many powers, Brother Pakler. The ability to guide you on a task from afar is one of them."

"Huh. I'll be." He scratched his head, which he had *not* combed when he got up this morning, so he would look tousled and untidy, and less like Herald Mags. *Well, this is not good. He doesn't know that* I *have Mindspeech and could hear him if I chose, so this other Mindspeaker is powerful enough to talk to people that don't have Gifts themselves. I thought* I *was the only one around that could do that!*

And that left him with another problem. Now he didn't dare use Mindspeech himself, lest this other Mindspeaker pick it up. He wasn't even certain he dared talk to Dallen directly . . . at least not while he was in the Temple. And not while there were so few other minds around his. He'd have to be somewhere very crowded to try it, and he had the distinct impression that "in a crowd" was the last place his "brothers" would let him be right now.

"So since you have no objection, Brother," the Novice continued, smoothly. "We will move on to the next phase of your testing."

Mags allowed himself to look a bit alarmed. "I ain't gonna lose m'place here am I?" he asked anxiously. "Iffen I cain't hear this stuff? I wanta serve Sethor, I wanta stay—I did all right last night, t'other Novice said so!"

The Novice smiled soothingly. "Don't you worry about that, Brother Pakler. We do not direct *every* Soldier of Sethor with Mindspeech. Just the most special ones. We are sure you will be one of the special ones."

Which means either that they know I'm Gifted, which is a big damn problem, or their Mindspeaker is as strong as me. Or maybe not. Mags could Mindspeak to literally anyone. But this Novice had implied that *their* Mindspeaker could only talk to some of the unGifted. So maybe he wasn't quite as good as Mags.

Don't count on it, and don't get cocky.

"For now, we would like you to rest. You will be performing your task by night, as you did last night. If you wake and are hungry, you may go straight to the kitchen and help yourself. I will show you where it is. You already know where the privies are, yes?" The Novice seemed utterly oblivious to the roil of anxiety and racing thoughts under his shield. And surely if the Mindspeaker had detected all of this, he'd have informed the Novice. *I might still get away with this.*

"Aye, sor," Mags said humbly. Then he smiled shyly. "Don' mind sleepin' th' day. On'y time I ever bin let t'do thet was when I bain't got work. An' then, a empty belly don't make fer good sleepin'."

"I can imagine," the Novice replied carelessly, and Mags got the distinct impression this fellow had never known a hungry day in his life. *Highborn? Maybe. Definitely better than a farmhand or a craftsman's helper.* "All right, let me show you the kitchen. We'll be serving you better food than we dole out in the Fellowship Hall, as I am sure you learned this morning."

"Aye sor," Mags repeated, this time sounding eager, as would any man who'd lived lean for a very long time, when told he was about to be able to enjoy all he could eat. There seemed to be two sorts of men here; the ones like Mags, the common working man—or just as common thug and layabout—and the ones like these, who came from a slightly better, or significantly better background. And the latter treated the former like . . . children to be indulged as long as they were good little children who did exactly as they were told.

He followed the Novice to the kitchen, which was just off the smaller hall where he and the others had eaten this morning. It was enormous, scrupulously clean, and warmer than the rest of the building. To his surprise there were *women* here.

Women who kept their heads down, didn't speak, and scuttled around like frightened mice. Mags restrained the impulse to say something. Here, it was clear, the principles of Sethor the Patriarch were put into practice . . . and when one of the women raised her head for a moment and he saw her bruised face, it was painfully clear just how Sethor's discipline was enforced.

They didn't look starved, and they were well-clothed, a little too well, actually, and identically, in shifts that were tied tightly around their necks, with sleeves that ended at their wrists, skirts that went all the way down to the floor, and aprons over it all. If this kitchen hadn't been in the cool of this stone building, they'd have been suffocating. As it was there was enough heat from the fireplaces and the ovens built into them to make them all sweat enough that their hair sent out little damp straggles and curls from under the kerchiefs they all wore.

The Novice smiled smugly. "Whatever you need to eat, you may take from here if it is not a mealtime," he said. "And . . . if you pass this second test, you may take *whatever you want* from this room." His nod as Mags looked from him, to one of the women, and back again, made it quite clear he meant the women workers. And to drive that home, he added, "Just do not leave the female incapable of her duties afterward. Otherwise you may do with her as you wish. That is the privilege of the Soldiers of Sethor."

Mags had never wanted to strangle anyone so much in his life, but he managed to grin—it probably looked a bit feral, which was all for the best—and say "Aye, sor!" And if that came out a bit fierce, well . . . a man who had been without a woman for quite some time might well sound fierce when told he could have one.

Told I can have one . . . as if they're pocket pies to be passed around and eaten by anyone, and not people! But it was quite clear that to the Novice, while these poor things might be intrinsically more valuable than a pocket pie, they were accounted to have no more free will than one.

The Novice left him, and he resisted the urge to grab these women and herd them out the door to freedom. It was a very powerful urge, but it would probably terrify them, and would end up exposing him for what he was. So he didn't. Instead he went back to his room like a good little Soldier of Sethor, and laid himself down on the bed as he had been instructed to do.

At least he was able to take better measure of his quarters; stone all around, no signs that the walls had ever been decorated; weak sunlight came through the slit near the ceiling, showing him that the outside wall here must be as thick as his forearm and hand.

He stared at it for a moment; he had thought of escaping through that slit, but it was quite clear now that it was too narrow and the wall was too thick for anything of the sort. One of his littles in Aunty Minda's gang might be able to, but not he.

All right, then. I'll have to see this through and take the hard way. He closed his eyes. He was going to have to do one of the most difficult mental tasks he had ever attempted. He was going to have to construct, quite literally, two minds. The first one, which would remain shielded, would be the real one. The second would have only the surface thoughts of the common sort of thuggish laborer he was supposed to be. The only time he'd ever tried anything like this, was when he'd tried to hold the kernel of "himself" intact through the barrage of drugs and memories that the Sleepgivers had put him through. He wished he had Dallen here, or dared to contact the Companion. This would have been a *lot* easier with Dallen's help.

On the whole he was very glad that he'd been given the day to "rest." He was going to need the entire day to build his "overmind" and rest from the labor.

First things first. The shield, which needed to look to a fellow Mindspeaker not like a shield at all, but like the murky bottom of a very stupid mind.

* * *

He emerged from his work at the ringing of a bell; there had been a similar bell rung this morning, when a Novice had come to take him to breakfast. Mindful that someone might be watching him, he stretched and got up slowly, as if he'd been sleeping.

I ain't goin' into that kitchen, no matter how hungry I be. If he couldn't rescue those poor women, then at least he wouldn't terrify them by going in there and making them think he was about to drag one of them off and rape her. Let whoever was keeping an eye on him believe that he was being very careful about minding the rules. This was a *mealtime*, therefore, he would eat with everyone else.

He kept his head down and appeared sleepy, and inhaled everything that he was offered. Mental work was *hard*, and he was ravenous.

After he'd eaten, he went straight back to his bed, and resumed his work, making his mental shields as tough as he ever had in his life, and setting a few dull thoughts about food and nice beds and sleep and how the women deserved everything they got to coat the surface of those shields. By the time he was done, the bell was ringing for dinner.

There were real windows in this room, and as he ate with the others, he watched the sun set and scarcely tasted what he'd been given. It wouldn't be very much longer before his ruse was tested . . . and he honestly did not know what he would do if he was found out. Try to call for Dallen of course, and any other Herald he could reach, but, what if he was prevented? The Sethorites could kill him and get rid of the body and deny he'd ever been here and there was *nothing* to show that he had been. Or . . . even worse, with a Mindspeaker as powerful as *he* was among them, the Sethorites could do what the Sleepgivers had not been able to accomplish, and wipe out his mind. Then they could just turn him loose on the street, a drooling idiot, and deny that he'd been inside their walls. No matter what Dallen and Nikolas said, the Sethorites could claim immunity from Truth Spell, and he had no way of leaving any token that he had been here. Even his original clothing was gone. With a Farseer possibly watching his every move, he didn't even dare scratch some identifying token in the stone of his cell.

Such were the gloomy thoughts that occupied him when he went back to his room, and waited to be contacted. The room grew dim, then dark, and still there was nothing. Grimly, he kept up his shield and the slow, dim thoughts of "Pakler" on the other side of it, keeping himself busy by changing them from time to time, from food, to runs over the rooftops, to memories of destroying that herb shop, then back to food again.

And finally, when he had begun to think he'd surely been detected for the fraud that he was . . .

:Soldier Pakler.: The Mindvoice was . . . odd. Not like any Mindvoice he'd ever heard before. Flat, expressionless. *:You will take your knife, but nothing else, go out into the hall, and turn right.:*

Obediently he did exactly that. From there he was directed to a small door that proved to be an entrance into a walled herb garden. He was told to climb the wall, using a ladder that was in a shed, and use the wall to get to the rooftops.

From there, the strange, flat voice guided him. Twice he was told to hide, once behind a chimney, and once by hanging over the side of a steep roof. Both times, he had no sooner gotten out of sight than he heard the sounds of men in the street—didn't dare try to get a glimpse of them to see who they were, but he suspected they were some of the augmented Watch patrols that the Prince had promised.

While he waited, he dared an experiment. He let another, not entirely anomalous thought creep over the surface of his shields. The suggestion of another, better path to travel, one with surer footing and more hiding places.

If the one Mindspeaking to him noticed the thought, he didn't even acknowledge the fact.

Finally, the voice directed him to drop down into a small yard in the back of another shop, and enter it. This was a small yard with some small, smelly vats of unidentifiable liquid in them, and he suspected they were dye. It was even easier to open this door than the last one; just pass his knife between the door and the frame and he could flick open the latch.

He walked into the shop, which had a generous window in front—a glass window, which was unusual. He looked around, as the smell of good leather hit his nose. Then it was obvious why he'd been told to bring his knife.

The shop belonged to someone who made small, fine leather objects; gloves, fancy belt-pouches, leather vests and bodices, cases for small, expensive objects, like fine tools, pens, or delicate instruments, all beautifully tooled or embellished. It broke his heart to do so, to see all that delicate work ruined, but he used his knife as the Mindvoice directed, and put defacing slashes through every single thing in the shop, no matter how small.

But he worked slowly, feigning that his knife was duller than it actually was, hoping somehow to be able to save some of these things. And whenever possible, he slashed the backs, not the fronts; the backs might be mended, and the owner would have to discount the items for the repair, but at least she wouldn't lose everything.

But he had only been at this "work" a short time when the Mindvoice suddenly interrupted him. :*Stop*,: it said. :*You must leave, now! Return to the Temple at once, as fast as you can.*:

Repressing his relief, he bolted out the back, clambered up the drainpipe to the roof, and ran for it.

The Mindvoice directed him to come in the front of the Temple— and the same Novice that had met him last night met him there tonight. "Well done, Pakler," the Novice told him, slapping him on the back. "Sorry we had to interrupt you, but there was a special patrol of the Watch who had keys to every shop in that area. They were opening every door and checking inside before moving on." The Novice frowned as he led Mags in. "Obviously the sluts went to whine at the King, and got him to order this. We'll have to put a halt to our night-work for a while, at least in the better parts of town, and there aren't any women owning shops elsewhere that we haven't already dealt with."

"Does thet mean ye ain't gonna need me?" Mags replied in feigned alarm, stopping right there in the hallway, and widening his eyes like a frightened horse.

The Novice's frown turned to a smile. "Not a bit of it. We'll just put you to a different sort of work. Now that we know you can hear the Mindspeech, you're being appointed as one of the Elite Soldiers of Sethor." He paused at the door to Mags' room. "Is there anything you need tonight? Food? Drink? The kitchen women have gone to bed, but I can have one brought to you if you're not particular."

Mags thought for a moment he was going to gag, but evidently neither the Novice nor any other watcher noticed. "No, sor. Uh, no, thet ain't true. I'd admire me some wine."

"That's easily done. I'll have some brought to you." The Novice left him at his door, and he went inside, leaving the door open so the light from the torches in the hallway shone inside.

He'd taken off his boots by the time a boy turned up with an open bottle of wine, it looked about two-thirds empty, which suited him. "Novice Tarenton said ye was t'hev this, Sojer," the boy said from the doorway. "What'd ye do tonight?"

Mags held out his hand, and the boy came into the room, handing him the bottle. *What would Pakler do? Boast. Definitely boast.* "Well," he said, inflating his chest as the boy stood there in the light from the door, looking at him, wide-eyed and worshipful. "Seems I got skills."

He spun a wild tale of running across rooftops, evading a dozen patrols of the Watch, utterly destroying the stock of a woman who was *clearly* some kind of witch, based on all the arcane symbols he saw carved and stitched into her goods. "Up to no good, she were," he lied. "Bet she were puttin' evil spells on poor fellahs t'make 'em do whut she wanted, like i' th' old, bad times. But Sethor done give me strenth! An' when I left, there weren't nothin' i' thet place could harm a flea."

The last, at least wasn't a lie.

"Cor!" breathed the boy. "I cain't hardly wait till I'm a Sojer like you!"

Mags reached out and ruffled the boy's hair. "Ye will be, soon 'nuff," he said. "Now be off. An close door behind ye."

He really *did* feel in need of the wine—which was quite good. Not really *excellent* wine, but then, someone like Pakler wouldn't know excellent wine if it stood up in the bottle and announced its quality to him. He drank it slowly, while he thought.

Now he knew exactly how the Poison Pen had been delivering letters up on the Hill. There were three people involved, the delivery-thug, a Farseer, and a Mindspeaker. The Farseer would keep track of their delivery man, while the Mindspeaker gave him instructions on where to go and which letter to deliver to whom, warning him if anyone was about to see him at work so he could hide. There may even have been more than one delivery man up there; that would make the job go quite a bit faster.

That was why the Poison Pen was no longer able to deliver letters personally once the shield against Farseeing had been put up.

So, he thought, finishing the bottle. *I know the how and the why. I just need to find out the* who. *And somehow I need to let Nikolas know. And all without the Mindspeaker figuring out I'm not what I seem. . . .*

There were only two candles burning in the room, giving just enough light that the people sitting in low chairs around an equally low table could see where to put their wine glasses. Gauze screens on the windows let in the lovely, cool breeze that stirred the curtains, but kept out the insects. It was too bad no one was in a mood to enjoy their surroundings.

". . . so Dallen is lurking passively in the background of Mags' mind, and not even *Mags* knows he's listening," Nikolas told Amily, Jorthun and Lady Dia. And Prince Sedric, who was attending this little meeting—which they were holding in the Prince's rooms, well inside the protections the spirit of the stone was holding against Farseers.

I can't believe how lucky we were that the Sethorite Farseer never learned enough about Lord Jorthun to keep an eye on him, she thought. Then again, Jorthun's identity as the King's agent was known only to a very few, and none of those people were ones that were being watched by the Poison Pen. *Except perhaps me, now . . . . I can only thank all the gods that I never led him to Jorthun.*

"So Dallen is talking to your Companion, and also to Rolan." Sedric chewed on his lower lip as he thought. "I am tempted to ask him to add my Companion to the list, but I think perhaps—"

:Tell him I will speak with his Companion,: Rolan interjected, before he could finish his sentence.

"Rolan says he'll keep you informed," Amily said, as Sedric mulled over his next few words. "It's all right, I think he can handle it. *I'm* not in danger of being discovered by a lot of dangerous fanatics."

Sedric's face cleared. "That suits me. I don't want Dallen to be overburdened at a time when he needs to be watching closely for signs his Chosen is in danger."

"Is he in danger?" Amily asked, finally asking the one thing she wanted to know. "Can we get him out if something goes wrong?"

"Well, we know this system works without their Mindspeaker detecting anything," Nikolas went on. "I was down in Haven last night; I was able to alert the Watch to check that leather-worker's shop, and according to what the Novice said to Mags, none of the Sethorites guessed the interruption was due to anything other than bad luck and vigilence on the part of the Watch." Her father's voice took on tones of admiration. "I can't believe the mental work he did, creating a false mind on top of the true one, with hardened shields in between. That's the work of . . . well the most talented and skillful Mindspeaker *I* ever heard of."

"He did manage to keep himself sane when he was a slavey in those mines for a good six months or more after his Gift emerged," Amily reminded her father. "And that was without any teaching at all. But you haven't answered my question. He's in the equivalent of a fortress, and I don't know how we'd get to him in time if they discovered he was a Herald!"

They all looked at her soberly, as if to remind her that a Herald's life was not . . . safe. Then her father spoke. "Dallen is confident that Mags can keep up his 'double mind' quite easily. He is also confident that the Mindspeaker is not going to pay much attention to him, since he obeyed every command immediately and to the letter. Given all of that, Mags can do this."

She nodded, slowly. *All right. If he doesn't know we can follow what is happening to him, he might actually be safer. I can see that.*

"Let's get to the point of this meeting," Nikolas replied, with a little nod to Amily of encouragement. "We know the why, the how, and the when this monster has been acting. But we still don't know *who* he is."

Amily sipped absently at her wine. It had to be someone higher than a Precept, because this person was obviously giving orders *to* the Precepts. Did the High Priest know about all this? He had to know about a great deal of it at the very least; he'd be a pretty poor leader if he didn't know that his underlings were destroying shops under his nose. But he probably had some sort of plausible deniability set up, just in case the rest were caught. *I knew I didn't like him the minute I set eyes on him.* Did he know about the Poison Pen, though? He might not. That would only require one or two people at most, and perhaps the Poison Pen himself to write all the letters. *Nice thing about being a priest. No one really questions you about what you're doing if you're writing.*

"I have already gotten answers to my letters, thanks to you, Sedric," Jorthun replied, looking distinctly uneasy. "I have a strong suspect, and a theory. But I don't yet have any proof. If I am wrong—I do not feel it is right to make accusations, for one thing, and for another, if I name the wrong person, then the right one will be alerted and might act swiftly and impulsively . . . and that would quite literally put several lives in jeopardy. Of course . . . those people may already be in danger. I don't know, and I have no way to be sure just how far this man will go."

They looked at each other, but it was Amily who spoke. "That's all very well, but if those people are already in danger I think *someone* should know. Who *are* they?"

"You," Jorthun said to Amily. "And Lady Tyria, and possibly Helane."

She was a bit taken aback by the fact that *she* was in danger . . . why? But then it struck her, all those letters telling her she should die and let her father be King's Own again. She might not be a threat to another woman's man, but by the Sethorite beliefs she was certainly stealing a man's job. "I can take care of myself, but shouldn't we warn *them*?" she asked, saying what Nikolas and Sedric were surely thinking.

"That is a problem," Jorthun replied. "Warning them, or at least, doing so openly, would warn our target. But we should certainly take steps to protect them."

Since that was pretty much a direct echo of what Mags had told her the last time they had been able to "speak," she nodded. "Mags had an idea," she said. "That I should befriend both of them; that way I have an excuse to keep an eye on them. We really can't take the chance that whichever Sethorite this is hasn't got more ordinary eyes and ears up here on the Hill."

"My thought exactly," Jorthun agreed. "I was going to suggest just that, and I think that will go a long way toward protecting them.

"But I have another idea," she continued. "Can we tell all of Lord Lional's children *except* Helane? Mags and I have had dealings with the other three, and they're clever, steady, and Lirelle is the one that made Helane talk to her mother about the improper conduct of that so-called music tutor in the first place."

Jorthun pondered this. "Do you think you can trust them to keep quiet? If so, then they would be ideal. They can alert us at the first sign of trouble."

"I think we'd be foolish *not* to include them." Amily frowned. "Part of me is saying to tell Lord Lional, but we all know what he'd do—he'd take them all home, and home would be even less safe for them than here is."

"That's sadly accurate," Nikolas agreed. "This Sethorite has made up his mind to act, and running—well, it would be like running from a predator. It will only make him attack. If he has the resources, he could probably even ambush them on the road, where they are *utterly* unprotected."

"I only have one more suggestion—Dia, do you also breed a smallish guard dog? Something the size of a rabbit-hound perhaps?" Amily asked, but Dia shook her head.

"No, I am sorry, but the only dogs I have that are trained to alert and to guard are the mastiffs," she said regretfully.

"All right, this is as much of a plan as we can manage for now," Sedric proclaimed. "Amily, you approach the children in the morning. Nikolas, I'm making your *only* duty to be down in Haven, at the ready, in case Mags needs help. You might set yourself up in the nearest Watch post. Jorthun—try and get me some more real evidence, something we can actually use to *charge* this man before he can act."

"It probably won't be possible," Jorthun warned.

"Try anyway." He looked around at them all. "All right. You all have your tasks. Nikolas, yours starts now."

In the morning, with Dean Caelen's help, Amily intercepted all three of Lord Lional's younger offspring, and got them all spirited up to the library, as being the one place there could not possibly be any Sethorite spies. They were clearly perplexed at being intercepted, and even more perplexed when they saw who was waiting for them in the middle of the library. Before any of them could burst out with questions, she said, "We think your mother and Helane are in danger."

Lirelle, as she had suspected, was the first to catch on. "From the man who's been writing all those letters! The one that killed the dog!" Then her face betrayed uncertainty. "But why? I mean, why *Helane*? She didn't get any more letters than anyone else. And why mother? She didn't get any *at all*."

"We think the letter writer may be the father of that tutor you disgraced," she told them frankly.

They thought about that for a moment. "And he wants revenge?" Hawken ventured. His eyes darkened with anger, and he clenched his fist on the hilt of his belt-knife. "Just let him try! I'll—"

Loren punched him in the biceps. "Don't be *stupid,* stupid!" he said, crossly. "Weaponsmaster can wipe the floor with me, and I'm better than you are at everything. He's been really smart so far, do you think he's going to be so stupid as to send somebody that hasn't killed people before? We wouldn't stand a chance." Hawken opened and shut his mouth several times, but didn't try to contradict his younger brother. He went up several degrees in Amily's estimation at that. So did Loren. *Oh, I really like these youngsters.*

"We don't want you to try and fight anyone," she told them. "If he decides to hurt your mother and sister, we just don't know *what* he would send. But what you absolutely can do is watch over them all the time. Here." She gave each of them a silver whistle, disguised as a pendant. Hawken's was an ax, Loren's was an arrow, and Lirelle's was a bird. "If you see *anything* suspicious, blow that whistle. We've already tried them; they're loud. The Guards have all been told to come on the run if they hear it. And having an alarm raised will probably unnerve anyone that was sent. That will give you a few moments to try and get them to somewhere safe. We're telling you and not your mother and Helane because we want them to act naturally. They are the ones that any spies will be watching."

"Shouldn't we tell Father?" Lirelle asked doubtfully.

"Absolutely not," Hawken exclaimed, before Amily could say anything. "He'll either not believe it and tell Mother, and then she'll be nervous and give the whole thing away, or he *will* believe it and try to take us back home. We'll be open to ambush at ten or a dozen places along the road, and *if* we get home, we won't have Guards everywhere. I know it's horrid, but it's safer here."

Amily let out a sigh of relief. These younglings had real sense. And they proved it in the next moment.

"Tell us exactly what you do and do not want us to do," said Hawken, as his siblings nodded agreement.

As Amily left the Collegium, she saw yet another series of laden carts, followed by a pair of very fine traveling carriages and a string of riding horses, heading for the Palace gate. A string of servants, looking a bit worn, shuffled in the direction of the Palace. It looked as if whoever was leaving had commandeered everyone possible to load the carts. She intercepted one of the Palace porters before he could go back to other duties.

"Who's leaving now?" she asked, as the man paused; her Whites got her his attention, where anything else other than a Guard uniform probably wouldn't have. He looked ready for a tall drink of water and a moment of rest.

"Lady Harmitege an' her pretty chickens," said the porter. "Eight of 'em. Eight! *And* all their fripperies and all." He looked perfectly happy to stand in the shade of one of the garden trees and gossip—and Amily was perfectly happy to let him. It wouldn't be "gossip" in his mind, obviously, it would be "informing the Herald."

"Eight!" he repeated, shaking his head in disbelief. "'Course, four of 'em is cousins, but 'ow she 'spected t'get 'em all married off—well ain't my problem, thank the gods. Can't blame 'em for leavin' either. Six of the eight was gettin' them nasty letters. The dog was the last straw, I reckon."

"Thank you," Amily replied, and then stopped stock still as a brilliant idea occurred to her. Lady Harmitege had inhabited—of course, with all those girls—the largest suite of rooms available to courtiers. And the Farseer *couldn't see what was going on here on the Hill anymore.* If she moved Lord Lional's family there, that would be one more significant layer of safety.

Now, as Nikolas and the others had pointed out, the Poison Pen might have ordinary spies up here . . .

But I doubt he will in the courtier's wing. We've gone over and over every single servant that does so much as pull weeds under their windows, and they are all good, loyal, and have been with us for a very long time.

:I agree, Amily,: said Rolan. *:The Seneschal is in his office. You can arrange to have Lord Lional's family moved immediately. I doubt very much that they will object to a change in quarters that allows them each a private bedroom.:*

She hurried to the Seneschal's office and caught him just before he left it. It took no more than a few words and he was happy to make the arrangements.

"Can you leave their old suite empty?" she asked hesitantly, when he agreed.

He arched an eyebrow at her. "I know exactly what is going on, you know, Herald Amily," he said to her. "I'm one of your father's—special circle. He's kept me informed of everything, so I can take proper precautions. You might as well tell me what you have in mind."

"I thought that I might as well spend the nights in that suite," she told him, with no hesitation. "Of course, the fewer people who know *that,* the better."

"Ah, set a trap. That's a good idea." He pondered it a moment. "Well, with courtiers fleeing—not that I blame them—there isn't anyone exactly clamoring for those rooms. I don't see why I can't leave them empty for a fortnight or so. *If*—" he looked at her sternly "—you will consent to an extra Guard or two under the window."

"I was going to ask for that," she replied, with a shrug. "I'll have Rolan tell my father, and anyone else he thinks should know, too."

"Good." The Seneschal brought his eyebrow back down. "One always hopes you Heralds will be sensible, but one never knows."

"Oh pish," she said, managing a faint smile. "Next you will be complaining about us cluttering up the lawn, and shaking your cane at us, and calling us 'young hooligans.'"

"Herald Amily—" he called after her as she turned to go.

"Yes, Seneschal?" she replied, turning back.

"Good hunting." Without waiting for her reply, he hurried off on whatever errand he was on before she interrupted him.

19

It had been a full sennight since that last aborted run on the leather-worker's shop, and Mags had not left the confines of the Sethorite Temple. He had exercised with the other Soldiers, and sparred with them, careful to show no more skill at weaponry than a simple laborer should have—but also taking care to seem to "learn" some of those skills quickly. Not so quickly as to excite suspicion, but enough to make him look as if he was earnestly trying with all his might to do what his masters wanted him to.

When he wasn't exercising, sparring, and sleeping, he was taking religious instruction, twice a day, some with all the other Soldiers, and some on his own. He had been given a copy of the ponderous Book of Sethor, which was every bit as misogynistic as he would have expected, and was told firmly to read it in his free time. So read it he did. And he was completely unsurprised to see a great many examples of the sort of raving that had been in those letters and scrawled on walls repeated word for word in the Book. He had already decided to smuggle his copy of the Book out as soon as he could manage; he'd marked the relevant passages by dog-earing the corners. It was more corroborating evidence that the Sethorites were involved, since they never let copies of their Book out of the Temple. 'Enough pebbles make an avalanche,' as they used to say in the mine. Hopefully, even if they didn't catch the Poison Pen himself, this would be a big enough avalanche to bury the entire Temple.

For the rest, if it hadn't been for the work of holding a double mind, this would have been something of a holiday. He was fed very well indeed by the standards of his persona. There was meat in his stew, his bread wasn't half sawdust, and there was butter on it. His oatmeal pottage in the morning was full of currants. There were fruit pies and seedcakes. And there was good ale and wine with every meal. If he had been who he claimed he was . . . well . . . this life would have been extremely seductive, and he probably would have succumbed to it by now, as had his fellow Soldiers. After all it was a fine thing to be told that your proper rights had been stolen from you by pernicious women, that your lack of success was not your fault, but theirs, that in the proper order of things you would be a master whose orders were obeyed without question. And it was an intoxicating thing to be solemnly told how important you were, and to a god, no less! And then to be treated with *respect*, fed well, housed better than Pakler would have been in his life, given everything he could possibly want, including a woman whenever he wanted . . . not that he made use of that. He had been afraid at first that this might tip his hand, but . . . no, he wasn't the only one to ignore the kitchen women. So he kept his mouth shut and read the Book.

It was not surprising that his fellow Soldiers were not thinking *at all* about what they were doing—unless it was to relish the "revenge" they were getting on women who should have been treating them like kings. It was in their self-interest not to think too hard about all the laws they were already breaking and believe everything the Precepts told them.

He did notice one thing, however. Every time he tried to go to the Fellowship Hall, where he might meet Teo, he was carefully, and subtly, steered away.

He thought about trying anyway, but that would damage the impression of complete and unthinking obedience he was trying to give, the picture of someone who was completely taken in and ready to do *anything* that was asked of him. So after three days, he stopped trying.

And as the days passed, he became more and more certain of his "double-minded" disguise. Either the Mindspeaker never spent much time on him, or he—it had to be a "he," given the Sethorite bias—never bothered to look past that false upper layer.

Mags wasn't going to press his luck, though, by trying to contact Dallen or Nikolas while he was inside the Temple. And he hadn't been allowed outside it to try. Before he did that, he needed to be away from the presence of someone who could potentially sense when another Mindspeaker was present.

But tonight . . . tonight he got the feeling that something was afoot. Tonight's dinner had not been a heavy stew, but venison steak—and the drink had not been wine, but something else, a tisane of some sort, sweet with honey and so pleasant none of the diners appeared to miss the wine. It left him feeling alert and very clear-minded. *I need to find out what this stuff is and get the Healers to look it over. It seems like something we could use.*

And when the dishes were cleared away, and he returned to his cell, there was something new there. A lit candle on the bedside table next to his copy of the Book—he'd never been granted a light in here until now. A sheet of folded paper on top of the book. And lying on the bed, laid out for him, a new outfit. There was a close-fitting suit of all-black clothing, with a hood and gloves, a set of long knives, and a simple robe of the sort that the Novices wore.

He unfolded the paper and began to read the closely written instructions.

You will memorize these instructions, it began. *You will put on the suit, leaving the suit hood down until you need it, and put the robe over all, leaving the robe hood* up. *Once you are clothed, you will go to the courtyard where you have been taking your exercise. You will join the Brothers who go up to the Palace twice a week to collect food from the feasts for the poor. You will be watched. Once there, you and three of your fellow Soldiers will slip away from the rest at the earliest opportunity. You will go to the dairy to wait. The dairy is just past the kitchen door where your cart will stop. It is a separate building, painted white, with a slabbed stone path leading to it. You will go in there and hide until full dark. When it is full dark, you will discard your robe, put the hood of the suit up and pull the front down over your eyes. When you have adjusted the hood to your liking, you will begin the mission.*

The directions continued, sending him to Healer's Collegium, then in through the door of his very own rooms. *There you will find the blasphemy that holds the title of "King's Own," and you will slay her, that a proper man may once again take the position that is rightfully his.*

For a moment, he sat there, trying not to shake with combined rage and anguish, chilled by how narrow an escape Amily had had. Then—well it was a good thing he was sitting, because if he'd been standing, he would have been weak-kneed with relief that it was *he* that was supposed to kill her, and not one of the other three. At least he knew for certain Amily would be safe tonight!

He covered all this by staying bent over the page of instructions, as if he was memorizing it, bracing himself to keep from trembling. He was supposed to be stolid and unimaginative. He shouldn't be at all moved by the orders he had been given. Controlling his emotions was almost as hard as holding the double mind. *So close . . . so close.*

Buck up, he told himself sternly. *She's safe. No one's gonna hurt her. An' even then, they know what's goin' on, they gotta be prepared up there. She kin take care of herself, and ye kin count on that. Ye need t'get yerself up the Hill so's ye kin make sure all t'other targets are safe, too.*

Well, the first thing he needed to do was get himself ready. Quickly he stripped to his breeks and began donning the black clothing. He found it oddly stretchy—how had they managed to do that?—and as a consequence, nearly form-fitting. Certainly ideal for sneaking about in the dark. He tried pulling the hood over his head as he'd been instructed, and discovered there was a slit right where his eyes should be. With some adjustment, he could see perfectly. He pulled it back down as directions had told him to do, discovered that the two flat knives fitted into sheathes on the soft boots, and donned the light robe, tying the flat fabric belt that came with it around his middle, snugly. He put the hood of his robe up, pulling it forward so it partly concealed his face and hid the black fabric at his neck. Then he went to the courtyard, where he found a milling group of what looked like about eight Novices in the same robes he was wearing. Since they all had their hoods up, he couldn't tell which of them was wearing the same black sneak-suit he was.

"Come, Brothers," said a Precept, beckoning from a door into the courtyard that he had never used before, and had never seen used. He went along with the rest, in the middle of the pack, following them down a corridor lined with empty rooms that could probably be used for storage, until they came out into the open again, in a stable-yard. There was a plain box-wagon with a mule hitched to it in the middle of the yard, which all but two of them got into. The last two mounted the front of the wagon and perched on the seat, one took the reins, and they were off, plodding out onto a different street than the Temple faced. He had no doubt that the Farseer and Mindspeaker were watching him now; possibly watching the other three as well, but definitely watching *him*. He had brought his copy of the Book with him, and without making any great fuss about it, opened it and began reading. This, he had discovered, was the easiest way of feeding his upper mind. Just fill that with the words from the Book, and everything would look completely normal to the Mindspeaker.

According to his instructions, he'd been reading from various assigned sections of the Book until now. Without any direction to follow, he started at the beginning, which was, of course, the creation story. In his limited experience every religion had a creation story, but most of the ones he'd had anything to do with gave at least a sideways acknowledgement that there were other gods that were just as important as the one their story talked about. Not this Book. Sethor started by dividing darkness and light, then created the heavens and the stars, *then* created the other gods, making them definite inferiors to himself. Then Sethor created earth, and one of the goddesses rebelled at her status of mere "helper" and he cast her to earth. Then he created everything else. When he got around to making people, he made man "out of the breath of life," but he made woman "out of the mud of the river," and designated her as man's perpetual servant. Then the cast-down goddess, now designated a demon, infested woman with her rebellion. And in the eyes of the Sethorites, that's when everything went to hell.

Even as loosely woven as this clothing was, he was getting overly warm, but at least the sun was going down; as they wound their way through town, then up through the residences of the wealthy and privileged, most of the time they were in shade. He glanced up from time to time, and couldn't help but notice they were taking the alleys and back ways, however. *Let's not trouble the highborn with the sight of our uncouth wagon.*

He went back to the Book. The writing was florid enough, and padded enough with praises to Sethor, that Mags had only just reached the part where "the demon spake sweetly to the woman, and she was weak and yielded to it," when they got to the top of the Hill and joined a line of three other carts. They were all coming in through the merchant's gate on the "working" side of the Palace.

He was going to put the book inside his robe, when he heard *:Leave the book in the cart,:* in his mind.

Obediently he tucked it under the wagon seat. They definitely had been watching him, and his double-mind was still holding. They were taking no chances that he might leave behind this bit of evidence of the Sethorites' guilt. Too bad. There could not be enough evidence, so far as he was concerned. *Hopefully I impressed them with my piety, anyway.*

Their wagon was checked over by the Guards, who gave each of the brothers a cursory search—

Too cursory. Unless that's on purpose. He wished he knew what was going on up here!

He reminded himself that he'd gotten warning through. He'd sent word out with Teo. He'd been able to Mindspeak a bit with Dallen. They *had* to have realized that something was being planned, and had planned a counter-move.

The Guards waved them through. They pulled up with the other three wagons at the kitchen door. By this time it was dusk. Dinner was well over . . . and servants were bringing out food. But there was far, far more than he had expected; these were actual supplies, not leftovers, in barrels and boxes and big burlap bags.

For a moment, Mags was taken aback, because he had no notion of what was going on here. Surely they weren't *stealing* this food! But then he realized, as he helped load these things into the wagon, that the Palace was actually supplying more than leftovers for the poor. It was providing some supplies for Temples as well. Hence, the wagon, and the eight men to load it. He looked things over quickly, and realized that this bounty was what the Sethorites were probably using to feed the folks in the Fellowship Hall. And he recalled vaguely that the Crown distributed its supplies to feed the poor through all the religious orders. *Well, I reckon th' Crown hasta treat all Temples and whatnot alike . . . but I sure don' like the fact that Sethor don't feed nobody but men.*

By the time the wagon was half loaded, it was dark, and

following his orders, Mags took the first opportunity to slip away from the rest. Of course, knowing the Hill as well as he did, it was ridiculously easy to get out of sight. But he did not go to the dairy as he'd been ordered.

As soon as he could, he slipped in through the doorway to the kitchen wood-room, to hide himself for a moment from passing Guards or servants. No one was going to be coming after wood at this time of night.

It was dark in there, with wood piled up close to the door. He backed into it, feeling the ends of the logs with one hand to make sure he didn't get snagged on them. *:Dallen!:* he called urgently, with anxiety clutching at his throat, and once again, he felt a rush of relief, this time when his Companion answered calmly.

:Take a breath, Chosen. I've been listening the entire time. I just stayed in the back of your inner mind; I knew if you had no idea I was there, no one else would either.:

:You have? You did?: He sagged against the woodpile, holding himself up with one hand braced against the end of a log behind him. It was going to be all right. They had a plan.

:Everyone has been warned. We don't know where the other three got themselves to—we are fairly certain that they are the same men who've been coming up here to plant letters, so they probably know the Hill as well as you do by now—but we'll find them. Lord Lional's family is safe. We moved them, and of course the men that came for them don't know that. Amily is waiting in their old quarters—:

:Wait, what?: he shouted. Amily wasn't safe? Amily was, in fact, in the one place that *wasn't* safe?

He tore off his robe, grabbed a stout stick from the pile and ran for the Courtier's Wing, his heart hammering with fear. *:Amily!:* he screamed at her. *:Amily!:*

Amily had been sitting on the bare floor of the suite, staff across her lap, monitoring all the muff-dogs along the hallway in turn, when her concentration was jolted by Mags' unexpected scream in her head. So she missed the exact moment when the door to the suite opened—but the light from the hallway caught her attention, and she didn't miss the door closing, the soft *shh-sh* of a blade leaving a sheathe, or the momentary gleam of steel in some fugitive light from the window. And he wasn't far from her. Fear hit her and coursed through her like a bolt of lightning—

And then it was gone, replaced with a cool calculation. Her hands steadied, she clutched the staff, she took a silent breath, and counted soft steps coming from where she had last seen that fugitive gleam of metal. *One . . . two . . .*

That was when she swung the staff she'd been holding where the invader's legs should be.

But the sound of the staff cutting the air must have alerted him; a darker shadow in the shadows leapt out of the way, then came at where she had been.

Damn. She scrambled to her feet.

He cut the air with his knife, stabbing where she had been a moment ago.

She had already moved, sliding her feet on the wooden floor to avoid making any sound, shifting around to the side.

There he is. She hit him from behind with a blow of the staff, aiming for a solid hit across both kidneys. The staff hit with a satisfying *thud,* and she heard him stagger toward the window. Now she could see him; there wasn't *much* light outside, but there was enough that he stood out against it. She swung and connected with his head, and the only reason she didn't knock him cold was that he managed to get his arm up in time to intercept the staff.

He grunted with pain, but quicker than she would have thought him able to, he wrapped his arm around the staff and pulled. Instead of resisting, she yielded, and the two of them stumbled across the room together, with the staff keeping him from grabbing her. The furniture was mostly gone, but he ran into a table that had been too big to move, and grunted in pain. He let go of the staff involuntarily, and she snatched it away from him. Reversing it, she swung at him again, but she couldn't see him now, and her staff met only air.

I'm between him and the window! she realized, and dropped and rolled until she met the wall, crawled along it for a bit then stood up, slowly, listening. Her heart pounded in her ears, but she was still in that cool, calculating state, and somehow wasn't at all afraid.

But her mouth was dry. And her neck tingled. She couldn't see him . . . but he couldn't see her, either. Now no longer a visible target, she felt her way along the wall, moving silently, and still listening as hard as she could.

She heard a soft shuffling of feet, but it stopped before she could figure out where it was coming from. *Now* she began to fear. Not much, just enough to galvanize her into action.

All right. Time to end this right now! She fumbled for the whistle around her neck, stuck it in her mouth and blew.

And with exquisitely bad timing, the whistle shrilled just as the door opened again, and two more dark figures entered. One of them shut the door, and she heard the bolt slamming home.

Now she was locked in here with all three of them. Mags was certainly coming. So were the Guards.

I just have to keep them off for a few more moments. . . . She slid along the wall, quickly, to at least get away from the spot she had stood when she had blown the whistle. Had any of them seen her?

"It's three against one," whispered a voice. "You can't win."

She kept her mouth shut. No point in giving her new position away. She kept the staff balanced horizontally in her hands, about waist high, and close to her body. She'd feel it if anyone approached her from either side; they'd run into the end of the staff.

"You in there!" This voice came from the window. "There's an entire squad of Guard out here, and more are coming down the hall. You can't escape. Surrender now!"

Just a few more moments. . . .

"God will protect us, unbelievers!" one of them shouted back shrilly.

"Shut *up*, you idiot!" hissed another. "We need a hostage! Find him!"

She couldn't help but grin at that. *Him, indeed.* What would they think if they knew they were being bested by a woman?

But at just that moment, the left-hand end of her staff moved— was bumped—and the man who'd bumped it was quick-witted enough to realize she was there and lunged for her.

Unfortunately for him, as he lunged, she did, too. She slammed the butt of the staff into something soft, and from the sound he made, it was his stomach. But the satisfaction she felt was short-lived as someone seized her from behind, and the staff fell from her hands with a clatter.

Someone was pounding on the door.

Panic hit as arms closed around her, but trained reflexes were faster. She rammed her head backward, hoping to get him in the chin, and slammed her foot down where she thought his arch might be. She did better than hitting his chin; she felt teeth on her scalp as the back of her head crunched his nose. She missed the arch of his foot, but not by much, and she heard another crunch from the floor where her hard heel hit his toes in what felt like cloth boots.

He howled with pain and let go, and once again, she dove and rolled across the floor, not stopping until she hit another wall.

The door slammed open. Light poured in. And Mags charged through it.

One of the Sethorites lunged for him; Mags pivoted, and smacked him in the side of the head with a log. She spotted another heading for him, and dove for his knees, intercepting him before he could reach Mags. She caught him completely off-guard; he lost his balance completely and went down, hitting his head on the floor with a *crack* that made her wince.

Movement as she rolled away from him made her cry *"Mags, look out!"* as the man whose nose she had broken came lunging at Mags out of the dark, knives ready.

Mags whirled. Her heart was in her mouth, as all she could see was a whirl of limbs and knives, and all she could hear were grunts of effort.

It was over in moments; there was a *thud*, and the man dropped to the floor, leaving Mags standing, panting. He dropped the log, and peered into the darkness. "Amily?"

"Here!" she said, springing to her feet and into his arms.

They clung together as the Guard poured into the room, bringing torches and lanterns. He was shaking just as hard as she was now, and their hearts hammered in double-time. *Now,* now she felt real fear, and she was ready to weep with it.

"It's over," he said, holding her tightly, as if he was afraid she would vanish if he let go. His trembling hands caressed her hair and the small of her back. "It's really over. We got 'em now."

"From your mouth to the gods' ears," she murmured into his shoulder, feeling every bit of nervous energy running right out of her, and wanting nothing more than to go to bed and sleep for an age in his arms.

"So long's it ain't Sethor," he replied.

20

The three captured Sethorites, wounds tended and bandaged, with wrists and ankles bound in iron manacles, had been shackled to three iron chairs that had been brought into the Lesser Audience Chamber. King and Prince both were on their thrones; Amily behind the Prince, her father behind the King. Jorthun stood before the dais and to the right, while Mags stood next to the manacled, would-be murderers, ready to cast the coercive Truth Spell when it was needed. The chamber was still, close, and a bit uncomfortable. This was Jorthun's idea. It was also Jorthun's idea to play the rule of "chief accuser." He wanted the attention on anyone *but* Mags.

The three felons had not said a word so far. Mags was not at all surprised. He would not have expected anything else, once he'd spent some time observing them in custody. These weren't just ordinary thugs like "Pakler" had been; they were fanatics, probably had been planting letters and destroying shops from the beginning, and they were prepared to die for Sethor.

He didn't think they were prepared for what was coming. Then again, it didn't really matter. They were mostly here as props; he didn't think Jorthun really cared if they confessed, or if he cast Truth Spell on them or not. They were here to rattle the bigger fish.

The door opened, and Theodor Kresh, the High Priest of Sethor, stepped through it, escorted by no less than four of the Guard, and accompanied by a single attendant—Mags recognized him as Kresh's second-in-command. It looked as if the Guard had collected them shortly after their three flunkies had been captured. That had been Jorthun's plan; grab them before they realized their mission had failed, and hold them until the King and Prince were ready to see them. Both of them were wearing rumpled robes that had clearly been thrown on in haste, and looked very indignant and ruffled—and both of them stopped dead when they saw the three bound men.

Jorthun stepped forward a single pace, and bowed slightly. "Master Kresh," he said smoothly. "We are about to invoke coercive Truth Spell on these men, and we thought you should be here. After all, they are known to be members of your . . . organization."

Kresh looked startled—and began looking in every direction *but* the three men, as if he was seeking a way out of this predicament. *He* was clearly unprepared for this. Whatever he had been imagining as he sat in that bare, guarded room, awaiting the King's pleasure, it obviously had not been this.

But his assistant suddenly lunged at Mags, who didn't move a hair, as the Guards piled on him and seized him. The guards hauled him back with quite a bit of effort; Mags yawned in his face, and did his best to look bored. "You are *all* cursed," he screamed, eyes wild, spittle flying, as he fought the men holding him. "You, your get, and yes, your Kingdom, that you let be ruled by perfidious whores and man-aping sluts! Death to all of you, but a fiery death to those demon-creatures who lead you all into ruin!"

Good thing I don' believe in Sethor, or his curses.

Four more Guards came racing in, and took over holding the assistant—whose name Mags could not recall—leaving the original four to go back to their positions.

This went on for quite some time. The ranting grew increasingly unhinged; Mags cast a quick glance over to the dais. The King was cleaning his fingernails. The Prince was tracing a little design on the arm of his throne. Amily was twirling a strand of hair around her finger. Her father looked half asleep. And Jorthun had his arms crossed and was visibly tapping a toe with impatience.

One of the Guards got hold of Kresh, though it didn't appear as if he intended to try to fight or run. Instead, he stared at them all, hollow-eyed, while his underling ranted.

Finally they all grew tired of the hysterics, and one of the Guards called out over the raving, "Anybody got a cloth?"

He took a handkerchief Amily gave him and gagged the man. That left him rolling his eyes in impotent fury. Jorthun turned to Kresh in the resulting silence. "You might as well cooperate," he said, coldly. "We have more than enough evidence to allow Coercive Truth Spell on all of you."

Kresh finally gathered the shreds of his dignity about himself and drew himself up. "The God will protect me!" he proclaimed, and snapped his mouth shut.

Jorthun smiled, thinly. "I'm sure *you* think so, but you might want to consider why your god allowed us to seize you in the first place," he replied, and motioned to Mags. "Kresh, or his underling first, Herald Mags?"

Mags eyed both of them. Kresh's nostrils were flaring in alarm; the flunky's attitude didn't change a particle. "Reckon the crazy one knows the most," he said. "But let me get the Spell on 'im first, so we can cut out all the rantin'."

Mags closed his eyes for a moment to get himself in the proper frame of mind, then invoked the Spell. The blue mist settled over the man as Kresh's eyes bulged. "You kin take the gag off 'im," Mags said to the Guard, then nodded to Jorthun. "You know what you wanta ask, so do it, milord."

Jorthun waited until the Guard had pulled the gag completely free of the man's mouth, then cleared his throat. "Is your real name Renn Haladane?"

"Yes," the man said, the words clearly coming from a violently unwilling mouth. He had turned bright red with the effort of resisting.

"And was your twin brother Roan Haladane, a musician who failed to get a position at Bardic Collegium?" Jorthun continued, as Mags wondered where this was going to go. Jorthun had been playing his cards very close to his chest, and hadn't let any of them know what was coming.

"Yes," the man growled.

"And your father was Taryan Haladane, a chief priest of the Temple of Sethor, as you were a Precept under him?" Jorthun continued smoothly, as Mags suddenly saw all the pieces falling in place.

"Yes." His teeth were gritted, brows were furrowed, and still the answer was forced from him.

"And was Roan Haladane not employed as a music tutor for Lord Lional's two daughters, Helane and Lirelle?" Jorthun continued, steadily, as enlightenment dawned on all their faces.

"Yes, damn you!" the man shouted, shaking with rage from head to toe. "Father died of grief after they drove him to his death! And if it had not been for the demons in your hearts, I would have had my revenge on them all! I would have had that harridan Tyria killed, I would have taken Helane for myself as was destined when my brother died, and I would have destroyed that bitch that stands beside the King so that Sethor could make me King's Own and begin the cleansing of this—"

"That'll be about enough," Mags said, and the Guards, taking that as their signal to gag the man, did so with alacrity. The King did not even appear remotely disturbed, only cold and a trifle angry. The Prince, however, looked furious.

"Take him away," the King said, sternly, and as the Guards dragged Haladane off, he turned to Kresh.

"I knew nothing about this!" Kresh proclaimed, his eyes wide, waving his hands frantically in negation. "Nothing!"

The King snorted, and looked utterly unconvinced. "Mags?" he said.

With a little smile. Mags invoked Truth Spell for the second time.

"Which of you was the Mindspeaker?" Jorthun asked Kresh. Kresh's eyes bulged in shock and surprise, but his mouth opened despite a visible struggle to keep it closed. "Haladane," the Priest said.

"Did his father bring him into the Temple because of this Gift?" Jorthun continued.

"Probably." The High Priest clearly did not know the answer to that, and Jorthun let it slide. It would have been logical, though. *Temple'd be about the only place he could get trainin' so he didn't go crazy.* Mags thought about that a moment, then amended his own thought. *Crazier.*

"And you were the Farseer?" Jorthun continued.

"Yes," the Priest answered unwillingly. Jorthun turned to the thrones.

"So, it is exactly as Mags thought. Kresh would use his Gift to make sure that the agents delivering the letters—*or* the vandals going to ruin the shops of honest craftswomen—were able to evade any of the Guards or Watch, and elude detection. Haladane would use Mindspeech to direct them." Jorthun nodded a little at Mags. "As Mags can testify."

"Aye, Majesty," Mags agreed. "I recognized the feel of 'is mind when 'e walked in here. Seein' as I was deep in their Temple as one of their bullyboys." He sighed sadly. "Wrecked one herb-shop, an' 'bout a quarter of a leather-shop."

Kresh made strangling sounds, presumably because he realized at the moment how completely, utterly and thoroughly hung he was.

"So, allow me to fill in the rest of the story," Jorthun continued, turning back to Kresh. "Feel free to correct me if I am wrong. When Haladane's brother killed himself, he and his father were already in your . . . service. You knew of his ability, you knew he would turn utterly fanatic when both his father and brother died, and you saw an opportunity. You would Farsee to watch over your pawns, he would use Mindspeech to direct them, and as a sideline to your campaign, you would help him get his revenge." Jorthun cocked his head to one side. "The only question I have left is this. Did you *really* think that your 'god' would allow him to become King's Own after he murdered Herald Amily?"

"Of *course*!" Kresh shouted, now losing any semblance of control. "Sethor is—"

"Impotent," King Kyril snapped. "And as of this moment, bankrupt and out of business in this Kingdom. Prince Sedric, I will rely on you to take a detachment of the Guard down to the so-called Temple, and round up everyone you find there. We'll sort them out after they're in gaol."

Sedric got to his feet with a speed that suggested he was as thoroughly sick of what the Sethorites had done as *any* of the women they had persecuted. "Aye, Majesty. We'll go now."

Kyril turned to Kresh. "As for you, your position and title will not save you. The *first* thing I will do will be to have the Healers shut down your Gift, and that of Haladane. After that, I will shut down your Temple, confiscate everything in it, and turn the Temple itself over to the Sworn of Betane." He smiled at the outraged look on Kresh's face. "I think they can make better use of a fortress than you. Though how they are going to move that ax—well, that's not my problem. Perhaps there will be a miracle. Every copper you have in your coffers will go toward repaying the women whose shops you ruined, and to the Sisters of Ardana. And then your punishment will begin, as determined by the Council and myself. I promise you, it will not be an easy one. At the least you attempted three direct murders, and one indirect one. Then there are the vandalized shops, and the sacrilegious desecration of the Temple of Betane and the Scriptorium of Ardana. I do not think you will see daylight again, except through iron bars. Guards, take him away."

Mags dropped the Truth Spell, freeing Kresh to say whatever he wanted. But he was utterly silent as the Guards took him to a cell, where there were Healers waiting to shut down his Gift, as they had probably already shut down Haladane's.

Then at the King's nod, the Guards took out the three would-be murderers, who after all, had needed to say nothing at all. Their punishment wouldn't be pretty either. *I wonder if they'll squeal, since their Priest is cooked.* Probably not. Fanatics only held firmer to their beliefs, the more they were proven wrong.

"Well," King Kyril said, with a little smile of satisfaction. "That was well done, you four."

"Four?" Mags replied, blankly. "Oh! Jorthun an' me an' Amily an' Nikolas. Thenkee, your Majest—"

"Kyril," the King corrected, laying his crown aside on the Prince's throne. "That really was astonishingly well coordinated. *And* I should thank your Companions as well, of course."

:Of course,: Dallen said smugly.

"I really do think having Father act as King's Own, even if he isn't, is an awfully good idea," Amily said slowly. "It felt wrong at first but now . . . it gives Sedric and me an extraordinary amount of freedom."

"I'm glad to hear you say that, Amily," the King replied. "Because I would like to be the first King of Valdemar in recent memory to abdicate in favor of his son, and having you and he firmly in harness together is a large part of that plan. Not immediately—" he said, holding up a cautionary hand at Amily's gasp of alarm. "—not for some time yet. I would like a few more grandchildren before I do this. But within the foreseeable future, while I can still enjoy my freedom in reasonable health."

"I approve," Jorthun replied, smiling. "We three old men can leave the younger set to handle all the difficult matters while we sit comfortably, sipping brandywine, and complaining how they are doing it all wrong."

"I see nothing at all to criticize in this plan," chuckled Nikolas. "Well, shall we leave the youngsters to handle the cleanup of their successful operation while we go put in some practice on just that?"

"I think I have a candlemark or two before the Council meeting," Kyril agreed, and looked to his other friend. "Steveral?"

"Nothing would suit me better," Lord Jorthun replied. And the three of them left the Audience Chamber together.

"I think that was a hint we should go help Sedric," Amily said into the silence.

"Huh," said Mags, looking after them. "Reckon they got our lives all planned out for us—"

"Maybe not our lives, but certainly our *day*," Amily corrected. "Let's go help Sedric. I'd like to see things properly tidied up."

"I want t' make sure that nobody slips the net. An' let Teo know how everythin' worked out." Mags gave her a quick hug and a kiss on the top of her head. "An' this time . . . there weren't no hostages or kidnappin's. I reckon we're improvin'."

"So we are!" she laughed. "So we are!"

ABOUT THE AUTHOR

Mercedes Lackey is a full-time writer and has published numerous novels and works of short fiction, including the bestselling *Heralds of Valdemar* series. She is also a professional lyricist and licensed wild bird rehabilitator. She lives in Oklahoma with her husband and collaborator, artist Larry Dixon, and their flock of parrots.

www.**mercedeslackey**.com

THE COLLEGIUM CHRONICLES

MERCEDES LACKEY

Follow Magpie, Bear, Lena and friends as they face their demons and find their true strength on the road to becoming full Heralds, Bards and Healers of Valdemar.

Book One: Foundation
Book Two: Intrigues
Book Three: Changes
Book Four: Redoubt
Book Five: Bastion

TITANBOOKS.COM

THE ELEMENTAL MASTERS

MERCEDES LACKEY

Mercedes Lackey's bestselling fantasy series set in an alternative Edwardian Britain, where magic is real—and the Elemental Masters are in control.

The Serpent's Shadow
The Gates of Sleep
Phoenix and Ashes
Wizard of London
Reserved for the Cat
Unnatural Issue

Home from the Sea
Steadfast
Blood Red
From a High Tower
A Study in Sable

"Fantastic… this is Lackey at her best." *Publishers Weekly*

"Intriguing and compelling." *Library Journal*

VALDEMAR OMNIBUSES

MERCEDES LACKEY

The Heralds of Valdemar
The Mage Winds
The Mage Storms
The Mage Wars
The Last Herald Mage (March 2017)
Vows & Honor (September 2017)
Exiles of Valdemar (March 2018)

For more fantastic fiction, author events, exclusive excerpts,
competitions, limited editions and more

VISIT OUR WEBSITE
titanbooks.com

LIKE US ON FACEBOOK
facebook.com/titanbooks

FOLLOW US ON TWITTER
@TitanBooks

EMAIL US
readerfeedback@titanemail.com

4 /11 /16